EPHEMERIS

THE QUESTRISON SAGA: BOOK TWO

J. DIANNE DOTSON

J. DIANNE DOTSON

CONTENTS

Dedication	vii
Acknowledgments	ix
A Note to Readers	xi
Prologue	1
1. The Herald	3
2. Galla-Deia	5
3. Flight	12
4. The Representative	18
5. Rikiloi	24
6. Aula	30
7. The Device	35
8. Sumond	42
9. Independence	49
10. Scintilla	54
11. The Abyss	60
12. Enlightenment	65
13. Crystalline	72
14. Fracture	78
15. Internecine	85
16. Ephemeral	87
17. Bitikk	93
18. Chatelaine	99
19. Magic	104
20. Departure	107
21. Perpetua	112
22. Descendent	119
23. The Curator	125
24. The Path	132
25. Enthralled	136
26. Legacy	139
27. Fledgling	142
28. Rendezvous	146
29. Valemog	155

30. Interception	156
31. Pheromonic	163
32. Splintered	167
33. Invader	172
34. Reunion	175
35. Matriarch	182
36. Convocation	187
37. Syntax	193
38. The Jewel	198
39. The Planetfinders	205
40. Storms	214
41. Voices In The Wind	222
42. Respite	231
43. Temerity	237
44. An Echo From The Past	240
45. Dance Lessons	246
46. Interwoven	250
47. Mind Cave	261
48. Befallen	266
49. Behest	273
50. Quondam	279
51. Portentous	283
52. Propulsion	287
53. Fusillade	292
54. Amalgamate	298
55. Machinations	304
56. Cutting The Wake	311
Pronunciation Guide	315
About the Author	317

EPHEMERIS: THE QUESTRISON SAGA: BOOK TWO

Copyright © *2020, 2019 by J. Dianne Dotson*

All rights reserved.

ISBN 978-0-9994082-4-7

ISBN 978-0-9994082-5-4 *(EBook)*

Published by *J. Dianne Dotson 2019*

San Diego, California, USA

No parts of this publication may be reproduced, stored in a retrieval system, or transmitted in any form or by any means, electronic, mechanical, photocopying, recording, or otherwise, without the prior written permission of the copyright owner.

This book is sold subject to the condition that it shall not, by way of trade or otherwise, be lent, resold, hired out, or otherwise circulated without the publisher's prior consent in any form of binding or cover other than that in which it is published and without a similar condition including this condition being imposed on the subsequent purchaser. Under no circumstances may any part of this book be photocopied for resale.

This is a work of fiction. Any similarity between the characters and situations within its pages and places or persons, living or dead, is unintentional and coincidental.

Cover Graphic Design by **Dash Creative LLC**

Cover Art from **Leon Tukker**

www.jdiannedotson.com

❦ Created with Vellum

DEDICATION

For my parents.

ACKNOWLEDGMENTS

I want to thank my husband and children for their love and guidance. I also want to thank my readers. When I published *Heliopause: The Questrison Saga: Book One* in 2018, I took a massive chance. I shared years of dreams with the entire world, and you supported me. Thank you to my delightful copy editor, Laurie Gibson. Thank you to my proofreader, Lisa Wolff. A huge thanks to beta readers Pam Magnus, Anne Sturgill, Chris Schera, and Nathan Camp. Thank you to helpers and supportive friends Paige Kirby, Carine Harambillet-Sharp, Alicia Noll, Malina Brown, Carine Alard-Poplawski, Jessica Springer, Dez Blanchfield, Mya Duong, and Chandler Johnson. Thank you to Dash Creative, LLC for the updated cover design for the 2nd edition. Thank you to cover artist Leon Tukker for the fabulous cover art. And thank you to my women friends, friends from when I first began this adventure as a girl: Tammy Cox, Erica McMurray, and Michelle Morales. In *Ephemeris*, the culmination of over thirty years of planning and dreaming really bursts forth. Thank you for following on this journey.

A NOTE TO READERS

As a guide to readers, it should be noted that the events of *Ephemeris* take place before, during, and after the events of *Heliopause*.

PROLOGUE

Every android has a purpose. The purpose of Oni-Odi changed with time. For millennia he served the legacy of the Seltra race, long vanished beyond the galactic plane. For that purpose the Seltra bequeathed him the star-city of Demetraan, which traversed that galaxy slowly, and as Oni-Odi, with purpose.

The Associates named him Elder, the sole remnant of the Seltra beings. He could withstand time, as he was designed to do. He shepherded his city of androids, which in turn tended the Seltra legacy of worlds long gone. The androids cultivated vast gardens and small ecosystems: glories of machines and devices, which turned all their diligent purpose to Oni-Odi. This Elder android tended his mechanical flock through epochs in order and harmony. The Associates would always aspire to, and never achieve, the manner of Oni-Odi.

But time stretches oddly. Only the Seltra ever truly understood it, and they transcended it. Oni-Odi rarely noticed the passage of time. Civilizations rose and fell, sometimes stars went nova, sometimes comets tore through worlds. The universe remained intact and changed little. The Associates discovered it first: the universe began to change.

There was a ripple. Everything seemed to stop: somehow, every race and every creature knew something had happened. The more primitive races wrote of deep mythology from the Event. The universe had ruptured, just the tiniest ripple, which left behind a wake, a portent.

How do the smallest things affect the larger whole? Everything changes. The Associates, through their grief and horror of losing a whole star system, knew this awful truth. And there were those who fed upon the suffering of the survivors: the greater the magnitude of the incident, the stronger they grew.

Oni-Odi and his androids drifted impassively through it all. But the Associates needed him, beseeched him to allay their fears. He told them, logically, that a hole in Existence needed to be stopped.

The hole had vanished, however. No one knew why it came, where it vanished to, or whether it would appear again. The shadowy feeling was that not only would it appear again, but also it could be far worse.

1

THE HERALD

The Governor waved away his court audience. His lambent eyes gauged the messenger before him: a boxy, compact creature from Seventh Dijj. *I must speak with the Associates about their couriers,* he thought, a fire kindling in his gaze. *Such complete filth.*

"I accept your message," Aeriod droned to the courier. "Now be off, will you? You tarry, and it is my dinnertime."

The creature clicked a reply: "Your answer is required before I can gain leave of you."

Aeriod's teeth flickered at the Dijjan in a malevolent grin.

"Very well," he said. "If I must endure your presence, take yourself to that window and air your wretched hide! The stench maddens me, nearly to murder."

The wretch from Seventh Dijj took note of Aeriod's fire conjurings and shuffled away. In a great huff, Aeriod settled back in his chair and awakened the message. The vision of the Elder, android Oni-Odi, wavered to life.

"Your presence is required at the summit of Associates. My Candidate is chosen and ready for training. Please come at once to discuss testing my Candidate."

And that was all.

Grudgingly, Aeriod bellowed, "Take a guest parcel from my staff and be off with my reply. Naturally I will attend."

The Dijjan quickly left with his treasures. Aeriod shot him a final baleful look and retreated to his chambers to dine.

Troubling news. He crumbled his sweets absently, barely tasting them. *I've heard little of Oni-Odi's pupil. What were the Associates thinking, representing humans? This must go against the credo of half of their people. Oni-Odi has never once kept a human before! How would he know what to do with one? Much less one that isn't even truly human. Poor judgment from the Elder.*

2

GALLA-DEIA

One day, Galla-Deia tried with no luck to locate Oni-Odi. He had mentioned briefly to her the night before that he was to have a full schedule the next day: service meetings with his androids, a visitor, and routine surveys of star fields. Galla had only half-heard him. She was quite accustomed to his having duties away from her. But sometimes she could be imperious. Oni-Odi always took her moods with his full grace and care, and usually placated her by stopping what he was doing to brush her misbehaving hair.

On this occasion, however, when the fit of petulance seized her, Oni could not be found. She tried her best to communicate with him via link and called out to him in the air. While he usually responded quickly, sometimes there could be a delay, depending on where he was in the City. Certain areas distorted communication. In those events, Galla went looking for her mentor herself.

She snatched a small, knee-height silver dome from a closet, gave it a light spank, and set it on the floor. This was her companion bot, Pliip. While it was not an emotive android, Oni-Odi had instilled it with certain precautionary features, as he came to realize that his ward could be most impulsive and downright unruly.

What Galla did not realize was that Oni-Odi could locate the youthful lady wherever she was, not only via Pliip, but also by the very floors she walked on. Galla cared little about this, unless it meant Oni could get to her more quickly, or she to him, when she was in a needy state. Tantrums must be avoided at all costs, lest the other Demetraanian inhabitants complain. Nor did Oni-Odi mind her adventures. It relieved him that she had developed something of an imagination. And Pliip could contact Oni-Odi if his charge had an outburst.

On this particular day, Galla felt her boredom slide over into frustration, which percolated nastily. Finally she could not resist exploring.

"Come on, Pliip," she called, as the bot whined behind her.

She carried the bot along at intervals through a narrow notch near the cooling system that regulated her block.

"It's so dark," she said. "Can you see which way to turn up ahead? I don't want to crawl."

Pliip squeaked. Galla bit her lip.

"Fine. Just a bit further and I'll put you back down."

And whatever other attributes Galla might have, strong night vision was not one of them. So she stumbled along and yelped, not seeing the tubing at her feet.

"Awk!" she cried, almost dropping Pliip, who volleyed indignant clucks. "Sorry, Pliip. Tell me we'll be out of this soon!" Pliip snorted back, and she sighed. "You don't have to be mean about it. Here, I'll let you down."

By and by, she grew more accustomed to the dreary slot they traversed. A constant whirring and echoing drips of liquid began to unnerve her. Perpetual breezes full of dank smells made her crinkle her nose. She could make out various panels along the way, low along the floor.

"Wait up," she called to Pliip. The little companion obeyed and turned toward where she now knelt. She placed her fingers around the edges of a panel and stuck her fingernails in them. With a clang, the panel fell to the floor. Inside, there was another bot, dormant.

"So," she murmured, "these must be the bots that maintain this hall. Let's keep going." She pushed the panel back in place.

"It's a really long hall, though," she said to the bot. Pliip kept rolling and hopping alternately over the obstacles along its path.

Eventually the hall curved almost imperceptibly. And beyond this curve, a faint light flickered. Galla shuddered. But she charged ahead, glad to see any light. When she and Pliip reached the guttering lamps, she beheld a door. The hall continued on ahead, but this door . . . Galla was determined to see what lay behind it. She placed her hand on it. It did not respond. She struck it—nothing happened. She tried to pry it open with her nails again, without success. Finally she gave it a good hard kick, and the door flew open.

Galla backed up and stumbled over Pliip in surprise. Inside she found an opulent chamber, gilded and curtained and smoldering with a thick haze of incense. And opposite her, a dark figure rippled to and fro across the floors.

Presently the figure whirled around. Its cold, sparking eyes sliced through the smoky air between them, and seared her resolve. She backed away from the door, snatched Pliip in her arms, and turned to run.

"Do stay," the figure hissed. The swirling form walked with great strides on two long legs over to her.

Galla swallowed with a very dry mouth and looked up. Fierce, glinting platinum eyes met her copper-hued stare. Long strands of silvery-white hair swung forward as the figure bent his head down a few inches to face her. The hair and eyes were all the more striking against his matte black attire . . . so black it seemed to absorb everything, including all her bravado.

"Come in, won't you?" the low voice drawled courteously. Her eyes went huge. Then the white hair flew back and the figure laughed openly. "I don't believe it! You're a naïf! For all your fire and spunk, you're actually shy! Oni-Odi did not tell me this."

Galla squeezed Pliip in confusion until the bot squawked. Trembling, she set it down.

"I don't know you," she said in her quietest voice; but she straightened, emboldened by her mentor's name.

"Oh, how *disappointing*," the enigmatic person sighed. "I did so hope Oni-Odi might let slip one or two details about me, before just such an incident as this. Enter."

This was a command, and Galla found herself following it. When she did, the door flicked shut behind her, severing her from Pliip.

Galla stared up at those silver-pale eyes. Their pupils dilated just barely, but she noticed.

"Sit," came his next order. Galla again obeyed, more from the novelty of being commanded than for any other reason. The ruby-hued sofa she sat in nearly absorbed her. She burrowed down into it a bit, as if it might protect her from this being.

"Who are you?" she asked, experiencing an uncomfortable feeling in her midsection. Gradually she felt this feeling creep up her back, into her throat, over her head.

"Aeriod," he replied. "And since Oni-Odi has not managed to enlighten you, despite all his other accomplishments, I will assume you know nothing about why I am here, either. Mm? No reply? Ah. Very well. I am here to discuss your training."

"My training?" Galla echoed, her voice quaking. She seized her throat as if to will it to behave. *Why do I feel like this?* she wondered.

"Ah. Even more a naïf than I imagined. Though a fair-looking one, I must say." And Aeriod studied the woman indulgently for a moment where she squirmed. Every hue of warmth and light and fire rippled in her hair, and her coppery eyes unmoored him. "I daresay Oni would . . . *disapprove* . . . if I revealed much more.

"As I've said, I'm here to meet with your *esteemed* Elder," he went on, and Galla frowned at his tone, "to discuss your training, among other things. He can provide you with details."

And Aeriod quickly pulled her up from the sofa and pushed her toward the door. He raised one finger, and the door opened.

"Perhaps," suggested Aeriod silkily, "we shall meet again soon."

Not knowing what to say, Galla simply nodded.

Aeriod herded her out of the room, gave her a rigid smile beneath his furrowed brow, and let the door shut between them. Galla looked down; her Pliip sat still beside her. She moved away from the door, gave it an uncertain look, and slowly continued her path back down the hallway. Pliip whistled, and Galla shook her wild hair out of her face.

As she walked, the odd sensation she had felt before slid its way through her body. She had never needed to feel it before, so she couldn't know it protected her. She finally exited the hallway and stood blinking in the bright light of the dome above. A breeze struck her face, and she shivered. Fear left her.

"Pliip, please stay here until your next duty," Galla instructed her little bot.

She walked under trees and giant fungus pods and breathed the sultry, biota-laden air. She walked for some time, until a blue flicker shone among the foliage. Galla cried out and ran toward it, thrashing the underbrush carelessly. Worker bots instantly converged on the ravaged trail to repair the damage.

"Oni-Odi!" she called, and she ran up to the android and looped her arms around him.

He patted her arms affectionately and held her back. He was blue and silver and bipedal, humanoid in form for Galla's sake, although he could alter his shape when needed.

"You damaged the trail," he observed.

"Oh. Yes. Sorry. Oni, I met someone," she panted. She gripped his hands, which warmed just for her, and looked into his unreadable, solid-blue eyes.

Oni's face remained still, so she went on, "His name is Aeriod. He told me I would be training soon. Training for what, Oni?"

"Let us walk back to your wing," Oni suggested.

Galla strolled happily beside him, her lithe arm draped around his metallic one. Relief cascaded over her. There was no more of that awful sensation she had felt after leaving Aeriod.

When they reached Galla's apartment, Oni-Odi extended his hand into the air, palm up. The palm opened, folded panels back, and three small jewel-like bulbs appeared. His palm closed; the bulbs hovered just above it—ruby, emerald, and topaz-hued.

"These are information globes. They contain instructions for you, Galla-Deia. When I came upon you, I suspected, but did not know for certain, that you might be of assistance to me. You already know I am affiliated with activities outside Demetraan. One of these is a group called the Associates."

When Oni-Odi said this, the topaz globe opened. The globe showed Galla a miniature image of a long table, around which were grouped fascinating beings, each more unusual than the last. Galla leaned forward and stared, her eyes huge. A model of Oni-Odi stood at one end; at the other end stood Aeriod. Galla wondered at his icy posturing, evident even at this tiny scale.

"Here you can see most of the Associates," Oni told her. "Aeriod and I attend occasional meetings with them. Aeriod is currently here to discuss your tutelage for a task of the Associates.

"You see, the Associates represent several different species of sentient beings throughout this galaxy. Among them, a Representative resembles its species in many ways. However," and the image grew to life size, so Galla could see each Associate more closely, "there is more than one profound difference. The Representatives live among and physically look like their core species. But the Associates are *not* members of those species."

"I don't understand," said Galla, marginally interested in Oni's speech, but mesmerized by the images themselves. Again her gaze drifted to Aeriod, as if pulled. She shivered.

Oni-Odi patiently said, "One important difference is that the Representatives, compared to their member species, are essentially ageless. Many have lived as long as the civilizations of the member species themselves.

"Another difference is that the Representatives cannot reproduce. They do, however, function in the utmost role for species preservation: protection. In order to achieve this goal, each Representative must be trained by the Associates. This returns us to you."

Galla blinked. "What do you mean, *I* represent a species?"

"That is correct," Oni-Odi answered. "You represent a species called humans. It is my responsibility to see that you are trained for this potential role."

Galla began pacing; she reached out and touched each Associate's hologram.

"What if I don't want this role?" Galla asked. Her fingers trailed the holographic shoulders of Aeriod's elaborate cape. She pretended he was solid, so her hands did not penetrate his image. Then she backed away from his form and blushed.

"It is still your choice," Oni said, and the hologram collapsed back into the topaz sphere. "I will leave these globes for you. If you decide to proceed, examine the red globe. After viewing that one, if you should still wish to proceed, examine the green globe. They must be viewed in this order, or they will not function. I will know if you have chosen the path. Then we will meet with the Associates.

"I must now meet with Aeriod; we have a full agenda. Good day, Galla-Deia."

Galla gave him a hug around his neck; he gave her another pat on her hair and left her with the globes, and her decision.

3
FLIGHT

Galla sat in a funk, swinging between wretched boredom and indecision. She occasionally walked over to where Oni-Odi had left the shimmering orbs by her desk. She would look at them, almost grab one, and then back away. Eventually she wearied of this unusual dilemma and stalked out of her chambers in a sullen mood. Even Pliip was off somewhere else, working or charging.

She slipped along a quiet walkway in the star-city's dusk. Above her wavered tiny pollinator drones with glowing skins; these sylphlets sang above her as she walked. She smiled up at them, and suddenly felt a crushing sadness. This heavy feeling confused Galla. Here was another new sensation, just a few days after the fear she had experienced with Aeriod.

Three of the glowing sylphlets alit on her shoulders. One rose into the air and lapped at her tears with its tiny, furred tongue. The three hummed in a low frequency a kind of song. Galla smiled again.

"Thank you," she told them. The sylphlets trilled tiny replies and drifted off to a group of flowers in benign sparkles. Galla left them and headed for the stellar meadow, which rose to a headland that seemed to drop into the inky black of space. From this spot, Galla could look up, and down . . . down into infinity, at brilliant lights of faraway stars and pale smudges of nebulae.

Galla knew what these things were, from Oni's teachings, but she had never experienced them herself. She then realized she would eventually have to go back to her room to those colorful globes. She understood Oni-Odi could never show her those places out there, in that deep black realm.

She said to herself, and to the stars, "He's always going to be running this place, or helping the Associates. He won't have time to do anything more. I'm alone."

Galla felt absolutely hollow, as if her insides had opened to a yawning abyss and loosed all her happiness into it. She might have wept, but this vacant feeling engulfed that small luxury. She shivered, and turned away from her headland perch.

She walked back along a different route, among long, draping violet-frond forests, where tending androids rattled and rustled in their secluded depths. The star-city pulsed with both organic life and machines.

But Galla knew this was only part of it. She knew there were whole worlds out there. Worlds of sand, forest, sea, creatures, and civilizations. What if she went looking for them? Could she protect them as well as explore them?

She thought about what Oni-Odi had said. If she chose to become a Representative, that meant she would protect an entire species. In what capacity, she could not guess. She wondered what that species was like. When she looked at herself, she knew she resembled humans. But Oni-Odi did not concern himself with humans whatsoever, and had never met one. Galla was the closest thing to a human he knew, and he was convinced that she must represent them. She lived among androids, and had for her entire life.

Would I fit in with humans at all? she wondered. *I want to make Oni-Odi proud of me. I can't stay with him forever. I feel like I have to leave, I have to grow. If I choose this path, I won't let him down. I will protect the people I represent, no matter what. He would want me to. And I want to. If they let me. If the Associates let me! I want to try. I want to prove to them I can do this. And then one day I can come back to Oni-Odi and show him that I did.*

She felt her steps quickening. She tripped a few times in her haste, and finally she began running, to the wonderment of the creatures and robots in the Demetraan night. Then she launched herself through her chamber doors, and reached to snatch one of the globes.

She grabbed the emerald-hued one: nothing happened. Or did it? She felt the vaguest hint of a tingle.

"Oh," she muttered, remembering Oni's instructions. She picked up the ruby-colored globe and sat down on the floor to watch a parade of color, light, and sound unfurl around her. While she did not fully grasp what she saw, she felt an irresistible draw to proceed. She then picked up the green globe again.

Oni-Odi's voice came through her room. "You have made your choice. In the morning, I would like for you to demonstrate some skills for our guest."

That night, Galla wriggled in her bed, and struggled to sleep. Crackles of anxiety pulsed through her.

"I don't like this," she whispered to the air. She shut her eyes and tried to calm herself. She squeezed her eyes tightly together until finally she slept.

She woke in shock, gasping at the memory of the day before. She pushed at the blankets with her feet and tripped trying to get out of bed. Galla bunched up her rakish hair into a knot, smoothed her jumpsuit, and left her room. She felt a thundering sensation in her chest, heard ringing in her ears. At one point she even had to stop and sit down on the floor of a corridor to calm herself. Her body confused her. Her thoughts confused her even more.

Why do I feel this way? she wondered, staring at her shaking hands.

She pressed her back against the wall behind her and sat for a few minutes. Soon a dome bot scuttled to her feet and prodded her and crooned concernedly.

"I think I am feeling better," she told the bot. But she stood up on legs that threatened to jackknife. "Please take me to Oni-Odi. I don't know if I can remember how to get to his meeting room; I'm having trouble."

The bot led her back to that room, but she found it empty. For a moment she sighed in relief. Maybe all of this was not necessary after all. Then the dome bot bumped into her foot and squeaked.

"Why would Oni want me over there? That's an odd place for a meeting," she answered. The dome bot simply swept forward, goading her to follow.

Galla strolled under buttresses of plants and made her way to a field. As she hiked up a small hill, she caught sight of Oni-Odi's blue form. That dreadful feeling came back to her midsection: there was Aeriod. Staring at her. She tilted her chin up and avoided looking back it him, choosing to look only at her beloved mentor. She could see behind Oni-Odi a little skyhopper, one of her favorite vehicles.

"Galla-Deia, thank you for coming so quickly," Oni-Odi said, implacable.

Aeriod had followed Galla with his eyes the entire way, and watched with a knitted brow as she fidgeted where she stood. Galla could not help but pick at her jumpsuit and try to smooth it. She felt the beginnings of a new sensation rising in her now, akin to one of her righteous old tantrums, but a little slower to boil up. Her cheeks burned.

"Galla, would you please demonstrate your piloting for Aeriod?" Oni-Odi asked.

She thought, *I would do anything for you, Oni-Odi. Anything you ever asked.* She nodded at the android, and took care to avoid acknowledging Aeriod.

He, meanwhile, had pulled his vacuum-black cape snugly around his arms, covering them. He looked to her like a silver-headed obelisk. Not that she was really looking.

Galla-Deia jumped on the skyhopper and jetted upward. In a moment of mutiny, she darted off out of sight of Oni-Odi and Aeriod. She spent several minutes swooping past the field and skimming treetops, and then began to feel a stab of guilt. This made her turn around. She did not want to disappoint Oni-Odi. She flew back to the two waiting figures, glided in an elegant circle around the head of her mentor, and finally settled her craft beside him. She leapt off and flashed him a broad smile.

"Well?" she asked Oni-Odi.

"The maneuvers are without error, Galla-Deia," the android responded, his cobalt eyes penetrating her confidence.

"Then why the look, Oni?" she asked, taking off her helmet. Her brilliant hair sprang in all directions.

"Let us go to the orchard," Oni-Odi suggested.

This pleased Galla. She dearly enjoyed the orchard. She wondered why Oni-Odi did not comment on her flying skills. Then she noticed Aeriod was closely following them, and she scowled.

"Why is he coming?"

Aeriod stepped next to her, and she found herself looking up at the tall governor's sharp face.

"Oh, I don't need to, Galla-Deia," he said to her coolly. "Elder, I will meet with you later."

"As you wish, Aeriod," Oni-Odi responded.

Galla watched the dark figure slink off behind them. Then she turned around and clung to Oni-Odi's warm arm.

They sat on a fine rock bench beneath heavy boughs of tree fruit so that Oni could brush her hair. He was always careful with her tangles, and there were always tangles. Today they were in rare form, jutting out everywhere, a visual display of her feelings.

"You are ready for your first exam, Galla-Deia," the android told her quietly.

Galla jerked upright, and the brush jammed into a mat of tangles. She faced him and clasped his hands.

"Am I?" she cried. "After I saw the globes, I thought it would be a long time from now—ages! Am I that good?"

"Galla," said Oni-Odi, in as serious a tone as possible, "you are ready for testing by the Associates. It is not a matter of how 'good' you are. I cannot prepare you further, not as I have been instructed. My own training is approaching its end. Please do not become overconfident."

Her shoulders slumped. "So I'm *not* that good."

Oni-Odi took up the brush again. "You will succeed, I am certain, Galla-Deia."

She relaxed a little. She knew that Oni-Odi had tried to be honest with her. Her mind then lilted off to daydreaming of those enigmatic Associates. She would stand before them soon, proud to become a Representative. And she would be only too glad to be away from the likes of Aeriod.

4

THE REPRESENTATIVE

Galla-Deia felt as if the air shimmered with greatness. She had been dressed in a simple, dark grey robe and sent around a vaulted room to meet each Associate. Her lips felt stiff from smiling and talking. The many faces of the aliens blended together, it seemed, and she suddenly forgot all of their names. In a panic, she reached out and touched Oni-Odi. He looked fondly at her.

"My Candidate is ready for her examination," Oni-Odi announced, to her horror.

She gathered herself up in what surely took hours, although of course within seconds Oni-Odi had led her to an exit.

She gasped, "Oni, I don't think I can do this! There are so many watching! And they're all so . . . so *ancient!*"

"As you will be, one day, my student," the android remarked. "Remain centered, Galla-Deia."

Galla made her way to her simulations feeling things she did not understand. When she was to find herself tightly curled up later that evening on her bed, she would research and name one of those emotions as dread.

That day, Galla performed aerial maneuvers without flaw. She resisted fire conjurings, survived blunt force, and took out targets. But in her showdown with bot fighters, she screamed in frustration. She could fight them off, but they kept coming, and her temper flared. At one point she threw off her helmet in a rage, and it struck an oncoming bot until it screeched and crumbled into the ground. Then she stopped and looked in horror at what she had done. And she balled her fists and glared up at the dome of the conference arena. At last she composed herself, took a deep bow, and left for her quarters, her cheeks flaming and glistening from embarrassed tears.

Audible displeasure rippled through the conference arena. Aeriod gave Oni-Odi an agonized glance. *Of course he's just standing there! He's an android!* thought Aeriod bitterly. In other company, or preferably none, Aeriod might have let his face fall into his hands. Instead his throat tickled him, and he laughed long and with derision.

"Enough, Oni-Odi," he gasped at last, swearing to himself that he would never forget the scandalized looks from the committee.

"Clearly," he said, standing with a flourish of cape and hair, "she's not what we want or need. This creature, a Representative? That may be true, were she a representative of everything wrong with the human species!

"Consider, my Associates, the care with which all other Representatives were chosen. Not one failed so utterly as this toy of Oni-Odi's!"

Oni-Odi turned his metallic face to stare at Aeriod with his unblinking eyes.

"You defy the Elder?" Vedant's whistling voice pierced through the room. Vedant rose, towering over Aeriod with its branched neck, its slits of eyes gleaming. No other indication of wrath was needed. Aeriod's pale skin blanched even further.

Aeriod hurried over to the stricken android and grasped him by the arm.

"I dare not," he assured Oni-Odi smoothly. "I do, however, reject the girl. She is idiotic! Who ever saw such an atrocious test result! And after all, while it is my judgment needed at this council, I can little afford to have my opinion ignored."

Cold anger shone from his eyes.

The Speaker of Bitikk then drifted forward, its sparkling, suited figure unnerving Aeriod. With no discernible face, the Speaker's mask folded into a new display, interpreted as agreement. All hushed at this. The Speaker of Bitikk then entreated Oni-Odi for his comments.

Oni-Odi waved Aeriod away.

"The counsel of Aeriod is sound," he acknowledged, "and is quite as I expected. I do offer my guarantee, however, that Galla-Deia will improve. She will be suitable for her Task, for she is the only one who can be."

The shrouded, enigmatic group of Associates called the Summoners then spoke: "This may be truth. We have sent forth what we may, and we have found no other." Gestures of interest traveled around the room. "We suspect she possesses unique abilities that can aid us in the Event. She may even be useful against Paosh Tohon. There are further tests that can discern this."

"What, then, do you propose, Oni-Odi?" asked Aeriod, exasperated.

Oni-Odi responded with feeling, "She is a fine pupil. She demonstrates poorly under such scrutiny. But I have seen her promise. She is diligent. She has fire and daring. She is stubborn. I will train her for as long as necessary, and leave each of you to train her in turn. She will have humans to teach her, as well. She must interact with them to gain their trust in the difficult times ahead."

He loves her! Aeriod thought suddenly. *No; absurd,* he reassured himself.

The silver-haired governor said aloud, "If we cannot change the obstinacy of our honorable Oni-Odi, there is really little else to do but wait. Know this, however: I will require her tenure at my home world. If she will learn from each of you, so shall she learn from me."

Oni-Odi bowed. As he suspected, the Associates resigned themselves to Aeriod's decision. Oni-Odi knew how much Aeriod's charisma could carry a vote. He did not wish to know how close

Aeriod had come to denying his pupil a chance to proceed with her training.

The android thanked each Associate, and then hastened away. He decided to tell Galla quickly about the outcome of the meeting. He thought she would feel elated.

Aeriod, however, moved faster. He swept over to Galla's quarters and rang for entry.

Galla jumped up to answer quickly, eager to hear from Oni-Odi about her results. She had been dozing, trying to recover from her excruciating display before the Associates. She yawned and noted that her skin looked creased.

She opened her door and faced Aeriod. Silver eyes met copper ones, and hers grew wide in surprise. Aeriod stood there examining her. There was that feeling she had again. Rather it was a mix of feelings, and they all threatened to rise up in her throat as a howl. She blushed, and this fascinated Aeriod.

She managed to say, "What are you doing here?"

Aeriod smirked at her. "How incredibly rude! Has Oni-Odi taught you no manners? Clearly you need a fair bit of training in *that*. Are you going to invite me in?"

Galla tried to slow her rapid breathing. She could not believe this individual dared invite himself into *her* room. But she knew he was Oni's guest. So she stepped aside and let him in.

Thinking rapidly about societal norms from her lessons with Oni-Odi, she raised her head loftily and said, "How may I assist you, Aeriod?"

Aeriod fingered his chin and looked down at her.

He said, "Perhaps you do have some promise after all. I'm here, Galla-Deia, to inform you that you will begin your training. In fact, I shall be your first tutor."

He twitched his long, dark cape like the wings of some great nocturnal animal. Galla felt certain those wings would sweep her up and carry her far away.

"I've come to the decision on my own, and the Associates have given me full support. I think it benefits everyone. We would not want you overly contaminated by the humans, so soon in the process, or overly shielded by your mentor, Oni-Odi."

At that moment, Oni-Odi rang her room. Galla let him in, and the android observed the looks on her and Aeriod's faces. Even he noticed the strange mix of ferality and intrigue in Aeriod's expression as he had considered Galla.

Aeriod frowned at Oni-Odi. *Damned machine,* he thought brutally. *I could have learned more if he hadn't shown up!*

With a long, dramatic bow to the android and an important glance to Galla, Aeriod whirled away in silence.

Galla fell to questioning: "Is it true, Oni-Odi, that this . . . person, Aeriod, made it possible for me to pass the test?"

Oni-Odi felt an odd, unpleasant stirring in his innards. "You owe him nothing," he said, "and I had hoped to tell you everything about the proceedings myself."

"So had I," remarked Galla sullenly.

"What more did he say to you?" asked Oni-Odi. He picked up a brush and began working it through her mussed hair.

Galla shrugged.

"He said that the Associates approved him as my first tutor. Something about not wanting me contaminated? Oni, you're pulling too hard—"

Oni-Odi actually stammered an apology. He could not understand this distracting, chaotic string of thoughts. Nor did he understand his next behavior. He put the brush down and wrapped his arms around her.

"Oni, what's this?" exclaimed Galla, responding to the embrace. "Are you all right? You've never done this before!"

Oni-Odi remained silent. Galla felt his skin change from cool to warm. As she looked at him, he changed even further: all his hard lines blurred and softened, and his face and eyes shifted into more than just a change of expression. He seemed more real than real to her. Less of an android.

"Galla-Deia," he said quietly, "I did not consider until this moment that you would really be leaving. I should let you gather your things now."

He loosened his embrace and stared at her through brilliant eyes. Her eyes filled with tears, but she held them at bay, and set her jaw stubbornly.

With a long sigh, Galla said, "I want to see you before I leave. I don't know how long he'll . . . need me. I'm—I'm scared, Oni-Odi. I don't like this feeling."

Oni-Odi disliked it also. *I had been happy that she was allowed to continue. Now I regret this. I cannot—she is meant for this—I will be pleased for her.* So he petted her hair soothingly. Then he left.

5

RIKILOI

Aeriod's assistants, in their black and scarlet wrappings, took the last of Galla's personal belongings. Galla stood and looked solemnly at Oni-Odi. *He's so solid,* she thought. She tried to be amused by the android's stiffness. She failed.

In all the time I have spent with him, now I know it wasn't long enough. She reached out her hands to his smooth face; it was warm again. She wished it had been cold, mechanically brittle. When she let her hands slide away from his cheeks, she still felt their warmth.

"Thank you, Oni-Odi," she said, and finally she turned away. She advanced toward the tall robed figure, which watched her with pale eyes that smoldered.

When their craft left his star-city, Oni-Odi activated every sensor in his possession. He no longer had probes that stretched so far as Aeriod's home. But he traced the craft as far as he could, until he could detect it no more. He cursed his own design for the first time, and stood alone, holding the brush for Galla's hair.

Galla was relieved it was a quiet ride. She remained on edge and fought her sadness over leaving Oni-Odi. Aeriod had also prevented her from bringing Pliip, which shocked and angered her. He had insisted upon having no bots in his home. After some time, she could hear the engine of Aeriod's craft whining. They were descending. She shook her hair back and plaited it in a lame attempt to control it. Then she found she could not do enough with her hands. *What was I thinking? That we would never actually arrive?*

She chewed on her lip; she pulled the braid apart and twisted it into a chignon. She clenched her fists and tried to look out her window, tried to be excited about this rust-hued world. After all, she had never before visited a planet's surface.

Rikiloi curved quickly up at her, as she bent her head to see it. It all happened in a flash of colors: they buffeted through the upper atmosphere amid brilliant plasma swirls and eerie, colorful phantom shapes. Galla watched, enchanted by this display, but too quickly she jolted in her seat from turbulence. She gasped and gripped her seat.

She heard Aeriod's chilling drawl over the speaker: "Calm down, Galla-Deia. I have eons of piloting skill behind me."

This did nothing to console her; in fact she flushed with outrage. She closed her eyes until she felt the craft angle into its final descent. Then she looked out, and her lips parted in awe. To the distant horizon of this world stretched long ridges of crinkled, eroded hills, rose and russet and umber-colored, all hues of soft reds from carmine to brick. Yet among the ridges stretched vast valleys of palest blue-green, vivid against the red hills.

As lovely as this scene was, Galla sat upright in amazement at the final destination. She knew of asteroids from her stay on Demetraan; yet here was one perched in the air of the world itself, floating perhaps a mile above one of its long valleys. Upon this mysteriously captured meteor stood Aeriod's palace, gleaming with deep red metal and black stone, in fiery contrast to his icy pallor. How he had coerced this planetoid along its continued migration, Galla could not guess.

Aeriod's ship glided sleekly into a catacomb near the base of his sky island. Within seconds, he swept into the cabin and loosed Galla from her belts before she had time to react.

"Really," he murmured, eyes glowering at her, "you're going to have to work on your reaction time. We'll add that to the agenda, lest a *human* take full advantage later on."

He laughed sharply, but offered his arm. Galla felt helpless: *I'm here, and no way out—what else can I do?* So she took it.

He led her past a throng of assistants, all elaborately dressed, many with jewels on their limbs, or even on tentacles. Galla's fretful mood vanished at seeing a new, diverse group of beings. She sensed immediately they were far kinder than the Associates. Just thinking of the Associates sent a small shiver of displeasure through her.

Aeriod glanced at her and slowed for a moment, watching her nod and smile through the pleasantries of his staff. He grimaced, pulled himself taut and straight, and led her on—after the occasional barked command at these assistants—until they reached a lift.

Inside the lift, the walls depicted views of one of the valleys below them. Galla watched the scenes, rapt, and was disappointed when the lift halted.

"Oh," she said, really more to herself than to Aeriod, "I would have liked to have seen more of that."

Aeriod stared down at her inscrutably.

"Come along," he said tersely.

They entered a hall lined with even more assistants, who each bowed, saluted, or otherwise gestured in respect to *both* of them, Galla noted. Aeriod led her to an intricately designed doorway, whose carvings changed every moment, as if alive. The doorway melted away to reveal a suite of rooms that smelled sweet and floral. Aeriod beckoned for her to enter; he followed, and the door reappeared behind them.

"Go on," he said, "it's yours."

"Mine?" Galla asked, and she gave him such a clear, open look that his silver eyes wavered and flashed away to another part of the room.

"Yes," he replied quietly. "Well, go on! I didn't fashion these for you just to stand there and gawk at." He walked over to a jewel-colored chaise and fingered a throw that lay on it. "It's all meant to be used, by *you*, so long as you are here."

Galla stepped tentatively forward and marveled at the luscious flooring, so soft under her feet. The ceiling hung with warm suspended lights, some of which followed above her head as she walked; the little tables here and there were covered in flowers and baubles and fabulous, unnamed objects. She stood and turned completely around, mouth agape, and Aeriod laughed.

"You're surely not entranced by the mere *sitting room,* Galla-Deia?" he asked with a grin.

Galla replied in a snap, "A real smile! You look better for it." She clapped her hand to her mouth, and there was a nasty silence. Aeriod's smile eroded.

"Come," he said crisply. "There's much more for you to see. Besides, you must change out of that ghastly uniform. Then you're to attend dinner with me. I will send one of my staff for you when I'm ready."

He strode from room to room, briskly describing each room's function, for which Galla was grateful. Oni-Odi did not have rooms akin to these—these were sumptuous, cozy, and intimate. Looking at them, Galla felt a pleasurable excitement. At the same time a prickling, warm sensation crept down the back of her neck. Every time Aeriod drew near to her, it intensified.

Aeriod insisted on showing Galla her wardrobe. In her naïveté, she had not thought about bringing special garments with her. Oni always gave her serviceable outfits, and Galla did not want for anything else. Aeriod knew this, of course.

While Galla had marveled at her new apartments, she was completely floored by her wardrobe. Nearly everything in it sparkled with jewels or glowed with iridescent fabrics. She stood dumbfounded until Aeriod gave her a nudge forward. She shuffled into the great closet, not really knowing what to do, until Aeriod sighed impatiently.

"What do you think?" he asked.

"Er . . . well," Galla stammered, "it's all—it's very—I mean, everything is gorgeous. But I guess I want to know, what if they're not really —for *me?*"

"What do you mean?" Aeriod bellowed. "Of course they're for you! They were made *for you.*"

"But how do—what if they don't fit?"

Aeriod rolled his eyes and snapped, "Do you really think I *don't* know your shape and size? I am a mage after all!"

Galla slowly nodded. *He certainly seems to know a good deal about me, without really knowing me,* she thought.

"Well, go on, pick something out!" he barked.

"But how? There have to be hundreds of outfits! I don't know the first thing—"

Aeriod made a strangled sound and then sighed again.

"Very well," he hissed. "We will do this my way."

Galla winced; some of her previous fear returned. But Aeriod left her standing there, his cape whirled after him, his hair tossed back. As she watched him go, Galla felt a curious sensation sweep her body. She looked down and gave a cry—her clothes were coming off of her—they were being snatched off, one at a time, by unseen hands! She gave an indignant howl of protest, but Aeriod had already left. Then she stilled herself and watched as, just as quickly as articles were removed from her, her skin was buffeted by warmth and scent—all invisible—and immediately re-clothed as if she were being instantaneously bandaged. In this way, she did not spend even one second nude.

The same warm sensations moved over her face and hair, until finally she stood looking at a very different vision of herself in the wardrobe's mirror. Aeriod's unseen assistants had dressed her in an exquisite gown, deep red in hue, so encrusted with rubies, garnets, and copper filigree that she thought she might not be able to walk. Yet she could, easily, as if the dress anticipated all her moves. She felt just as comfortable as ever . . . until a pair of copper shoes appeared at her feet.

She stepped into the delicate things with apprehension, then scoffed, "How can *anyone* wear these?" At that, the shoes eased into a different shape with a softer sole. "That's better," she muttered.

A bell sounded in another room. She walked, at first uncertainly, toward the sound. A small entourage of beings stood at the enchanted door. One of them spoke:

"The Governor awaits your presence."

Galla wondered at it all, and for a moment she considered what might happen if she refused to go. *If he can undress and dress me with a mere wave of his hand, maybe I had better accept!*

"Please take me to Aeriod," Galla replied.

6

AULA

She followed them along magnificent, high-arched hallways: some had, to her delight, views of the planet below through open windows; some showed interstellar scenes like pulsars and nebulae; one hall revealed a green land dotted with small seas and lakes. She marveled at these scenes but remained silent, as did her companions. When she finally arrived at Aeriod's dining room, her face shone with pleasure, despite her general uneasiness about the entire situation.

Aeriod welcomed her inside and sent his staff away. He stood near Galla and looked down at her, and his gaze lingered over certain points of her gown. He deliberately took her hand and pulled her a little ways away, so that her entire frame was reflected in a large mirror on the opposite side of the room. Galla remained oblivious to this; Aeriod smirked to himself.

"Well done," he said in a low growl.

"Then I can thank you for that," Galla shot back, feeling rebellious. "After all, you gave me no choice."

"You dithered. I've no patience for dithering," Aeriod said loftily.

Galla pushed her lips together, since she had no comeback for such a statement.

"Sit," he advised, waving to his table. He joined her, sitting practically across the room at the other end. The table then shrank, bringing them within a few feet of each other, so that she faced him.

He moved his hand, palm down, above the surface; food and drink appeared. Galla sat and stared at the opulent display.

"You do eat," Aeriod said casually. "I know because I spied you picking fruit on Demetraan."

"Yes," Galla admitted, "but I don't have to."

"Ah," said Aeriod, taking a cluster of voluptuous fruit and holding it out to Galla. "We're very fortunate in that regard, Galla-Deia. There are many pleasures for us that others are bound to by necessity. Food is only one of them."

She took a bit of the fruit and ate it, but refused any more of it. She instead chose several different items from the table, and busied her thoughts by eating. Aeriod laughed softly, and began eating as well. Neither said a word for some time, though Galla's thoughts bounded about nervously.

She became more unsettled the longer she was alone with Aeriod. She felt a thrill of longing for Demetraan, its paths through the many habitats, its gentle robots, even little Pliip, and with a wince, Oni-Odi.

"When do I begin training?" she asked abruptly.

Aeriod set his glass down and considered her.

He replied, "You've already begun. You've spent a considerable amount of time with Oni-Odi, haven't you? Long enough for a certain torpor to grow in you, frankly. A lack of refinement, as well. That place is all you know. I can promise you, that experience prepared you for very little."

"So this," said Galla slowly, and she smoothed her hands innocently over her bodice, "this is part of my preparation?"

Aeriod threw back his moon-pale hair and laughed richly.

"Definitely," he replied, and Galla noticed a new look in his face, one of warmth. It dissipated so quickly that she thought she had imagined it.

"There are many facets to your training," he went on. "I do hope to teach you some measure of culture, naturally. But there are other items on our agenda—intensive challenges that should prove invaluable. I will address them as they come up."

"As I become more experienced?" asked Galla.

"Exactly."

They sat in another long silence until a tiny tone rang, and Aeriod exclaimed, "The time! We must go aloft."

He froze and closed his eyes. Galla could hear a high whistling of wind. He opened his eyes again and smirked. He stood.

"Come with me," he said, offering his hand. "I've lifted the palace higher, for the sunset."

Aeriod opened a curtain in the room to reveal a broad balcony, and he led Galla onto it. She gasped. Aeriod peered over the edge of the balcony and gave the ground below an appraising gaze. He glanced over at Galla, who watched him with uncertain eyes.

"On to practical matters tomorrow, I think," he told her. "I want you to enjoy yourself for now." She stepped gingerly next to him and looked down. A bank of fog had begun to creep into the valley floor, to obscure the fungus fields, turning teal in the fading light.

"What will I be doing?" asked Galla, feeling apprehensive.

"You will see a bit of my operation," replied Aeriod. His shining, pale eyes rose to look at the last glowing edge of sunset beyond the hills. Galla felt that strange tingle on her neck as she watched him. "And you will also assist."

"Really?" cried Galla, intrigued. "I'll be farming?"

"In a way," said Aeriod in a low voice. He seemed restive; he sighed. "We'll soon be coming to harvest, which is a busy time. Farming is not vital to your training, of course. It is, however, an incredibly useful skill, and you'll see it in many cultures.

"You need surface experience, first off. You could do with a bit of mechanical expertise as well. But," and he shot her a sly look, "there are other skills to learn down there."

"Like what?" asked Galla.

"Oh, you'll see in time," he responded softly, the faintest grin curling at one corner of his mouth. As the light grew dim, chilling winds whipped around the two of them.

Galla trembled.

"Are you cold?" asked Aeriod, and for a moment Galla caught a spark of genuine concern in his face. He took off his cape and draped it around her shoulders. It pooled around her sparkling feet, and smelled somehow of fire. "How do you like the view?"

Galla could not stop shaking, and she did not understand if it was from the cold, or from stress, or both. "It's . . . it's so beautiful," she chattered. She felt the cape warm her, and Aeriod took her hands in his and blew on them. They warmed instantly. She began blinking.

"You're exhausted," he said. "Come, I'll take you back to your suite."

He led her to her rooms, and she tried to retrace the way so that she could remember better the next time. She did not want to rely on Aeriod for this in the future.

Galla stood blinking and yawning inside her door.

Aeriod let her keep his cape, and said crisply, "Rest. I'll wake you when it's time to go down."

After he left, Galla fell upon on her plush bed, lazily keeping her entire outfit on, glinting red jewels and all. She swaddled herself with Aeriod's jet-black cape. She tried not to wonder too much about Oni-Odi, or about tomorrow's lessons. She could still smell something pleasant in that cape, so she took long breaths with it pressed to her nose: smoke (incense?), fruit, other things that she did not recognize. The smell of the cape seemed so warm, unlike the person who wore it.

She drifted off and dreamed of odd scenes: Aeriod holding her about her waist, walking her through a garden.

"There are our palaces," the dream Aeriod told her. *"To the north, south, east, and west we have our palaces."*

And he took her through a bright golden field toward a large white structure. In the next moment, they had changed direction. They walked toward a forest, still arm in arm, and Aeriod announced, *"Here is our family."*

And in the shadows of the forest, Galla could see large, black, glinting eyes with no irises, stealing looks between the leaves. Those eyes were huge, ominously dark, and disturbing. Galla felt herself shiver in the dream.

7

THE DEVICE

"Up, I say!" cried a voice. She jerked awake. Aeriod leered over her, holding an outfit above her head.

Galla leapt up, nearly hitting Aeriod in the face. "What are you doing in my room?" she demanded.

"You didn't answer my call, and you've missed breakfast," Aeriod retorted. "Quickly now. We're late, and I've little time left for today's session. Put this on."

Galla grasped the thing, a plain red jumper, and chirped, "Wow, no jewels!"

Aeriod's sniff was his only response. So she dashed to her closet and changed. When she emerged, Aeriod was frowning, looking down at the floor. She remembered how, in her dream, he had looked peaceful, pleased. Not so in reality.

Thinking about the dream caused her to shudder. Those huge dark eyes tilting toward her among the shade.

Suddenly she asked, "Aeriod, who does the farming?"

"My assistants, of course," he replied in surprise.

"What do they look like?" she asked hesitantly. She really felt she did not want to see creatures with eyes like those, ever again.

Aeriod raised his eyebrows bemusedly and replied, "They look like simple folk. Bipedal. Quite charming when they follow instructions. You shall see shortly. Ready?"

"I am," and Galla felt her cheeks sting. "But first, do not wake me like that again!"

Aeriod dipped his head. "Very well. But! Try to answer your messages, will you? I'm running a farm. No sleeping in on a farm."

Galla scowled at him. "Fine."

She followed him to a small ship, onyx-black and sleek. In it they soared out of the floating palace and skimmed above the vibrant valley below. Aeriod slid the craft artfully into hovering mode above a patch of farm machinery. He helped Galla make the small leap to the ground and waved the ship away. It launched upward toward the sky island.

She could see a few great beetle-like creatures moving slowly and steadily through the valley. As she and Aeriod approached one of them, she discovered these were not creatures at all, but rather large, bulbous harvesters. The beastly machines had domed windows for eyes and long, sophisticated pincers extending out like great mouths at the front. Their skins shone in iridescent violets, pinks, and greens. Galla had rarely seen such organic-based technology: Oni-Odi's Demetraan favored more utilitarian lines.

Aeriod stood taut and tall, wind-lashed, his striking platinum hair like white fire in the gusts. Galla took in his imposing appearance, combined with the harvester, the blue-green fungus, and the ruddy hills. The richness of color, light, and life dazzled her. She felt as if her many years on Demetraan were being siphoned off of her in the wind of this strange world. She wanted to hold onto something, Oni-Odi, Pliip, anything from her former life. But the wind snatched all those thoughts away from her.

The nearest harvester slowed at their approach. Aeriod held up his hand to command its pilots: the harvester stopped. The great eyes lifted up on either side, now like wings, and three beings emerged. Galla realized she was holding her breath.

She exhaled in relief: these beings were small, attractive bipeds, hairless with sparkling mauve skin, shorter than her by at least a head. They had no frightening huge eyes, but instead their eyes were soft, grey, keen, and—maybe she was imagining it—amused. She saw two of them look at each other significantly. However, they supplicated to Aeriod, kneeling briefly, until he spoke sharp little syllables. Then they rose. Galla blushed; the three now bowed low to her. They watched her intently from then on, but not unkindly.

Aeriod told her, "These are my field workers. They are the Indry-Kol. You surely have heard of their world?"

Galla strained to remember, and then gave a start. The Indry system had been ravaged by nova; only those who had emigrated prior to the catastrophe endured. Galla wondered how many colonists there were.

Aeriod answered for her, quietly, "This is the only substantial remaining population known."

Galla stared at him, then at the Indry-Kol. They were now looking at the ground, their charming and shimmery mauve faces unreadable. Galla impulsively stepped forward, her hand outstretched.

"I'm sorry," she said.

They were clearly taken aback for a moment, and then glanced at each other. Aeriod gave her a sour look. But then the three Indry-Kol assistants bowed again, of their own accord, and their expressions made Galla's eyes sting in empathy.

"This is Galla-Deia," Aeriod told them. "She will be learning some basics down here, so that she understands how everything works."

He looked sidewise at Galla, and she raised her eyebrows.

"Very well," said Aeriod stiffly. "Pleasantries aside, it is time we got to work."

Galla could not help but wonder what actual "work" Aeriod had ever done. She also wondered why he hosted the population here. Was he actually kinder than he came across? Had she known what the Indry-Kol felt toward her at the moment, she might have ducked under Aeriod's cape to hide her face.

As it was, Aeriod asked the farmers about their shift, the weather conditions farther up the valley, and then finally, he asked (not commanded, Galla noted) them if he and Galla could join them. Galla peeked at them as they murmured in hooting, melodic voices to each other, and they knelt again to Aeriod.

"That will do," he told them, but warmly.

He turned and gave Galla a sidelong, piercing glance. She flinched. He beckoned her to him and held her arm.

"Come along, my dear student," he told her, with a little weaving of sarcasm in his sleek voice. "Apparently these good people want you to have my seat." His mouth twitched in amusement. "Your charms already stir not only the firmament, but the surface as well."

This last comment flew past Galla's naïveté. She felt a swell of pride and excitement to climb aboard the beetle-craft. Aeriod guided her in after the Indry took their seats. Galla sat between and slightly behind the farmers, with an excellent view out either "eye" window. Aeriod sat immediately behind her. The eye-doors sealed into place, and the vehicle lurched a bit, and then rumbled forward.

Galla laughed in a high voice and shouted, "This is fun!"

Her laugh startled the crew, including Aeriod, but they kept rolling forward along a long thread of road down the valley. Galla could see that on either side lay amorphous fields of green lichen and cerulean fungus; here and there small adjunct roads shot off into patches for harvest. They passed more beetle-crafts, their pincers embedded in the fungus, chewing up choice specimens as if eating; the harvest was propelled and processed into the gullet of the craft, and any waste flushed from underneath the vehicle.

"Where are we going?" asked Galla. Again, the other four passengers jumped. She thought perhaps nobody ever spoke while operating the machine, which struck her as a dreary way to do things.

"Our pilots are taking us to another field that has a quite interesting topography," Aeriod replied. Galla's eyes widened with curiosity. He asked her, "What do you think of it—the land, the farms?"

Galla whipped around excitedly and cried, "I love it! It's a wonder!"

She did not see Aeriod's expression as he gripped his seat a little more tightly than normal. He watched her incessantly for every reaction.

Galla soon found, however, that the red dust blowing down the hills, and the fungus fibers kicked up by the harvesters, managed to creep into the craft and set her sneezing. And despite its comfortable design, the craft bumped and tossed with every turn of its wheels. Finally, after enduring a good hour of this, Galla asked, "Is it much farther?"

Aeriod chuckled, though it sounded more like a low growl. "Patience, Galla-Deia, we're nearly there," he told her.

"I've been quite patient," she snapped back, and then crossed her arms defiantly.

"I'm sure you think you have," responded Aeriod, "but the view from *my* seat is that of a fidgeting, sighing, restless chit."

"It is *not!*" cried Galla, straining in her seat to glare at Aeriod with her lips sucked in at the corners.

"It does you no good to sulk," said Aeriod calmly. "Do you want to return to the palace? Or would you rather I left you down here? Show some respect."

Galla fumed. She could swear that she saw the Indry pilots shift uneasily after her reprimand. Then she felt a crushing longing for Oni-Odi's quiet guidance. She sat dejected and confused, and sneezed explosively on occasion. She felt that perhaps she would not enjoy this Task of hers.

That sent her fantasizing about a meeting with the Associates, telling them all . . . what? That she didn't want to continue? That Aeriod seemed toxic? That her place was on Demetraan? For even as she thought these things, she felt turmoil and guilt. She had assured Oni-Odi she would perform her training. What would he think if she let him down? She could not disappoint Oni-Odi! He was revered and respected, and he had been her mentor. No, she thought, she must prove herself worthy of him.

She swallowed any simmering epithets for the moment. Luckily the craft was slowing and its passengers were preoccupied by its final destination. The fungus fields stretched around a yawning hole, and at its lip the harvester parked. Everyone left the vehicle and approached the edge of the hole. The Indry people peeked in and, seemingly satisfied, returned to their craft.

Aeriod took Galla's arm.

"No falling in," he muttered.

Before her eyes a fence appeared all around the hole, which was easily four times the size of a harvester in diameter. Galla noticed a small gate to her left.

"What is this?" she wondered aloud.

Aeriod waved impressively, sending his cape flapping in the breeze that funneled down off the warm hills. "This," he told her, "is one reason I reside here. Did you think I was only a part-time mage-governor, farming in retirement?"

"Well," Galla stammered, "no, not exactly. You don't look like what I imagined a farmer to look like, anyway. I mean it seemed—for a moment, anyway—you were here to protect the Indry-Kol."

"Ah yes, an added enhancement to my image," Aeriod whispered just so she could hear. Louder, he declared, "Of course that is part of what I do. Yet this gaping hole you see here—this is one of the main reasons why I live on Rikiloi. I am its guardian."

"Well," Galla goaded him, "what is it?"

"It is an entry to an old Device—far older than I, if you can imagine... Never mind. One day you will understand *that*."

"A device?" repeated Galla. "Like a machine?"

"Oh, no doubt some would call it that," Aeriod replied. His eyes peered into the darkness of the pit. "It is, however, much more. It's a remnant of a culture that existed eons ago. It is not the only such Device. However, there are few of them known. And not every one of them has a decipherable purpose. For you see, in that pit, there is a series of catacombs, lifts, passageways, and locks. I have spent many years exploring these things, and have learned much about them. However, I am nowhere near finished with my survey. And this is only one Device!

"Your assistance exploring this could prove useful to the

Associates, as part of your training with me. Our shared knowledge might help find and decipher the other Devices as well."

Galla considered this, and then asked, "Is this my Task then?"

"No, not exclusively," Aeriod replied. He gave her an inscrutable look. "Consider this a necessary prerequisite, one of many."

"Hmm," Galla answered.

Aeriod returned her to the harvester. When she peeked back at the hole, she could not see it.

"I hide it," Aeriod answered her gaze.

Galla felt a sense of unease.

"From what?" she asked.

"You really ought to make an effort, Galla-Deia, to learn some patience," replied Aeriod archly. "You've seen enough today. You'll have plenty of opportunity to help with the harvest soon enough, and with exploring the Device. Let's return to the keep."

Aeriod invoked a call she did not understand upward to the sky; his ship hurtled out from its dock in the floating asteroid and arced sleekly down to hover close by. Aeriod allowed the harvesters to resume their work, and he led Galla onto the ship. As they sailed skyward, Galla's thoughts frothed with questions.

Finally, just as they docked, she asked, "So, you trust the Indry-Kol with this Device?"

Aeriod jutted his chin high. "The Indry-Kol owe me that," he replied shortly.

Galla cringed. Somehow, she thought, the Indry-Kol should be exempt from owing anyone a thing, especially since they were an endangered race. So once again Galla felt a tug of dislike for Aeriod, and thought him conceited.

8

SUMOND

The next day, Aeriod did not materialize for breakfast in Galla's quarters. At least, not in physical form: when Galla awoke, his face leered at her from a hologram. She groaned.

Aeriod told her in an onerous voice, "I have been called to a meeting offworld. It may be a few days before my return. I have no tasks assigned for you, so enjoy your brief respite."

And the image vanished.

Galla felt an eruption of joy pervade her, so she laughed and jumped back into her bed. She lay there and wriggled comfortably, basking in the luxury of Aeriod's absence. She planned out her whole day: she would lie in bed an extra hour, eat breakfast, and then explore the gliding palace.

She tucked her covers around herself and thought about Demetraan. She wondered about Oni-Odi. But since it was a good day, she didn't wallow in missing him or the City. Her thoughts would bounce back and forth, to what she could wear, to what kind of food she could ask for from the kitchen. And then she fell to wondering, where *was* the kitchen?

The second she thought that, she sat up. Of course she could visit the kitchen. *Does he even have a kitchen?* She stopped and wondered.

Maybe he just waved his hand and that made the food. Then she considered the farms she'd just seen on the surface below. He did not wave his hands for that, but rather let the Indry-Kol subsist for their livelihood. She could not understand it.

Galla bathed in her suite's tub of swirling, scented water. Then she yanked one of the few plain outfits from the closets, pulled it on, and stumbled out of her room, electrified by her small quest. What she failed to grasp was the true extent of the palace-island. And while Aeriod had placed various educational panels along certain visitors' corridors, he took no chances that someone could discern the true contents of his fortress. Naturally, he had ensured Galla could not, either.

After the first hour of investigating each hall, passage, or stairwell near her own suite, she took a different tack. She at first consulted a panel, and asked for the kitchen's location. After hearing "access denied" a few times, even after carefully rewording the request each time, Galla stalked off.

But she returned, and asked casually, "Perishable shipment docks."

This gave her a response, and she pelted along to seek out a docking bay. She soon discovered that Aeriod made passage difficult even if you knew where you were supposed to go. Inconveniently for Galla, some passageways were blocked, ramps and stairwells disappeared, and eventually she became lost.

She did find the docking bay, but only after using her nose. Despite having an efficient air recycling system, Aeriod could not block everything, and Galla recognized the scent of fuels and machinery from her own experience in Demetraan's docking bays. She took the chance and managed to find the entrance. It opened without incident, and she stepped into the bay.

Dockworkers moved to and fro, so she kept out of sight behind crates and containers. She could just see a small group surrounding a set of orange containers; one of them was a passionate, bluish character with multiple limbs, by the looks of it. Its several arms waved and thrashed in a high temper. Shouts rang across the bay, but the other dockworkers ignored them.

Galla moved closer, until she could see the creature better. She stifled a laugh; in each "hand," the character held a piece of fruit. Suddenly, each arm rotated in windmill fashion, and launched the fruit in rapid fire into the chest of a poor pilot.

Nevertheless, the pilot bowed and hastened back to its ship. The multi-limbed creature barked commands at its fellow stevedores, who followed with orange cylinders in tow. Galla crept quietly behind them.

The party continued along corridors she had not seen listed on the information panels. Galla just managed to slip into these halls behind the orange cylinders, before the section doors closed. At last they reached a lift.

Galla balked and hid herself. Although this freight lift was quite large, there was no way she could escape being seen. From where Galla stood out of sight, she heard the voices of the food workers. She recognized the multi-limbed creature's voice; instead of shouting, it now spoke quietly. Then the voices silenced. She didn't dare look, but she knew they had entered the lift.

"You!" snapped a voice.

Galla jumped. Before her stood the many-limbed, high-tempered food thrower. The being towered over her and folded all its arms in an unmistakably reproachful fashion. Galla shrank back against the wall, but crouched to run if needed.

The being stared down at her through deep-set black eyes and opened its several gill-like nostrils wide, as if sniffing. Its skin was deep blue and mottled with brown. Its arms were long and wiry, although its midsection bulged under a tunic. Its appendages varied in shape, and even changed shape.

"You have followed us," this being accused her. "Who are you? Why do you spy on us?"

Galla replied defensively, "I've just been going for a walk. I've not been spying on anyone."

The being replied with a huffing sound, and some of its arms unfolded menacingly.

"Really," stammered Galla, "I'm not doing anything wrong. I was . . . just trying to find the kitchens."

"Why?" bellowed the creature.

"Because . . . well, I was curious," responded Galla weakly.

She hugged herself in apprehension. Would all those blue limbs come at her rapid-fire, and hammer her to the floor?

"That is no answer," the being declared. The limbs loosened. "I think I know who you are: you are the mage's pupil."

Galla nodded.

"He did tell us you might try to apprehend us. He did not mention you would use subterfuge!"

Galla then stood as straight and tall as she could.

"Oh, he told you that, did he?" she cried. "I wonder what else he told you. Fine, I'll leave. I just wanted to see the kitchens. And Aeriod has made it impossible to find them on my own. I hadn't seen any of you, so it's not as though I could have asked you. Anyway, he is away on some *very important* business or something."

At this, the being let out a long humming noise and closed its eyes. Its face turned from blue to more of a purple-brown.

To Galla's surprise it said, "You are *funny!* You may see the kitchens. Come with me. I am Sumond, the head chef here."

Galla eyed him warily, but said, "I'm Galla-Deia. Call me Galla."

The being Sumond bowed with all arms clasped to his abdomen. Despite his ungainly appearance, he walked elegantly along, his clothing fluttering. He led her to the lift, now empty, and it shut and began moving up. Sumond stood quietly, not looking at Galla, though she took many looks at him.

Soon the lift opened to reveal a short hallway, and on the other side of that, a gigantic space opened before them. Galla drew in a long, satisfied breath, for here was yet another marvel.

All around her workers rushed back and forth, carrying trays of steaming food, carting produce, or rolling canisters along. Above her, all the way to the ceiling, workers perched on platforms, with small lifts connecting each of them. In the center of this space sat three huge vats, with ramps and platforms built all around them. And at the ceiling, long tendrils of plants stretched down, their branches clustered with many different kinds of fruit and vegetables. Around the plants, workers hovered in the air, picking them.

From where Galla stood, the smells of fruit, hearty meals, delectable sweets, tangy ciders, and unnamable foods filled her senses. She stood stunned at this giant sphere of activity, its sheer size, its many facets and wonders. Sumond leaned over and touched her shoulder.

"We are proud of our kitchens," he told her. "Please, come with me to my workplace. You can tour this area at any time. And I do mean this: the mage has limited jurisdiction here."

"Oh?" Galla turned to look at Sumond. "Why is that?"

"Because," replied Sumond with a hint of smugness, "in our sector of the galaxy, having a chef is an utmost luxury. You did not know? Well then, I should tell you—chefs require a great deal of money and power, and we wield those things also. Because of this, chefs are some of the most powerful figures around! Oh, we don't run governments or anything. But I do wonder how many civilizations would remain intact, without chefs!"

Galla laughed; she liked Sumond already. She followed him to a great room full of rich smells and discovered a new pleasure: purple tarts. Their sweet yet tangy scent drew her over to them and gave her a strong craving. She sighed rapturously after eating one of the small, flaky tarts.

Sumond in turn warmed quickly to Galla, for he held a captive audience as he crafted his confections with his many hands.

"Although," he went on thoughtfully, "we may not have a choice about governments and civilizations. Things are changing, and we are entering a dark time."

Galla looked at him with huge eyes. She asked, "Are we safe?"

Sumond lowered his eyelids and formed a circle with all of his hands.

"No one is safe now. Aeriod gives us a veneer of safety, with his 'protected' worlds. But he is one person. And there is only so much he can do to stop . . . Well, I am not sure he can really stop anything. Move things around? Hide things? Those are his skills."

Galla did not know what to say. After Sumond plied her with small vials of liquor and candies, she made her way back to her quarters in a dreamy state. Somehow staying in Aeriod's soaring palace had become a little less chilling.

She returned each day after that and spent more and more time talking to Sumond as he worked, and listened to stories of roaring parties he had previously prepped for the mage.

"Do you know anything about humans?" she asked Sumond one day. Sumond's skin color faded to sky blue and he exhaled with a low whistle.

"I know what I have heard from Aeriod, and what other observers have told me," he answered. He squinted at her. "I do not think you are much like them, after all."

"Well, no," Galla answered. "Not yet. I think I will be, one day."

"Why would you want that?" gasped Sumond.

"Why wouldn't I?" asked Galla, genuinely curious.

Sumond hissed.

"Vicious things. Messy, dramatic. Temperamental. Primitive reproduction methods."

"Like what?" Galla pressed.

Sumond shook his chins at her.

"Messy," he repeated.

"I want to know," insisted Galla.

"I'm not going to tell you! Go and look it up over on my panel if you must. Disgusting."

Galla laughed and did as Sumond suggested. She began asking the panel questions and soon found answers she had not expected. Those led to more questions. Sumond watched her slyly as she straightened her back and cried, "Oh! How does that work?" and then he guffawed. She soon learned Sumond took great amusement in her self-education.

Galla began to realize she had been the only guest here for a long time. Despite not wanting to think about him much, she still could not keep Aeriod far from her thoughts. She simultaneously feared and was fascinated by him, and she dreaded the undercurrent of malice that shone in his gaze sometimes, or that quickly made its way to his lips. She began to wonder why he was so acerbic. But Sumond revealed little that explained the mage's behavior.

Sumond asked her what she would be studying from Aeriod on her last day before the mage's return. Galla shivered where she sat, avoiding Sumond's stare.

"I think," she said slowly, fidgeting with her hair, "I probably shouldn't talk about that."

A breeze struck her and sent Sumond's flour aloft into a cloud. In that cloud appeared a face—Aeriod's.

His voice boomed, "Correct, my student. You will return to your quarters. Now," and the cloud disappeared with a loud *crack*.

Galla trembled. Sumond reached out to her with four hands and squeezed her shoulders gently. She looked up and he smiled at her with fondness.

"Don't worry, Galla," he told her. "When you dine, remember where true power can lie. And should you fail at your studies, perhaps you would consider becoming a chef!"

9
INDEPENDENCE

Galla gave Sumond a quick hug, smelling sweetness on him, and fled the kitchens. She walked swiftly and her nervousness faded. In its place she felt resentment. She tried to control it so Aeriod would not see it. She entered her rooms and paced slowly, breathing deeply and calming herself.

Just as she relaxed, Aeriod chimed and entered her parlor. They looked at each other: Galla defiant, chin high, her hair untamed; Aeriod cold and stiff.

He towered over her and bellowed, "What have you done? What have you *said?*"

Galla stilled her trembling hands by clenching them into fists.

She said quickly, sharply, "I have done nothing important. I have explored the grounds and expanded my knowledge of its people and its workings. *You* left me with nothing to do but stare at trinkets in my rooms!"

"You lowered yourself!" Aeriod cried, his own hands opening and closing like claws. "You affiliated with my *staff*, you *exposed* yourself."

"*You* would have me isolated, then?" Galla shot back in the same tone. "A prisoner?"

"No. No; but I will not have you walking openly among the keep's people," replied the mage. He said quietly and terribly, "You risk your very purpose, the purpose of the Associates. You are not ready for social exposure."

"No. You are wrong!" flashed Galla, shaking. "You don't know my true purpose, do you? Because if you did, you wouldn't risk delaying me from it. You wouldn't insist on having me first."

Aeriod blinked and wrinkled his brow. Galla looked smug, but he placed his hands on her shoulders. She tensed under his long fingers, but kept her chin set.

"While you are within my territory," he hissed, "you will abide by my rules, by my teaching. This is your *immediate* purpose. Beyond that I will not speculate. You must tell no one of the Associates, and say nothing of your Task, not even a hint of it! Do you understand?"

Galla folded her arms haughtily.

"It's clear that I don't. But Oni-Odi wants me to complete my Task, whatever it is. If that means I have to deal with you, I guess I don't have a choice." She pushed Aeriod's hands off her shoulders. "But if you think I will spend all my time with you or down in that dark hole on the planet, forget it. Oni wouldn't want that either."

"He has no authority here," snapped Aeriod.

Galla raised an eyebrow at him but said nothing.

That was a fast answer, she thought. *I think he's lying.*

"Well then, if you're finished . . ." Galla began, looking pointedly at the door.

"I am not," Aeriod replied. He composed himself and smoothed his black clothes. "It is time for dinner."

"I've already dined!" Galla shouted, her whole body shaking, her feral hair twisting this way and that.

Aeriod swept forward in a ripple of cape and hair, seized Galla about her waist, and threw her neatly over his shoulder. She shrieked and thrashed with rage.

"Put me down!" Galla howled.

Her clothes were changing. She brought forth as many curses on Aeriod as she knew (she had just picked up some zingers in the kitchens) and wailed in humiliation at being carried like a sack *and* being magically re-dressed in some elaborate frock.

He set her down abruptly once inside his quarters, and she flew at him, a streak of red gems and magically coiffed hair, and shouted, "How dare you! How dare you pick me up!"

"What?" Aeriod asked, genuinely surprised. "Oni-Odi told me that when you threw tantrums, sometimes he would carry you."

"Not like that!" cried Galla. She could feel heat rising up her neck and her face. She clasped her hands to her red cheeks. "Not like a sack of food! Sometimes he would *gently* cradle me until I calmed down."

"Ah," Aeriod said, and he put his hands to his mouth. He groaned. Galla stared at him, amazed, as he said, "How embarrassing. I apologize, then."

"You still dressed me against my will!" Galla raged, and Aeriod watched her, bemused, as she shook her fists at him, the low light flashing on her gemstone dress.

"Behave!" he gasped.

"Freedom!" she snarled back. "Give me more freedom, or I'm leaving!"

Aeriod laughed. "And how would you do that? You're ridiculous!" He held out his arms, placating to Galla, and she folded hers in defiance.

Galla glanced up and noticed the light had changed, and she recognized a whiff of the incense from when she had met him on Demetraan.

"Why are we here? These are your quarters, yes?" she demanded.

"Yes," said Aeriod.

"Why?"

Aeriod looked uncomfortable. "I thought we would dine here when I returned. This did not go . . . quite as I envisioned."

"You can't control me," she told him, jutting her chin.

"Oh?" Aeriod replied. "You wouldn't be where you are, this moment, if I could not."

Galla seethed, knowing any response was damned. If she agreed she admitted failure, and if she scoffed, he still controlled her by her allowing him to anger her. So she decided to improvise.

"I don't want to dine with you," she said, glaring at him. "You're harsh, demanding, and unfriendly."

"Allow me to apologize, Galla-Deia," Aeriod proffered, and again he tried holding his hands out. "I am sorry for . . . seizing you. That was an error in judgment."

Galla snorted.

Aeriod went on, "Perhaps we could arrange . . . something . . . a compromise. But you can't just go poking around when I'm offworld. It is still *my* home."

"Fine, I accept your apology," Galla reluctantly said. "But I have my own rules. First of all, there will be no more throwing me over your shoulder."

Aeriod grinned.

"And this undressing and re-dressing . . . this has to stop!"

Aeriod nodded.

"You can't force me to dine with you. You have to ask if I would like to."

"Very well," agreed Aeriod. He bent down a bit. "Would you please join me for dinner? I would very much like to hear more about your adventures."

Galla lifted a skeptical eyebrow and studied the mage. *He seems friendly for now. I wonder how long it will last?*

"That's much better. Yes, fine. I will join you for dinner," she replied. "This time."

Aeriod looked visibly relieved. He waved his hand and a table appeared, loaded with food and drink. He offered his hand once more, and this time Galla took it. They sat at the table and stared at each other for what seemed to Galla several minutes. Aeriod's face was unreadable.

Galla said to him, "I've been learning from . . . your kitchen staff about some general societal rules." She felt reluctant to bring up her panel education.

"Well then, I suppose it's a good thing you've done *something* useful in my absence," retorted Aeriod.

"Why are you so harsh and cold?" she asked him suddenly.

"You're young, Galla-Deia, too naïve and inexperienced to understand."

"There you go again! Patronizing," Galla snapped. She seized the glass in front of her and nearly bit it in fury as she took a drink.

"Look," he told her, "you must see the truth in what I'm saying. You're a Representative. Have you thought about what that truly means?"

"Only a little," Galla admitted.

"I daresay it's better that way," Aeriod said quietly. "The point is, when you get to where *I* am, you know what you want and don't want. It takes a long time to get to that point; at least it did for me. For myself, I want things to be a certain way, and I expect them to be so."

"Is that why you're alone?" asked Galla archly.

Aeriod scowled. "Do not assume things about me, Galla-Deia."

"I sort of have to, because you seem too cold for me to know otherwise."

Aeriod sighed. "Just how much have you been talking to the kitchen staff?"

"Does it matter?" Galla asked. "I'm getting an education."

"I'm not sure I like its quality," mused Aeriod, lifting a glass to his lips. Galla could see his other hand clenched the edge of the table. "Now that I'm back, I can give you more of a tour. I do have to leave every once in a while. I have missions beyond this world. You might as well know how things work around here, while I'm gone."

Galla relaxed a bit. "I like the sound of that," she said, and she also took another drink, this time more gently. They ate quietly for several minutes. Then the unease between them crept back in, and Aeriod rigidly walked her back to her suite. Galla entered her rooms feeling a bit overwhelmed and exhausted emotionally.

Aeriod, meanwhile, walked the length of his wing several times through the night.

I wonder how much longer, he thought as he paced.

10

SCINTILLA

She sat excitedly at the controls of her craft. Aeriod had instructed her to navigate the canyons and valleys, solo. He had given her a sampling task as well.

"I've seen your piloting skills," he had remarked acidly. "So I won't be joining you."

Galla flew out of the launch bay and sped out of its immediate area with a sense of liberation. She swept through the air, marveling at the feeling of flying in a proper atmosphere. Eventually she made her way to the valley with the Device and hovered over the area. She could not see the pit.

"Surprise!" crackled Aeriod's voice in her helmet. "I did not give you unshielding capability yet."

"It doesn't matter," Galla responded. "You've not ordered me to work on it."

"Complete your survey," said Aeriod flatly. "Take the measurements I asked for, and return."

Galla whizzed on from the pit area and flowed up and over some low hills. She liked the rise and fall of those red hills; the gentle undulation soothed her. From time to time she could see small Indry-Kol outposts, and hangars for their farm equipment. She swept down through several new valleys, halting only to launch her sampler spheres and await their return. She carried on until dusk, when the hills began to turn purple and the hues of zenith, horizon, hill, and vale resembled a great rainbow. She grinned the whole time, ecstatic about the beauty of Rikiloi.

Aeriod chimed her. With her cue to return, she altered course and zoomed back, a mix of melancholy and pleasure tugging at her. She went to the mage the moment she returned, flushed from her day of flying. He frowned at her.

"What's this?" he hissed. "Full pilot regalia, in my quarters?"

"I just wanted to—" she began.

"Go change. Now. Then return."

Galla harrumphed.

"Do wash up, while you're at it," Aeriod said serenely, one side of his mouth curled in a smirk.

She loped to her suite, headed straight to the bath, and found the tub steaming and full of flowers and oils. She yanked off her clothing and slid into the frothy basin.

"Don't you dare watch!" she shouted at the air, and she ducked under bubbles.

She bathed at ferocious speed, sending soap flying, and then wrapped herself in a simple robe. She strutted to Aeriod's quarters. He allowed her to enter, and his eyes widened at her appearance.

"Your hair—" he began.

"Yes! It's wet!" she cried.

But she could feel her hair misbehaving. It betrayed her mood, and she blushed.

"It's—it's just that it's sticking up in—ah, never mind," Aeriod said.

"I got your precious samples," said Galla expectantly. "Now how did I do?"

Aeriod regarded her with amusement and even some admiration. He unsnapped a small brooch on his cape, and the cape lifted into the air and swirled over to Galla, where it wrapped her up and warmed her. He raised his hand when her mouth opened.

"Your flying," he told her, "improved as the day went on. But you should know—before you implode from overconfidence—your piloting skills were beyond horrendous. Now they are *merely awful.*"

"Oh, well then," sniffed Galla, leering at him, "I've learned *so much* from *you,* after all."

"And," Aeriod continued, ignoring her, "the samples are quite satisfactory. Not that you had anything to do with that, besides deploying the samplers."

Galla slumped into a chair and closed her eyes. "So does this mean I won't be learning anything new?"

Aeriod bent over her and lifted her face with his hands.

"You, my darling student," he said, "will learn very soon not to ask such things. But since you have, I will say that it is time for you to study the Device down in the pit."

Galla stood quickly, and collided with him. He caught her and held her back, a little reluctantly.

"Do you mean it?" she asked earnestly. "Don't look away. Please, tell me the truth, no teasing. Am I ready?"

Aeriod did look at her directly, and replied firmly, "Yes."

Galla's face glowed, and her smile flooded him with such intensity he held his breath. She then dropped her smile and cautiously studied him.

"Aeriod," she said slowly, "you look . . . like something's bothering you. What is it?"

"Nothing pressing," he replied easily. "Ready for an evening meal?"

Galla agreed to this. They sat in another awkward silence while Aeriod busied himself with his wine and food. Galla decided something had changed with the mage, but she could not figure it out. So she tried to be social, having acquired a few skills from the kitchen staff.

"Why are you alone?" she blurted out.

Aeriod studied his wine in the light. "Don't be stupid, Galla. There are many people here, including yourself."

"I mean, why don't you have any companions?" pressed Galla. "I've not seen anyone with you."

"That would be because you're with me at the time."

Galla thought about that statement.

She asked, "Does that mean that when I'm not around, someone else is with you?"

"Is there a point to your badgering?" demanded Aeriod, his voice hardening. He flicked back his long, pale hair. Galla noticed how pointy his ears were. She had a sudden, strong desire to touch them.

Galla felt her cheeks go hot. "I just wondered. I mean, it's a huge and gorgeous place. It seems like you'd want to share it. I don't know, just seems like it would be lonely otherwise."

She watched as he stared moodily down at his glass. His face looked sad to her, his eyes cloud-grey and dull. He sat that way for so long that his lamps began fizzing on and ambling slowly toward the two of them through the air. They hovered by and sent warm light onto Aeriod's pale hair. His sharp face did not soften in the light. Galla hesitated, then reached over and clasped his free hand.

"Are you all right?"

Slowly, as if thawing, Aeriod rotated his wineglass in his other hand and brought his gaze back to the bright-haired woman. *How long?* he wondered again.

"I am tired," he said eventually. "You may go."

Galla again squeezed his hand, with its fine long fingers, in her own small hands. "Are you ordering me out?" she queried.

"No," he replied, his voice hollow.

"Then I would like to stay a bit longer," said Galla, taking in a deep breath, "so that no one else needs to keep you company."

Aeriod replied, "Then you may stay." He sighed heavily. "I must tell you, Galla-Deia, you are oddly persuasive. It is your innocence that worries me."

"Why?" wondered Galla.

"I had agreed to train you first, before . . . before other influences changed you. I thought I would not recognize innocence anymore, Galla. But now it stares at me with your eyes."

Galla looked away.

The mage went on, "I wanted to preserve that while you remain here."

Galla declared, "You want me before anyone else gets me, you mean."

Aeriod jerked upright, sloshing his glass. "What!" he exclaimed.

She shrugged. "That's what it seems like."

Aeriod pierced her with one of his sparking looks. Then he let out a great gale of laughter. Galla glared at him.

"You've learned too much from the kitchen staff! Haven't you?" he asked.

Galla smirked. "Maybe."

"Damn that chef!" cried Aeriod, eyes crinkled. Sobering, he said, "Sumond knows many things, some of which he should not tell you."

"Oh, I didn't mean to get him in trouble," Galla said quickly. Her forehead pinched together in stress, and she realized at that moment how fond she had grown of Sumond.

"Ah—wait—I'm not going to fire him, Galla! He's the best there is. But I will have a word! Let me guess: you heard something and had questions."

"Yes," she admitted, turning deep rose.

"That's the problem with having Sumond for one's chef," mused Aeriod. "He's omniscient, that one."

"Was I right, then?" Galla asked.

"Not entirely," Aeriod replied impishly.

"Am I safe with you?" she asked, her insides turbulent. She was feeling warm, and her neck tingled. She started peeling off Aeriod's cape.

His fingers entwined with hers. "Always."

"Aeriod, you annoy me, but I still like you somehow," Galla said.

"The feeling is mutual," said Aeriod quietly. He admired Galla's small hands, and her amber eyes, her funny little smirk, her brilliant hair. He realized he had stopped breathing.

Abruptly, he stood and pulled her up. "I think it's time to say good night," he said. "Busy day tomorrow, you know. Shall I walk you back?"

"No, I've learned the way," said Galla. "Good night." Aeriod bowed, and Galla left the room. Once in the hallway, she sprinted back to her suite, hoping to rid herself of the intense heat coursing throughout her body. She lay awake for some time and hugged herself to sleep.

11

THE ABYSS

Galla awoke to Aeriod's hologram face above her. She shrieked and sat bolt upright.

"Time to get up!" his face told her. He wore a wicked smirk.

"Could you please *not* wake me like that?" Galla asked.

"Well, you weren't answering, and it was effective, yes?" said Aeriod. "When you start answering your alarm, I'll stop waking you like this."

She moaned and slid back down under the covers. "Can I just have breakfast in here?"

"You may," Aeriod answered, "but it's time to examine that Device. Head down in your craft. I'll unshield it for you."

Galla hastily readied for her work. She ate the sugared bun and fruit that suddenly appeared on her nightstand. She donned a jumpsuit that phosphoresced, and fled to the bay. She loved this. Aeriod might think her a dreadful pilot, but she adored how it felt. She could scarcely wait to begin, even if it took some time and effort to get her hair to behave for the helmet. She would shove the curling tendrils in, and out they would spring again. She jumped onto the little survey craft and shot out of the floating fortress, and dropped rapidly.

Aeriod, watching from his balcony, felt like covering his eyes. *I should not be worrying about her, but it's difficult not to.*

She pulled up just before skimming the surface (Aeriod had turned away, having covered his face with his hands), and then sped back upward with a joyful whoop. She headed straight into the wind, loving the feeling of it sweeping away any uncomfortable thoughts, just simple motion at high speed. She wove around the hills and headed for the pit.

Galla soon found it, and flew all around it before landing near its rim. She took off her helmet and set it on the seat of her survey craft. She peered over the edge and recoiled. There was something about this gaping thing that seemed unsettling to her.

"I've made it," she said to her wrist communicator.

"Good," said a relieved Aeriod. "Now look for footholds and make your way down. Take note of everything you see."

"Got it," said Galla.

"Be careful," Aeriod told her.

Galla slinked slowly down the footholds. She ventured farther down for several minutes. The air temperature seemed cool, like a cave. It smelled metallic, like rusted machinery. Deep into the hole, she could just see dim red lights. The light emanating from her glowing clothing did not reach the other side of the pit, so she was grateful for the red lamps. She carefully stepped farther down again. It was silent except for a whistling breeze. The blackness of that pit unnerved her, even with the lights.

She shuffled her feet on a solid surface. She let out a sigh.

"I've reached a platform," she said aloud.

Aeriod's voice said, "Well done. Now hold steady—and calm yourself."

Galla felt, but could not see, the edges of the platform. She sat with her legs crossed and waited. Gradually a humming sounded, and a series of whooshing noises came from somewhere in the pit.

"Something's happening," she whispered.

"Don't move until after the platform stops," Aeriod told her.

"You'll be beyond communication range soon, due to interference. Proceed and be cautious."

The platform suddenly shot down into the darkness. Galla had no time to shriek in surprise. She sat perfectly still, her hair blown upward from the speed of descent. Quaking, she watched the disk of sky above her become smaller and smaller. She eyed the wall of the pit, its red lights streaming in a vertical blur. And then, *clack!* The platform stopped.

"I've stopped," she breathed. No answer. She exhaled shakily. Aeriod could no longer hear her.

She stood and turned around. A panel had slid open behind her, taller than Aeriod and thinner. More dim light shone beyond. Galla entered the door and found a long hallway. The panel slid shut behind her.

She blinked; the light grew brighter. Soon she could see well enough to orient herself. Before her were other doors, all opening into various passageways that branched downward. She moved to one at her left, and began walking down its hall.

She traveled for some time along the metallic halls, looking for anything interesting. No other doors and no markings were visible, even after nearly an hour of searching. There was, however, a rhythmic sort of humming, soft and barely perceptible to Galla. And while she had been accustomed to many machines and their sounds on Demetraan, this humming heightened her anxiety.

I don't like this place, she thought as she walked. *I don't know how Aeriod explored this pit all by himself. There's something not right about it.*

For an awful moment, her thoughts returned to the dream she had about Aeriod and the beings with the great, dark eyes. She hated thinking of that: she began obsessing about those eyes, staring coldly, unflinching. The humming-thumping rang in her ears and she began to realize she was afraid.

She had stopped, but now she began walking again, thinking, *What is this place? What is it for? Who built it? And why would there be several of these on different planets?*

She had finally staved off some of her anxiety about it all, when she heard a hideous clanging and scraping sound. She twitched where she stood: *There's something in here!* she thought frantically. She wanted to run back out to the platform and skyrocket out of there.

A vibration flowed through the floor, followed by a deep, low-octave hum. The clanging stopped. Galla could see the hallway light up in the distance, revealing a broad space like a courtyard. She decided to walk toward it. Inside, she found nothing but empty space, and several other doors heading off from the courtyard like spokes of a wheel. The air was still and stagnant in this space. She began to walk toward one of the doors.

Then Galla froze. Images entered her mind, things she did not understand: faces, other planets, fire, clouds. At one point she saw something that seemed familiar—a great piece of rock, larger than her, split open, lined with violet crystals. Another image showed her a star collapsing, then vanishing suddenly before any ejection of material. She stood transfixed, and the visions kept rolling. In one scene, there was a shadowy place filled with hive-like cells. Another image showed her what looked like a city made of copper. Finally, one image made her clench her own arms tightly: a great web, with herself caught in it and cabled up as the web enveloped her, pulled her arms and legs far apart, threw her head back, and thrust into her mouth, suffocating her.

A quiet voice said to her, *"You cannot stop us. If we cannot harm you, we will take everything from you. We will feed upon the pain of those you love."*

She fell to her knees, wheezing. The scraping sound began again. The buzzing and thumping grew. The place was roaring, shaking.

She cried out, "Oni-Odi! Aeriod!" and staggered up. She ran, pounding the metal floor as it pitched and rolled below her. She reached the exit and the door slid open. She nearly missed the small platform, and clung to it ferociously while looking back at the door behind her. It had shut.

Desperately, she yelled, "Go! Go up!" and held tight. The platform surged upward and she gasped in relief at the small light above.

As soon as the lift stopped, Galla clambered up the footholds in mad haste and threw herself onto the ground. She covered her face with her hands and curled into a ball, shaking.

"Galla!" cried a voice.

"Aeriod," she moaned. She felt hands lifting her, holding her steady.

"You're safe. Try to stop convulsing," the mage told her in a calm voice. She began to remove her hands from her face.

It was dusk. When Galla had gone down, it had been morning. She shuddered. Then she noticed three Indry-Kol standing behind Aeriod at a distance. They bowed to her respectfully; she recognized them from her first harvesting trip.

Aeriod murmured an incantation to prevent Galla from curling back up. He put an arm around her and walked her toward the Indry-Kol. They looked up at him with frightened expressions.

"She will be all right," he told them in their language. "Come along with me; we'll all go back together."

They entered Aeriod's craft and soon arrived within his keep. Aeriod led Galla and the three Indry-Kol to her chambers. The mage coaxed her onto her bed, where she turned away from all of them and clutched her covers about her.

Aeriod turned to the Indry-Kol and spoke to them in whispers. They bowed to the mage and left the chambers. Aeriod swept over to Galla and moved her tangled hair from under her head.

"Rest now," his voice came soothingly, but she could not hear him.

12

ENLIGHTENMENT

In the morning, Galla tried desperately to awaken, but each time she did so, she found herself sliding back to sleep. She had never experienced this before, and she found it frightening and frustrating. Eventually she stayed awake and lay blinking at the ceiling, which was masked with several levitating flowers.

"Are those for me?" she asked aloud. She watched them swirl down to her and onto her bed. She picked some of them up and breathed them in. "How lovely!" she cried.

Her door chimed.

"Come in," she called.

Aeriod swept over to her and knelt next to her bed. She leaned back on her pillows and looked at him. His face looked haggard, but his silver eyes shone.

"How do you feel?" he asked her.

She pushed herself up and said, "Very strange. But better, I think."

In truth, she still felt drowsy and even a bit numb. "What happened down there?" she asked.

"I'm not entirely sure," he replied. He held out his hand. She plopped her hand into his.

"So I take it that's never happened to you?" she asked.

"No," he said. "Tell me what you saw."

Galla hesitated, struggling to remember. "There wasn't much to see at first: the pit itself, the platform, and hallways, and doors . . . until I had these images in my mind," she said.

"Images? What kind of images?"

Galla recounted what she could, but the memory confused her. She felt uncomfortable, with the nasty feeling that maybe she had panicked over something stupid. She shuddered, thinking of the voice from those images, but she could not remember exactly what it had said. She braced herself for a potential berating.

"Did I do something wrong?"

Aeriod rose and paced around her bed, his hands behind his back, his brow pinched. "No," he said.

"Then what is it?" Galla asked, disquieted by his expression.

Aeriod continued pacing as he answered, "This has never happened while I have explored the tunnels. And I've been down through many of them. Yet you say—and I believe you—that the hall you went down was empty and began to reverberate. And then you saw images. The scraping sounds, I've heard those. Though perhaps this was more extreme than what I heard. But the images in your mind . . . that voice . . . It eludes me, what they could be."

"What put them there?" Galla wondered.

Aeriod glanced at her, and then turned away. He thought rapidly. *This portends something I had not foreseen. What does it mean for my world? Has this happened before, to anyone else? I dread telling the Associates.*

"Galla," he said, still turned away from her, "I must tell the Associates what happened to you."

At first Galla went cold. Then she lit up with excitement.

"Could I speak to Oni-Odi?" she asked the mage.

Aeriod turned to her and frowned. "You know you cannot!"

Galla trembled. "Aeriod, could you at least pass a message to him? From me?"

Aeriod sat beside her and gave her a hard look. "Galla, it is forbidden that you contact him. It could jeopardize everything."

"You could arrange it—"

"I will not," he said shortly. "Even if I wanted to—which I do not—I would not take such a risk. Now I must contact the Associates to see what they think of this."

"When can I see Oni-Odi again?" Galla asked, tears in her eyes.

"When your training is over," Aeriod answered.

"*When* will that be?" she cried.

"Long from now."

She gave herself up to a slow spilling of tears and breathed in little gasps of anguish. Aeriod left her and raged inwardly.

The response from the Associates both relieved and infuriated him. The Summoners had not yet detected an impending Event, and his world would remain intact by their analyses. The Associates as a majority were intensely interested in Galla's experience in the Device, but did not wish to speak to her. Their consensus was, for the moment, to allow Galla to continue her exploration when she became ready. Aeriod said nothing to this. He would not order her back into the pit, despite the suggestions of the Associates.

When he returned to Galla later that morning, he feigned a smile.

"What did they say?" she asked. She sat hugging her knees, and her face betrayed the runnelling of prior tears. But she felt calmer.

"You're to take a break from the pit," he answered benignly.

"Oh, well, that's a relief," Galla retorted. "Any word from Oni-Odi?"

"I did not speak with him yet."

Galla recognized his tone of finality. She decided not to push the subject. At the moment, she was too tired to object.

"You're going sampling again, first thing tomorrow morning," Aeriod told her. "I think it would be a good idea to keep you busy for a few days, to keep your mind off of what happened."

He left, and she began to get out of bed to dress. The flowers tumbled from her covers. "Oh!" she cried. "Thank you for the flowers," she called out to the air. Aeriod did not answer her, but the flowers all swept together in a bunch, and a large vase appeared next to her bed. The flowers sank into the vase. Galla cocked her head to one side and smiled.

"He's not *all* that bad," she said to herself aloud.

She had decided to go for a walk and try to shake off the haziness she had had since her encounter with the Device. She nearly made it to an upper balcony, when Aeriod appeared behind her.

"Galla," he said, with stern eyes, "something has come up. I need to be offworld again for a few days. As usual, if you need anything, ask the staff or Sumond."

Galla did not like his expression. "What is it? You look worried."

"I'm not worried," said Aeriod stubbornly, as if convincing himself. "I'll be back soon, hopefully with some answers."

Galla blinked. Something seemed off. *Is he lying to me?*

"Can I come with you this time?"

"No," he said firmly. "Just do your work, as I asked. Sample each day. And," Aeriod added, looking amused at her arched eyebrows, "enjoy yourself."

"Have a good trip, then," Galla said lamely. They stood facing each other. Galla stepped forward, and so did Aeriod, and they quickly embraced. Aeriod breathed in the scent of her hair, and she leaned against his shoulder. Then he stepped away, bowed, and stalked off without looking back.

After watching him leave, Galla seized on an irresistible idea. While Aeriod was away, she would ask Sumond some choice questions.

She made her way to the kitchens, finding more staff bustling to and fro as she grew closer. They all lowered their heads as she passed them, and she squirmed every time. This was not the sort of treatment she wanted, but this was not her home. *If I ever do have my own home, this is not how I will run it,* she thought.

She realized that she wanted to do things herself, more and more each day. And she wanted no one to feel subservient to her. Aeriod seemed to thrive on his arrogant arrangement, and it seemed to her he would never give it up. This was one of several things she struggled to understand about him.

When she reached the kitchens, Sumond raised all of his hands in greeting.

"Oho!" he called as she made her way to him. "Master's away, is he?"

Galla giggled. "He is. So I've come to talk about him." She breathed in the warm, savory-sweet-spicy air of the kitchens and grinned happily.

Sumond cackled. "Ah! Good. I was in need of some good, quality gossip. Have a seat!"

"What are you making?" she asked, leaning in closer to inspect.

"Oh, it's a surprise, special order from the boss," and Sumond winked. "You'll never guess who it's for."

"Did I ruin my own surprise?" Galla asked. She felt a little crestfallen.

"Not to worry, it's not finished—you'll see it this evening."

And Sumond pushed his project out of the way. Little puffs of green arose from the mixture.

"Aeriod said you were feeling ill, so he meant to cheer you. You look well enough at the moment, though your eyes are a bit droopy."

"I am tired," admitted Galla. "I had a strange adventure yesterday. Anyway, that's not what I'm here to talk about. I want to ask you more questions."

"What about this time, my dear?" Sumond asked, each hand occupied with a different tool while he worked on another dish. "I hope this isn't another question about humans, because I never met one, nor do I wish to. No offense. I can only tell you what I've heard."

"No, no questions about humans today," Galla reassured him. "I'll find out soon enough, because eventually I'll be training with them."

Sumond made a clucking sound. "I hope not," he confessed under his breath. Galla heard and grimaced.

"Anyway, I want to know, why is Aeriod alone?"

Sumond slowly closed his eyes. "Well, he's never alone, is he? We're all here, aren't we?"

"You're evading me, like he does," said Galla, wrinkling her brow.

"Oh, you're learning quickly," said Sumond. He opened his eyes again and chuckled.

"Why does he have no mate, then?" asked Galla, and she felt a strange sensation in her throat when she asked it. She had thought about it many times, and had tried to ask Aeriod, but always the question seemed to stay inside her. They had ventured along this line of conversation, but she still felt the answer had been deliberately vague.

Sumond considered his interrogator, with her large, curious eyes. Her hair swirled of its own volition, despite there being no breeze.

"You know he's lived a long time," Sumond said slowly.

"Why alone, though?" Galla persisted.

Sumond huffed. "Well, of course, he's had his share of courtships over the ages, but he can be ... difficult."

"Yes," agreed Galla emphatically.

"Lately he seems ... softer," Sumond mused. He watched Galla's cheeks turn pink. "He finds you a bit of a conundrum. I think he was prepared to treat you like a servant, or a collection piece, but you've surprised him."

"Did he tell you this?" Galla whispered, trying to remember to breathe.

"No, but I've known him a long time myself, so I have eyes, and I see."

Galla crinkled her nose in confusion. What was Sumond trying to say to her? She was not sure how to feel, or what to ask next.

"He knows what he wants," Sumond went on, "but I think he's too long overlooked what he needs. Until now."

"I don't understand," she said, and she hugged herself to stop from trembling.

Sumond thrust all his arms into the air. "How can you not see it, my dear? But then, you've had such limited experience. That is too bad. Galla, he wants and needs *you*."

Galla stood up and shook her head. Sumond studied her pityingly.

"I should go," said Galla, and she held onto her burning cheeks and raced out into the hall and back to her suite.

When she got there, she curled up on her chaise. Sumond's words echoed in her head, and she found herself suddenly fearing Aeriod's return.

13

CRYSTALLINE

Galla kept herself busy over several days, and tried to push Sumond's words from her mind whenever they threatened to return. She went on her sampling missions and became a better pilot. She focused on improving her flying every day and set new goals. *Today I won't do the drop.* Or, *Today I'll learn to glide more smoothly.* It worked, so by the time Aeriod returned, she had a small cadre of Indry-Kol applauding her moves.

Aeriod did not alert her at first, but slipped along in his own craft to meet up with hers as she returned from a day's work. At first she did not see him, and she sped elegantly along the small rises in the land, eyeing the shadows forming as the sun dipped. Then he pulled alongside her, and she nearly fell off her craft in shock.

"Keep going!" he called to her.

Galla panicked, and shot ahead of him. He raced her all the way back to his fortress, up into the bay. She jumped from the craft, cast off her helmet, and eyed him anxiously. He removed his helmet, revealing his silver hair pulled back in a plait. She tried to avoid his gaze.

He marched over to her and took hold of her chin, lifting it up so she would look at him. "You were amazing!" he exclaimed. He smiled openly at her, and she felt herself shaking. "Your piloting improved tremendously. I am proud of you."

Galla blinked at his eyes, which looked bright and eager. She had never seen such warmth in his face before.

"You are?" she asked.

"Very," Aeriod answered. "Come, I'll walk you back to your quarters."

Galla fought her galloping nerves long enough to say, "You seem excited."

"I am," he told her, smiling again. "I'll tell you why very soon."

"Thank you, by the way," Galla stammered. Aeriod looked surprised.

"For what?"

"For the special treats," she said, blushing. "I liked them."

"Ah, good," said Aeriod, and he looked so pleased and tranquil that Galla grew flustered. Then he stopped outside her door and looked down at her, and touched her shoulder.

"Is something wrong?"

"No," said Galla quickly. She took his hand off her shoulder and held it for a moment. "I'll see you at dinner?"

"Yes, please do," Aeriod said, and he smiled again.

Galla felt pensive. *Why is he so happy all of a sudden?* He left her and walked off, looking buoyant, as she had never seen him before.

He's changing. I'm changing. I'm so confused.

She chose a gown only after several minutes of indecision. She loved the copper one best, but still had not worked up the nerve to wear it. She chose a silver one. *Silver like his eyes,* she thought, and she shivered.

She walked to his door, and it opened for her. Aeriod stood waiting, his hair loose and brushed. The air smelled of smoky incense. She inhaled it and felt herself grow warm all over. She took his hands doubtfully, and for a moment rashly considered running back to her little craft and flying out into the night, never to return. But he looked so kind and so excited, it hurt even to think of such a thing. *What is happening to me?* she wondered.

"You're magnificent," said Aeriod, pulling her into the room and surveying her gown.

"My hair's a mess," Galla said obstinately.

"I like it," he said, and he took one long, vivid curl and wound it around his finger, then released it. "Come! Let's eat, and then I'll tell you what I found."

"Oh, you found something?" Now Galla was curious. What could excite someone like Aeriod, who she presumed had seen everything?

Aeriod said brightly, "I did. Just in time, too, I think."

As they ate, he asked her about her work, and complimented her on her samples.

"You've improved in many areas," he commented. "It seems like you've put a lot of focus on work since I've been away. I'm glad you're feeling better."

"Mm," said Galla.

"You're unusually quiet, though," he pointed out, and for the first time that evening, his brows twined together. He stood and offered his hand. "Come, I'll show you what I found."

Galla walked with Aeriod to his personal launch bay, which she had not seen since her arrival. She enjoyed having more time to take it all in, for Aeriod had an eye toward design. The ornate ceilings and drifting lights again seemed a far cry from utilitarian Demetraan. Aeriod's ship represented him just as well, sleek and stealthy and finely detailed.

Galla noticed something unusual behind the ship. She walked in a semicircle around it to get a better angle, and then stood befuddled looking at it. It was a large grey object.

"It's a rock," she said flatly.

Aeriod sighed. "Keep looking," he said impatiently. He followed her as she walked slowly around the boulder.

Galla reached the other side and gasped. The great rock had been split open, and its interior sparkled with violet crystals. She put her hands to her mouth, and slid down onto the floor to sit in front of it.

"Do you know what it is?" Aeriod asked her.

She looked up at him with huge eyes.

"I remember, just barely," she said softly. Her eyes filled with tears. "I remember Oni-Odi picking me up out of it. My very first day."

"The stone that birthed you," said Aeriod, his pale eyes sparkling. He knelt beside her.

Galla took a deep breath. "How did you find it?" she asked as she touched the spiky interior of the huge geode reverently. She felt warmth from the crystals. "Oni-Odi said he'd set it adrift."

"It turns out he left a beacon on it, with a very specific signal," Aeriod told her. "I received the signal information from him before I left to get it."

"So you've heard from him?" Galla stood and reached out to Aeriod. "How is he?"

Aeriod looked cagey. "I didn't actually hear from him on a personal level, no; he only sent me the code. I assumed he wanted me to retrieve it for you, and keep it safe."

Galla frowned. "That sounds odd."

Aeriod said slowly, "That's what I thought, too."

He frowned a bit, thinking to himself, while Galla stepped forward and held onto the opening of the enormous geode.

The crystals flashed in hues of lavender, rose, magenta, violet, and every gradation of color between red and blue. Galla ran her fingers along them, feeling a pang of emotion, remembering Oni-Odi's warm robotic arms holding her, fully formed, when she opened her eyes. She placed her fingers around one small knob of purple stone and pulled, and it snapped off. It was small and egg-shaped, and felt cool in her hand.

Aeriod's eyes widened. "How did you do that?"

"What? I just pulled it off," said Galla. Then she found a much darker, larger crystal that seemed to wink and flash at her, and she pulled it off, too.

"But if I tried to do that, Galla, I could never succeed," Aeriod said, and he demonstrated. He pulled with a tight grip on various crystals, and even braced his feet on the floor to pull with all his strength. Nothing yielded.

"It's *your* diamethyst," he marveled. "No one else will be able to remove the crystals, or harm them in any way."

Galla's face lit up. She held the two crystals in her hands.

"I rather like this one," she said, feeling the heft of the larger, darker stone. She looked up at Aeriod. "Here," she said, holding the smaller stone out to him. "You take this one."

Aeriod's mouth fell open. "I can't accept. It's too precious."

Galla shook her head. "You found this for me. And if you don't mind, may I keep the geode here?"

"Of course," Aeriod said graciously. "It is a great honor."

"Then can I give this to you, for safekeeping?" Galla pressed him, holding out the little pale purple stone.

"Let's say I borrow it," Aeriod offered. "Then, if you ever want it back, you can have it."

Galla grinned. "That sounds good to me. Now we need chains for them."

"You're going to wear that big thing around your neck?" laughed Aeriod, pointing at her larger stone.

She jutted her chin. "Why not? It's mine."

Aeriod shrugged. "Suit yourself. I know just the sort of chains for both."

Galla took a glance back at the geode as they left the bay.

"I'll store it for you, and no one will have access to it but us," Aeriod assured her.

They walked slowly back to his quarters, each admiring their stones. They went in, and Aeriod conjured a fire, then went to an old cabinet of his. He drew out various metal blocks and held them out.

"Which metal do you like?" he asked her. "I will make the chains."

Galla considered, as the metals shone in many different colors. But since her gem was so vibrant and large, she chose simplicity. "I like the copper one best."

"And I'll choose the silver," said Aeriod.

"They match our eyes," noted Galla.

"They do!" said Aeriod, looking at her eyes. She blushed.

They sat in front of the fire and he began to spin the metal manually into a long thread, and then deftly wove it into plaits. As he moved his hands about it, his eyes glowed.

Galla watched the final chains form. "How lovely," she breathed.

Aeriod fashioned clasps for both gems, out of their necklace metal, to hold them in place. "They won't fall out," he assured her. He took Galla's stone, flashing darkly in the firelight, its copper chain glowing, and placed it around her neck. She took his silver chain and placed it, with its smaller, smoother stone, over his neck. She admired the little stone, flashing on his black shirt with silver embroidery.

"Thank you for this," he said, taking her hands.

"Thank *you* for bringing it back to me," Galla replied. "Maybe tomorrow you can ask about Oni-Odi for me?"

"Nice try, but remember what I said," said Aeriod with a smirk. Inwardly, however, he was troubled. *Why hadn't the Elder contacted me, other than giving me that code?* He would have to look into it.

Galla leaned in toward Aeriod. "Do you know what a kiss is like?"

"What humans do, you mean?" asked Aeriod, startled.

"Yes," answered Galla.

"I suppose so," said Aeriod. "How do you . . . Ah, Sumond again. How does he know everything? Anyway, why do you—"

But Galla impulsively leaned forward and pressed her lips against his. They felt warm and soft, which surprised her.

"How was that?" Galla asked him nervously. She felt very warm all over, and not simply from the fire.

He stared at her, and drew his fingers along her cheekbones.

"Maybe we should try again," Aeriod advised. So they did. "I am not an expert, but maybe a bit more." He pulled her to him in an embrace.

"I like kissing," she sighed.

"There's your training," Aeriod said with a laugh.

"Oh," said Galla. She raised her eyebrows. "Is this what the Associates had in mind?"

Aeriod smirked. "It's fair to say they did not," he said.

14

FRACTURE

Galla woke in her suite to find a set of copper bracelets on her bedside table. Aeriod had walked her there the night before, and after another practice run of kisses at her door, she had settled into a delicious sleep. She remembered how his lips had felt on hers, and she pushed away any previous misgivings she'd had about him. Now she sat up and examined the bracelets.

"He must have come back while I slept," she said aloud. She put the three bracelets on her left wrist and watched them shrink to fit her. Looking closely, she saw that the bracelets were carved with the tiniest leaves, barely perceptible, and they moved as if blown by a gentle wind.

Aeriod had indeed made the bracelets in his room the night before, for he could not rest. He took them to her, found her asleep, and lingered next to her for a few minutes. He had wanted nothing more than to stay there, but he did not wake her. He drew himself up, gently adjusted her diamethyst necklace where it lay under her neck, and left.

Galla dressed, had a lichen tisane (its bitter-sour taste thrilled her tongue, even if she didn't love it), and went to her closet to choose a jumper for the day's harvesting work. She fought her hair, managing to twist it and tie it, but bits of it sprang out, and it frizzed moodily. She groaned, irritated, and gave up on it. Instead she focused on her gemstone, holding it in one hand and admiring it. She considered taking it off, but felt uncertain.

"It seems like it belongs there," she muttered to her reflection. It rested between her breasts. She tucked it into her jumper and patted it.

When she stepped outside, Galla nearly rammed a member of the staff who was standing by her door.

"Oh! So sorry," she said quickly. The older female, tall, pale green, and delicate with a very thin neck, bowed.

"Lady Galla-Deia, I apologize," she said. "The mage has sent me to accompany you to the high turret."

Galla wrinkled her nose. "Why didn't he come himself?"

"My lady, the mage has been in a conference all morning." And the wizened alien lady, with her long, spindly arms, motioned for Galla to step ahead of her. Galla refused, and chose to walk beside her.

"That's interesting," Galla said as they walked to the lift. "I wonder why he wants me up there? Normally he does his business without me."

The assistant made a clicking sound in her throat, but said nothing. They reached the lift, and once inside shot up to the uppermost turret of the keep, and Galla's companion bowed to her as she stepped off. The woman disappeared, and Galla stood standing in wonder of the turret.

Aeriod had never brought her up here before. It was open on three sides, with nothing but a thin, clear shield enclosing it from the outdoors. The ceiling and framework were covered with long, scrolling designs in silver and deep maroon. The floor shone in onyx tiles. On the fourth side of the tower, Aeriod kept a small office. Its door was beautifully carved, with more silver scrollwork, and it stood wide open. Galla peeked in. There was a desk of sorts, and several ornamental but apparently functional small tables and globes and oddments. Two long sets of golden beads hung from the ceiling, and she thought she glimpsed shifting faces in each bead.

He was sitting, staring at an image of the sky outside, and Galla realized it was another shield. He sensed her and turned, and she paused. He swept his hand, and the two chains of beads disappeared. His face looked grim.

"Good morning," he said to her, and he rose and came to take her hands.

"Good morning," Galla replied. "Is your conference over?"

"Yes," Aeriod answered, and he looked pained. He took her face in his hands. "Something has happened."

Galla felt a strange flutter inside. Her eyes grew wide, and she took hold of Aeriod's hands and held them.

"Oni-Odi?" she asked, her breath caught in her throat.

"Yes," said Aeriod. "Now, hold on, have a seat for a moment."

Galla sat down, tremors of fear rippling through her, and stared at Aeriod.

He said, "I followed up on our conversation this morning. I contacted the Associates and asked if they had had any recent communication with Oni-Odi. They had not. It would appear his last known communiqué was the code he sent to me."

Galla took a deep breath. "But that could mean anything. Maybe he just didn't want to, maybe he's busy," she stammered, but she knew Oni-Odi well.

"I tried contacting him and received no response. Not even on our most private channel," said Aeriod, his voice steady and low. "The Associates, out of caution, did the same. No one has been able to reach him. And his last known coordinates, five days ago, were checked by scans. No one has found a reading on the star-city. Demetraan is gone."

Galla's hands flew to her ears, and she bent her head down to her knees. She felt like something extremely heavy sat on her chest, so that she could not draw breath. It pressed her down, and she thought she would break under it.

Aeriod stepped over to her and placed an arm around her shoulders.

Galla finally breathed, and said shakily, "How can it be gone? Just vanished? Maybe he just moved the City somewhere else? He does that sometimes."

"I know he does," said Aeriod. "We've checked every system. Every waypoint. It's nowhere."

"How?"

Aeriod grimaced. "I do not know, and I fear it portends the Event."

Galla looked up at him. "I know something about the Event. This doesn't sound like it. What about . . ." She pursed her lips and thought for a moment. "What about that one force that Sumond has talked about? The one that attacks people, and freezes them in pain?"

A memory shot through her, and she grew still. The voice in the Device. Was that . . .?

"Paosh Tohon," said Aeriod. "I thought that too, but it doesn't make any sense to me. Demetraan is filled with androids. It doesn't track with previous targets." He sighed heavily. "This defies any explanation. And there's no evidence of any explosions; we'd have detected that. Just . . . gone."

Galla sobbed.

"He'll come back, though," she said stubbornly, shaking the tears off her cheeks. "He'll come back for *me*."

Aeriod winced. "We don't know that," he said.

Galla threw her head back and stood, her face scarlet. "How *dare* you?" she shouted. "I will find him myself, if I have to!"

Aeriod stood away from Galla, the force of her rage was so intense.

"Get out of my way," she hissed. Her copper eyes looked like embers in a fire. "I'll take a ship, I'll take *every* ship—I'll do anything, but I will find him."

Aeriod reached out his arms to her. "Galla, please, you have your training, and you must keep at it. Running off to do this helps no one, least of all Oni-Odi. You know he would want you to continue!"

"Get away from me!" Galla snapped. She clipped his shoulder as she charged past.

"Where are you going?" Aeriod called to her as she left the office. "Please don't try to go. Not alone, anyway," he pleaded.

Galla glared at him. "Are you saying you'll come with me to find him?"

"We can't find him! He's. Gone," and Aeriod walked toward her.

"No," she said as he reached for her once more. "Look, I'm going to work. I'll be back later, and then we'll talk."

"Galla—wait," Aeriod began.

"You can't stop me!" she spat.

"Galla! Stop! We've moved, for the harvest—there *is* no work today," Aeriod said rapidly, before she could leave. The lift stood open. She hesitated.

She stepped over and looked outside. Aeriod was right. The asteroid fortress was currently migrating on, as autumn had come to the north.

"I was going to tell you," he said, "this morning, before I got into all this mess. The Indry-Kol are moving, too, to follow the harvest south. We'll be having a celebration for the season change."

Aeriod walked slowly toward Galla, whose fury had extended to her hair, and it twisted in all directions and glowed in the sunrise as she looked down.

"I wanted to throw a party, for everyone, but especially for you, Galla," Aeriod said cautiously. He came within arm's reach of her, but she held her hand up, and he stopped.

Don't even try it, was all she could manage to think for several minutes. Her thoughts could not even form proper words, her anguish was so great.

Finally she declared, "I don't want a party. How could I possibly celebrate? Oni-Odi is my only family."

Aeriod sighed. "No, he isn't," he said. "I'm your family now too. *They're* your family, the farmers who have worked so hard. Sumond, he's family too. And we're your friends, Galla. Don't you see? Why don't we at least do this, and then if you want to jet off for a bit, fine. But let's celebrate the harvest. Please?"

Galla took large, deep breaths. She felt so inflamed by her anger and grief, she wished she could sprout wings and fly out of that fortress, and up into space, and off to look for her mentor, alone. Aeriod could never understand what this felt like, she was certain. A missing city! And an enormous, ancient, technical marvel of a city, gone! It was too incredible, and too awful.

"Please stay," Aeriod murmured, and now he dared to stand next to her. "You won't be here much longer, either way."

She snapped her head back to look at him ferociously.

"Good," she said. His eyes went wide.

Galla felt nauseated. She had hurt him. She stood aloof and turned her back to him, and walked to the lift. It was too much right now. She could not look at him, so she shut her eyes.

"Take me to the launch bay," she commanded the lift. It shot down to the bowels of the keep, to where the harvesting craft rested momentarily. Aeriod had allowed them to be stored here, while his asteroid keep moved south.

Galla felt a pang, looking at the resting equipment. A few Indry-Kol were refurbishing things and cleaning up, and their moods seemed high and merry. They had worked hard, and now they would have a break, and soon, they would celebrate. Galla felt dreadful. They deserved the harvest party, and Aeriod would have one with or without her. She had made everything about herself, at the expense of all the others around her.

Feeling wretched, she found her favorite craft, and started it. One of the Indry-Kol farmers rushed up to her and said, "My lady! We are not working today, as the keep is relocating. No need to go out!"

Galla managed to smile at him. "Thank you. But *I* need to go for a drive."

And the bay door opened just enough for her to blast out. She let herself drop this time, and charged up again, and flew off west, away from the fortress. It had moved several hundred miles overnight, so the terrain looked wholly unfamiliar to Galla. The higher terrain necessitated a higher orbit. Galla skimmed along low mountains and noted that farther west, the mountains grew taller, and were covered with ice and snow. She sped toward them, and landed on a thin neck of land between two peaks.

She stepped off her craft, which hovered in waiting, and sank into snow up to her waist. Soon, she realized, the lower terrain of the north would also be covered in snow. She fought her way up out of the drifts and looked out on the land below. The sky fortress floated on the eastern horizon. She felt an enormous urge to fly farther west, out of its sight completely, but she hesitated. Instead she looked down where the snow ended and the tree line began, and she could see thawing water tumble among the rocks. She clambered back onto her craft and set its course for the small alpine valley below. When she landed, she could only see a ring of mountains, and no sign of Aeriod's keep. She breathed in relief.

She sat by a rushing river and let its thunderous current cover the sounds of her sobs.

15

INTERNECINE

"Final check. Cleared for launch," voiced the crackling image on the screen. Instantly the image distorted. The effect of the singularity on the transmissions grew by the second.

"Stand by," replied the slender figure, its long, gripping fingertips slipping across the controls. It sagged in exhaustion, but precision was key. All checks made, it made a final return transmission.

"Crew and passengers secured. Ready," it said.

The screen went black, as did the controls. The creature raised its arms aloft, appalled. Far off, a long screech rang through the bowels of the ship behind. Echoing hoots and screams roiled through the decks. The pilot tried the controls again, to no avail. It sent an emergency communication on its wristband. Nothing.

A terrible rip tore open the cockpit, and the pilot stood agape at what came through. A twitching, grinning thing: one of the passengers the pilot recognized. The being stood in that ragged hole, which no creature of its size should have been able to open with its own power. Its limbs seeped blood and fractures from the attempt. A glint in its great, sunken eyes sent a horror through the pilot. The pilot backed up against the controls, but there was nowhere else to go.

"You need to get back to the decks!" shrieked the pilot. "The singularity is nearly upon us, and I need to send an emergency beacon. We've stalled!"

"We will make it better," the being responded, its eyes lolling. It shimmied and hopped in the door, but edged closer to the pilot.

"Get out of here!" The pilot reached for its holster, to find something, anything to repel the deranged creature.

"We will make it better!" the creature replied, edging closer.

The pilot could see something forming in the creature's eyes. The air changed, and a stinging developed in the pilot's feet. A gnawing pain grew and crept up its legs and through its tail.

"Stop! We're going to die here, we'll be torn apart by the gravitation!"

"You will not die," said the creature, edging in closer. "We will make it better! You will live forever, and your screams will make it better!"

And the pilot's screams began, and reverberated through the ship. The singularity twisted and warped and shredded the ship, and its passengers wailed until they could scream no more.

The pilot's mind crinkled and smashed, not from the singularity itself, but from the being's power, as its eyes shone like diamonds.

"We will make it better. Let us begin."

16

EPHEMERAL

She had fallen asleep that night near the river, in a small glade, and while she slept, small animals came by to sniff her. Larger beasts kept a wary eye on her and stayed farther away. When she awoke, Galla found herself ringed by tiny mushrooms and flowers that had grown in the night. They were nowhere else in the glade. She sighed.

"Aeriod," she said aloud.

She stood and wiped off the detritus from the ground, and looked around. She liked it here, and she felt much calmer. Something tugged at her, a conflicting desire to stay and to leave. She wrestled with it for a long while. She looked up at the dawn sky, where two amorphous moons reflected their sun's morning light. Beyond the moons, beyond the star, beyond the system, somewhere out there, Oni-Odi and Demetraan must surely be. She must find them.

But she struggled to admit that Aeriod had been correct, about everything. She bent down, grabbed a twig, twisted her hair with it, and placed the helmet back on her head. She looked all around her at the mountain scenery and said, "Time to go back."

Galla zoomed up and over the mountains, headed east and south, and eventually saw the familiar shape of the turreted asteroid. Her eyes stung. She was glad to see it, but she was afraid of how she would be received there. As she approached, she could hear music and laughter, which surprised her.

She swung her little craft into the bay and looked around. The Indry-Kol were nowhere to be seen, and their machines sparkled. She realized from the distant sounds of music and merriment the party must have already begun, and she smiled ruefully.

She headed straight to her room, took off her helmet, pulled the twig out of her hair and set it on her desk. Now she had a line of little objects she had collected: dried lichen, small pieces of machinery, dried flowers, and little baubles. She took her necklace off and laid it on the desk, and admired everything. Aeriod had stopped insisting on its formerly museum-like quality, and now it was all truly hers.

She did find a hot bath waiting for her, and little fizzy lights floating above it. She enjoyed the warmth, but she felt the urge to hurry. She went to her closet. *I'll wear the first thing I touch,* she thought, her eyes closed. She grabbed something, pulled it out, and opened her eyes. It was a deep sapphire gown, covered in starburst patterns. She had not worn this one yet. She put it on, looked at herself in the mirror, and then instinctively touched her chest.

"Oh!" she said, and she stepped over to her desk and put the copper and amethyst necklace on. She paused for a moment, then reached down and grabbed her helmet.

She walked the length of the hallway, followed the sounds out the open windows, and took the lift to a great hall. She came upon a haze of activity, with kitchen staff racing to and fro, and heard and saw the guffaws of the farmworkers, all at long tables loaded with food and drink. Music bounced everywhere. Sumond caught sight of her and held up a glass in each of his hands, and rapidly drank three of them. And at one table, she spied Aeriod, leaning in to talk to an Indry-Kol supervisor. Somewhere a long, clear tone rang, and everyone looked up, including Aeriod, to see Galla standing there.

A great, delighted sigh rose among the crowd, and she turned a very deep rose. Every eye looked at her, but the two silver ones pierced her. Aeriod stood and stared at her, and time seemed to stretch.

Aeriod took in every bit of her, in her blue dress, with her violet stone, her masses of hair, and lastly her fiery copper eyes. "You came back," he said, and held out his hand.

"Yes," said Galla. She took her helmet and threw it along the floor so it rolled to Aeriod's feet. "I'm no longer your student, and you're no longer my teacher."

Aeriod looked from the helmet, to her face, and back again, uncertain.

She rushed to him, took his hand, and laced her arms around him. She could barely hear the applause and the squawk of celebratory music rising to encircle them.

Later, after the revelers had gone, and Sumond's team had removed all the food, the music faded softly into the background. Galla joined Aeriod on his balcony to watch the last bit of sunset. She leaned her head against him, and he slid his arm around her waist.

"I'm sorry, Aeriod," she said.

"You already apologized, just by coming back, and I already forgave you," he said into her hair.

Galla looked at his face, saw his mercurial eyes lit in the purple dusk. "I've made a home here," she said.

"And you'll always have it," he assured her, stroking her chin.

"I'll miss it when I have to leave," said Galla.

They walked slowly back to her quarters, and lingered by her door. She pulled him into her suite and the door shut behind them, and they stood awkwardly at first.

"Will you stay?" Galla asked.

Aeriod grinned, and reached down and picked her up.

"You're not going to throw me over your shoulder again, are you?" she teased.

"Only if you ask me to," he said.

"I'm asking you to stay," she stammered, "and I'm asking you to be with me."

Aeriod met her eyes squarely and asked, "Are you sure?"

Galla's smile shook. "I am." And then they said nothing more.

In the morning, Galla lifted the small purple stone from Aeriod's chest and studied it. She watched his breathing and pulled his long white hair away from his neck, and she nuzzled there. He woke and smiled at her, and pulled her up onto him, her hair spilling over his face. They heard a tone.

"Really?" said Galla, resting her elbows on his chest. Then she sat upright. "What if it's news?"

"Hmm," said Aeriod, and he pulled her back down. "News can wait just a little bit."

A voice rang through the air, and they both jumped.

"High Mage," said the voice, "my apologies, I know you insisted on no disturbances. But I thought you should know, a ship approaches. It bears Associates insignia."

Aeriod's face froze. "Thank you," he muttered.

"Associates?" Galla asked. "What would they—oh." And she hastily dressed. "You don't think it's . . . Is it . . ."

Aeriod took her hands and kissed them. His face looked ashen. "It's time."

"Oh," said Galla numbly. *Now? Now it's time? How, why?* She could not concentrate. She felt cold prickles marching up her back, into her shoulders.

She looked rapidly around the room, and said, "What should I bring?"

"Nothing," Aeriod advised. "Come, we have to meet them."

"What about this?" asked Galla, clutching her amethyst necklace.

"You'll have to leave it for this," Aeriod said. He sighed, and took it off of her. They stood in stunned silence for a moment.

The tone rang again. "Sir, the ship has landed in the bay. Requesting permission to deboard."

"We'll be right there," Aeriod called. He held Galla's hand and they left her suite.

They walked hastily toward the bay, not looking at each other, and Galla could not speak. When they entered the great bay, she gasped. The visitor's ship, a large pulsating thing unlike anything she had ever seen, squatted on the floor, and unrolled a tentacle closer to where Galla and Aeriod stood, and from its innards slid forth a being Aeriod recognized.

The figure stood in dark, iridescent garb that seemed to rearrange itself into different geometric shapes. Where a face might have been rested a metallic mask with strange insignia. Aeriod stretched his hand before it: the Speaker of Bitikk.

Galla noticed the faintest tic in Aeriod's cheek. He let his hand fall to his side and he turned to her.

He said, "Speaker, I present Galla-Deia to you."

If the Speaker made any acknowledgment of Galla, she could not discern it. Aeriod's face twitched again. He pinched his lips together and squinted at the Speaker's insignia-face.

"She is not ready," Aeriod said in a low growl. He stepped back to see the Speaker's full response. Deep, shimmery green appeared in its raiment.

"I realize that certain lessons have been . . . delayed," Aeriod hissed.

Galla watched in confusion. *Are they talking to each other? Is the Speaker telepathic?* She stood in respectful silence. The two figures moved away from her; Aeriod motioned for her to stay where she was. Galla thought she could see changing hues and shapes moving across the Associate's robes and mask.

Aeriod stood rigid, his jaw clenched. But she could only stand and watch, and occasionally hear the rise and fall of his tone of voice.

He eventually gestured to Galla to approach them. This time, she discovered, the mage bore no expression. But his voice cracked.

"Galla-Deia," Aeriod announced, "the Speaker of Bitikk will take you to your next phase of training."

"What! When?" Galla exclaimed.

"Now," he replied, his jaw set.

She stared at the Associate, aghast. "For how long?" she asked bluntly.

"Galla," Aeriod said, his voice melting, "you'll never know how long. No matter who trains you. This is all I know."

She looked at the Speaker and felt she would have dived off of the station, down into the Device pit, and faced whatever it held, rather than join this being on a journey for any length of time. She felt leaden with fear.

"You have to go now, Galla-Deia," said Aeriod in a neutral voice. "Speaker, a moment please. She will join you shortly."

The Speaker trailed away to its ship and entered it seamlessly. The ship smoldered.

"Aeriod," Galla gasped, grabbing his hands. "I can't do this. I can't go!"

"You must."

Aeriod bodily turned her away from him. He held her close from behind, smoothed her hair, breathed in any bit of her he could. She stood still then, arms hanging limply. "Come back," he whispered, and she nodded stiffly. Aeriod released her, and pushed her gently toward the Speaker's ship. When Galla turned to look at him, Aeriod had vanished. His cloak hung around her shoulders.

She clenched her fists to her chest and choked back a sob, but she turned again and walked toward the ship. It extended itself to her and she entered. The Speaker waited for her and indicated a round object on the golden-hued floor. It stretched into an oval. Galla sucked in a breath as the ship began powering up. The pod on the floor opened. She wrapped Aeriod's cloak about herself and settled into the pod. It sealed around her and she fell unconscious.

17

BITIKK

In her pod, Galla began dreaming. She could see a dim web all around her, above and below. She reached out to touch this web and it moved away from her. She found she could never quite reach the web, no matter how many times she tried. Then she heard a voice, whispering something.

The voice spoke to her, low and resonant like a murmur: *"I waited for you."* And even in this netherworld, she felt the love in that voice she did not know.

"Who are you? Where am I?" Galla asked, and then wondered in surprise at the clarity of her own voice.

The invisible stranger continued, ignoring her questions.

"I tried to bring something to this. I wanted to bring memories to you. Quiet days with the rain outside, listening to the floors creak from someone walking. Do you remember?

"I brought you a present and your eyes filled up. I dried your tears with my sleeve. You apologized, but I laughed. Here I had brought you something and it upset you. And you told me it was because you loved it.

"And when I helped you get ready for the party, my hands were shaking, helping you dress. It almost hurt to look at you. You were going off to dance, but I wanted to dance with you, Galla. For the rest of my life."

The dream ended and Galla wanted to awaken. But the pod sensed her movement and constricted about her like a cocoon. She relented and wafted into a deeper sleep.

As for Aeriod, he sat in his levitating realm and brooded. Days rolled into weeks, and then months, and the harvests below finished, then it was time to head north again. He had gone to several meetings offworld, but he could scarcely focus on any of them. Sometimes he raged at Sumond, and sometimes he just asked him to bring him his meals personally. This suited Sumond, for he had noticed the mage had stopped eating. While Sumond knew he would survive, he also knew Aeriod's fondness for fine cuisine.

Sumond took the risk at last.

"It is because she is gone. One day, she will finish her training, and she will complete her Task, whatever it is. But she will need you to help her. If you sit here and burn yourself out on everything you know, you insult any good memories she has of this place and of you."

Aeriod had been tempted to pick the chef up and toss him bodily away from him. Sumond had got off easy.

Aeriod seethed and mourned in his chair during the day and much of each night. A long time passed before he could even bring himself to look at the grams Oni-Odi had given him of Galla. In them she looked so untamed, feral yet innocent, and Oni-Odi so patiently brushed her hair. When Aeriod could bear to watch these images, he sat mesmerized but empty.

The Associates had given him the expected order not to pursue contact with her, lest he lose his position. While they respected (and some feared) him, the Associates made clear his status remained tenuous on this point. He suspected darker workings than this.

They give her to Bitikk, so inexperienced, he ruminated. *All Bitikk need do is probe her to know any weakness she may have. If she comes out of it intact, she will still remain vulnerable. Probably she will never be fully conscious during her training. She may never truly recover.*

Aeriod wrestled with the rawness of his emotions until it finally dulled. He began focusing listlessly on the increasing number of reports of Paosh Tohon expanding. The long-term goal of coping with an Event would remain, but these other reports troubled Aeriod. He realized Sumond was right. He could not help Galla achieve her Task without doing something to stop Paosh Tohon, which threatened to undo what the Associates and Representatives had been working on for centuries. If Aeriod in his most morose moods could be nihilistic, it was nothing compared to those who sought suffering or obliteration at all costs.

And how did the Device on Rikiloi and other worlds figure into this equation—if at all? Or was it simply a relic left behind, to remain a question he could never answer? He wished he could talk about it with her. He felt the least he could do was try to get things moving forward, for Galla's future Task, and for himself.

One difficult morning, after staring at the ceiling for far too long and ignoring his staff, he squeezed his small amethyst-like stone, and it began to glow in his hand. He jumped up and looked at it. What could it mean? In a rush he headed to the alcove where he had stored Galla's geode. He looked at the great boulder for a long time, thinking. *It's part of who she was, who she is, and who she will be. I can't live in the past. But maybe I can help her future.* He had one piece of diamethyst, and he dared not take Galla's other one, in case she came back soon. For the first time in over a year since she had left, his eyes flashed again. It was time to see what this stone could do. And it was finally time to see what *he* could do.

Aeriod called for Sumond and his senior staff. "I'm heading off for a long while," he told them. "Please contact me the moment she's back. I'm asking a great deal from each of you, and I am grateful. You've kept me moving, even when I didn't want to move."

"What is a 'long while,' sir?" Sumond asked cautiously.

"I'm not sure," Aeriod admitted. "But I might as well be proactive."

Sumond folded all of his arms and said, "Good. We will keep things running here."

Aeriod sighed gratefully and thanked everyone again, and headed off to his ship.

GALLA NEVER BEHELD the Speaker of Bitikk's true form. Only certain sensations alerted her to the Associate's presence: feelings of suffocation, a piercing pain in the nape of her neck. Other times she might feel dizziness, nausea, falling sensations, and electric shocks. Bitikk taught her intense suffering, testing the limits of her body and her sanity. She had never known true pain, or anxiety, or paranoia, before Bitikk suspended her in each of these states for long periods. Her dreams became far less pleasant.

At rare times, Galla regained consciousness long enough to look around. The beings kept her caked into a sort of cocoon. When one session finished, she was moved to a new cocoon. During those brief moments when she became aware of her surroundings, Galla could not open her mouth. They plugged her mouth with a sentient resin, which also prevented her from screaming. The resin would quickly detect her alert state and inform the Speaker's assistants. Despite this, she could see she was not alone.

There were many shadowy alcoves filled with cocoon-like pods of various sizes. Sometimes she would see beings hovering around them or walking by to inspect them. She could never make out what was kept in the other pods. The assistants always came to her quickly, as soon as she showed any alertness. Then she would feel her body become very light, and her thoughts would spiral away to an oblivion of disturbing visions.

A day came when they broke open Galla's cocoon and floated her away from the great catacombs. They took her to a globular sort of chair, which twisted around her and forced her to sit. Her head hung, hair matted, until she could sense her surroundings. She found her mouth and hands free, so she rubbed her lips for some time and pushed her hair from her eyes. She wheezed a bit and said huskily, "Where am I?"

She realized a large, diaphanous membrane separated her from silhouettes she could not discern. They had gathered all around her. One of the silhouettes raised a long appendage or tentacle and barely touched the bubble.

"*Questions,*" a voiced hissed around her.

"What—what do you mean?" Galla asked nervously, wishing she could see her interrogators. "Who are you?"

The tentacle slid a bit where it rested on the bubble. The voice came again, ominously: "*Answers.*"

And Galla screamed. Blinding plasma fire burst around her and crackled. Her body jerked, but the chair seized her and held her still, allowing the lightning and swirls to course through her. She ceased screaming and sank unconscious in the chair.

She woke some time later, not knowing the passage of time, and found herself lying on a hard platform, fully dressed, clean, and groomed. She shivered and sat up. She was in a roughly dome-shaped room with dark grey, faceted walls. Soft light shone from the tips of the crystals on the walls. She felt as if she were suspended in space, surrounded by stars.

She stood, and the second she did, the facets opened into a door. She walked out and found herself in a long hallway. A being approached her. She felt herself seize in anxiety: it was the Speaker of Bitikk. She suddenly understood, and did not know whether to feel dread or relief. Her training with Bitikk was complete, and she did not even know what she had learned.

The Speaker of Bitikk led her through faceted hallways in its ship of deep green; they might have been walking through a great emerald's heart. Finally they reached a launch bay and found perched there a tiny craft of dull grey.

"Here is the craft to take you to Rikiloi," said the emotionless Associate. Galla stared at the creature, in surprise that she could understand it at all. "You will have a brief respite. The craft will alert you when it is time to leave for your next training."

Galla's lips opened to speak, but the creature had moved off at astounding speed. The green pathways closed behind the Speaker as if there had never been a door. The craft hissed. She climbed in, and the Speaker's huge ship opened as if it had a mouth, and her craft tumbled out into the atmosphere of Rikiloi.

She fought the controls and managed to brake the ship before it impacted the surface. She got her bearings, and realized she was a few hundred miles from Aeriod's home. She felt her insides twist, thinking of him. But she sped ahead and by and by, the fortress loomed on the horizon.

"Home," she said to herself, but she felt uncertain now. Nothing felt the same.

18

CHATELAINE

The first unusual sign Galla noticed was that no one attempted to hail her. Had the Speaker of Bitikk informed Aeriod that she was returning? She steered the little grey ship up to Aeriod's private bay, and it opened for her. So at least the keep was functioning properly.

She stepped out of the craft and looked around.

"His ship is gone," she said out loud. As soon as she spoke, music began playing, and lights bobbed above her.

Doors opened for her as she walked slowly through the hallways. Where was everyone? She saw no staff. The music and art displays activated for her as she walked. She came to her room and stopped. She held her chest, remembering her last night in that room, with Aeriod.

The door opened for Galla, and she felt disoriented. Everything looked exactly the same as when she had left. The trinkets and dried flowers still sat on her table. She walked over to the desk and lifted her amethyst necklace fondly, and put it on. This gave her a sensation of normalcy and relief.

Still, she felt uneasy. As if she should not be here, as if she had stolen secretly into a stranger's home and looked at the stranger's things.

"Hello again!" said a voice behind her, and she jumped.

"Sumond!" she exclaimed, and she gawked at him where he stood in her doorway. He looked bent and weathered, his arms flaccid, his eyes sunken, his skin more mottled.

Sumond bowed.

"Come! You must be hungry."

"Sure, let me change," said Galla, derailed for a moment by her old friend's appearance. Sumond bowed and left to wait outside.

Galla went into her closet and stared at it. She had that feeling again, that these were not her things. But hadn't she *just* been here? She thought of how Sumond looked, and shivered. Sumond had not been young when she had first arrived here, but now he seemed so aged and shrunken.

"I just want something simple to wear," she said out loud, and her wardrobe shifted, and she pulled out long pants and a tunic. She belted her waist and joined Sumond in the corridor.

"Galla-Deia," he puffed, "it is such a pleasure to have you here again."

"I'm glad to be back," she confessed. "Glad to be away from . . . from . . ."

"No need, I understand it must have been quite the ordeal," Sumond assured her.

"But where is Aeriod?" she asked, feeling anxious. "I was surprised I didn't have a greeting from him."

Sumond looked at her fondly.

"He has come and gone a few times since you left, but he's been on a mission for some time. So we've been running things around here. It's been very quiet, as you can imagine, but we adjusted. Would you like to go to the kitchens?"

"Oh yes," Galla said emphatically. "Would I ever!"

She sat and watched Sumond make his pastries, and noticed how slow and shaky he had become. Sumond glanced at her and saw the concern on her face.

"Do not be sad," he said. "You are back in your home, and I am going to make your favorite purple tarts."

"That's lovely, Sumond," said Galla gratefully. She drummed her fingers on his worktable as she watched him.

"Sumond, how long was I gone?"

Her friend focused on his pastry and did not look up.

He mused, "Well, it's all very confusing to me now, your and Aeriod's leaving, and his returning, and his leaving again. I think you left some fifty-two years ago. Don't trust me in my old age, though, dear."

"What!" cried Galla, stunned. "Oh. Oh my," and she pressed her hands to her cheeks in dismay.

"Yet you look exactly the same," Sumond noted. "As pretty as ever. But there's something in your eyes that's different."

Galla slumped a bit. "I guess . . . I guess *I'm* different. I . . . went through . . . some things. And I'm not even really sure what all they were. I saw things I've never experienced, I felt things I hadn't before, and so on. People I've never met. I heard voices. And I felt . . . stuck."

Her shoulders tensed from recalling her befuddled memories. She did not realize it, but her hands formed fists while she spoke. The chef noticed, however.

Sumond whistled. "It sounds dreadful," he said.

"Yes," agreed Galla with a shudder.

"There now, all done. Let me get you a draught to go with them," said Sumond, serving her the tarts piping hot.

Galla enjoyed the treats. She sat in silence and drank cider from her tall glass, and tried to readjust. Not having Aeriod around seemed wrong. He had left before a few times, but she sensed this was different.

"Do you know when he's coming back?" she asked hesitantly. She thought without asking, *Is he coming back?*

"I do not," said Sumond. "He did say to alert him when you arrived, so I have sent a message to him. None of us has heard from him in some time, in fact. Oh, do not worry, my dear. It's Aeriod, after all."

Galla managed a little laugh. "I suppose so. Did he ever hear anything from Oni-Odi?"

"Not that I'm aware of, I'm sorry to say," replied Sumond.

Galla sighed sadly. "All this time, and nothing. I don't understand it."

She caught her breath, and realized that Oni-Odi had not been the first individual she had thought of when leaving Bitikk.

"I think I should go for a walk and get some fresh air, and reacquaint myself," she said quietly.

"Very well. Let me know if you need anything," said Sumond.

She walked around to him. "Thank you," she said, hugging him. She noted with alarm that he felt frail and weak. With a sigh, she left to explore the empty halls.

The surreality of Aeriod's absence shook her. It all felt so discordant. But Galla came to realize it was not simply his absence, but her presence, that seemed off. This was a place that had existed without her for a long time before, and now over half a century later, she had arrived again. She felt keenly that it really was not her home anymore, though it had felt so at one time. Oni-Odi was gone, Aeriod was off somewhere, and now she had years of a bizarre experience behind her, which she barely remembered. She was a stranger again.

She thought about the voice that she sometimes heard in her strange dreams, which seemed so kind and friendly. It seemed like something she had been missing, and she realized now, she craved hearing that voice again. The love, the steadfastness in it . . . there was something there. She had never seen whose voice it was.

Galla shook her hair and walked self-consciously through the halls. She poked into doorways that had been off limits to her in the past. She took the time to look more closely at the art, and saw it with new eyes. It was a quieter place, but it still held many wonderful things, and now that she had come through her ordeal, she appreciated them more.

Her favorite discovery was a map room, with projections of various systems in the galaxy. There was one framed map hanging on a wall that intrigued her. It looked incredibly weathered and aged, cracked and frayed, but its artistry was very fine. It showed a few continents of some other world, not Rikiloi. She stared at it a long time, and tried to read its smudged and aged script. It was the only such map in the entire room. Why would Aeriod keep this antiquity? She lifted it gently and found a list on the back of it in a language she did not know, despite her years of learning on Demetraan.

She thought of something. "Show me the human homeworld," she asked the air. A yellow star appeared projected on the ceiling, and all around it spun a haze of several planets and asteroids. One smaller world, closer to the star, glowed brighter than the others. Galla studied it intently. She asked no other questions, but instead looked at each planet in turn, and then sighed. She would learn more about the people of that system at some point, and she thought it best to keep more of her questions for them.

As Galla continued her exploration, she delayed walking to Aeriod's suite. She felt the pull and fought it until the very last, and finally she decided to approach. The door opened for her, and she realized she had been holding her breath. She exhaled and entered, and lights winked on for her and followed her around.

He's left his permissions open for me, she thought with a pang. She did not want to venture any farther, but she did glance around for his amethyst necklace and did not see it anywhere. She backed out of the rooms and headed to the balcony down the hall. The sun was setting, so she decided to lean into the updrafts and watch the colors mingle. Then she felt a blast of hot wind from below, so she stood back a bit from the edge. A large shape rose and hovered in front of her. It was a black and silver ship, and its cockpit reflected her image. It tilted a bit, flashing a light on her, and she could see inside the cockpit.

Aeriod had returned.

19

MAGIC

She ran to his private bay. Her cheeks burned, her chest hurt, and she felt as if her head would burst. Everything fell away for a moment, the years on Bitikk, the pain, and the dreams: there was nothing but this. Aeriod climbed down his ramp and they faced each other. Then he loped swiftly over on his long legs and seized her, and held her up to look at her, and brought her down again to bury his face in her hair.

"I can't believe it," he said, tasting her tears as he kissed her. "You came back."

"Of course I did," she said.

Galla smiled at him and marveled, for his face wore a serenity she had never seen before. She wondered how far he had come himself, in their years apart. She noticed he was carrying a bag on his shoulder.

"I have something for you," Aeriod said eagerly, "but it can wait."

They grinned foolishly at each other and walked quickly back to his quarters.

Aeriod swept his hand in a circle and a ring of flames appeared on the floor around them. "Ah!" he exclaimed. "I can't tell you how good it feels to be able to do *that!*"

"What, you didn't have your abilities while you were away?" Galla asked, confused.

"They were . . . limited, shall we say," Aeriod explained.

He set his bag down and opened it, and brought out what looked like a large blanket covered in colorful patches and designs. He looked at it fondly and said, "A friend made this for you, for when I would see you again. It's a quilt."

Galla knelt down on it and ran her fingers over the diamond-shaped fabrics in purple, turquoise, and copper, admiring the little hand-sewn designs. Someone had taken great care to embroider vines throughout.

"I love it!" she exclaimed.

She looked at Aeriod, who watched her with his silver eyes glinting.

"I missed you so much," he said.

Then for a long while they had nothing to say and everything to feel.

Galla draped her arms around his neck as she lay on top of him, and nudged the little purple stone aside to kiss his chest.

"This was quite useful," said Aeriod, holding up the diamethyst. "I was reluctant to take it off, but it really helped. We should talk more about it, because I think it's incredibly important material. Thank you for letting me borrow it."

"I want you to keep it," said Galla. She picked up her larger stone from where she had placed it on the floor near the flames. "Thank you for keeping this here for me. I felt more at home after I found it. It was so *empty* here earlier. I can't imagine what it must have been like, all those years, for the others who live and work here."

Aeriod sighed, and his brow creased, as he ran his fingers through her hair, down her back, and to her waist. "It was not ideal, but it looks like they managed. It was difficult for me to come back very often, because I had work to do elsewhere."

Galla felt a strange twinge, wondering where he had been.

"Was it a success?" she asked delicately.

"It was!" Aeriod said firmly. "I'm pleased. But it raised more questions than answers. And also, I've got a few people clamoring to meet you. All in good time."

Galla laughed nervously. "What did you say about me?"

"I couldn't say much," Aeriod admitted. "I had to keep a low profile."

"Hmm," said Galla, a bit troubled. Aeriod caught her look and laughed.

"Are you jealous?" he cried. Galla shook her head. "I think you are! You preposterous, fabulous thing, you. As if I could ever meet anyone else like *you*."

Galla answered that with another kiss, and their words stopped as they gasped and sighed together.

Aeriod was in no hurry to leave their rooms that day or the next, with Galla next to him. *How much longer?* he caught himself thinking, and he felt ashamed. Every second could be the last for a long time. It had already been so long. And Galla seemed matured, and quieter, but he worried about her, and tried to ask her about her time with Bitikk with sensitivity.

Galla had no desire to go into details, as what she remembered disturbed her. So they reached an agreement only to talk about it when she was ready. She felt vulnerable enough as it was, having been isolated for so long.

"I do love you," she said quietly, as she plaited his long hair. Since she also felt keenly that their time was limited, somehow it seemed important to tell him. Aeriod smiled at her with a shattering openness. *He has come a long way,* she thought.

"I love you," said Aeriod. "I always have. I'm sorry I did not show it well at first."

Their shared dread of her eventual deployment gave them urgency and intensity, and they were reluctant to leave each other's side. Galla felt sure that things would change again when she left.

20

DEPARTURE

Five days later, Aeriod received a message from the Associates. He sat alone in his office and put his head in his hands. "It's too soon for this," he said to no one, and his old simmering anger flared.

Galla had gone flying each day, to see and assist the farmers, many of whom were younger and she did not recognize, and also to feel the wind. She sometimes felt the suffocation and pain from her time on Bitikk. It would seize her suddenly, and at times she entered a fugue state for several minutes. It always happened when she was alone. She hid it from Aeriod, though, and when she would come out of it she would race to him, to feel comforted. But she never felt this anxiety when she flew.

On this day she skimmed the fungus crop, rose and fell and turned in the air, and then she caught sight of the pit. Aeriod had unshielded it, in case she wanted to explore it. She pulled up alongside it, hopped off, and peered over the edge. She felt a chill, looking at the deep hole. At first she had no desire to descend, but gradually her curiosity overcame her. What would it be like now, after what she had been through?

"If I can handle Bitikk, I can handle you," she said defiantly to the dark maw.

She worked her way down to the platform, and its machinery clanked into gear and sent her descending, away from daylight. Once again she found herself in the empty hallway, and the courtyard with all of the doors leading off. Nothing happened, so she chose one of the doors at random, and it opened for her.

She stepped in and it shut, leaving her in pitch-blackness. She could not even see her hands at first. But then she noticed a glow coming from her diamethyst, and it grew stronger, giving off a rosy light. She touched it, and then she began to see things.

This time she was ready for anything, but what she saw intrigued rather than frightened her. *Who is that?* she wondered, for at first she saw a little ship entering an atmosphere. Next she saw a small person with long, dark hair, who Galla realized must be a human, and who stood looking out a window, which was reflected in her green eyes. In another image, Galla saw what at first looked like a statue. But gradually she began to discern something very wrong, as it looked like someone had been twisted into odd shapes and angles, and had an open mouth and closed eyes, as if screaming. She shivered, and the image changed again.

Now she could see a rusty-hazy sky, and a large, grey, angular structure, topped with what looked like some kind of creature she did not recognize. It turned its hair-lined face to look at her with bulbous, black eyes, and it began to rise on long, spindly legs. She gasped and stepped back. But then she saw a gleaming city, with vehicles flying between its buildings, and lush green and golden trees. Finally she saw a vast place, which looked like a city made entirely of new copper. It appeared empty, but the light was dim. She realized she had seen this place before, during her dreams on Bitikk. As she stood looking at this great, abandoned city, she felt a hand press into hers and squeeze, and she felt warmth for this person, as she had in her dreams over the years.

And then she looked all around her, and found herself in the dark room again with an open door. She walked out into the courtyard. Her necklace felt cool and no longer glowed. She headed back to the platform, thinking of everything she had seen, and barely noticed how quickly the platform shot her back up through the abyss.

When she reached the surface and approached her craft, she caught sight of something high in the sky, rapidly descending. She clapped her hand to her mouth and felt a stab of dread and sadness.

"Galla," Aeriod called on her communicator, "Galla, are you there? Are you back in range?"

"Yes," she answered.

"I've been trying to contact you. Your ship is coming," Aeriod said, his voice dull. "It's time."

Galla shakily climbed back on her craft and rose upward. She slowly circled higher and higher around the location of the pit, which had vanished from sight, and took a long, mournful look at Rikiloi. Then she hurtled her craft back to Aeriod's floating home and into his private bay.

I'm not ready to leave him again, she thought. Her throat had gone dry. *I don't even care where I go next. If only I could have a little more time.*

He was waiting for her. They embraced in silence for a few minutes, then held each other's faces.

"Any idea how long this time?" she managed to ask.

"No," Aeriod said. "I'll wait for you." He touched her forehead, her nose, her cheekbones, her lips, and his hands slid down her neck and her back. He then held her hands and looked into her eyes. "However long it takes, I will wait for you. I love you beyond anything else."

Galla kissed him. "Your opening up to me is the greatest gift. I feel like we grew together. I love you." She could say nothing more for several minutes, as her body shook from stifled sobs.

They walked to the main landing bay, hand in hand, and Aeriod gave her a bag.

"It's the quilt," he explained.

Galla took it absently, said "Thank you," and then eyed the small grey ship. It was very similar to the one that had returned her to

Rikiloi, but it had markings on its side and a small painting of an animal she did not recognize.

A door dropped open. She gawked at the figure that walked out.

The lean biped smiled. Galla's mouth fell open. She wiped her eyes. She had seen her own features, and other images, often enough to know that this really was a human, not one of Aeriod's or any other race. He had short, rumpled dark hair, a mustache, and warm, crinkly hazel eyes.

"So you're Galla-Deia," he said with a short laugh. "I'm Kein." He came forward, bowed, and shook her hand; she smiled.

She liked him instantly.

"I've never met a human before," she gasped.

Kein smirked. "So I've been told. Now I know why they picked *me* for this." He laughed more loudly this time and shook his head.

Aeriod had watched in silence, but now he stepped forward, and Galla noticed a peculiar expression on his face, as if he were trying to see something in the man that she could not.

"And I know you must be Aeriod," Kein said, reaching out to shake the mage's hand.

Aeriod's face broke into a huge smile.

"You look so like your great-grandfather Forster!" he exclaimed, and he shook Kein's hand enthusiastically. Galla thought this looked comical, and she realized just how tall Aeriod was.

Kein chuckled. "Well, that's not the first time I've heard that," he said.

"You have your great-grandmother's name," remarked Aeriod. Galla looked back and forth between them.

"You're right, I do!" said Kein. "Well, I have to say, it's satisfying to meet you at last. I've heard many things."

"Ah," said Aeriod with a slight grimace, "hopefully not too terrible."

Kein winked at Galla. "Not . . . entirely." His eyes crinkled up again as he took in Aeriod and Galla. He said, "All right, are you ready, Galla-Deia? Let's get you on board." He took her bag and turned to walk back to the ship.

"Please, call me Galla," she said.

She felt such enormous relief, meeting this pleasant person and seeing Aeriod's reaction to him. *There must be a story there,* she thought, *while I was on Bitikk.* She sighed. She wished she had heard it from Aeriod, but they were out of time.

She turned back to him, and they embraced for a long moment.

Aeriod said in a muffled voice, "It will be all right. He comes from a good family. It is the best we could hope for your first training with humans."

"So I have you to thank for this," said Galla, trying to smile, and failing.

"Do come back," said Aeriod, his face a mix of sorrow and adoration.

"Of course I will," said Galla, and she turned away from him, with every step dragging.

She climbed on board the simple vehicle and strapped in. She held her hand against its window. It droned to life, and took her away from Aeriod and his gliding island.

21

PERPETUA

Galla watched Rikiloi disappear behind her. Somehow it hurt more to see it falling away from her. When she had been taken before, she had not had the luxury. Eventually it grew fainter, and fainter, until she saw only starry space.

"You've probably had better transports," Kein remarked suddenly, startling her. She realized he had been watching her.

"I've had... stranger ones," Galla stammered.

Kein laughed again.

"You laugh often," she said.

"I suppose so," said Kein amiably.

He began running his fingers over the controls. He voiced commands and the craft moved farther and farther into the black emptiness. Then he turned back to look at Galla.

"So, you were on Bitikk, before this?" Kein asked, squinting.

"I was, yes," said Galla, and she visibly shivered.

"I just can't get used to that place."

"What do you mean?" asked Galla.

"Well, look at it! It's incredible. Looks like they grew everything. Right? But it's not like other organic construction. I think every speck of that place has eyes. Sure seems like it. Makes my hair stand on end."

"Why?"

Kein's crooked grin returned. He leaned over to meet her gaze squarely. "It's scary," he said. "Now don't ask me why. All I know is . . . I don't like it."

"Oh." Galla kept her mouth shut. *It's far scarier than you realize, I think.*

Kein fussed with the controls and said casually, "You didn't bring much with you, I see."

Galla opened her flight jacket to reveal her necklace. Kein noticed and raised his eyebrows.

"That's some rock!" he said.

"I didn't need anything else," said Galla.

Kein pushed his lips together in a funny way. He announced, "Well, we're at the junction now; make sure you're securely strapped in. Unless you want to be shattered and splattered."

This time, Galla laughed.

"I don't think that is possible, Kein."

Kein started to ask why, but his clearance for the junction was given. They launched into a pulsating stream of light that would carry them across the galaxy. He quickly shielded the view by closing off all the windows; he couldn't bear it. Some people could handle it and he was not one of them.

"I wanted to see it all," Galla said regretfully.

"Sorry, Galla," said Kein. "It gives me terrible headaches. I'm a genetically doomed person who still gets them."

The ship lurched out of pulsation into a new star system. Kein opened the view window again; this he did love. A green and white planet loomed quickly into view.

"That's where we're going?" asked Galla. She rose from her seat to stare.

"You sound excited," Kein remarked.

"I am. It's so . . ." and Galla stopped, realizing she knew too few adjectives.

Kein beamed as they began braking. He knew just how she felt. Perpetua, to him, was the most beautiful world, and for him it was home.

"Here we go. Hang tight!" he cried, and the ship raced through the atmosphere, roaring in slowdown.

"Oh! Oh!" Galla cried. "Look!"

She sat erect, pointing and then drawing her hands to her face. Mountains and forests whizzed past. Lakes reflected the cloudy skies.

They finally slowed and then hovered over a small landing pad. As soon as the craft settled onto the platform, Galla unhooked herself and stood quickly.

"Wait!" Kein exclaimed. "Let me finish. It's not safe yet."

He murmured controls and the ship whined to silence. "All right, Galla, *now* we can get out." The door fell open and she leapt through the portal.

She bounced a bit on her heels, and swiveled in every direction to take in the scenery.

"It smells so . . . so . . . I don't know," said Galla wonderingly. "Sharp, salty."

She thought back to the small alpine areas of Rikiloi, but she could not quite compare it.

"Moldy?" offered Kein, cracking up. "Welcome to Perpetua!"

He noticed her complete engagement with the environment as she drew in deep breaths and held her chin high. *She's an odd one!* he thought.

"Well, come on, then," said Kein, hoisting her bag onto his shoulder. "Let's get you situated. You'll be staying at my house, with myself and my husband, Rez. I'm afraid it's not up to flying city standards, but we like it. And it's close to town, so that will be good for you to get to know people."

Galla barely heard him, for she was too interested in the enormous trees, the leaden, fast-moving clouds, and the grey streak on the horizon. The wind blew fiercely from that direction.

"It wasn't the best flying weather," Kein remarked, "but it never is. I'll take you to the ocean later."

"The ocean! I've never been to an ocean," said Galla, wonderingly.

Kein looked sidewise at her, and said, "Oh, you're in for a treat then, I think."

She followed him along a paved trail through tall conifers, which led them to a clearing with a bungalow. Galla smiled broadly at the sight of it, having never seen its like, and again she stopped to take in deep breaths of the sea air. He set her bag down on the long porch, opened the door, and beckoned her to enter.

Whereas outside the wind had been bracing and the sky dark with moisture, inside everything glowed warmly and smelled of woodsmoke and something savory. There were chairs and a couch and shelves full of all sorts of interesting things Galla had never seen before. She liked the coziness of the place. Kein was right, it was nothing like her former home, but she found she adored it.

"Come, your room is back here," Kein called. She followed him down a narrow hallway to a wooden door, and Kein turned its little stone knob. Galla stood facing her small, tidy room, with a bed and a tiny desk, and a window where raindrops began collecting on the outside.

"Oop," said Kein, seeing the window. "Raining again, right on time. Anyway, you can have the small guest bathroom across the hall. I'll let you settle in, and then give you a tour of the house and grounds."

He set her bag down and nodded to her, and shut the door behind him as he left.

Galla looked all around the little nugget of a room. For a moment she had forgotten her sadness about leaving Aeriod, but she remembered it when she opened her bag and pulled out her quilt. She sighed, and spread the quilt out over the small bed. It suited the room, and the house, and Galla felt for a moment a sense of rightness. She found other things in the bag: a few jumpsuits, a small thick poncho, and a hairbrush, for Aeriod had thought ahead. She could tell he also didn't want to overwhelm her with anything too fancy. The sight of these things made her sigh. She found a closet, and discovered it also contained some basic outfits.

"A far cry from Aeriod's realm," she murmured, but it pleased her, and she tucked her bag inside and shut its little door.

She ventured out into the hall, and Kein poked his head around a corner and said, "That one, that's the bathroom." Taking his hint, she grabbed a new outfit from her room, went in, and looked at everything confusedly.

"Oh, do you need help?" he asked politely.

"Maybe?" she said uncertainly. "What is that thing?"

Kein walked over and looked, and snickered. "That's the shower. Wait, have you never seen a shower before? I mean, I get it; it's kind of old-fashioned. I'll show you how it works."

She jumped back as water cascaded from the spout above the tub, and watched Kein adjust the knobs. "And you just turn that off when you're done," he said.

"Thank you," said Galla gratefully, clinging to her fresh clothes. He had already left and shut the door.

She stripped and stepped in, and the warm water rushed over her. She grabbed a vial of soap and scrubbed herself all over, including her hair, and when she turned off the shower and dried herself with a towel, she noticed in her foggy mirror that her hair began to frizz in all directions, seeming to curl before her eyes. She sighed in frustration.

She walked out, fully dressed, and found Kein in his living room. She noticed then that another man had joined them. He was a large, barrel-chested man, with fiery ginger hair and a massive orange beard.

His voice boomed, "Hello!" and she jumped, but his huge smile charmed her.

"Galla," said Kein, "this is my husband, Rez. Rez, Galla."

"Hello," said Galla with a nod.

"Nice to meet you," the red-haired man said pleasantly. He turned his grey eyes to Kein and said, "You don't want to know how long you were gone."

"I can tell by the season," murmured Kein. "Hate going too far away."

Galla lifted one eyebrow. Kein said to her, "Time dilation. We live pretty far out here. If I hop through too many junctions, years will pass on Perpetua while I'm gone. That's why my great-grandparents never went back to Mandira, much less Earth. Rikiloi and Bitikk are as far as I've been willing to go. You're so lucky, Galla. You'll never have to worry about that."

I never did before, you mean, thought Galla. *There's so much humans have to deal with!*

Kein yawned and said, "It's getting a bit late, so we're going to have supper soon, and settle in for the night. I'll give you a better tour of everything tomorrow."

"Actually, supper's ready," Rez announced. "Galla, would you like a beer?"

Galla raised her eyebrows. "What's beer?"

Kein and Rez looked at each other, smirking. "Oh boy," said Rez.

"Oh girl, more like," said Kein, and they chuckled. Galla gave him a confused look and he dipped his head.

Kein said, "What about wine, do you like wine?"

"I've had some wine before," said Galla slowly, "but I have a feeling it's not like *your* wine. Anyway, I want to try this beer of yours." She held her chin up.

"Good!" said Rez enthusiastically. "We make our own. We brew a few different kinds, so come and have a look in the kitchen."

Galla lit up. "I love kitchens!" she said. When she followed Rez, she stood and blinked for a moment.

Rez did not see her face, but Kein did, and he quipped, "Well, like I said, it's no palace."

"How do you do anything in this tiny space?" Galla wondered.

Kein and Rez guffawed.

"Whew," said Rez. "I keep saying we need to expand; maybe now we'd better—got royalty and all that."

Kein coughed into his sleeve.

"I'm not *royalty*," said Galla in a huff, and with a toss of her hair.

Kein's face had turned purple from suppressed laughter. He fled the room. Rez's beard twitched, but he remained silent. He had pulled an upright wooden lever on the side of a barrel and filled a clear goblet with a dark, frothy liquid. He held the goblet out to her while bowing deeply.

"My lady," he said with sincerity, but Kein had completely lost it and was cackling outside the door.

"Thank you," said Galla, her cheeks reddening. "I'm really not, though."

"Of course," said Rez dryly. "Now tell me what you think."

Galla took a sip and sucked the head of the beer right up her nose, and she sneezed. She could tell Rez wanted to laugh one more time, but he politely handed her a napkin and nodded for her to try again. She did, and took a good long drink, and licked her lips.

"Oh, I like this," she said. "It's very rich, and has a good tang to it."

"Hey, Kein," called Rez, "got a new taster here, I won't be needing you anymore."

Kein entered again, composed, but with his eyes twinkling. "Hey now! I'll take one," he said, and Rez pulled him a draught. The three of them stood in the small kitchen and raised their glasses.

Kein said, "Welcome, Galla, to humanity!" and the glasses clinked together.

Finally, she thought.

22

DESCENDENT

Galla fell asleep with a swimming head, a full stomach, and the sound of rain pelting the roof. She awoke to a pearl-grey foggy window and a mild sense of vertigo and disorientation. She looked around her small room and breathed in. She picked up the corner of her quilt and smelled it, and it smelled like Aeriod. She lost herself in the scent for several minutes, letting her tears flow.

But she was determined to make the most of everything. Already she was excited about the day ahead, and relished talking with Kein and Rez. She found them slightly infuriating but kind, and she enjoyed their interaction with each other. She could sense they had been together a long time and had fallen into sort of a habit. She could not guess how quickly her presence reverberated through that household.

Kein, meanwhile, had spent the early morning hours reviewing any records he had of Galla-Deia. Kein had received all his information about her from a shadowy figure working for Bitikk. He knew there were no human Associates. He watched very limited grams of Galla practicing under Oni-Odi.

Oni-Odi's own eyes had apparently recorded some of the grams, which he had in turn given to the Associates. Kein watched these with intrigue. He was convinced the android was not watching just her training all the time. The clip with a hairbrush really puzzled him; why include *that?* What useful information could be gained from that, for training Galla-Deia?

Kein sat up in his chair. "Do they expect *me* to brush her hair?" he said aloud. "Forget it!"

But he could not shake Oni-Odi's perspective. Galla waved to him in these images, smiled strikingly, eagerly tried to please him. When she erred, this was painful to watch. Kein felt voyeuristic, reviewing the grams. The young woman—and he simply had to call her young, though he knew she was not—seemed so childlike, of such a fragile disposition. *Maybe,* he thought, *that's why she's with me this time. They want me not just to teach her about being human, but about being socially equipped for dealing with other humans.* She did seem close to Aeriod, though.

He delved as far as he could into her records; no footage existed of Rikiloi, to his disappointment. *What I wouldn't give to see one of those legendary parties,* he thought with amusement.

He shrugged those thoughts away and searched again, this time for Galla's history. Abruptly his information ended. All that he could discern was the fact that Oni-Odi had housed her and given her principal training. He mulled this over. His informant had merely told him that she was not like humans in many ways, that Kein could train her to fit in, and that he had better ask no more questions about her.

Kein managed stealing an entire ten-minute block of morning to himself, to kick back on his deck with a huge mug of tea. It was just enough time to imagine business as usual: typical low fog wisping the hilltops, usual rustling of wilderness. His kind of morning, his pre-dawn world.

Thump-thump-thump.

"Shit," Kein groaned.

Out of the house tumbled an over-eager, too-awake, shining-faced vision—complete with unintentionally lovely, bed-rumpled hair . . . and clean teeth. She looked at him with eyes like russet half-moons.

"Hello, Kein!" piped Galla.

"Good morning," came the gruff reply. "Morning person, hey?"

"What do you mean?" she asked.

"Never mind. Listen: give me ten more minutes. I'm not human till I finish my tea."

Galla drew back from him with a puzzled look, and asked soberly, "Then what are you?"

Kein bent over and guffawed. He slapped his knee and cried, "First lesson today! Figure of *speech!* Now please, let me finish this tea, then I'll come get you."

She nodded and reentered the cabin. She slipped into the kitchen to admire the various crockery and tools and pictures on the walls.

"All right," said Kein, coming in a few minutes later, rubbing his hands together. "About that first lesson—that's a work in progress. Now, before you ask what I mean, I'll just say that you're in a process. Hell, *I'm* in a process, too. I'll learn more about myself by teaching you.

"You're going to hear a lot of human talk, because that's something humans do a lot of. And we don't always mean what we say, or say what we mean, and even though we love to talk, we still run into problems communicating. And that's just in *our* own species!"

Kein poured a steaming mug of tea and gave it to an utterly bewildered Galla.

"Next up, rituals," he declared. "This is one ritual I *have* to have every morning, to feel normal, to feel *human.*"

She held the hot mug and let its vapor steam her face. She liked the smell of the tea, but the taste was bland to her.

"This makes you feel human," she repeated, looking at him with wide eyes. She set the mug down and let her mouth curl at one corner. "Well, I don't feel any different."

Kein nodded. "I'm sure you don't. You look like us, but you're not quite like us. And even if you were, you might not like tea! But it's a start. Humans like rituals. This one is one of mine, and I don't like being bothered during it."

"Oh," said Galla, blushing. "Sorry."

Kein shrugged. "It's a process, like I said."

She remarked, "I used to have a ritual. My hair—"

"Let's get one thing straight," Kein quickly interrupted, his hazel eyes hard, "I'm not going to brush your hair."

Galla laughed out loud. "I hadn't thought about asking *you!*" she exclaimed. "I just thought that was something Oni-Odi could do, when I didn't feel like it myself."

Kein whistled.

"Good," he sighed with embarrassed relief. "Anyway, find some rituals just for you."

Again Galla thought of Aeriod, and how she had adjusted to his rituals for dining and sunset watching. Yet Kein did not want Galla to be a part of his dawn ritual. It was just another difference. She felt intensely glad that Kein was at least amiable enough.

Kein went on, "Now, clearly this is no palace like what you're used to. So I'll show you around. Things are rustic here from anyone's perspective. You'll have to get used to it."

Galla joined Kein for his tour of the house and land. There were a few small rooms on the main floor of his cabin, including the one Galla had slept in. Upstairs, a loft room spread across the entire floor. There, Kein kept various pieces of wooden entertainment equipment, none of which he described to his new companion, so Galla was left wondering what it all was.

Kein took her back to the deck, and then down a set of stairs that connected to a boardwalk over a wetland. This boardwalk extended to a large pond, and then disappeared into a forest as a regular dirt trail. Galla wanted to explore that trail, but Kein steered her away from it and they walked back along the pond.

"So this is pretty much it," he told her. "You have free rein of the house, except of course the deck before dawn. There's a lake nearby. I have kayaks. Nothing fancy, but I did make them myself."

Galla watched his eyes crinkle in pride. He then said offhandedly, "The woods are off limits."

"Why?" she asked.

"They're just not—" and Kein paused, throwing a look back at the forest. Galla looked too, and thought the trees seemed as harmless as anything on Demetraan. Kein said simply, "They're not safe. Just don't go there."

She frowned and shrugged. Kein led her back to the house, moving along with a fluidity she admired. He was someone who was good at what he did, and he seemed to dabble in many things. Whereas Aeriod could by turns seem menacing or imposing, with different degrees of stiffness and yet with a sense of latent power, Kein ambled along simply and confidently, with a casual jauntiness of step.

And Kein was gritty. His fingernails were stained black, his face showed stubble, his wiry hair looked a bit smashed on one side. Even his canvas pants were streaked with stains from polishing his kayaks. Galla learned quickly enough that Kein mostly looked dirty, and rarely actually was. He truly lived a relatively austere life most of the time.

He had been thinking about what to show her next, carefully treading around certain information until it was necessary. So as he prepared a breakfast for both of them, he also considered his rugged nature. He reflected that the Associates could have—and perhaps *should* have—placed Galla with a woman for her initial contact. Kein thought that perhaps the Associates wanted to minimize contact for her among humans at large. They knew he would never abuse his task of training her. He was renowned for reliability.

Rez had made the whole situation sound like some kind of honor.

"Think about it," he'd told Kein. "They've chosen you, in this backwater, to ease her into humanity. That's a pretty big responsibility. But you're known for consistency, and everybody likes you. You should feel proud somebody finally rewarded you for who you are."

Kein knew there was more to this than honor. For one thing, he had worked out his own deal to keep development out of his region for the length of his life, or the length of hers, whichever was longer. That was paramount to him. The Associates also provided him with a considerable pension, although he felt he could have asked for more.

And then, of course, there was Aeriod's connection with his

family. Much had been made of the fact that he came from some of the first humans to live outside the solar system. His family had grown a successful eco-touring business for Perpetua. While his sisters had chosen to move on to other careers, Kein managed the family business from afar, and employed only the most reliable beings to maintain his company and his accounts. This gave him the luxury of living simply.

Either way, Kein was grateful for the opportunity to train Galla, even as he wondered how to go about it. Ultimately he decided she must meet other women. He soon thought of the most innocuous one he knew: a curator in town. He seized on a plan. He would show Galla a bit of local culture first, and work up to more complex social events over time.

Galla, for her part, listened raptly to everything Kein and Rez told her, and absorbed her surroundings with fascination. She felt stimulated enough that she had not thought much about her prior life until nightfall, when she sat with her elbows on her windowsill and watched clouds dash past in a starry sky. Seeing the stars gave her a hollow feeling.

I like it here. I might even be happy here, for a time. But somewhere out there, Oni-Odi and Demetraan are hidden, and Aeriod plans and waits. I do not know how I can help either of them from here.

But she swaddled herself with her quilt in her small dark room, and for a moment she felt a sense of home.

23

THE CURATOR

The next day, Kein took Galla into town. There was little to make it much of a town; it was more an assemblage of shops, a bar, warehouses, and hangars to protect any crafts from the wild climate. As Galla walked along, she stretched to see glimpses of the grey ocean, white-capped in a brisk wind.

"When can we go to the sea?" she asked, staring so intently between the dark evergreens for any glimpse of it that she tripped.

"You're that eager, huh?" Kein said, and he smirked. "Okay, we can go and look after we've done our business."

Galla scrunched her nose up at him.

"What is *oakay*?" she asked.

Kein stared at her and then snorted. "I forgot. Sorry. It means . . . sure, or fine. Sometimes we just say it."

Galla shook her head. "You have a lot of strange words. Like *shit*."

"Um," said Kein, "I'm guessing you heard us say that. Sorry."

"No, I like it. It's good and crisp." Galla lifted her chin, sure of herself.

"It means *poop*, Galla," said Kein.

"Oh! That's a nasty word. I hate it," Galla replied, shrugging. Kein snickered.

They met other humans, and some outright stared at Galla until she self-consciously plucked at her hair and tried to pull it down from its wind-chiseled heights. She glanced nervously at Kein.

"Why are they staring at me?" she hissed.

Kein looked around and then nodded. "Well, you are new here. And you ... well, you ... turn heads."

"How?" she asked.

Kein rolled his eyes. "I'm not going to tell you how. You can figure that one out yourself."

Galla sniffed. "So where's this curator person? Oh! Who are *they*?" She pointed at a group of tall beings with grey skin, bulbous proboscis noses, and leathery attire.

"Oh God, don't stare," whispered Kein. "We do share the town with others. They are Veedlt-Ka. They settled Perpetua before we did. And we also get other visitors."

"Do you like them?" Galla asked, wondering why Kein had whispered. She resisted staring again, but stole glances at them. Four of them walked side by side, and she could see they had long arms and long feet. Their hands were hidden in mittens.

"They're fine." Kein shrugged. "We get along, but we don't intermingle much. It's always been that way."

"So they are *okay*," pondered Galla aloud.

"Yes!" Kein smiled. "Exactly."

They walked up to a small box of a house, wind-lashed grey with white window trim. Its yard was all gravel, with intricate patterns raked in it. Galla could hear a hollow, melodically knocking sound and a twinkling metallic sound as well. She walked with crunching steps along the front of the gravel yard until she could see a little behind the house, and from one of the eaves hung two wind chimes, one of wood, the other metal.

"Now," said Kein, "we knock, and see if she's in. Go on," he encouraged her.

Galla took little mincing steps up to the simple white door and turned to look at Kein. He nodded, and she knocked four times with her knuckles. She stood back, looked up and down at the door, and then returned to Kein.

The door creaked and opened, and it was Galla's turn to stare.

The Curator stood in brilliant scarlet and yellow robes. She held her hands together and looked serenely at both Kein and Galla with dark eyes set among high cheekbones, and under steel-grey, closely cropped hair. She looked about Galla's height, and her face was lined with wrinkles that made her look as if she smiled most of the time.

"Kein!" she called out to him, and extended her arms. "So good to see you! Would you like to come in? Who is your friend?"

Before Kein could stop her, Galla bounded forward, her hands clasped under her chin.

"I'm Galla-Deia! But you can call me Galla." She jerked forward her right hand and held it out to the woman. They shook hands.

The woman said, "And I am Loreena. So nice to meet you, Galla!"

Kein had stepped up beside her, amused but a bit embarrassed.

"I should have called first," he said, "but I knew we would be coming this way for other errands."

"Oh, it's fine, Kein, I'm so happy to meet Galla here," Loreena said with a smile. "Now come in. I'll put some tea on. Have a seat, and make yourselves comfortable."

Galla walked in and smelled thick incense. Not like anything of Aeriod's, however. Something more rustic and herbal. She blinked in the light, for there were many candles and hanging lanterns, and two low, orange couches along with floor poufs of vibrant colors. She sank into a couch and faced a low table. On every wall hung pictures or documents or framed paraphernalia. In the warm, dim light, it was hard to make any of them out.

While Loreena had gone to the kitchen to make the tea, Kein said quietly, "Loreena is our Curator. Like me, she's descended from the original human settlers here. Her ancestors have kept different things from our history here. A little legacy. When she is gone, I'm not sure who will take over. She is an only child."

Galla thought about that for a moment, and realized with a jolt something she had forgotten. Humans did not live very long, not compared to Oni-Odi, or Aeriod, or even herself, although she was not sure how long she had lived. Oni-Odi had never told her. Suddenly it was the one thing she wanted to know.

But she stifled that line of questioning, since she couldn't ask Kein anyway. Loreena returned with a tray bearing a teapot and three mugs, and a small plate of spice biscuits. Galla could smell spices from the tea as well, and she felt her hair lifting a bit on her head in excitement. Kein glanced over and watched the drifting mane in amazement.

Loreena made a clucking sound and Kein turned to face her. Galla could not read her expression, but understood that they were to pay attention to her. She sat cross-legged opposite them.

"Tell me, Galla, where did you live before coming to Perpetua?" she asked in a warm voice. Her eyes were nearly black in the dim, warm light. Galla felt locked in place by them.

"I lived on Rikiloi, and before that, on Demetraan with Oni-Odi," Galla replied. She did not mention Bitikk. But the dark eyes seemed to pierce her.

"You have traveled," said Loreena.

"Yes, some, especially on Demetraan," Galla responded. She took a biscuit and let it dissolve in her mouth, the spices warming her tongue. The tea intrigued her. It was golden-clear and not sweet, but both tart and savory, almost a broth.

Loreena smiled, and rubbed her cropped head. "I think you have walked an interesting path. Only the beginning of the path."

Galla nodded slowly. Kein glanced sidewise at her.

He said, "Loreena, thank you for the tea. I wondered if I might leave Galla here while I run some errands? Would that be all right?"

Galla smirked at him. *"Okay,"* she said. Loreena laughed softly. Kein bowed and left. Galla faced Loreena.

She said to the Curator, "You are the first woman I have ever met."

"That isn't true, Galla-Deia," said Loreena kindly. "You've met yourself!"

Galla grinned. "I meant, the first human woman."

"Do you think you are so different from me?" asked Loreena.

"Well, I . . . yes, right? I am not really human, I only look it. I am not made of the same things as you. I do not live the same way." And Galla found herself twisting coils of her hair around her fingers.

Loreena closed her eyes for a moment. She said, "You were born."

Galla's eyes grew large. "Yes," she replied.

"You were brought up by someone, Oni-Odi?" Loreena questioned.

"Yes," said Galla.

"And you have lived," said Loreena.

"I mean, yes, of course," said Galla, confused.

"Then we are no different," Loreena proclaimed.

Galla straightened in her seat. "I never thought of that," she said.

Loreena clasped her fingers together in her lap and her eyes lowered nearly to slits. Galla could see the candlelight just barely reflected in them.

"You have suffered," said Loreena, very quietly.

Galla shuddered: the stabs of shadowy memory from Bitikk, the haunting images in the Device. She hugged herself.

"Breathe, Galla," said Loreena. "Breathe deeply. Exhale, inhale; just breathe."

Galla followed Loreena's calming words and felt a sense of release.

"We all suffer," said Loreena. "That is the way. I do not know your strengths, or your weaknesses. They do not matter. What matters is that you understand the nature of suffering, that it is cyclical, and that all beings must endure it. But we can try to stop it, we can wish for it to end. And that is my goal."

"Is it my goal?" Galla wondered aloud without thinking.

Loreena's eyes opened a little more. "You must decide that for yourself."

Galla whispered, "Do you know about Paosh Tohon?"

Loreena opened her eyes fully. "Oh yes. We may seem immune here, thanks to Governor Aeriod. But I know of it. And I know that our immunity will not last forever. Paosh Tohon is far more vast than Perpetua."

"How is this world protected? Is Aeriod able to do that everywhere?" Galla wondered.

Loreena shrugged. "I do not know all of his skills. The worlds he governs currently are well protected, or outright hidden. But where there is suffering, Paosh Tohon can find a way in. Where there are telepaths, it is drawn especially."

"Are there telepaths here?" Galla asked, looking around the room.

"You came with one," Loreena answered.

"Kein?" cried Galla. "He never told me!"

Loreena said in a hushed voice, "He does not know, as yet. Some of his ancestors developed their abilities only in midlife. I think he resists it, but I am not sure since I am not a telepath myself."

"So he will not be safe here?" gasped Galla, standing.

Loreena waved her down. "I know he is protective of his family, and wants to maintain the peace of this world. He is safe here for now. He just needs a bit of a nudge, I think. When the time is right. Now, let's go outside. I want you to see the backyard."

Galla followed Loreena through the small kitchen, noting its simplicity, as it looked very clean and tidy but with no remarkable decor. They exited the back door of the house into another gravel yard. Circles of gravel and winding paths met their feet. One of the paths extended to the edge of a woods and stretched into its quiet depths.

"Have you been along the path at Rez and Kein's house yet?" Loreena asked.

"Only a little way," Galla answered. She was following a small labyrinth made of stone. "Kein told me not to go any farther."

"Did he," Loreena mused. She glanced at Galla, and Galla met her gaze. Loreena lifted her chin and nodded.

Galla felt a spark of excitement. She made up her mind.

"What will I find?" she whispered conspiratorially.

Loreena laughed. "Maybe nothing. But you won't know unless you look, will you?"

Galla gazed at Loreena wistfully. "I don't know how long I will be here," she said.

"None of us knows that, Galla. So you may as well make the best of it. Now come, let's finish that tea."

Galla felt so at ease around another woman. While some of Aeriod's assistants were female, she'd never sensed she could connect with them. But even within an hour's visit with Loreena, something in Galla felt comforted for the first time in her life.

She held her teacup and stared at the memorabilia on the walls. She looked at pictures of the settlers, and spotted Kein's ancestors. He did indeed look like his great-grandfather, but perhaps he had his great-grandmother's broad forehead. She stared at them, and realized they had also known Aeriod.

Loreena had sipped her tea in silence while her guest perused the collections. Galla eventually sat and held out her hands.

"Thank you," she said.

Loreena nodded and smiled. A knock came at the door.

She and Galla both stood and clasped hands. "You are a good person, Galla. Do what you must. It will not always be easy. But that clear fire that shines in you, draw upon that. It will never steer you wrong." She bowed her head, so Galla did the same.

Kein met her at the door and Galla waved as she left. Loreena stood in her bright robes and smiled. Galla felt a strange, sad tug in herself as she glanced back at the maternal gaze of the Curator.

24

THE PATH

Kein had bought some treats for Galla to try, bread loaves and pastries and fruit from the market. She helped him carry the items as they dashed through drizzle to get back to the cabin. She could not see the ocean at all now, as a thick fog had rolled in. Dusk approached and she realized they had not seen the sun all day. Then the pang of memory set in again, as she thought of Aeriod and their sunset views.

But it vanished when she remembered Loreena's suggestion. Galla helped set the table a bit absently, bumping into things and stammering apologies. Her mind flitted to that path behind the house. She knew she should explore it soon, since she never knew when an Associate ship would arrive to take her away.

"You know, Galla," Kein said abruptly, as she dreamily munched on a roll, "it's acceptable to talk at the table."

She blinked at him. "Oh. Yes." She turned to Rez and asked, "How was your day?"

Rez wagged his ginger beard and boomed, "Great day! Got home before the downpour. Always a good thing. How'd it go today?"

"I met the Curator!" Galla exclaimed.

"Oh! She's neat," said Rez simply, and with a nod, he took in a spoon of stew and then swallowed a big slug of beer.

Galla worked on her plan for sneaking out to the path. She ate methodically, and only when she heard Kein's exasperated sigh did she offer to help clean up.

"I'm sorry," she said sheepishly. "Thank you for the dinner. I've just... I have a lot to think about."

Kein nodded. "Loreena has that effect on some people."

Galla stole a long look at Kein as he dried dishes. *He doesn't know. Or he doesn't want to know. So I've got to find out more.*

She wished Kein and Rez good night and huddled under her covers, listening to the rain and wind coming in sheets. Later, she heard distant snores from one of the men. The rain stopped. She raised herself up on her elbows and listened. No one was awake. She chucked aside the sheet and quilt, pulled on a jumper and a jacket, and unfastened her window. A moment later, she landed on soft moss. She blinked in the darkness and tried to figure out where the path was. Finally she found it, and began picking her way along it farther and farther into the woods.

The wind had calmed, but still moaned high in the trees. The branches creaked and the undergrowth rustled. Clouds scattered to show stars at times, but otherwise it was a moonless night. Galla then pulled out her amethyst and squeezed it instinctively. It began to glow, a soft pink-violet light. While not very bright, it gave her just enough light to see where to step. She walked along happily then, but as she went farther and farther away from the cabin, she grew uneasy.

I should not be afraid of anything here. Nothing is going to hurt me, she assured herself. But she could not help feeling watched, as if the trees themselves stared at her balefully, a trespasser in their midst. She had begun breathing shallow breaths when she noticed everything started to look more defined.

"There's a light coming from somewhere," she said aloud, and then smacked her hand over her mouth in horror at speaking. Skittering noises erupted in the woods. Her eyes stung with near panic.

But she pressed on, and the light increased. The path grew wilder then, and suddenly she reached a fork. One branch curved off to the right, back toward the water. The other one forged ahead, and that was where the light was coming from. So she edged forward toward it. She reached a clearing and stood dumbfounded at what she saw.

Another pond lay at the end of the trail. It stretched back into the woods among the trunks of the trees. And in its depths something shone, illuminating the woods.

Galla stared into that pond, yet could see no defined shape of any animal. The entire pond glowed. But as she stood there, a single ripple spread outward from the center. It slapped the edge of the shore with a *plop,* and she froze. Every part of her body pulsed with the urge to turn and run away, back to the cabin. But there came another ripple. And another. And another. And then, a lurching, sucking sound rose from the pond. A long, glowing tendril extended from the water and onto the ground. More tendrils joined it, and it flowed out and along the ground toward her.

She scooted back, every hair on end, but then she stood firmly. Loreena had wanted her to see something, and she felt sure this was it. The glowing sludge crept toward her feet, halting just at her toes. It stayed there. So Galla swallowed and bent down to look at it.

There were no markings, no discernible limbs. It was just a glowing slime, palest green-blue. Taking a chance, she reached out her finger and poked it. Her mind crackled, and she flew back and hit a tree.

Gasping, she pushed herself into the tree and watched, horrified, as the slime approached her again, and then it wrapped itself around her ankles. It jolted her with something akin to electric shock, but did not hurt her.

Her mind filled with words:

"You have sought us. Do not be frightened. We know who you are, and you are welcome in these woods."

The slime bulged upward, and an appendage of sorts reached out and touched her forehead. All she could see then was pale aqua light everywhere. But the presence spoke again.

"We belong on this world. But we are elsewhere as well. You must listen to us and understand.

"What you call Paosh Tohon is not unlike us. But it metastasized long ago, and spat out stalks throughout this galaxy. Its world hides while it stretches forth, to maim and entrap. Your mage cannot stop it. One day, it may come here as well. Even now it overtakes core worlds and siphons upon those in pain. Interlinked minds drive its hunger for more. It must be stopped, or all worlds will fall.

"The great cataclysm you call the Event will give it unlimited capacity to feed upon the suffering. Those it feeds upon wish for death, lest it keep them in perpetual agony. Those it twists to its will reside in another form of purgatory, inescapable. Those who worship it are damned."

"What can I do?" Galla managed to ask.

"Find the worlds with Devices. Gather a force to purge it from the galaxy. You will need strong minds to help you, and they will need you to protect them. We all need you, Galla-Deia."

And with that, the tendrils fled her body and slid beneath the surface of the pond. It went dark and stilled. The only light that shone now was Galla's diamethyst. She wrapped her fingers around it and ran to the cabin.

25

ENTHRALLED

I *made it, I made it. I'm out.*
 The man gripped the little shuttle's controls and plowed ahead. He had smashed the speaker so he no longer heard the squawk from the station. Freedom. He didn't even look back, to see the blue-green world and its shell-like orbiter and its golden sun.
 He chewed his lips and looked at his groomed nails. He scratched his chin, once shaven sleek, now peppered with stubble.
 Where's the junction, where's the junction? Find the pulsing light, right?
 He gnawed on his lips some more. No one followed. *Well, fuck them anyway.*
 A tiny prick of guilt settled into him, but not for any of them, none except Marshall. Why hadn't she come too? What was left? They had no place there. It was a beautiful prison. They could never risk going far, so they were told.
 Bullshit.
 So he left.
 "I'll tell you when I find something better," he'd told her. She had stared at him with her slate-blue eyes, but he refused to see the horror in them. Marshall had gone soft. That was all.

There it is.

He could see the pulsing light of the junction. It grew iridescent as he approached it. He began to sweat, not knowing what to expect.

Almost there.

At that moment his controls glowed and a shape developed on his screen. Aeriod.

"Officer Derry." The governor looked at him, aquiline, even predatory, Derry thought. "Return at once with your ship. If you go farther, you'll be out of my protection."

"Your *protection,* is that what you're calling it?" Derry spat. "You made a birdcage. To hell with that. I'm out."

Aeriod sighed and said, "I understand, you feel you do not fit in. Something else can be arranged. Please do not go through the junction."

Derry held up his middle finger.

"'Bye," he said, and he drove his fist through the screen.

He pulled in front of the junction, and for a moment, he hesitated, and wondered. The tremble in Marshall's face haunted him. Why couldn't she have come too? And at the fleeting second when he might have turned around, the junction grabbed him and pulled him through.

He covered his eyes, as the blinding lights spun outside the windows. He staggered and pressed controls to cover them. His stomach protested to the stretching, strange sensations and he vomited all down his front. Then the turbulence began.

Derry shouted, "Is this supposed to happen?" and the ship seemed to ricochet off something, bashing and spinning. He screamed as it spun. And then a great shriek blasted in his ears, followed by a buzz. A repeating buzz, over and over.

"The fuck is happening!" he yelled.

And then the ship stopped, completely without power. And Derry beheld with wonder as a shape emerged from his controls. A woman! And not just any woman, but a voluptuous, dark-haired, violet-eyed woman. He stared at her body and did not register her face until she had crept up to him and straddled him, her breasts touching his mouth. She licked his vomit-stained lips and smiled with the whitest teeth.

"We will make it better," the woman murmured. "Just relax."

Derry knew then. But he was too late.

26

LEGACY

When she reached the cabin, Galla found Kein sitting outside on the back deck in his coat, waiting. He glared at her and she gulped. Still, she climbed the steps and faced him with unflinching eyes.

"You went on the path. I *told* you not to!" he chided. His mustache lowered in a frown. "Something could have happened to you!"

She interlocked her fingers and twisted them. "Well . . ." she began.

"Something *did* happen! Jesus! What?" cried Kein, and then he lowered his voice, for fear of waking Rez. "Are you all right?" he whispered.

"I am *okay*," she reassured him, with a smirk settling in one corner of her mouth. "But I think we should talk."

Kein shook his head. "I don't want to go there," he said.

"You don't have to," said Galla archly. "Because I did. And I *know*."

Kein could not meet her gaze. "What do you know?"

"I know what you are," she said, and she could feel little pops of anger well in her. The old urge to have a tantrum grew mighty. At another time of day, and in another place, she might have slid right into that rage. For now, she lifted herself on her toes repeatedly while staring at Kein. Why would he evade her like this?

Kein threw his arms up in the air. "Fine. What am I?"

"A telepath! Just like your great-grandfather," said Galla, crossing her arms.

"I am *not like him*," hissed Kein, putting his finger to his mouth. "And please, do *not* mention this to Rez!"

"Wait, what! You haven't told him!" cried Galla.

"Shh! Shhhh!" Kein threw his fists in the air and then brought them down again to cover his eyes. "Damn. It!" he said quietly. "Look, I have the gene. I know I have the gene, because I get those headaches. And apparently great-granddad started getting them, triggered by another telepath. But nothing like that's happened to me! I don't have any real powers!"

"Because you're the only telepathic person on this planet!" said Galla. "I think if you go to that pond in the woods—"

"Like hell I will! I made that mistake years ago, and had nightmares every single night for months!"

"But Kein, maybe you weren't ready yet! Now you are!" she insisted. "Look, this glowing thing in the pond, it told me—"

"What the fuck!" Kein cried, and this time Galla put her finger over her lips.

"Stop it! Let me finish! It's a being in the pond! Ugh!"

Kein threw his arms out wide and slapped his hands down onto the tops of his thighs. "Go on."

"It told me that I needed to gather a group of strong minds to help stop Paosh Tohon, and we need to go to these different worlds with these Devices and . . . I don't really know what else, but somehow we work together and get rid of it!"

And now she threw her hands out and shook her head. "Don't you see? I could take you with me!"

"I'm not going *anywhere*. Let me be clear: I am not leaving Perpetua." Kein chopped the words like chunks from a tree.

She dared to sit next to him, and pleaded with her eyes in the starlight.

"Ohhh, no. That's not gonna work on me, Galla." Kein shook his head. Then he glanced at her soft, open, concerned gaze. "Shit."

"Listen," said Galla. "I think that's why I am here. Right? The Associates wanted me to train with you. Because you're needed in the times ahead! It's so obvious! You're a telepath, and I'm . . . well, I'm not sure what I am, but clearly I'm necessary for this Task. Now I know what the Task actually is, and I can start working on it! But I need your help."

"Galla, I really don't know if the Associates even know what your Task is, to be quite honest," said Kein. "They have some vague idea, but no specifics. And, I mean, I'm probably an evolutionary dead end. I'm one man. My sisters don't have the gene. I'm probably not going to have any kids, to pass it on. This is it, the end of the line! And I just . . . look, I've heard what Paosh Tohon can do. I've heard about its wanting telepaths. I've been so lucky that I've never come across it, but that's also why I don't leave Perpetua for long. And I've got Rez here. I can't just bail on him. I'm happy here. Can't you see? I don't want to go with you. I'm sorry."

She felt tears welling. "I wish you would," she said. "I like you, and I wish I didn't have to go alone."

He sighed. "I know. But I really think you're going to be fine; you'll find a good team."

"Where?" she wondered.

"I don't know. But not here. And not right now. Come on, it's wicked late and we need our rest. I've got more human stuff to introduce you to, tomorrow."

"If you change your mind—" Galla began.

"I won't," Kein said.

27

FLEDGLING

Galla could almost feel the twilight of her time on Perpetua. Kein had introduced her to everyone, and he and Rez had been generous hosts. They had thrown a small party for her one evening, and the settlers came in waves with food and drink. It overwhelmed her, but she blinked away grateful tears. Then she asked her two hosts if she could walk to the beach with them.

She had visited it a few times, but never at night. She could make out a few faint lights along the shore, of others' homes. The wind lowed and sighed, and the sea thundered and fizzed and sucked at her toes with its stabbing cold foam. They made it to a promontory called Auna's Rock, and Galla climbed up on it and let the bracing wind yank her hair to the night sky. She loved the sea.

She lay in her bed for a long time after, and as Kein and Rez turned the lights out, she went to her window and knelt there, elbows on the sill, her forehead against the glass. She looked up at the swaying trees. And the familiar sensation of dread and excitement crept into her. It would be soon.

She could hear muttering, and rose up to turn her head to listen. Kein's voice mumbled softly in another room. She opened her door and craned her neck. Then she decided to slink along the floor, avoiding the center where it creaked, to listen more closely.

"I think so," she heard Kein say. "I mean, there's nothing more we can really do. She's just got to get out there. She's been great. But yeah."

"I urge you to reconsider my offer," another voice replied.

Galla stiffened. It was Aeriod's voice. She covered her mouth to prevent herself from making any sound.

Kein sighed loudly. "Look, I'm sorry. I feel like I've done enough, on my end here. I don't have these... abilities. And even if I did, I'm not leaving."

"Your ancestors—" Aeriod began.

"They're gone," snapped Kein. "Don't you think they've paid you back enough? Don't you think all of us have? Maybe all we really have left is here, if things get as bad as you say. Why not just let us live in peace? Or die in peace, if it comes that? No. I'm not coming. I'm done."

And Galla heard Aeriod sigh in return. "It could jeopardize everything the Associates have worked toward. That I've fought for. If there's anything I can offer—"

"Okay, we're done here. I'll make sure she's ready for her deployment."

She heard a *vvvipp* sound from Kein's communicator, and the scuffing of a chair. She fled as quietly as she could on her toes back to her room and shut the door behind her.

She felt sick. What had just happened? What was Aeriod trying to get Kein to do, go with her? Like she had suggested? She knew there was no convincing Kein otherwise. And she had accepted that. But something in Kein's response to Aeriod bothered her. What did he mean by his ancestors paying Aeriod back? A cold, heavy feeling burrowed into her. What had Aeriod done in the past?

Galla tried to sleep, but her dreams and her experiences made her twitch all night. She woke up and stared at her sunken-eyed reflection in the bathroom mirror. She cleaned and dressed, and looked for Kein. Rez stood in the kitchen, wiping the surfaces.

"Good morning!" he bellowed, grinning through his fiery beard. "I left you some breakfast. We thought we'd let you sleep in."

"Thank you, Rez," she answered gratefully. She picked at the food, working her thoughts through what she had heard the night before. "Where's Kein?"

"I think he was cleaning the kayaks."

"Rez," said Galla between chews, "I just want to say how much I appreciate you both. You've been so welcoming, and so patient with me."

Rez smiled and his bright eyes twinkled. "It's been a pleasure. Really. We've been able to wake up a bit, with you here. And you seem to have settled into our routines and fit in well."

She lowered her head and smiled back. She managed to finish her food, and then went out on the deck. Kein had returned and was sitting with his legs propped up on the railing. His pants were stained from polish, and he had not washed his hands. He stared out at the woods. Galla followed his gaze.

She took a deep breath. "I respect your choice to stay," she told him.

Kein grunted, or chuckled, she was not sure which. He glanced up at her, then back to the trees. They stayed silent, listening to the wind. Then the sky darkened and rain started again. The incessant rain, or so it seemed. Kein stood to go inside, but stopped to turn his head skyward. Galla heard it too: a high, whining sound that lowered in pitch and slowed. The treetops bent from the wind of a vehicle descending from above.

Galla and Kein looked at each other. She could not help it: tears sprang to her eyes. Kein turned pale.

"Let's get your things," he said gruffly. Galla's lips quivered, but he would not look at her.

She snatched her clothes and her quilt and stuffed them into her bag. Kein grabbed the bag before she could insist on carrying it herself. They met Rez at the front door, where he stood watching the small craft steaming in the falling rain.

"Is that it?" Rez asked what both Galla and Kein were wondering.

Kein stepped forward with Galla's backpack and peeked into the tiny ship.

"Yep," he answered, leaving empty-handed. "It's a drone ship. It looks programmed to go . . . somewhere. I'm not sure where. There's Associate insignia on it."

Galla drew a shaky breath. "Then it's time for me to go," she said, her voice tremulous.

Rez squeezed her in a huge hug, and his coarse beard brushed her ears. Then he stood aside and looked fondly at his husband, and mournfully, for he could see what Kein could not admit.

Kein stepped forward, and Galla rushed at him and peppered him with kisses. She could not see him through her tears. "Goodbye," she choked. "I love you both."

Kein kissed two of his fingers and touched her forehead. "Don't forget to brush your hair," he said with a little chuckle.

Galla sprang into her ship, and sat staring through the cockpit down at them as they waved. Kein looked aged as his face grew smaller to her. The little ship took her up above the trees, above the sea, into the clouds, away from Perpetua.

28

RENDEZVOUS

Galla sat in her ship, alone, sulking. She could not control the ship at all, and this infuriated her. It forced her to reckon with her sorrows, when she would have liked the distraction of piloting. Even through the boring junctions, of which there were many. This was by far the longest flight she had ever been on.

When the ship finally burst free of the final junction, a message droned in a deep monotone. "You have arrived at Fael'Kar. You will be located by an agent and given instructions." And that was it.

"How helpful, these Associates," she grumbled. She strapped herself in for the atmosphere descent. After breaking through, she beheld the surface of Fael'Kar. Or rather, the structures upon it.

It was night, and the glow of a vast city-continent shone in all directions. It flickered and smoldered. A thick haze gave her the sense of looking at candles through smoke. Nowhere could she see trees, or mountains, or water, and she hoped this was only because it was night. The ship banked and evaded the air traffic, which rose and fell over the land constantly. Galla realized then that her ship was cloaked.

It brought her down through skyscrapers and maneuvered horizontally into canyon-like alleys. Finally it perched in one of those alleys, and she hesitated before getting out.

"Is that it?" she asked the ship. No response. The door hissed open.

She grabbed her bag and stepped out into the night. A sulfurous scent burned her nose instantly. Just as she adjusted to it, the ship behind her revved up and shot into the air.

"Oh," she said feebly, and she lost sight of it as it blended into its surroundings.

She looked all around her, at the stretching, dark alleyway, at the tall buildings on either side of her, at the orange lights everywhere. Small bot lights drifted hither and yon, and voices echoed. She could make out little else. But as she shouldered her bag, she felt her stone press into her skin. She pulled it out from her shirt and stared at it.

"You're glowing," she marveled. While it did not offer much light, its lavender glow comforted her. She straightened up and headed out of the alley.

Someone bumped into her and gave her a disgusted look out of its third eye.

"Sorry," she stammered. She held the stone. It grew warmer. The sidewalk ahead of her steamed and she could see little besides the throngs of beings of all descriptions moving through the area. The lights of the city overhead did not penetrate all the way to the street level, and despite the light bots, everything either lay in shadow or had that hideous orange cast from above.

She felt compelled to keep going, as her stone grew warmer. She held her hands over her chest and looked ahead, then left, then right. She pulled her rucksack tightly to secure it. Street-cleaning bots chided her, and she stepped off into another alley. A light bot bobbed through it, malfunctioning, and bumped into things with a *sproing*. She stared at something it had revealed: a lump leaning up against the alley wall. She moved forward, toward the figure, and clutched her jewel.

"Hello?" she called. The figure stepped into the middle of the alley. Two-legged, she noticed, and just a bit shorter than herself. It approached her. She stood still and watched anxiously.

The person said, "You should have a helmet," and stepped a few feet before her. This person did wear a helmet, obscuring eyes and mouth entirely.

"I don't need a helmet," said Galla. "The air isn't bothering me. Who are you?"

"You should have one anyway," said the figure. "You stand out too much."

Galla squinted. "Do I know you?" she asked.

"No, but I know who you are. We should go somewhere else."

And the figure moved swiftly down the alley, a slippery shadow, and Galla sprinted to keep up. It turned a corner out of sight and she followed, looking to and fro, having lost sight of it.

"Up here," its voice called. A small bike hovered above, and lowered. The helmeted person sat expectantly and patted the long seat.

"I don't even know who you are," Galla pointed out.

"I can tell you that later," said the voice. "But you really should get out of here; you have people tailing you."

Galla looked behind her and noted three veiled figures, and just above them, another craft hovered.

She hesitated. "Where will you take me?" she asked.

"Somewhere safe."

"How can I trust you?" Galla demanded.

"You have to try. Now climb on!"

Galla took another glance back and leapt on the bike, and it rose upward into the haze and lights above. It shot forward and then arced off to the left, and Galla held onto her handles. *This person is not terrible, but I think I'm a better pilot,* she thought, grimacing. A few near-misses with other craft and a couple of blaring sirens later, and they began to descend to another district.

Galla wondered what the pilot could be doing, bobbing in front of an old, debilitated factory. Then suddenly they shot into one of its large exhaust vents, and around one bend, they came to a halt.

The bike wobbled as the two got off, and Galla took in her surroundings: the dark, curving tunnel of the vent she stood in, a barely perceptible door in its side, the bike, and the figure next to her.

This person held up a hand to the door and it quickly opened. Galla saw a small hand reach for hers, and the person said, "Come."

She took the gloved hand in a tight grip and stepped through the door. The door slammed behind her and beeped softly as it locked. The figure dropped her hand and moved swiftly off out of sight. Galla blinked.

Little overhead and wall lights flickered on, and Galla found herself in the short hallway of a tiny living space. A rudimentary and minuscule kitchen blended into a small table, and farther down the hall she could see a small cot.

Presently the figure returned and said, "Sorry. I really had to pee," and took off the helmet.

Long, dark hair spilled down the back of a young woman with grime smeared on her pale cheeks, and large green eyes staring out. Galla stood very straight: she had seen this face before, somewhere. Where? When?

"I'm Ariel Brant," said the woman, holding out a gloveless, clean hand.

"Ariel," said Galla, feeling the wistful familiarity of a similar name to Aeriod. "I'm Galla," and she shook Ariel's hand. "Are you my contact?"

"Definitely," said Ariel, with a knowing smirk.

"Then who is our mutual friend?" Galla asked pointedly.

Ariel's smirk deepened. "A certain guy with a little purple stone."

"Like this?" asked Galla, pulling out her large amethyst.

Ariel's eyes bulged.

"My God, that's huge!" she said, and she stepped forward a bit to look at it, then composed herself.

Galla eyed Ariel with a furrowed brow. "Is he here?"

"Aeriod?" Ariel asked, nonchalantly. "No. I've been doing a few odd jobs, and he asked me to find you if you ended up here."

Galla let her bag slide onto the floor. "Do you think he's coming back?"

"I don't know, I've not seen him in a while," Ariel answered. She had gone to the little wall of a kitchen, and poured two small cups of water. She handed one to Galla, who took it gladly. Ariel watched her drink.

"Who was tailing me?" asked Galla.

"Not sure," said Ariel. "I think you'd better lay low here for a bit. Hungry?"

She wasn't hungry, but she saw Ariel reaching into a cupboard for something with a slight tremble in her hands. "I could eat," Galla replied. Ariel grabbed two small packs and opened them, handing one to Galla.

"Thank you," said Galla, and Ariel nodded as she quickly wolfed down the soup in her packet.

"Sorry," Ariel said, slurping. "I've been out all day. Starving."

"Good thing you found me, then," said Galla.

Ariel motioned back to the little room with the cot. Galla followed her down the dim hallway and watched her pull little chairs out of the walls. Galla sat in one, facing Ariel. She did not know what to think of this young woman, whose green eyes looked very hungry. There was something on edge in this Ariel; Galla could see that.

Again Ariel stared at Galla's gem.

"I see now why Aeriod wanted us to meet," she said.

"Oh? Why?" Galla asked, but she felt the warmth of the stone and felt sure it was not Aeriod, but the stone, that had led her to Ariel.

Ariel said, after setting down her finished soup packet, "His little stone amplified my telepathy. And here you are, with a much larger one. So, you're the original owner of his stone, yes?"

Galla gawked at Ariel. "You're a telepath!"

"Yes," said Ariel. "I can't read *you*, though. You're like Aeriod."

Galla shook her head and her curls bobbed. "I'm not like him, no," she said so emphatically that Ariel raised her eyebrows. Galla could not explain her own reaction, but felt strongly she was not like him.

"I meant I can't read him either," Ariel said, course-correcting quickly.

Galla bit her lip. "I wonder why he would want us to meet, though."

Ariel considered and said slowly, "Now that I've met you, and know you have this stone, I think he must be concerned about the workings of"—and she lowered her voice to a whisper, almost unconsciously—"Paosh Tohon."

Galla lifted her chin. "Oh," she said. "I still don't know how I do anything against that. Just so you know."

Ariel twisted her fingers together absently. "Aeriod's stone—your little stone, that is—gave us the ability to resist that force, but it only covered a couple of us from direct attack. We did amplify our telepathic ability, though, along with Aeriod's own powers. We moved a space station across the galaxy!"

Galla's eyes lit up. "Oh! Is that the station Kein's great-grandparents were on, I wonder?"

"Kein?" asked Ariel, looking excited. "As in Auna Kein?"

"That was his great-grandmother," said Galla. She noted Ariel had flinched at the word "was."

Ariel said slowly, "And so his great-grandfather..."

"He was Linden Forster," said Galla casually. "I learned all about how they first came to Perpetua. The first humans on that world, or in that part of the galaxy. It's pretty far away from here."

"Yes, I know," said Ariel quietly. Galla watched the woman's eyes glaze a bit, as if remembering something from long ago.

"Are you all right?" Galla asked. As with Kein, she felt an immediate warmth for Ariel.

Ariel shook herself.

"Yes. Yes, I am. I wish I could meet Kein. I knew Forster and Auna. Forster was the other telepath who worked with me to move us all to Ika Nui. So they called the world Perpetua! Of course. Like Cape Perpetua on Earth."

"What's Ika Nui?" Galla asked.

"Oh, it's a lovely place; Aeriod helped put the old station in orbit around it," said Ariel, almost offhandedly.

"Why didn't you stay there?" Galla asked.

Ariel glanced at Galla. "I'm a wanderer, I guess," she said. She tucked her lank, dark hair behind her ears. "Mama said she would follow me anywhere, but she's getting up in age now. I think she may like to return to Ika Nui."

Galla held the warm stone and felt her face creasing into a smile. Ariel could not resist looking at it.

"Here," Galla said, "you can see it if you wish," and she took off the copper chain, caressing it lovingly as she did so, and handed the large gem to Ariel.

"It's heavy!" Ariel exclaimed, feeling it in her small hands. She tilted it back and forth to catch the small lights in her apartment. "How beautiful," she murmured. She handed it back to Galla.

"Are you tired?" she asked. "I know I am."

"I suppose," said Galla, but really she was quite excited, and wanted to ask Ariel many questions.

"Tomorrow I'll go over what is going on and what we hope to do, and all that," Ariel said. "Has Aeriod told you anything?"

"No," said Galla. "No one has. I was flown here alone, and I assumed I was on my next training mission for the Associates."

Ariel frowned. "I don't know who that is," she admitted. "But if Aeriod trusts you, I do."

"I think he does," said Galla, blushing, and Ariel caught her and grinned.

"I have to ask," said Ariel rapidly, as if she had wanted to ask the entire time, "are you two married?"

Galla gasped and laughed. "No!" she said. "No," she reiterated, more firmly.

"Okay. Sorry," said Ariel. "He just . . . he's always spoken about you with a certain . . . change in his voice."

Galla's cheeks burned. "He's spoken about me," she repeated.

"Not enough," said Ariel, "because I really wasn't expecting you to be so . . . so . . ."

"So what?" Galla wanted to know.

Ariel sighed, trying to find the words. "Well, let's just say, you're not as much like him as I thought you would be. You're more like . . . us."

"Human?" Galla asked. She squeezed her stone in excitement.

"Yes," said Ariel. "The only difference is . . . well, there are a few differences, but I can't read you at all. And you look . . . you don't look . . . typical."

"That doesn't sound good," murmured Galla.

Ariel threw her hands up in the air. "Like I said, you stand out. I mean. Well, you're *hot*."

"Oh," said Galla, crinkling her nose. "I guess I'm a little warm, and my stone is warm, but I don't feel hot."

Ariel burst out laughing.

"No, not that kind of hot." She stared unabashedly at Galla, taking in the wild, bright hair and pointy chin, and her vibrant copper eyes. Galla smiled serenely back at her. "Well, I mean that you . . . you're the most beautiful person I've ever met in my entire life."

"Oh!" cried Galla, and her cheeks stained pink. "Thank you!"

Ariel shook herself and cleared her throat.

"Now, here's all I have, this cot and a Murphy bed," Ariel said, shoving the chairs back into the wall and pulling out a small bed from it.

Galla loved the clever storage. "I'll take the cot," she said.

"No, please take the bed," Ariel urged. "If you don't, Aeriod will kill me."

Galla stared. "He would never!"

"It's a joke, Galla," said Ariel. "Oh, I think I see now. You're here to normalize a bit. Maybe you'll end up as jaded as me."

"I lived with Kein and his husband for a time, and met several humans," said Galla defensively.

Ariel tilted her head to one side and took in the lady before her.

"Still," she said, "you'd better take the bed. I don't want Aeriod to get angry with *me*. That's never fun."

"No," said Galla. "But I'm pretty good at getting him worked up, so I will handle him if he dares say anything to you."

Ariel burst into giggles. "This is the best thing ever. I'm so glad I finally met you. And I really see now why he's loved you for so long."

Galla blushed again. She could not look at Ariel for some time. *Just what had Aeriod said about her? And to whom?* She dragged her rucksack forward and said, "Thank you for the bed," and pulled out her quilt.

"Oh!" cried Ariel, and without thinking she reached out to touch the quilt.

"Yes, isn't it pretty?" said Galla, and then she noticed Ariel's glistening eyes.

"My mother made that for you," said Ariel quietly.

Galla beamed at her.

"Thanks to her, then. I love it." She spread out the quilt over the small Murphy bed.

Ariel in turn brought out a quilt of her own. It looked a bit frayed along its edges, but was obviously sewn by the same maker. Each woman lay on her bed and they looked at each other for a moment, under their quilts, and grinned. Ariel fell asleep within seconds. Galla tucked her quilt around herself, listened to the constant thrumming sounds of the old building, and watched the lights continue to dim until she fell asleep.

29

VALEMOG

"You will make it better!"

The voice rang among the throng of thousands. Derry took it all in, the lone human. So far.

He could see everything now. Why hadn't he seen it before? The deception, the control. Now that he knew who and what the Associates were, he knew his purpose. The shepherdess had saved him! Guided him to the promise!

They would all join. Or they would face unimaginable pain. But Derry knew the spaces between. He knew manipulation. He smiled to himself. He could follow, and he could lead. He could recruit. And he would be believed. The galaxy grew weary of the relics of its leaders. It was time for strength! Time for a new era!

He breathed in the sour air, which made him feel more alive than his former life, as a toady for MindSynd, and even worse on Mandira. There, he had no purpose. They had moved him without his consent, and there were others chafing as well. He could convince them. And if not? He would find a way to make it back to Earth. And make it better.

"*We are Valemog!*" He joined in the chorus.

30

INTERCEPTION

Galla stretched and rose up on her elbows. Ariel stood in her tiny kitchen over a steaming pot. So Galla walked behind her and poked her head around Ariel's shoulder to see what she was doing.

"JESUS!" yelled Ariel. "You scared the *shit* out of me!"

Galla looked at her, owl-eyed. "Sorry!"

Ariel threw her hair back over her shoulder. "I keep forgetting I can't read you. I would have known you were coming. But you were very quiet."

"Can I help?" Galla asked.

"Nope." Ariel shook her head and poured two bowls full of a thick paste. She handed one to Galla. "It's not much. Nothing like you're used to, I'm sure."

Galla raised her arched eyebrows. She caught something in Ariel's voice, something she was unsure of. Anger? Maybe that wasn't the right word.

"Thank you," she murmured, tasting the concoction. "It's very good, as good as anything else," she added. "Salty-sweet."

Ariel sighed. "Do you want to sit down? Usually I just stand and eat, then head out."

"Um ... sure," said Galla. She helped Ariel pull the little table and chairs from the wall.

"I'm used to eating alone," Ariel explained.

"I can understand that," said Galla eagerly. "When I was on Demetraan I was the only one who—why are you looking at me like that?"

Ariel's eyes grew larger than usual as she watched the bright coils of Galla's hair drift up and out as if of their own volition. She pointed at Galla's head and Galla snickered.

"It's my hair again, right?" she laughed.

"How ... how is it doing that? There's no wind in here," said Ariel.

"I ... don't know. My hair is very ... moody. It seems to respond to how I feel."

"Are you ... excited?" Ariel suggested, ogling the warm masses of hair. There were strands of bright gold and bronze and auburn all throughout it. The red parts of it almost radiated a purple sheen. She found it very difficult not to reach out and touch that hair.

Galla considered. "Yes! I am. I was talking about home and—" She stopped. For a moment she had forgotten about everything: about Oni-Odi's disappearance, about Aeriod. She had been in the moment with Ariel and she had been happy. Now the emotions flooded back, and her hair drifted down again. She pulled it back and twisted it into a low bun. Then she straightened herself.

"I suppose we should get down to business," she said, her voice flat. "What instructions do you have?"

While Ariel could not read Galla's thoughts, she could read her face and her body language. She thought that Galla's great weakness, no matter what hidden strengths she might have, was her completely open nature. Ariel cringed inwardly, thinking of how someone like that could be taken advantage of. And that brought her back to the job.

"Aeriod"—Ariel noted Galla's jolt in her seat—"sent a communiqué overnight. I haven't looked at it yet," she drawled. "Figured we could at least eat and get you settled first."

Galla, flushed from the mere mention of the governor's name, quickly finished her breakfast. She was more than ready to get to work. She didn't want to think about *him*. But she could feel her curiosity boiling up.

"So, what sort of things have you been working on?"

Ariel tried to prevent Galla from taking both their empty bowls, but relented, and watched Galla turn on what Ariel called the Blink, or blinding sink, to clean them.

"Thanks," she said. "Well, he's had me following different people over time. Listening in on their thoughts. Working a few deals for him. Lately, things have changed. Not much happening locally. It's as if something's up; people are skittish."

"Why, do you think?" asked Galla.

Ariel frowned. "I don't know. I picked up on some thought-bleed and there was something about an Event. And a lot of general anxiety. From everyone. Just in the past couple of weeks."

"Do you mean, *the* Event?" Galla asked in a rush. "The cataclysm? Has it started?"

Ariel rubbed her sunken eyes. "I don't know. Whatever it is, it's bad for business. And maybe that's for the best. I get a little bit of a break. It's tiring, reading alien minds. Honestly, it's kind of a relief I can't read yours."

Galla felt a little chill go through her.

"Am I so alien?" she asked. She could not help it.

Ariel smirked. "Yeah, but you're not like any other alien. Don't feel bad. You'll never fit in, so don't worry about it!"

Galla shook, and felt hot tears at the corners of her eyes. "I *have* to fit in. I'll never be much help if I don't."

Ariel stood and reached out a hand to her. "Hey, I'm sorry. You'll be fine. That's partly why you're here, right? To learn to fit in? We'll make it work."

And Ariel clasped Galla's hand in hers and gave it a squeeze. Then she gasped.

"What is that?" she breathed. Galla stared at her.

"What?"

Ariel reached her fingertips to Galla's face and touched her cheeks where the tears had dried. She brought her hands back quickly and looked at them. On her fingers, tiny violet sparkles shone. The remnants glinted on Galla's cheeks, almost imperceptible, but Ariel could see them.

"It's like the stone," she murmured.

"What, my tears?" asked Galla. "They're like your tears, I think."

"No," insisted Ariel. "Not even remotely. They dry purple, like amethyst! I can barely see it, but it's there!"

"Oh, is that all," snorted Galla. "Well, the stone is me. I'm made of the same stuff."

Ariel's mouth fell open. "My God," she said. Her mind bounced around, trying to comprehend, but ultimately she could not fathom it. "You're not like anyone else! But don't get upset! This is amazing."

Ariel's face shone with wonder, and Galla sighed. *I hope she doesn't treat me like some sort of creature,* she thought. But soon enough, Ariel was preoccupied by a blaring sound.

"For fuck's sake!" Ariel cried, and she huffed over to her comms. "Fuckin' Aeriod, *again*. Oh. Sorry, Galla."

Galla laughed. "You'd better answer that. He's very persistent."

Ariel rolled her eyes. "Okay. It's just a message, thank God. I can't deal with him right now. I really can't."

"What does it say?"

Ariel read and reread the message, and furrowed her brow. "Wants me to confirm your arrival ... Says we need to find a Dijjan in the Circuit District by the name of Klelk; he may have some information. Says to lay low and not ... use ... telepathy. Why?"

"That's it?" asked Galla.

"Yeah."

Galla felt suspicious. *Something isn't right. Everything Ariel said earlier, and now this message from Aeriod.* Dread crept into her. Flashes from her time in the Device. The being on Perpetua warning her.

"Ariel," she said aloud, "I don't like this."

"Neither do I. But we have our job, so let's roll."

"One condition," Galla said.

"What?"

"You can tell me where to go. But I'm flying this time," she insisted, and she set her jaw. Ariel lifted her eyebrows and smirked.

"Okay, pilot. But helmets this time. Show me what you got!"

Ariel quickly regretted the agreement. The second Galla sat on Ariel's bike hovering outside the apartment, and Ariel looped her arms around Galla's waist, Galla let the bike drop in freefall. Ariel screamed, and Galla laughed and engaged the accelerator. They shot back up and swerved among the canyon of buildings.

"Th-th-that way!" Ariel gasped, shuddering and clinging desperately to Galla.

Galla whooped in glee, free to fly again, and to show off her skills. Ariel winced and groaned and yelled and swore, but directed them above the thick, rusty morning haze of the vast city. Finally she pointed downward and Galla dropped them again, to Ariel's agonized yelps, back among the shadows of the alleys below.

Alongside a brilliantly lit building, Galla brought the bike down more gently, and swerved into an alcove in one of the alleys. She jumped from the bike and almost yanked off her helmet, but a shaky Ariel held her hand up.

"Keep it on," she said. Galla nodded.

"So where is this Dijjan?"

"I don't know," Ariel replied. "I could try to read people—"

"No," said Galla, "don't do it. There has to be a good reason you were told not to."

Ariel sighed in frustration. "So what do we do?"

"Do you know his last known location? We could work it out manually," suggested Galla. Ariel nodded and consulted her comm bracelet. Galla leaned over the young woman's arm to see the picture of the Dijjan.

"He's definitely here," said Ariel. "He's checked into Circuit Prime, which is a block west."

"So let's go," said Galla, exhilarated from her flight.

Ariel walked with her a few steps and then stopped. She ran her hands along her neck.

"What is it?" asked Galla.

"I don't know, I'm . . . I'm picking up something. I'm not reading anyone, don't worry. It's almost like . . . an interference . . . but it's also —wait. Do you smell that?"

"Smell what?" Galla wondered. "I smell exhaust, and air pollution, and something metallic from the power stations."

"No," murmured Ariel, looking behind her, and left and right. They had joined the workday throng of surface workers. Ariel touched her lips and her neck. "It smells like . . . spices . . . cinnamon, allspice maybe . . . delicious."

Galla furrowed her brow. "I am not smelling any spices. I wish I were. It's kind of disgusting here," she said, and she grabbed Ariel's elbow to prevent her from stepping in what looked like intestines on the ground.

But Ariel seemed to be in a reverie. Galla pressed her, "Well? Let's find this guy." And Ariel shook her head and seemed to snap out of it.

"Okay. Right. Circuit Prime."

And the two women evaded getting trammeled by the various alien species making their way along the streets, with flocks of vehicles flying above and around them. Galla would have liked to take in the scenery and the diverse crowds, but she urged Ariel on, and grew dismayed at her distraction.

They had just reached Circuit Prime, sleek and lit with many colors, abuzz with crafts all up and down its towers. A bright flash and a giant clap of sound hit them, and the two flew along the ground on their backs. Shrieks and sirens met their ears. Ariel tried to stand but was disoriented. Galla rushed over to her and pulled her up. Amid the smoke, two figures emerged.

One yelled in a deep voice, "Are you all right?" And then another flash, and that person yelled, "Get out of here!" and ran off as if in pursuit. The other figure faded away.

Through the smoke and the wails, Galla helped Ariel along until she could stand on her own. Galla led her away from the Circuit Prime building to another alleyway. Another figure approached them, bent over. Galla and Ariel stood to face this creature, when it fell toward them and wheezed. The Dijjan!

"Shit shit shit!" hissed Ariel. She and Galla tried to peel away the being's wrappings, but its wound gaped, embedded with shrapnel. Galla held its head.

"Can you speak?" asked Ariel. The Dijjan, Klelk, looked balefully up at Galla and tried to reach toward her face.

He hissed to Galla, "Valemog! Tell . . . them!" and collapsed.

She stared. "Is he—"

"Dead," Ariel muttered. "Shit!"

Galla held the Dijjan and trembled all over. She placed it gently on the ground. And then she noticed something in its hand, the one that had reached up to her face. A small silver diamond. Ariel gasped.

"That's one of Aeriod's communicators!"

"Ariel," Galla said urgently, "we should leave; the smoke is clearing and there are a lot of people around. If there's another bomb—"

"Yes. Come on. Leave him."

"No!" cried Galla. She had never seen anyone die before. She could not leave the Dijjan by itself.

"Look, we can't carry him," said Ariel.

"I'll carry him," said Galla firmly, and Ariel watched amazed as Galla picked the massive Dijjan up and carried him swiftly back toward the alley they had parked in.

There, Galla knew she must leave the body. The bike would not hold three. She placed the Dijjan's arms across its chest and held its hands for a moment. "I know you helped us. Thank you for your life."

And she and Ariel hopped on the sky bike and fled back to the apartment.

31

PHEROMONIC

Galla could not shake the finality of the Dijjan's death. She knew about death, but to her it had seemed so abstract. This creature had died in her arms. She felt empty. She sat, sullen, alongside Ariel at her comms panel.

Ariel placed the Dijjan's silver diamond on the panel and did nothing more.

"It recorded everything, hopefully," she told Galla. "I don't dare say anything on the comms. We'll let the diamond do its work."

She looked askance at Galla, who rocked gently where she sat. "Why don't I get us a drink? I have just enough Stroffy liqueur left for us both. It's very special."

And Ariel brought out of her cabinet a small, clear vial of ultramarine blue liquid. She poured two tiny glasses of it and handed one to Galla. Ariel tossed hers back in one mouthful.

But Galla sniffed her glass and sat up, alert. "It smells like flowers," she said. She sniffed again, and forgot for a moment her anguish. Then she took one sip.

It seared through her chest, all through her innards, and her hair began lifting and her eyes shone. "Ahhhhh!" she sighed, and a lazy grin crept across her lips. She drank every last drop of the liqueur and licked the glass.

"Oh my God," said Ariel, for Galla stood and twirled.

"Do you have more?" Galla asked breathlessly, swaying.

"No, and good thing," retorted Ariel. "It gives me a pleasant buzz. I'm not sure what it's doing to you. Maybe you should sit down."

"I want to dance," insisted Galla, and she had never felt so delightful. Every part of her body tingled. "Let's hear some music!"

And at that moment a rushing sound met their ears, and the drone of an engine just outside the apartment brought both women to attention.

"Who's that?" asked Galla.

"No idea," said Ariel, and she reached for something on her counter and tucked it under her shirt. "Not expecting anyone."

They slowly approached the back door dock, when it sprang open and a tall, black shape swirled into the room. Long, pale hair blew forward from the thermal updrafts, and silver eyes found copper ones.

"Aeriod!" Galla and Ariel exclaimed together.

And Ariel moved aside as Aeriod rushed forward and seized Galla and lifted her just off her feet into his arms. He kissed her neck, and she threw her head back in ecstasy and then kissed him in return.

"Hi!" Ariel said lamely. "I'm just over here, wondering if we got what we needed! The Dijjan died and everything! Oh God, she's drunk. Great."

Aeriod turned to her long enough to say, "I got the message. We can discuss it in a bit. Galla, why don't you come to my ship for a moment?"

Ariel stared at them, the icy mage and the fiery lady, putting off waves that did not need mind reading to figure out. Every caress and kiss, she could not help watching. Ariel watched them leave, stroked her neck again, and realized she was sweating. She looked around her empty apartment and said, "Screw it. I'm out," grabbed her jacket and helmet, and hopped on her bike.

She skimmed the building tops and found herself drifting back toward the Circuit District. She could still hear sirens. She knew she should not get any closer. But something pulled her. Something warm. She parked out of sight and began walking. She did not know where. And she didn't care. She wanted to smell that scent from earlier. Feel that warmth. She could feel her heart racing, from watching Galla and Aeriod.

And then a figure appeared, tall, and she smelled the cinnamon. The comfort, the warmth. She walked toward it. And she looked up and found black eyes looking at her, human eyes—except for a brilliant gold ring around the pupils. It was a man, with umber skin, and he stared into her leaf-green eyes.

"You found me," he said. She recognized the deep voice. "I'm glad you're safe. I saw someone running and went after him, but he got away."

"Who are you?" Ariel asked. "You're ... human?"

The man smiled through his close-cropped beard. His shoulder-length, twisted black hair was tied at the back of his neck with a gold thread. He wore a dark grey tunic and pants and black boots, and bore no jewelry, but did have a long, vertical scar on his neck.

"I'm half human. My name is Dagovaby Ambrono." He held his hand out to her.

"Ariel Brant," she said simply. She took his hand. She breathed in. It was Dagovaby that she had sensed earlier: both the scent and the warmth. "Are you a telepath?" she asked.

"I'm an empath," he responded. "I felt you before I ever saw you. And you're putting out some ... uh ... interesting vibes right now," he said, grinning.

Ariel felt blood rush to her face, but she could not take her eyes from this man. *Can you read me?* she asked.

"Are you trying to talk to me?" said Dagovaby. "Please don't do that with your mind. Not here. I can only feel you. And I felt the question. I think you're not safe here, as a telepath. I wouldn't risk it again if I were you."

"Why?" Ariel asked, coming out of her reverie long enough to grow suspicious.

Dagovaby looked in all directions. "Maybe we should not be in the open. Can we go somewhere? A café or something?"

Ariel could sense the honesty in Dagovaby, and she relaxed. She wanted to say his name again and again, and let it roll from her lips. "Anywhere," she said finally.

32

SPLINTERED

The reunion with Aeriod confused Galla, and as the two lingered in his ship the next morning, she grew uneasy. She leaned on his chest with her elbows, as she had in the past, and swept his long, white hair off to one side and stared at his half-lidded silver eyes.

"Why did you come here?" she wanted to know.

The pupils in the mage's mercurial eyes dilated, and he ran his long fingers along her neck and down to her hips. Then he pulled her gently down to lay her head on his chest, and intertwined his fingers in her many-hued hair.

"It seemed like the right time," he said simply.

She rose again and fixed him with a glare.

"You weren't supposed to do this," she said.

"You didn't seem to mind last night," Aeriod said with a grin.

Galla sat upright, and reached down from their bunk for her clothes.

"I don't know what came over me," she said. "Maybe it was the Stroffy liqueur."

Aeriod laughed richly. "Should I stock it just for you? And

anyway, I *don't think* that's why we . . . indulged ourselves. I missed you. And it seems you had a little . . . ah . . . pent-up longing as well."

"Of course," replied Galla, adjusting her diamethyst over her clothes. She grasped it in her hands and looked down at Aeriod's smaller stone. "It's not like I haven't missed you, but . . . Aeriod, we had just escaped a bombing. Your contact died. I wasn't expecting you to come here in person and I just—I don't think we should do this. We have our jobs."

Aeriod sighed and sat up. He reluctantly dressed, and pulled Galla's small hands into his large ones.

"Duty, then," he said, with a nod. "If that's what you prefer."

Galla blushed. "I think we're risking too much. Anyway, can we talk about business now? Let's go back to Ariel's. I need to go over something. Make sure I'm remembering everything right."

Aeriod opened the door of his ship and Galla knocked on Ariel's door. It flashed open and Ariel stood with a cold stare. She looked even paler than usual, and she yawned.

"Back so soon?" she snarked. "Come in. I'll make tea for three."

Galla noticed something different about Ariel. She squinted at the young woman. "Were you out all night?"

Ariel shrugged, turning away from her. "I went for a drive. I met that guy we talked to, after the explosion."

Galla gaped. "What? You went back there?"

Ariel's cheeks flooded with color. "Well . . . not exactly. I met him close by."

Galla crinkled her brow. "Why did you do that?"

Ariel sighed. "Look, I'm fine, you're fine, can we just not talk about this right now? I didn't ask you about *your* night." And she shot a reproachful look at Aeriod.

Aeriod busied himself by looking at the silver diamond he had given the Dijjan. Ariel handed him a mug of tea, and he gruffly nodded.

"Tell me what happened," he said to the two women.

Ariel recounted everything but her meeting with Dagovaby. Galla mentioned the man, and Aeriod's eyebrows rose. She hastily continued, for she could see Ariel slinking back a bit, not wanting to talk about her evening out.

"He said, 'Valemog—tell them,' and then he died," Galla said, with a shudder.

"Valemog," Aeriod repeated, a frown forming on his face. "This is something new. I had better do a search."

"So you don't know what he was talking about?" Ariel asked. "Must be hard for you, not to know *everything*."

Galla smirked at that.

Then she said to Ariel, "Your comms panel is flashing."

Ariel slipped over and blocked Galla from seeing who it was. Galla watched keenly as Ariel smoothed her dark hair behind her ears. Those ears glowed pink when she turned back around.

"I have a guest. He's coming up right now," she told them, flustered.

Galla grinned impishly, and Aeriod raised one eyebrow and turned back to ponder the diamond's contents. Ariel pelted off to the bedroom and soon emerged in a different outfit, with her hair now brushed.

"Is it that guy?" Galla whispered too loudly.

Ariel rolled her eyes just as her front door chimed. She smoothed her pants and shirt and strode across to open the door. And there he stood, Dagovaby Ambrono, filling the door frame with his great size. He was nearly as tall as Aeriod, but far more muscular, and Galla noticed immediately his complete focus on Ariel, as if the rest of the place didn't exist. Galla stepped forward and extended her hand. It was time to test out her social graces.

"How do you do?" she said formally. "I'm Galla-Deia." She noticed the gold ring around his pupils and glanced approvingly at Ariel. "Call me Galla."

And she shook his massive hand.

"Dagovaby. You can call me Dag," said the man.

"I'm calling you Dagovaby," Ariel said enthusiastically, and then she blushed again.

It was Galla's turn to feel some heat between the two. Aeriod then stepped forward and introduced himself. He appraised the man, and began asking questions.

"What were you doing at the Circuit at the time of the explosion?"

"Helping," the man replied simply, but Galla caught the twitch in his jaw muscle.

"Really," said Aeriod. "You seemed to be conveniently close to Galla and Ariel."

Dagovaby's jaw clenched, but he smiled. "I was there on private business. I thought I saw the suspect, and went in pursuit."

"Aeriod," interjected Ariel, "what are you doing?"

"Making sure you're not deceived by a stranger," snapped Aeriod.

"Okay," said Dagovaby, "maybe this isn't the best time. Ariel, I'll call later."

Ariel's eyes grew huge and she scowled at Aeriod.

"Stop!" cried Galla. "This is ridiculous. Aeriod, what is this? Are you profiling this man? He really was there to help us. Dag, please stay. I get the sense there's more you're not telling us. But," and she glared furiously at Aeriod, "that doesn't mean any bad intentions."

The four sat tensely and drank their tea.

Finally Dagovaby said to Aeriod, "Look. I'm an empath. I'm half human. I'm not going to give you my family history. I don't know any of you very well, but I know what side I'm on. Something's happening out there. There's a movement forming. I think yesterday was a terrorist attack to try and prevent that Dijjan from getting information to you."

"I've been trailing him for some time," the man admitted. "Some friends and I have been keeping tabs on the underworld trading. Two were killed a week ago. So I knew we were close to finding something out. There's been some talk of a group called Valemog—"

"Valemog!" exclaimed Ariel and Galla.

"What is this Valemog?" Aeriod asked him, an urgency creeping into his voice.

Dagovaby clenched his fists. "I think it's a cult. A group of 'believers' who think Paosh Tohon is the answer to the galaxy's problems. I only know this much because I intercepted some messages being sent here from a ship at the nearest junction."

"This is . . . not good," said Ariel, who blanched at the mention of Paosh Tohon.

"No indeed," agreed Aeriod. He stood and swept his black cape around him like great wings. "I must go."

Galla stood as well. They embraced, but she pulled away first. Aeriod searched her face and sighed. She walked with him to his ship.

He looked down at her. "I'm sorry. I thought you wanted this."

"I thought I did, too," Galla said, unable to shake the thought of folding the dead Dijjan's arms over each other, "but people are relying on us with their lives. This just . . . isn't the right time, or place. You know that. We can't do this."

Aeriod sighed again, and swept her up in his arms. She closed her eyes tightly and held him too. She could smell a familiar whiff of incense on him that made her think of Rikiloi. One final kiss, firm and brief, and they pulled apart. He swooped out into the ship and it shot into the sky out of sight.

Galla walked back toward the table, to the wide-eyed stares of Ariel and Dagovaby.

"Did you just break up?" gasped Ariel.

Galla trembled. "I think we should get out of here," she said.

"I agree," said Dagovaby. "I don't think you're safe here. But where?"

"I have an idea," said Ariel. "But we'll need a ship."

"That can be arranged," said Dagovaby.

Galla was already stuffing her quilt into her bag. She bunched her wild hair under her helmet.

"Ready," she said.

33

INVADER

Dagovaby joined the two women on his own sky bike, and blasted ahead quickly to the south, down into the bowels of the city. There were signs of decrepitude, with dilapidated buildings and exposed pipes, and a strong metallic smell everywhere. Ancient, destroyed foundries were tangled in decaying roots throughout. After they swooped into an abandoned warehouse, Galla hopped off and looked all around. The place seemed infused with rot.

"What are we looking for?" she asked abruptly, and Ariel and Dagovaby put their fingers over their mouths. Galla noticed that the golden rings in Dagovaby's eyes glowed in the dim light.

They followed Dagovaby into the darkest part of the warehouse. He pulled a light out and shone it over a hulking shape. A dark green drape hid something beneath. They walked across thick dust and over squat, pale-eyed carrion eaters that slithered and snapped, and reached the large shape. Dagovaby pulled on the drape. It slid away with a hiss, sending clouds of dust everywhere.

The three stared at the ship, a boxy construct of dark blue, with black markings on its side. Galla did not recognize them. But she did not care about that; she merely wanted to get on board. Just as

Dagovaby reached his hand to the ship's door control, he groaned and doubled over. Ariel screamed and began folding into a ball. Galla stared, horrified. Then she turned around.

She could see something coming through the gaping entry of the warehouse. It snaked and twisted and spun in the air, forked like lightning but with no light, and seemed to be made of dead space, flat, impenetrable. The mass approached them silently, but she could make out a person's shape coalescing. Instinct took over, and she turned and shoved Ariel and Dagovaby onto the ground and lay on top of them, spread-eagle, and faced the shape. Her stone glowed.

She grabbed the stone and, unsure what else to do, yelled, "LEAVE US!"

A blinding, purple-edged light burst forth from her stone in every direction and cast shadows all through the huge warehouse. The carrion feeders shrieked and scrambled away from the light, and the dark, forked mass itself spasmed. She could hear a horrible, deep moan, unlike any other sound she had ever heard. She looked behind her, and Ariel and Dagovaby had recovered, and now stood behind her, eyes and mouths agape. She marched toward the mass.

It spat and moaned and writhed, and the former person's shape dissolved in a shriek. And then it was gone.

Galla's stone went dark, but it felt hot to the touch. She took in great gasping breaths and sank to her knees. Ariel knelt beside Galla, and Dagovaby put his hands under her arms and lifted her.

"Are you two all right?" Galla managed to ask.

"We're fine now," said Dagovaby.

"You did that!" Ariel gasped. "Do you know what it was?"

"No," said Galla, but she crawled with the feeling that she did, in fact, know.

"It was Paosh Tohon," answered Ariel. "And you destroyed it!"

"She didn't destroy it," Dagovaby said grimly. "She drove it away. It can appear anywhere, like a cancer, and can grow. It's drawn here because—"

"Because of me," whispered Ariel.

"Because of us," Dagovaby agreed.

"So there's more out there," Galla said in a low voice.

Dagovaby nodded. "Vast stretches. And if what I'm hearing is right, it's growing. System-wide in places."

Galla felt cold all over. How could she face such an immense force as that? Ariel suddenly seized her in a hug.

"You saved us! You blocked us before it could really take hold," she said, and then Ariel stared at the stone.

"It wasn't just the stone, was it?" she marveled. "It was *you*. You said you were made of the same stuff as the stone!"

Galla's head spun. "Yes," she replied, overwhelmed.

"Let's get on the ship and get out of here before anything else happens," suggested Dagovaby.

They clambered aboard and hooked into their seats. Ariel kept taking peeks at Galla, who looked excited.

"Glad I could help," Galla smiled wanly. "I feel like I need to sleep."

"You've never done that before, have you?" Ariel asked.

"I didn't know I could!" said Galla.

"What else can you do?" Ariel pressed.

"Why don't we let her rest. She just saved our asses," said Dagovaby with a wink.

"Right," said Ariel.

The ship spun up and Dagovaby piloted it out. Galla was disappointed that she could not fly the ship, but she realized she was exhausted.

"One thing is for sure," said Dagovaby, "and I hate to be a buzz kill here." The two women looked at him curiously. "Paosh Tohon knows about you now."

Galla leaned back in her seat and closed her eyes.

"So where are we going?" she asked.

Ariel's voice rose an octave. "To my mother."

34

REUNION

After a mildly turbulent ride through two junctions, the little blue ship shot forth into a new system. At that point, Dagovaby let out a long sigh. Galla and Ariel looked at him. Galla could see Ariel reading him with thoughts, just by the way she smiled to herself.

"That wasn't so bad," Galla noted. "Nobody followed us."

"That we know of," Ariel remarked.

Dagovaby shook his head. "I didn't sense anything."

"I just hope our senses are working properly," Ariel murmured.

"And I hope nobody can pick them up remotely," said Galla, and she quickly regretted it. Biting her lower lip, she added hastily, "But I'm sure no one did. We'd have picked them up."

Ariel grimaced. "I don't know what all ... it ... can do." Then she straightened in her seat and her mouth twisted into a wry grin. "But we've got *you*," she pointed out.

Galla nodded and smiled, but inwardly she quaked.

What can I do for them, though? I'm one person. I shielded two people, and that was it. And I didn't even know what I was doing! They're relying on me. And I can't seem to count on Aeriod. She sat on her hands to keep them from fidgeting.

Ariel leaned over to look at the controls in front of Dagovaby. "Can we send a message now?"

"Yes. Any particular call sign you think I should use?" he asked, looking over at her. Galla watched the two lean toward each other, and felt at once both a pleasure and an ache.

"Little Goose," Ariel replied. There seemed to be a current of warmth flowing between the two. She looked shyly up at Galla, who smiled and turned away.

Dagovaby chuckled, and then spoke. "Ika Nui Traffic Control, this is Little Goose. Do you copy?"

Silence.

Then a few clicks, and a chirp: "This is Ika Nui Traffic Control. Identify yourselves."

"Repeat, this is Little Goose," said Dagovaby, and then Ariel abruptly jumped in.

"Come on, you guys, it's Ariel Brant!" she cried, exasperated. "Can you send word to my mother, Meredith Brant? We need to know if we can dock."

"Negative to docking," the voice squawked back. "Security protocol. We will relay the message. Await your instructions."

Ariel looked at both Dagovaby and Galla with a creased brow.

"I take it this isn't normal?" Galla asked, and she shivered. Nothing was normal now, if it ever had been. She felt sure of that.

"No, it's not—" began Ariel.

"This is Ika Nui Traffic Control. You will be intercepted momentarily. Park yourselves." And the squawk ended in silence.

"What is going on?" Ariel wondered aloud.

"Easy," soothed Dagovaby, extending his hand. "I'm sure your mother's fine." Ariel clasped his hand and calmed immediately; her shoulders relaxed.

I wish that worked on me, thought Galla. She felt irritated and frustrated, thinking of Aeriod, for she knew he could have put a stop to such proceedings as this security check. *There are a lot of things he could do that he hasn't done. Like give us a road map to the Device worlds!*

It's not happening, though. I think we're on our own for that. And maybe for pretty much everything else.

She puffed out a sigh and closed her eyes. The ship hummed along at a lower pitch, then was brought to a full stop, hanging in space. She listened to its rhythmic drones and felt herself doze off.

"Galla," Ariel called quietly. "The ship is here."

With a jolt, Galla woke up. Her diamethyst felt warm to the touch, and she rubbed it in her hands. She could see Ariel squirming in her seat, eager to get up. Dagovaby sat waiting for instructions.

"Hello there!" called a man's voice across the comms. "I hear you have a little goose on board! Stand by."

"*Who is that?*" Ariel whispered.

They could hear laughter. Then, a woman's voice, low and serene, "Little Goose!"

"Mama!" cried Ariel, shivering in nervous excitement. She glanced at Dagovaby, and back at Galla.

"We're going to let you dock inside," the woman said softly. "See you soon!"

The little craft approached a larger ship, sleek, iridescent black with a sharp nose and curled wingtips, and unmarked. Galla knew immediately it was one of Aeriod's fleet from its design. Dagovaby piloted the shuttle in with a few rough thruster boosts, along with the help of the shuttle's navigation, and they perched inside. The docking bay door closed and air returned to the bay. Ariel sprang from her seat, and Dagovaby followed. Galla shouldered her bag and followed the two, feeling apprehensive suddenly. What would these new people be like? Would they be welcoming, or would she be judged instantly as not being one of them?

But the moment Galla saw Meredith Brant, her worries vanished. The sheer love bursting from the mother's eyes, as green as her daughter's, struck Galla with such unexpected feeling that she gasped and clutched her stone with both hands. Meredith was many decades older than Ariel, and lined by worries over time. Galla felt a keen urge to hug the woman on the spot, but she resisted.

Meredith, though, stepped toward her and Dagovaby.

"You must be Ariel's friends," she said warmly, and she shook Dagovaby's large hands and stared up at his striking eyes. He smiled broadly at her and bowed his head. "I'm Meredith Brant."

"Dagovaby Ambrono," he said.

"So nice to meet you," Meredith answered with a smile.

And Meredith turned her green eyes to Galla, and pushed her white hair behind her ears as her daughter might. Galla had never felt so shy before. She quickly swallowed the sensation, though, and surged forth to clasp Meredith's hands.

"I'm Galla-Deia," she said breathlessly.

"Yes, you are," said Meredith with a laugh. "Every bit of you as gorgeous as I have always heard you were. I'm so glad I finally get to meet you, dear," she continued. "I understand you've been training off and on at various places. And one of them was Perpetua!"

Meredith smiled over some old memory, and lowered her head. But she patted Galla's hands. "I want you to tell me all about it."

"But what about me, Mama?" laughed Ariel, nudging her mother with her elbow. Her mother looped one arm around her and held Galla's hand with the other.

"Come on inside. I want to hear everything," said Meredith.

Galla's eyes filled with happy tears of belonging.

Meredith led them to a room with a round table, where they could all sit and talk. The room's ceiling arched in a dome, with lights that illuminated the table. Some of Aeriod's style could be evidenced in the design of panels along the curved walls of the room. There was a great deal of black and silver everywhere in the color scheme. Several black seats encircled the table, attached to the floor. The room was cool and smelled fresh, considering the recirculated air. Galla noticed two other people poke their heads in. One of them, a young man with short, fiery hair, bright blue eyes, and freckles, lingered at the door.

He caught sight of Galla and full-on stared.

Meredith noticed him, and said, "Oh, you can come in, Rob."

The young man looked struck dumb, as if he hadn't heard Meredith, but he entered anyway and walked straight to Galla.

"How do you do?" he asked. "Rob Idin." And he even gave a little bow.

Meredith laughed. "Rob, this is Galla-Deia."

"Call me Galla," she said abruptly. She reached out to the stricken Rob and shook his hand, which seemed to come alive and squeezed hers in a firm handshake. He sat down next to her.

Ariel snickered mercilessly. She said, "Didn't you used to work on Bottom Deck at Mandira?"

"Uh . . . yes," said Rob, still openly staring at Galla. Galla turned scarlet and swiveled away from him to face the others seated at the table.

Dagovaby laughed with Meredith. He and Ariel glanced at each other, and he winked as if they were in on some secret. Galla would have liked to put her head in her hands, but she sat stiffly and politely, as if she were eating dinner with guests. Her training with Aeriod paid off in that regard, at least.

Dagovaby asked Rob, "I take it you're who I spoke to on our way here?"

Rob pulled his attention from Galla long enough to say, "Yep. That was me," and then turned back again. Ariel's shoulders shook from suppressed laughter and she caught Galla's eyes. Then Galla began giggling and could not stop.

"Well!" Meredith called out, grinning. "Now that we've acquainted ourselves, I thought I should explain the situation with the security. I know you're wondering, dear," she added to Ariel.

"As it turns out, we've lost someone. Ariel, do you remember Officer Derry from MindSynd?"

Ariel clicked her tongue and rolled her eyes. "Unfortunately I do," she sneered.

"Well, he's gone," said Meredith.

"Oh!" Ariel went pale. "I'm sorry."

Meredith nodded. "It was very strange. He had been slow to adjust to things after we arrived at Ika Nui. Never seemed to want to fit in, kept getting out of his duties. I think he was depressed, personally. Everything he had worked for, in his view, was gone. And he was

... is, I should say ... a bright man. He could learn anything! He just didn't want to. A real shame, but there it is. And so, one day a few weeks ago, he took off."

"You didn't try to stop him?" asked Ariel.

"I didn't. But Aeriod did," said Meredith grimly. Galla sat up a little straighter.

"And he refused Aeriod's orders?" she asked.

"He did," said Meredith, her mouth a thin line. "Took off to the junction. Aeriod says he lost track of him after that. Thinks something may have happened to him, as he didn't make it out at the other junction that's normally used."

"Damn," said Ariel. "That's too bad. But why the security situation?"

Meredith shifted in her seat and glanced at Rob.

"Rob, tell them what you saw."

Rob took a deep breath, dragged his eyes away from Galla, and said, "We—okay, some of us former Bottom Deck folks—perform routine patrols in the system. Aeriod provides a general network of security, but he still thought it was a good idea to do this. Gave us something to do, that sort of thing.

"So one day, right before Officer Derry went missing, I was out at the asteroid circle at the system edge, and I saw a ship. At first I wasn't sure it was a ship. And honestly I'm still not convinced. Anyway, it was *something* traveling very fast, and then it sped away to the junction before I could get a closer look. It set off every alarm we've got. But where it came from, we don't know. Just seems like that happening right before Derry goes missing ... too much of a coincidence, I think."

Meredith nodded. "We all thought so. Aeriod suggested we keep up patrols. I know he's needed elsewhere; the Associates have him taking care of things on their end. But something seems to have spooked him. So we are all a little on edge. Wanted to play it safe with whoever came through the junction next. And here you are, so that's a relief!"

"There's more to it than tha—" began Rob, but Meredith shot him a look.

"That'll do for now, Rob. Now if you don't mind, we need to get back to the patrol."

Rob nodded and stood to leave, but not without another glance at Galla, and a roguish smirk.

"Won't we go to the Station? Or Ika Nui?" asked Ariel in a surprised voice.

"I think we had better stay out here for now, Little Goose," said Meredith.

"Not to worry, though. We've got plenty of room, and we'll be fine. Now let's eat!"

"That's my mother, you guys," Ariel beamed at Galla and Dagovaby. "She'll never let you go hungry!"

Galla smiled, but she felt her stone's warmth and wondered. She picked up on what Meredith was saying. They didn't want anyone coming near their planet. And after what had happened on Fael'Kar, Galla could not blame them. The star-dotted blackness outside the ship held something terrible, somewhere out where they could not see. And yet she *could* see, and wished that she could not.

35

MATRIARCH

Meredith took Galla and Ariel to her makeshift quarters on the ship. It was a small room, but there was enough floor space to spread out. Galla put her bag on the floor, opened it, and unfurled her quilt. She held it in her arms and looked at Meredith.

"Thank you for this," she said, smiling. She spread the quilt out onto a sleeping pad Meredith had unrolled on the floor.

"Oh, you're welcome, dear," Meredith replied fondly. She then asked Ariel, "So how long have you known Dagovaby?"

Ariel's cheeks went pink. "About as long as I've known Galla here," she said, keeping her voice even. "Which is to say, not very long. But it's weird." And she smirked at Galla. "I feel like I've known you both forever."

Galla could feel her shoulders relax, and a surge of happiness coursed through her. "Likewise," she said.

"Well," Meredith said with a grin, "that's how you know you've made fast friends! I'm glad. For each of you."

"Dagovaby's an empath," Ariel said. "And he's half human."

Meredith raised her eyebrows. "Now that sounds like an interesting story! I thought us Mandirans were the only ones out here."

"I guess not," said Ariel, furrowing her brow. "I wonder if anyone else is?"

"I don't know, but I should tell you, not everyone wants to stay. It's been a bumpy ride since your last visit. Derry is just the latest example, and sadly that didn't work out for him."

"So, why can't people contact their loved ones?" Galla asked, confused.

"Aeriod specifically told us not to, that it would threaten our safety and theirs," Meredith replied.

"Really!" Galla raised her arched eyebrows high. "Surely there must be some way to get around that?"

Meredith and Ariel exchanged looks.

Meredith said, "Well, if there is some way, we don't know what it is. We've been going along with what Aeriod says. And in light of Derry's disappearance and that strange ship out there, he may be right. It's a big galaxy, and we don't know how it all works, and who's running the shots."

Galla sat cross-legged on the floor and considered the two women. She said, "Something about all of this bothers me. We seem so dependent on Aeriod. Why is that?"

Meredith nodded, and she and Ariel joined Galla in a circle.

"I've thought about this a lot over the years," Meredith replied. "He's done plenty of good for us, brought me back my daughter. Helped us to escape a bad situation. Brought us here."

"But he couldn't have done that without me and Forster," Ariel pointed out. "And for that matter, Galla. Without her stone, none of us would have made it out."

Galla breathed in deeply. "I'm glad it worked!" she said. "I can tell you who's running the shots, as you said. It's the Associates."

"Aeriod has mentioned them," Meredith replied. "They gave him the orders to come to Mandira, as I understand."

"And that would have been specifically to help them, not you," Galla said.

She watched Ariel shift uncomfortably.

"The Associates don't do things by accident. They have plans,"

Galla went on. "And I don't understand half of them. They work as an omnipresent group governing the galaxy as a whole. And they have Representatives for various spacefaring cultures. I am one of them. As far as I know, the only being in this galaxy that holds any authority over the Associates is Oni-Odi."

"Who's Oni-Odi?" asked Ariel.

Galla folded her hands together and cupped her stone. "Oni-Odi found me. Adrift in space, inside my stone, and he brought me onto his star-city, where he lives with thousands of androids, robots of every kind."

Galla's eyes went out of focus as she remembered. "He was the only parent I had, really. For many years I lived with him, until the Associates began my training to serve as a Representative. And then Aeriod came and took me away to train with him first."

A strange look came over Meredith's face, and Ariel squirmed, her cool eyes sympathetic.

"Galla, I don't want to overreach here, but did you want to go?" Meredith asked.

Galla blinked and clenched her stone. *I don't want to remember those days. There were some good days, but others I am not so sure about. And then the time on Bitikk.*

"Mama, I'm going to see if Dagovaby needs me," Ariel said suddenly. But before she left, she looked Galla straight in the eyes and put a hand on her shoulder. She turned and left, and Galla could see she looked troubled.

Galla looked down at her hands and realized how tightly she was holding her stone. She felt so trusting of Meredith, however, that she took a chance. "I had to go," she said in a shaky voice. "I had to go and train. Either way, that was going to happen. But he stepped in first. I was afraid of him."

"It's all right," Meredith said, her voice soothing and her eyes fixed on Galla.

She nodded. "I'm glad I didn't go to Bitikk first. That would have been so much worse. Aeriod and I did not get along initially, but we were attracted to each other. And I—I loved him. And he loved me. But something never felt right to me about any of it."

"He should never have stepped in as he did," said Meredith firmly. "You were naïve and young. That much is clear. He was not. And yes, he did love you; I know that because I got to know him. I did not know the whole story. And while he loved you, and still does, I presume, that does not mean that you are in any way beholden to him. You have to grow as your own person. Away from him."

Galla blinked through tears. Then she reached for Meredith and the old woman hugged her, and let her sob.

"Did he hurt you, dear?" Meredith asked into the wild, bright hair as Galla loosed her troubles.

"No," she said. She straightened. "I suppose he hurt my feelings a bit, at first, but no. He never hurt me. There was an undeniable attraction. I asked him to show me more. And I don't regret that. We enjoyed each other very much, for a little while. But I can see now, he wanted to keep me sheltered."

"Yes, that is an instinct we sometimes feel toward others we care about," Meredith said. "But that does not make it healthy. I think Aeriod was a lonely person. And here you came into his life: vibrant, beautiful, brash, wild, with a life of adventures ahead of you. All these things he was not. I can see why he was so drawn to you. And I can also see why you would be to him."

"I don't want to go further with him," Galla said, as much to herself as Meredith. "He wants me forever. And that isn't what I want. I don't know how long I'll live. I have work to do, and a purpose. And I feel that more now than ever. There's no room for me to be tethered by someone else."

Meredith sighed. "I'm so sorry. I know it must hurt. I think you're showing maturity here, though. Good for you!"

Galla rubbed her eyes and looked at Meredith's lined face.

"What about you? Did you love someone?"

Meredith grinned. "Oh yes. Ariel's father, Paul. We were friends for years before we ever decided to have a family."

"What happened?" Galla asked, delicately.

"He died many years ago," said Meredith.

Galla gasped. "I'm so sorry!"

"Oh, dear, it's been many years. The pain has lessened, and I've got my memories. But he was my best friend. That matters so much. I miss staying up late at night talking to him, sometimes. Or walking. Just walking and talking. The simplest things. It was never grand, just comfortable. But we had a good run, and a great daughter." Meredith pushed her hair behind her ears. She took Galla's hands.

"Don't rule out friendship," she said. "You'll need it. It's a beautiful thing. And if you're very, very lucky, it can grow into more than that. I've had a blessed life. I wish you the same, dear."

"Thank you," Galla said, her head bowed. "And thank you for . . . this. I didn't know how much I needed it."

"You had a father, and no mother," Meredith noted. "I've got enough love for two girls, dear. I'm here if you need me."

Galla could not speak, and could not see through her tears.

36

CONVOCATION

After a night on the ship, everyone met at the round table again for breakfast. Ariel sat next to Galla, and Dagovaby sat next to Ariel. Meredith sat alone, serving as a leader. Other crew scattered around the large table.

"We are here for a couple of things today," Meredith announced. "First, let's see how we can help Galla-Deia in her quest. It is my understanding she needs to find a number of planets with what she calls Devices on them. These are huge machines, apparently mostly underground. And many, or all of them, could be covered or shielded in some way. We have no idea where they all are, but we need that information. So! Any ideas?"

One of the crew, a middle-aged man with olive skin, downturned eyebrows, and salt-and-pepper hair, said, "Hi. Trent Korba here." He waved to Galla and her seatmates. "It's a big galaxy. If these things are hidden, it's going to take scans to find them."

"Wouldn't Aeriod have this info?" Ariel asked.

Galla spoke up. "He has not looked for the others, no. But I wonder about the Associates."

Meredith nodded. "You would think so. But we have no access to their tech, yes?"

"That's right," said Galla. "And they're not known for sharing."

Trent spoke up again. "If we could access their tech somehow, maybe we could find what we're looking for."

"You mean, hack in?" another crew member asked. This woman, with chestnut-brown skin and elaborately carved hair poufs, bore sparkling green gems down both her ears. She was adorned simply in pants and a T-shirt, but her demeanor radiated confidence.

"Thank you, Jana, yes," replied Trent with a nod.

"Jana Okoro," the woman said, extending her hand to Galla. "I can do that," she said assuredly.

"Then go for it!" Galla exclaimed, shaking Jana's hand. She smiled with impish glee, imagining the ire such a hack would draw. She realized how satisfying it would be to outsmart the horrible Speaker of Bitikk.

"One problem, though," said Jana. "How do I *get* to their tech?"

"We'll figure something out," said Galla.

At that moment, a looping alert sounded throughout the ship.

A voice crackled over the intercom, and Galla recognized it as Rob Idin's.

"Meredith," he called, "you might want to come up here. Um. We've got company."

The group rose and ambled toward the cockpit. Something drifted down, around the ship, like the long tendrils of a jellyfish.

"Jesus Christ!" Rob cried. "It's closing all around us!"

"What the hell is that?" asked Ariel, and Dagovaby glanced back at Galla.

Galla returned his look, and set her mouth in a grim line.

"It's an Associate ship," she answered.

"Ohhh shit," Jana said. "Did we just bring them here? Did they overhear us?"

"I don't know," Galla said, beginning to worry. *Why are they here? Here, of all places?* Her skin crawled. She could feel it to her core.

"They want *me*," said Galla, and everyone stared at her.

"I don't think you should go alone," Meredith declared. The others nodded.

"I'll go with you," Rob said instantly. Galla rolled her eyes, and Ariel snickered.

"Mate, give it a rest," chuckled Dagovaby.

"Rob," Meredith said, with an adoring look, "bless your heart. We need you to pilot the ship, dear."

"I'll go," said Ariel. Dagovaby and Meredith sighed. "What? Never know when you need a telepath."

Galla considered. "They won't expect me to bring anyone. But it's a good idea," she said, and she glanced at Jana. "Want to come along?"

"Hell yes," Jana responded, twisting one of her green earrings.

"Then you know what I'm going to ask you to do," Galla continued. Jana nodded and winked. "Whatever you can find, do so. We may not have much time."

The smaller craft was now fully covered by the enormous Associate ship. The comms screen glowed, and everyone turned to face it.

A hooded figure spoke: "We summon Galla-Deia. Prepare to board."

"Grab me!" Galla hissed to Ariel and Jana, and they linked arms. A ghostly blue light filled the room and enveloped the three women, and they vanished.

When Galla opened her eyes, her companions still clung to her arms. "It worked!" she breathed. The three looked all around them. They stood in an enormous, cavernous, dark space, seemingly empty. They were lit by an unseen source, bathed in blue. Ghostly shadows hung under Ariel's pale eyes, and blue glints shone on Jana's face. Galla's stone winked in deep violet sparkles.

"We requested only Galla-Deia," a deep, monotone voice sounded.

"They stay with me," said Galla. "Or I leave."

"You are summoned. You must step forward."

Ariel whispered, "There are several beings entering this room, and they're hard to read."

Galla nodded. "Summoners," she murmured, quietly.

Jana looked for any sign of a control panel, found none, and shrugged in frustration.

Galla obliged her command. "What do you want?" she dared to ask.

"We are here to address your training." Now the voices of dozens layered upon the first voice. Galla could just make out figures moving toward where she stood. They seemed to ignore Ariel and Jana. Galla noticed Jana slip farther into the shadows, while Ariel stayed where she was.

The voices rippled and echoed and folded back on themselves, disorienting Galla, and by the look of her face, Ariel as well. Galla sympathized, and wondered if everything echoed as much in the young woman's mind as in their ears.

Those voices now boomed, "The Event approaches. Your presence is needed."

"Is that so?" Galla asked, loudly. She felt a heat building in her. Something she had over time fought down as she had grown more mature. But it could not be stopped. A searing rage shivered through her and her voice shook.

"There is no stopping the Event!" she cried. "What is natural must be allowed to happen. You need to pay closer attention to what else is going on! Paosh Tohon is loose upon the galaxy!"

A roiling hiss of disapproval reverberated throughout the dark space.

"Paosh Tohon is not our concern. Our concern lies with the Event, as foretold by the Seltra. It is at hand."

"How stupid are you?" yelled Galla. "The two are absolutely related! Paosh Tohon will take advantage of the suffering the Event causes, and grow beyond anything it is now."

She dared to glance behind her. Jana was nowhere in sight. Ariel's eyelids were pressed together, as if she were concentrating.

Galla went on, "What you are really saying is, I've graduated, and you want me to go along with your plans as usual. I'm here to ask you this: will you grant access to me for all plans to Devices in this galaxy? You know what I'm talking about. You cannot lie to me." She resisted the urge to peek at Ariel.

"Your specific Task is to work to mitigate the Event!" the voices bellowed, their pitch higher, denoting disapproval.

"It's the least you could do for me!" cried Galla. "After all, let's talk about what *you* did *to me*. You manipulated Oni-Odi into turning me over to the Associates. Aeriod stepped in and began my training first. Then you shipped me to Bitikk! Where you *tortured me* for decades! I don't even know what all you did to me. I guess whatever it was, you feel like I'm ready now. So if you won't give me what I need to fight Paosh Tohon, forget it. I can't stop the Event. I *can* help the galaxy."

"You will do your Task!" The voices, louder, seemed to swirl around her now. The light flickered.

Galla felt defiance and anger course through her. *How dare they? After all they did to me ... and who knows how many others!*

"That's *your* task," Galla said firmly, her hands on her hips. "I do not follow orders from you, from *any* of you, anymore. Just look at you. All in shadows, not showing your true natures," and she swiveled on her toes to take in the dark spaces where the beings hid. "You're all cowards. And you know what? The galaxy knows it! That's why this . . . Valemog has grown now. A cult around Paosh Tohon. There's a vacuum of leadership and it's being filled with poison.

"You can't command any of us anymore. You can't rip us away from our families, you can't torture us. Not anymore," Galla thundered. Her stone flashed, as if reflecting her inner ire. "I reject you. Now send me back to my ship, and leave this place."

A horrible silence followed. Finally, a shape ventured forth. Galla winced, watching a long tentacle approach her from the figure. It was Vedant.

A whistling sound arose from Vedant, and it spoke:

"You defy the sacred Task of the Seltra! If you do reject us, we can no longer help you."

"I thought you might say that, Tentacles," Galla spat back. "Guess what! The Seltra are gone. The Seltrason era is over. This is a new era, whether you like it or not. You can be with us on the side of what's right, or you can wither and die. Your choice. I've made my choice. Send me back! Now!"

And Jana darted in next to Galla, while Ariel stepped beside her on the other side. They clasped hands. Galla eyed Jana, who winked very slowly. Ariel nodded. A long howl of confusion and horror rose from the crowd around them, but they were granted their wish.

Within seconds, the three women stood firmly on Meredith's ship again. The Summoners' ship dematerialized as if it had never been there.

Galla gasped and then laughed. She clapped her hands, and then hugged Ariel and Jana on either side of her.

"You did *that!*" Jana murmured in awe. Then she grinned. "And I did *this.*" And she brought out of her pocket a long, slender cylinder.

"You got the data!" Galla shouted, hopping into the air.

"Let's hope so!" Jana replied, handing Galla the cylinder.

"No, you keep it; you know more about this sort of thing than I do," she said. "That was amazing, Jana!" She turned to Ariel. "Did you pick up anything?"

Ariel exhaled. "Whew. That was a mess, and hard to deal with. But yes, I did pick up some things. Galla, you shook them hard! But I picked up on something else: some of them agreed with you."

Galla threw her arms wide and said, "Ahhh! I feel free now!"

The crew congratulated her, and she thanked them. "Now let's find these Devices," she said, fully confident for the first time in her life.

37

SYNTAX

Galla checked with Jana to see if she needed anything else to help decipher her cylinder's contents. Jana enthusiastically dove into her task and waved Galla away, which suited her fine. She was exhausted.

She entered the little room of Meredith's and collapsed on her quilt, not wanting to think about anything, and really needing to rest after the encounter with the Summoners. *I know that's not the last of them. I know I'll have to deal with more of this. But for now? A nap.*

A fizzy, crackling sound woke her, and she jerked up on her elbows. The room was dark, and Ariel and Meredith were sleeping. Ariel stirred but remained asleep. The sound came through again.

"Pick up, please," a voice sounded. Galla realized it was the comms. She gingerly stepped over the other two women and switched the comms on. It was Rob.

He waved, but his blue eyes shone wide.

"Hiya," he said, as quietly as he could. "You have a call up here. Want to come take it?"

"Sure," Galla replied. She left the room and followed the sleek hallway, with its lights lowered in simulated night, to the cockpit. Rob was the only person there, and he swung around and smiled rakishly at Galla.

"You know," he said, standing to greet her, "you could have said he was your boyfriend. I really don't need to be blasted by his silver eyes," and he snickered. Then he bowed his head sheepishly. He stepped toward the door.

Oh. Great. It's Aeriod.

"He's not—" Galla began, and she groaned.

Rob stopped mid-gait. "He's . . . not?" He smirked hopefully over his shoulder. Galla scowled at him and pointed to the door.

"I'll be back in a few minutes," he said, and he seemed suddenly buoyant.

Galla sighed and sat in the pilot seat. She twitched her hair back and tried to tame it, lest it betray her ricocheting feelings. She switched on the comms screen.

They stared at each other in silence, unsmiling.

"Yes?" she said finally.

Aeriod's face looked sharp, creased in anger: "How could you *do* this? After everything? This isn't some game!"

"I know it's no game," Galla answered, chin high. "Or if it is, it's a sick one played on our lives by the Associates. I want no part of it. They're out of their depth."

Aeriod put his hands over his face and sighed.

"You may be right. So what's your plan now?"

"I'm going to find all the Devices," Galla answered.

"And then what?"

She heaved a huge sigh. "I don't know. I have to figure out how to work them, somehow, to try and stop Paosh Tohon."

"Galla, you're being rash," said Aeriod testily.

"Maybe," she answered. "But at least I'm doing *something*. What's *your* plan, exactly?"

"I'm following some leads," Aeriod answered.

"Well. Good luck with that," snapped Galla. "The galaxy is changing, rapidly."

"I see it," Aeriod agreed. "But I don't follow all the Associates' rules."

"As well I know," muttered Galla, touching her lips. Aeriod noticed.

"I'm sorry," he said suddenly. He looked sorrowful. "Can we get past this?"

"I don't think so, no," said Galla. "I can't sit with you in some sky palace for the rest of my life. It's not who I am. I've learned that much."

Aeriod sighed, nodded, and reached out with his hand. Galla extended hers. They touched on the screen. She blinked rapidly.

"Whatever you need, however I can help, just ask," he said.

"Thank you," she replied, and she turned the screen off.

She swiveled around in her chair and saw a shadow at the door.

"You can come in now," she called.

Rob peeked in uncertainly, his ginger hair outlined by the lights behind him.

"That went well, I thought!" he exclaimed brightly.

Galla gaped at him. "You *listened?*"

Rob shrugged. "I was completely riveted. Couldn't help it. You have that effect."

"Ugh!" cried Galla. "I'm going back to bed."

And she stalked off.

They all met in the round room the next morning, everyone looking expectantly at Galla. She put on a bright smile, because it didn't make sense to her to be anything but encouraged. She turned to Jana.

"Can you tell us what you found?"

Jana produced her cylinder. She held it up and it winked in the light.

"I was able to get into the ship's memory, but it isn't anything like what we're used to, on this ship, or Mandira for that matter," Jana told them all. "But I think we may have what we need."

Everyone exhaled in relief. Galla bounced a bit in her seat.

"Jana the genius!" Trent cried, shaking his head in awe.

"Go on," Galla encouraged Jana, clasping her hands together against her stone.

Jana said, "There's what appears to be an old database, something different from that ship's. And it's accessed remotely, but I couldn't track from where. But I sapped what I could from it, and I cross-linked it with Aeriod's world and excluded Ika Nui and Perpetua."

"Excellent," murmured Galla.

Trent asked, "And then what?"

"Well," Jana said, touching one of her earrings, "there are worlds that fit a certain profile. None of them gaseous. All essentially Earth or super-Earth sized—that's our homeworld," she interjected to Galla.

"I know," Galla replied. "Go on, please."

Jana continued, "So on a subset of those worlds, I queried for known underground caverns, based on what you described on Rikiloi. I had to play it fast and loose with dimensions, because it sounds like we don't really know what those are. And honestly I wasn't sure it would work, because that database is some pretty weird shit."

"And?" Meredith pressed, twisting her hands together.

"There are twenty-one planets with a similar underground signature."

Everyone else gasped.

"Is there any pattern to them you can recognize?" Galla asked.

Jana shook her head. "Not that I could determine from the query."

"Let's find them all!" Galla exclaimed, standing.

"One thing," Jana warned. "We don't know for sure those are really the 'Devices' or if the signature is just similar, natural structures."

Galla nodded. "True. And we don't know if they would even still be intact."

"Or what security they might have," muttered Trent.

"What happens then?" Ariel asked Galla.

"I think we'd better make sure they're still there first," she replied.

"And then maybe something will happen—to me, as it did on Rikiloi."

Galla felt a surge of excitement ripple through her entire body. She felt sure, now, that they were on the right track. Where it would lead, she could not guess. But it was a road map.

38

THE JEWEL

Ariel sat on the floor of the makeshift room and rubbed her eyes. She had grown tired from the constant bombardment of human thoughts, after her recent years of interacting very little with her own species. With Galla she felt relief, but in turn she wished she could speak with her through her thoughts. She smiled thinking about her wild-haired, odd new friend. Galla simply could not effectively hide her feelings from anyone, and Ariel wanted somehow for her to stay that way forever. Galla seemed to her someone absolutely true, more so than even her own mother. To Ariel, Galla represented the ultimate free spirit. And while she was tempted to envy her, Ariel could not.

What she did want was happiness for her friend. There had been something so discordant, now that Ariel knew them both, about Galla and Aeriod's relationship. It seemed obvious to her, and she had picked it up in Dagovaby's thoughts as well. Ariel had felt a quake of relief when Galla broke up with the mage. He was simply wrong for Galla: Ariel felt this to her core. And that saddened her. For who could be a companion for someone who did not seem to age?

And then she thought increasingly of Dagovaby. Of stolen kisses. Of spice-laden air wherever he was. They could not speak in their thoughts exactly, but she could read his, and he could feel hers, and something inside her had begun to awaken. It had really been triggered by watching Galla and Aeriod in better times, her raw attraction to both of them in their moment of lust. And she had walked into that night and broadcast those feelings. And Dagovaby had picked them up, like a sailor lost at sea seeing the sweeping band of a lighthouse, unable to resist. Ariel curled her legs up to her chest and leaned against the wall. He was here, on this ship. So close.

At that moment, Galla swept in like a wild summer rain, sudden and crashing and warm and bursting with life. Ariel grinned at her. She loved Galla-Deia, she knew in that moment. Here was the friend she had always wanted. She need never feel out of time or place anymore, with this fully living creature in her life.

Galla spun around and sat next to Ariel, back also against the wall, and wound ringlets of her brilliant hair all in her fingers. She exhaled excitedly.

"I finally feel like I'm doing something," she admitted. "Like I'm on the path I'm supposed to be on."

Ariel leaned forward and looked into Galla's flushed face. Galla's copper eyes were blazing.

"I think you definitely are," she told her friend. Galla made a funny little squeal and hugged Ariel ferociously. "Ack!" she yelped.

"Oh! Sorry!" Galla gasped, all apology and nurture suddenly.

Ariel laughed. "You seem happier now," she said. "I'm sorry for what happened, though. But you deserve better than him. I hope someday, if it's what you want, that you find someone who 'gets' you." She pulled her long, dark hair back behind her ears and leaned her head on Galla's shoulder. "I just love you."

Galla nearly incandesced. "I love you too!" she cried. "What a great day!" and she excitedly went on, "Jana and I are working on a map with this ship, and we'll display it at lunch."

"Let me know what it shows," Ariel said. She squeezed Galla's left hand and stood. "I have something I need to take care of."

Dagovaby, she called. She did not hold back anymore. She let her body feel everything it had been repressing on the ship. She opened up her emotions and hoped he would feel them.

He met her in the hallway. The cinnamon scent seemed to swirl around her. The golden rings glowed in his dark eyes. She walked to him slowly, taking in the sight of him, strong yet gentle. She was a damaged person, and had spent many years in cold darkness and loneliness. And this man stood here, all embers and strength and openness. All the warmth she had ever wanted and needed.

"I'm ready," Ariel told Dagovaby.

They slipped into a little room off the hall, hands and lips and sweat intermingling. Clothes falling. In the dim light, her pale green eyes stared into his dark, gold-edged eyes and never looked away. And their feelings and thoughts swirled all together, crashing and tumbling, minds and bodies folding together, exploding, expanding, contracting, and completely entwined.

Galla, meanwhile, sighed in her room. She was excited, but it felt bittersweet. Aside from her friction with Aeriod, she could not help but think that Oni-Odi would have known exactly what she must do next. And he was gone.

Here, now, she had no star-city, but instead a loaned ship from her former lover, and a small crew of mostly humans. She did not know why any of them would want to help her, but for some reason they did. She clenched her jaw. She could not let them down.

She joined Jana in the conference room and noticed the dark circles under the other woman's eyes.

"Jana," she said quietly, "you look so tired. Maybe we should table this for now, and you can rest."

"No, no," insisted Jana, her blinking betraying her fatigue. "I couldn't sleep. I had to think about all this. I wanted to find a pattern, like you mentioned. And I think I did, but I don't understand it."

Galla's eyes widened. "Let's wait for everyone else, and then you can tell us!"

The others filed into the room—except for Ariel and Dagovaby. Galla raised one eyebrow, wondering, but kept her mouth shut. She remembered the looks they had exchanged.

"Good morning!" Galla said to them all. "I'm happy to report we may have something of a map."

"Well, not exactly a map," Jana explained, and she projected an orrery of sorts above the table. They all beheld the galaxy itself, its bright core, its spiral arms, and then a small illuminated shape between the arms and the core. "It's really more of a picture of . . . well—"

"It looks like a horseshoe!" Rob exclaimed. Meredith nodded.

"So the systems are all in that shape? That's the pattern?" Galla clarified.

"That's it," said Jana, enlarging the image.

"Why would the Devices be in such a pattern?" Meredith wondered.

"Maybe they're all pointing at something," Trent enthused.

Galla felt a thrill. That had to be it. She peered at the outlined shape, as if it were some enormous constellation. Millions upon millions of stars were in the same area, but for some reason those particular systems made a U-shaped arc.

"What could they be pointing *at*?" Rob asked.

"Could be anything," Jana said.

"Or nothing," Meredith reminded them.

Galla said, "I think there must be a reason for the pattern. Maybe by visiting each of them, we can figure it out."

"And that's it?" Rob asked. "I mean, as your pilot, I'll take you anywhere you want to go. But—hear me out. What if you need to do more than just visit? What are we really doing? Why would *you* be needed? I feel like we need to know that before we start gallivanting around the galaxy. Not"—he said quickly, with the slyest wink at Galla—"that I don't want to."

Galla blinked at him in surprise. *He's more resourceful than I thought!*

She let out a big sigh. "I don't know. I feel like I'm missing something here."

"Time for Mister Deep Space Booty Call?" Rob said, and the

second he did he clapped his hand over his mouth. Everyone stared at him.

Galla tossed her feisty hair back. "Definitely not," she answered briskly. Everyone squirmed, looking between her and Rob. "Apology accepted, by the way," she muttered. "You look like a bruise right now."

Rob sat down, mortified. Galla could feel her hair curling tighter from rage, but she breathed consciously to calm herself.

"We try to figure this out on our own," she said firmly. "Until such time that we need"—and she cleared her throat—"any *outside* assistance."

She leaned in to look again at the "horseshoe" and said very softly, "What is it? What are we supposed to see there?"

The door slid open, and Ariel and Dagovaby slipped in. Galla could almost feel Rob forming the words, and shot him a terrible glare. No one at the table said a word.

"Sorry we're late," Dagovaby apologized.

"Lunch," Ariel explained lamely. Galla could see Jana and Rob exchange quick glances and cover their mouths to keep from laughing. Meredith turned slowly to look at her daughter, and Ariel's already flushed face went scarlet.

"So *anyway*," Galla said, mildly exasperated, "we have a sort of map for systems with Devices, and they're arranged in a kind of pattern."

"A horseshoe," Ariel chimed in, nodding.

"If you say so," replied Galla crisply, frustrated that she had no idea what a horseshoe was.

Dagovaby asked, "Why would they be in that pattern?"

"We went over this, and we think maybe they're all pointed at something," Galla responded.

Dagovaby leaned in and Jana enlarged the picture more. Everyone stared at the image. "If these Devices all work together, there must be a focal point for them," he said.

"Nothing that we can see on this map," Meredith answered, looking intently at him. He glanced sheepishly at her, and then away.

But Galla could see the tiniest twitch in the corner of Meredith's mouth.

"Focus," murmured Ariel.

"What?" said Galla, her brow creasing.

"Dagovaby said *focal point*. So that's why we need to *focus*," said Ariel. She straightened and looked at Meredith.

"Like when Forster and I moved Mandira!" she exclaimed. "We had to focus our minds to do it!"

"That's it?" Rob asked in amazement. "That's all you did? You just . . . thought it away?"

"Well," Ariel admitted, "we had Aeriod's help."

Rob rolled his eyes and muttered, "Sorry I asked."

"That wasn't all you had," Meredith said suddenly. She stared at Galla.

Ariel looked at Galla and her eyes grew huge, as her gaze fell to the faceted violet stone on the woman's breast.

"Holy. Shit," breathed Ariel.

Galla threw her hands into the air.

"What!" she cried.

"We used Aeriod's little stone!" cried Ariel. "We focused our minds, and the stone amplified our abilities!"

"Wait," said Galla, thinking hard, "we also repelled Paosh Tohon. On Fael'Kar, *together*. With *this* stone."

"So you need that stone," Trent said slowly, squinting, "to repel Paosh Tohon. Okay. Got it. But how does that relate to this map? And to these Devices?"

Galla closed her eyes. What had she seen in the Device on Rikiloi? So many images had whirled past her, none of them making sense at the time. And yet that had never happened with Aeriod. Only to her.

"It's me," she said slowly. "I am the stone."

"I'm sorry, what?" Jana asked what everyone was thinking.

Galla looked at each of them in turn. "I am diamethyst," she told them. "I was borne of it, and I am made of it. This is only one piece of the shell I awoke from," she added, holding her necklace.

"But—but—but," said Rob, at a loss, "you look human!"

She bit her lip. "That's because I'm a Representative. I'm one of several beings that are chosen to represent a particular species. In this case, I represent humans."

Jana pushed her lips together. "Really," she said, an edge in her voice.

Trent rubbed his face in utter confusion, Rob stared at her until she thought she would scream, and Meredith, Ariel, and Dagovaby looked deep in thought.

Meredith spoke up. "You said that stone you're wearing is only one piece. We know there is another: the one Aeriod has. How much more of this do you have?"

Galla stood up stick-straight.

"I have the whole geode I was born in."

"So, a baby-sized geode?" Rob asked.

"I was always the way you see me," Galla told them. "I was never a baby."

Headshakes and blinks met her. She began to tremble.

Dagovaby raised his hand, and said, "So that means you actually have an adult, person-sized geode, full of these ... diamethysts?"

"Yes," said Galla slowly, her spirit sinking.

"Then where is it?" he asked.

"Rikiloi," said Galla.

Rob groaned. "Here we go again!"

39

THE PLANETFINDERS

Galla paced back and forth in front of the cockpit door. Ariel found her there and looked at her with her large, cool peridot eyes. At first Galla did not see her, for she was so absorbed in a mixture of dread and uncertainty that nothing else seemed to exist.

"Galla," Ariel said quietly. She approached her wild-haired friend. She could see that Galla's hair reflected her inner turmoil, as it shot in all directions.

Startled, Galla looked up from her pacing and blinked to focus on her human friend. *She is my friend,* Galla thought, with a stirring wistfulness. *I wish we were somewhere else, and could just . . . be friends. Be away from all this.*

"I know you've got to contact *him*," Ariel said pointedly. She watched Galla jut her chin upward. "But that stone is *yours* and he has no claim over it. Or you."

And she seized her friend's hand. "It's going to be all right. Just get it over with. The sooner, the better."

Galla nodded. Ariel studied every movement of her face.

"I can't read your thoughts," Ariel said with a sigh, "but I can tell you're pretty worked up over this. I can be with you when you call him. Would you like that?"

Galla's eyes shone like amber. "Yes, please!" She took a deep breath. They entered the cockpit and Rob swung around. Ariel shot him a warning look.

"Don't—say—it," she hissed.

"Fine, fine, spoon-bender girl," Rob grumbled. He stood and bowed down in front of Galla.

"Milady," he mumbled.

Galla snickered in spite of herself. "Go, Rob," she said. He winked at her from his precarious position and then straightened and left the room.

"I think if you'd been wearing a skirt, he'd totally have looked up it," Ariel sniffed.

Galla grinned. Then she stiffened her back and sat rigidly in front of the comms screen. "I'm ready."

Ariel gave her shoulder a squeeze and sat in the copilot chair.

"Aeriod," Galla rasped, and she cleared her throat.

The comms screen shimmered, and there he was, his irises like mercury, their pupils piercing even through the screen. She felt a jolt of roiling emotions, but fought them. Aeriod, for his part, sat completely still.

"Yes?" he asked, calmly.

"I need something," Galla replied. She bit her lower lip. "I need my geode."

Aeriod's eyes closed halfway, and even across space and time she could feel their intensity, as if he could see entirely though her. He arched his left eyebrow.

"Oh?" he responded coolly. "Why would you need that?"

"First of all, it's mine," said Galla, feeling hot. "So I should have it. Second, I think I may need it for my mission."

"Should I expect you here?" Aeriod asked, almost whispering.

Galla felt waves of anger, mistrust, attraction, and confusion, all coursing through her simultaneously. She could feel her resolve slipping. At this point Ariel reached over to Galla with her extended hand. Galla broke eye contact with Aeriod long enough to glance at her friend, and she reached out as well. Their fingers joined.

"No," said Galla firmly. "I'm not coming to your sky palace. We will meet you in a neutral spot. And I'm going to need something else."

Ariel's eyes bulged. Galla gave her hand a squeeze.

"Ah," said Aeriod, pinching his lips together. "What more do you need, Galla-Deia?"

"Protection," answered Galla, wincing from hearing her full name from him.

"You don't really need—"

"For *them*, Aeriod. Not for me."

Aeriod sighed. "Such as?"

"I want this ship shielded with everything you can spare," she demanded.

"It's already a fine ship," Aeriod remarked. "It's one of mine, after all."

"No. The Associates found it. I want it completely hidden from anything."

"I can't guarantee you that," said Aeriod. "Even if I try to boost the security, there will always be a risk."

"I understand," Galla conceded. "Will you do it? I'm carrying precious cargo, after all," and she grinned at Ariel.

Aeriod blinked. "Very well. I do wish Kein had agreed to join you, though."

"I know. I tried," answered Galla, sighing. She felt a great sense of unease without Kein playing a role in any plans. As if something had gone wrong. She did not want to tell Ariel, this, however. And maybe it would be all right, with Dagovaby on board now.

"I'll program your ship to come here," Aeriod announced.

"You're taking over the ship?" she asked, her voice stern.

"Only so that no one on board gets the coordinates," murmured Aeriod.

"Why would you worry about that?" Galla wanted to know.

"Do you want a secure ship, or not?" Aeriod countered, his voice bitter.

"Fine," snapped Galla. "Do it."

"Buckle up. I will see you soon," said Aeriod, and his image vanished. Galla stood and dashed to the door.

"Rob, tell the crew to strap in, we're off," she told him hastily.

Rob squinted with disdain. "What's he doing?" he muttered.

Galla and Ariel ran to the round room and strapped in. As soon as they had, the ship spun up and shot forth into the blackness. Within minutes they approached a junction and catapulted through its conduit of strobing lights, forking off a few times to other junctions, all beyond their control. In less than two hours, the ship snapped to a halt above Rikiloi.

Meredith projected the exterior of the ship above the table. A spindle-like structure appeared alongside them and blossomed into a larger ship: Aeriod's own, glistening black and silver. His ship drew the smaller one toward it. Galla could hear Rob down the hall.

"*...fucking pulling us along, sonofabitch!*" he roared.

She sympathized. Here again, Aeriod put on a display. Galla felt her hands close into fists.

The two ships now adjoined, a long set of locking sounds clattered in echoes through the smaller ship. Everyone sat uncertainly. Meredith's mouth was downturned. Dagovaby put his muscular arms behind his head and closed his eyes.

"You're all putting out some serious anxiety," he noted. "Well, except you," he said, glancing at Galla before closing his eyes again. "He's going to use that, you know."

"Don't let him," Galla told her crew. "I'll deal with him."

And she stood up just as Aeriod swept into the room, all in black, his cape spinning around behind him. Everyone stared as Galla approached him, her hair dancing behind her, her back straight, her fists balled. The silence of the room crackled.

"Did you bring it?" Galla asked him promptly.

"Of course I did," replied Aeriod.

They stared at each other.

"Thank you," said Galla. "We'll need to transfer it over. Can you work on the security while we do that?"

"I can," replied Aeriod, elegant and cool in the face of Galla's palpable fire.

"Then let's get started," Galla replied flatly, and she nodded to Jana.

"Jana, if you don't mind working with Rob and Aeriod to update the systems?"

"On it," Jana replied simply, but she did not look enthused.

"The rest of you, if you would please help me get my stone," she called. They all stood.

"I could help—" Aeriod began.

"No thank you," Galla said quickly. "You're already helping. We can do this."

She led Ariel, Dagovaby, Trent, and Meredith to the small docking bay that connected to Aeriod's larger ship. They stepped through and beheld the large, arching ceiling of Aeriod's bay, and the light flickering and winking in every hue of violet from the ruptured side of Galla's enormous geode.

Ariel gasped.

"You were born... from *that*?" she breathed, dumbfounded.

Galla stared at the flashing crystals inside the large rock. Oni-Odi's arms, her own hands plucking a stone off and giving it to Aeriod; these moments met her in a crash and seemed to reverberate through her.

Trent pierced her reverie. "How do we get it out of here?" he asked.

"He's already got it harnessed," Meredith noticed, and Galla could see two sled-like shapes underneath the geode.

"Nothing to it," Dagovaby remarked. "We can pull and push as needed."

And with everyone's combined effort of shoving and turning, the immense stone slid along on its sleds thorough the connector between the ships, and into the smaller ship's bay. Galla stood looking at it in triumph.

She turned to each of them. "I can't thank you enough. Just being near it again . . . Anyway. I don't know what to say. Other than thank you. I hope this is the answer to what we need."

They made their way, sweating, to the round room again, and sank into their seats with cups of water at the ready. Jana leaned into the room and tilted her head at them.

"Did you get the stone?" she asked.

"Yes," Galla replied. "How's it coming along?"

"Oh, we're finished," Jana responded. Her lips twitched. "I don't think Rob is very happy about things."

"What about you? Do you think we have a better chance of not being detected?" Galla asked.

Jana nodded enthusiastically. "I think so. Granted, we don't know what all's out there. But this gives us a fighting chance. So if we need to slip in somewhere undetected, this is as good as it's gonna get."

Galla let out a relieved sigh.

Aeriod appeared behind Jana, who ducked in and sat down.

"What will you do?" he asked Galla.

"I need a drop. And then I'll be back," she answered, avoiding his eyes.

"We're too high up. I'll lower us."

"Fine," she said.

"You're going down inside the Device again?" he asked, following her as she returned to her geode.

Galla walked up to the geode and felt the inside of it, raking her fingers across its purple bumps and spikes. She found a small knob of it and snapped it off. It felt lukewarm in her hand. She looked down at it, at her own stone, and at the stone around Aeriod's neck. Finally she stared straight into his eyes.

"I'm ready to drop," she declared.

"Galla—" he began, reaching for her.

She held her hand up. "No. I'm doing this. Get out of my way."

And she walked over to the wall of the bay and pulled down a compartment with a sky bike. Climbing on and donning a helmet, she yelled over her shoulder, "Seal it off! And let me out."

Aeriod sealed off the rest of the bay. Its door opened. Galla powered up her bike, hovered over the opening, and glanced at him, defiant. His face taut, he nodded. She dropped through.

The wind met her in a crush, buffeting every part of her as the world she knew so well pulled her toward it. For several seconds she allowed herself the thrill of the drop, never wondering what would happen if she let go of the sky bike. She gripped it and watched the colors of the sky flash above and the ground arch upward. Within a half mile of the surface, she powered the bike.

It jerked forward, and she leaned in, lowering until she almost skimmed the hilltops. She did not look for Aeriod's asteroid home. That was a luxury she could not afford, an indulgence that would only cause her pain. She would have liked to see Sumond, but knew she had a little team waiting for her in low orbit. So she thought of them instead. She rose and fell above the hills and valleys, and finally came to the spot. Aeriod had unshielded it for her. She stopped the bike, leapt off, shoved the helmet onto its seat, and looked down into the darkness.

"Here I am again," she muttered. The platform appeared, and she stood on it, hanging over the black abyss. It shot her down and down, and stopped at the familiar level. Where she had seen the visions. She stepped off the platform and faced the hallway with the doors.

"I don't know what to do," she said to the empty space. Her stones warmed against her skin, the one against her neck and the one in her pocket. She took the smaller one out and it glowed, and reflected in the floor and ceiling.

She stepped forward until she could see all the doors from before. Not knowing what else to do, she set the little knob of diamethyst onto the floor. A distant howl of wind dashed against the walls of the pit behind her, and met her as if some spirit had taken form to swirl around her. She looked down at the little knob, and it stopped glowing. It stood still, and the wind died.

She shivered. She would never get used to this space. The

metallic smell, the deadness of it all. Shuddering, she took one final glance at the little diamethyst, and then pelted over to the platform. It roared back up to the surface and she sprang away from it. Looking back, she found the abyss had disappeared, for Aeriod had shielded it again.

She climbed onto her bike, put on the helmet, and shot upward toward the adjoined ships.

Once Galla was inside her ship, Aeriod wheeled around. She could tell he had been pacing.

"What happened?" he asked, genuinely curious. He approached her, stepping very close, by habit and memory. She backed up, took off her helmet, and shoved the sky bike back into its dock.

"Nothing," she answered, but she was not sure. "I put the stone down, and I left. So. I suppose that's that."

Galla quickly strode away from Aeriod, though he walked in his long strides and kept pace with her. She entered the round room and faced her crew.

"That's one down," she announced.

Meredith sighed and smiled, and Rob and Dagovaby clapped. Trent nodded, smiling and looking relieved. Jana gave her a thumbs-up. Ariel watched Galla closely.

Galla turned back to Aeriod, who hovered just behind her.

"Thank you for helping us," she told him. Aeriod gave a small bow, flicking his cape aside. Galla could see Ariel roll her eyes.

"I'm only too glad to help," Aeriod said smoothly, as much to the room as to Galla.

"We'll be on our way, then," Galla answered. "If you don't mind."

"Of course," and Aeriod took her hand and led her out into the hall, away from the others.

"I don't approve," he said to her very quietly.

"I'm not seeking your approval," she whispered. "I have a job to do. You have... however many jobs you need to do. Farming. Governing, maging, scheming. It's none of my concern. And I should not be yours."

"But you always will be," Aeriod said to her.

Galla swallowed. Everything could be easier, she thought for the smallest moment, if she stepped up to him, let him sweep her into his cape, let him ferry her back to his keep. Let him find every pleasure she could possibly have, the galaxy be damned. But she blinked. She thought of her new friends, and she remembered: Aeriod had never really seemed like her friend. She remembered Meredith's words about her husband. She pulled away from Aeriod.

"My crew and I have some planets to find. Goodbye."

And he bowed again, turned, and swept back to his ship.

40

STORMS

Galla sat beside Rob as copilot more and more, to his glee. She did her best to ignore him, focusing completely on her mission. And much of the time this involved a great deal of lip biting on her part, as she tried to figure out what to do next.

The ship handled three junctions' worth of turbulence well. It jettisoned downward into their next destination in the Horseshoe, a binary star system. Galla called for Jana.

"Which planet is this one, Jana?" she asked.

Jana scanned her file. "Fifth one. I can't really figure out the name pronunciations."

"That's all right. Is it inhabited?" Galla asked.

Jana leaned her head to the side. "I didn't query for that. I'll do that now."

"Yes, we'll need to know that for each one," murmured Galla.

Rob opened the control screen so they could have a full view of the system. "Locked in for the fifth planet," he said. "Who goes there?"

Jana wrinkled her brow. "Nothing definitive here," she answered. "I'm confused, though. Someone's been here—someone's been to *all* of them, right?"

"Yes," Galla answered, "we just don't know *when*. I need to know if there's anyone there now."

"Your guess is as good as mine," replied Jana. "I'll check into the others. Though we don't know how current our info is. Let me know if you need anything."

Galla nodded and Jana left. Rob leaned over toward her.

"What's the plan?"

"Take us into orbit," said Galla. "Run a sweep for any signs of settlement. And then we'll hunt for the Device."

She and Rob stared out at the world they now approached. It was grey and brown, with long, dark cracks along its surface. The atmosphere looked thin, with no clouds. Galla furrowed her brow. The planet, to her, looked desolate.

"Not much here," Rob muttered. "We're in orbit. Scanning," and he turned to Galla. "You gonna do another drop like before? What if the sky bike doesn't operate in this environment?"

Galla shrugged. "I'm figuring it out."

Rob nodded slowly and pulled at his chin. "Confidence inspiring."

"Well? What?" Galla flashed at him. "I've only ever been in one of these Devices. Do you see anything or not?"

"Nothing yet," Rob answered. He called Jana on her comms. "You sure about this one, Jana? Not finding anything. I don't suppose you have any more details?"

"Nope," Jana called back. "Nada."

"It could be shielded," Galla said. "Like the one on Rikiloi."

"Don't you think *this* ship would have found it by now?" Rob drawled. "It's your ex-space-wizard's ship, after all."

Galla leaned to meet his smirking face.

"Are you really doing this with me? Still?" she hissed. "Just stop!"

Rob grinned. "I can't help it. He's an ass," and he shrugged and folded his arms, watching Galla's face contort between furious and resigned.

"See? Pegged it," Rob laughed.

"Yes! Fine!" snapped Galla. "He's an ass! That's why he's my *ex*-space-wizard. Or whatever he is."

"Good thing, too," Rob muttered, his smile fading. "You deserve better."

Galla rolled her eyes. "Such as? *You?*"

"What's not to like?" Rob smiled again, leaning forward, his blue eyes flashing under pale eyebrows, his face flushed to his ginger hair. She could smell a faint scent on him, a salty scent that reminded her of the sea on Perpetua. "I'm a good guy. And you're amazing."

Galla considered his amiable face, and for a second she wondered what it would be like to be with someone like Rob. There was a fire to him that she liked very much. She liked his vigor, and his presence. But he irritated her. She leaned back and yawned.

"Awwww," Rob howled, clutching his heart. "Savage!" But his eyes sparkled.

Just then, a chime rang out.

"We've got something!" Rob said excitedly. Galla stared at the screen. The ship had found an indentation near the equator, several meters across.

"That's about the right size, I think," Galla breathed.

"Galla," Rob said in a low voice suddenly. "Don't do the drop."

"Why not?" she asked, incredulous.

"That," said Rob, pointing at the image before them. A billowing dust storm arose just north of the indentation. Soon it would sweep across the area.

"What do we do? Wait it out?" Galla asked.

"I don't think we have a choice," said Rob. "The sky bike might lock up in those conditions, and you'd be stranded."

"Wish we had the Associates' teleportation," remarked Galla.

"Even if we did, you'd be right in the thick of that dust."

Galla tapped her chin. "Odd, don't you think?" she murmured. "That shows up as soon as we approach."

"The winds are reading ninety-five kilometers per hour," Rob told her. "Nasty shit."

Something tickled the edge of Galla's mind. She stood up straight.

"Ariel. Dagovaby," she called on her comms. "Can you come to the cockpit?"

When the two walked in, Galla noticed immediately the dark circles under Ariel's eyes.

"Are you all right?" she asked gently.

Ariel smiled wanly. "I'm a little tired. Have you found something?"

"I think so," Galla answered, gesturing at the window viewer. Ariel and Dagovaby moved closer to it and looked where Galla pointed. "Do you see that dust storm? It appeared right as we approached. I'm pretty sure it's covering an area above a Device."

She looked back and forth between Ariel and Dagovaby, spying how closely they stood together, their hands just touching.

"I'm curious," she said, "can you sense anything when you look there?"

"Do you mean, can I pick up any thoughts?" asked Ariel. Galla nodded. Ariel stared with her large, pale eyes at the mottled surface and especially the storm. She shook her head and tucked her hair behind her ears. Galla's eyes traced a couple of silver strands among Ariel's dark mane.

She looks so tired, Galla thought.

"I can sense something," Dagovaby said, and Galla's eyebrows shot up.

"And when I look down there, I can't read any thoughts, so I'm really relying on Dagovaby's thoughts to sort of translate what he's picking up," Ariel declared.

Ariel searched his face and tracked his thoughts as he watched the planet's surface.

"Broken fragments of something," she murmured. "Fear and anger, maybe?"

"Definitely alarm," agreed Dagovaby. "It's not one single emotion, but several mixed, as if a group were feeling many different things. One of them is terror."

"But why?" Galla wondered. "Fear of us?"

Dagovaby shrugged and sighed. "I can't figure that out. It's a swirl of feelings, almost as if the storm itself were made of feelings. Sounds ridiculous. But there are a lot of strange life forms out there in the galaxy. Maybe it's sentient?"

"A sentient storm?" a level voice said behind them. They turned to see Trent staring inscrutably at the image.

"We don't know," Galla admitted.

She heard a shuffling sound and wheeled around to see Ariel sag to the floor, Dagovaby seizing her just before her head hit the hard surface. Trent rushed forward.

Galla felt her own breath coming in short spurts as she watched the pale woman, limp in Dagovaby's arms.

"What's happened to her?" she cried. Trent checked Ariel's pulse and drew back her eyelids.

Trent said, soothing, "She's all right. She's fainted."

"Can you help her?" Galla asked, her voice rising.

Dagovaby looked fondly up at her with his dark, gold-ringed eyes. "She'll be okay, Galla," he assured her.

"I thought she looked tired earlier." Galla knelt and stroked her friend's cheek and squeezed her hand.

"Let's get her to her room so she can rest," Trent advised. Dagovaby lifted Ariel easily and carried her, with Galla close behind.

Once there, Trent held a sensor over Ariel and swept it along her body from head to feet. Dagovaby stood on one side of her and Galla on the other. They looked at each other for a moment.

"You love her, don't you?" she whispered to him.

Dagovaby's mouth twitched, almost into a smile, but his brow was creased with concern. "So much," he said in a quiet voice.

Trent cleared his throat. "She's dehydrated and fatigued. She'll need to get more fluids and more sleep, and she'll be good to go."

Galla exhaled in relief, and Dagovaby lifted Ariel's hand and kissed it.

Trent then said, "And there's something else."

"Yes?" Galla asked, not sure what she was seeing in Trent's face.

Dagovaby said, "It's all right, Trent, you can relax."

"Do you know, then?" Trent asked him.

Galla watched Dagovaby's expression change from worry to elation to worry back again.

"Are you sure?" Dagovaby asked him.

"Quite," said Trent.

Galla threw her hands in the air.

"What! What is it?" she demanded.

Trent looked at Galla and said, "Ariel is pregnant."

Galla opened her eyes wide. At that moment, Meredith rushed in.

"What's happened? Rob said Ariel fainted!" she said breathlessly. Galla stepped back to let Ariel's mother in next to her daughter.

Ariel stirred and blinked.

"Ohhh," she groaned. She pushed herself up on her elbows and looked at everyone standing around her. Trent brought her an electrolyte mixture and urged her to drink. She took two sips and leaned back.

"What are you all staring at?"

"You—you fainted," Galla began.

"Oh," said Ariel. "That's embarrassing."

"Ariel," Dagovaby said, and Ariel turned to look at him. She gasped loudly and sat up in a rush, but Dagovaby and Meredith cradled her.

Ariel looked from Dagovaby to Trent to Meredith to Galla.

"Holy shit, I'm pregnant!" she exclaimed.

Meredith cried out in a high whoop, then laughed. Palpable relief circled through the room. Soon Rob and Jana joined them, and offered their congratulations.

"But *how*?" Ariel asked aloud, zeroing in on Trent particularly. "I mean, we took precautions! I didn't think it was possible!"

Dagovaby looked at Trent with a questioning expression.

Trent smirked. "Hybrid vigor?"

Ariel shivered. "How else will this be different? Will I be okay? Will the baby be okay?"

Trent answered, "Well, so far I would say you're having a normal pregnancy. But you've got to stay on top of your own health. We can't know about the normal fetal development of this kind of hybrid, which is probably mostly human."

Ariel held her hands to her face.

Galla said quickly, "Ariel, we are here for you. All of us," and her eyes flashed around the room, both rallying and warning her crew.

"How can I help out like this, though?" Ariel moaned.

Meredith laughed softly. "You don't stop being who you are," she answered. "Keep doing what you want to do. When the time comes, I'll help."

"We need you, Ariel," said Galla, "so let us know how we can help you."

Trent said, "As you get further along, if this functions as a normal human pregnancy, you'll get more energy back. Your hormone levels will fluctuate." He sighed almost imperceptibly to himself, and Galla watched his eyes droop slightly. "I have to say, it'll be good to bring a new life."

Meredith pressed her hand onto his shoulder and they exchanged looks.

Then she turned to Ariel.

"Just let it roll, dear," Meredith said.

Rob chirped, "Well, congrats and all, but—Galla? What's the next plan?"

Meredith smiled fondly at Dagovaby. "I'll stay with her," she said. "Go and see how you're needed."

Galla joined Rob, who glanced back at a lingering Dagovaby and whispered, "Fuck! What now? We can't do this sort of shit with a baby on board! Do we take them back to Ika Nui?"

She scowled at him. "What for? We're in the safest ship we can get. You heard Meredith. Ariel's not down for the count. She's just . . . she's—well, she's making a person, but she's still her own person. As long as she wants to contribute, she will."

Then she felt a deep, hollow loneliness. She knew she could never experience what Ariel could. It felt like another gulf between them, one that could never be crossed. She was not sure what she was feeling. But it pulled at her in a sort of pain.

Rob glanced sidewise at her.

"Is that something you want?" He fumbled for words. "I mean. Do you want a family? One day? I never really thought about it before. Out here."

Galla still felt lost in herself. "I guess I hadn't either. But. I can't."

Rob searched her face and dared to reach out and touch her hand.

"What, duty and all that?" he asked softly. She looked up at him, his bright blue eyes focused on her. She did not mind his touch. But she felt confused and turbulent.

"No, I mean it's not possible... for me," she said to him directly.

"Oh," he said, not looking away. "I didn't mean to offend you."

"You didn't. It's just the way it is," said Galla.

Rob straightened up and squeezed both her hands. "There's nothing wrong with that," he said.

Dagovaby shuffled to make his presence known.

Galla stepped back from Rob, blushing, and he turned to shake Dagovaby's hand.

"Congrats, Papa," Rob said, grinning.

Dagovaby smirked back at him. "Thanks, man."

Galla took a deep breath and said, "Now. The storm. When it's died down a bit, I want to drop in. Dagovaby, can you join me?"

Dagovaby blinked and nodded. "Sure," he said.

"If we have a sentient storm on our hands," said Galla, "I want to know what's going on with it. I need to get in that Device, no matter what."

"I don't see any decrease in wind speed," Rob reported.

"Then I'm not waiting any longer," Galla declared, her hair drifting all around her shoulders. "Let's drop."

41

VOICES IN THE WIND

Ariel soon joined them in the cockpit. They all stared at her, and she rolled her eyes.

"I'm fine," she snapped. "I just have to remember to take some naps and drink more water. Did you think I'd miss this?"

Galla lifted her chin. "Absolutely not. It's totally up to you, what you want to do."

"I know it is," Ariel said with some heat. "No, Dagovaby, you can't go there," she warned, and the two locked eyes. "I want to work, and I plan to work in any way I can, for as long as I'm able to. I'm still *me*."

"We're headed down now," Galla told her, and she hefted her helmet in her hands. Ariel dashed forward and kissed her on the cheek.

"Be safe," she said.

Then Ariel hugged Dagovaby. "Well, this is a good test for us. Let's see how far apart we can be and still share a link."

Dagovaby lifted up her hair and kissed her neck, her cheeks, and her lips. Ariel flushed pink. Their foreheads touched, and then they pulled apart. Dagovaby sighed.

Galla shoved her helmet onto her suit. Dagovaby climbed into his own suit and helmeted. They nodded to Rob and headed to the bay.

"Are you sure the bike can handle this?" Dagovaby asked, his voice uncertain.

"Pretty sure," Galla answered.

But she was not entirely convinced. And if it had only been her on the bike, she absolutely would not have worried. But she was carrying Dagovaby as well. She swallowed. Her mouth had gone dry. She had to make sure this man got back safely.

It hit her suddenly. A crushing sensation pummeled her just as she sat on the sky bike. What if she caused him harm, not intentionally but incidentally? She could never forgive herself.

"You don't have to come," she said suddenly to Dagovaby. "I'm serious. You can stay here with Ariel."

Dagovaby looked at her with exasperation. "So Ariel can do anything she wants, but I can't? Come on. We'll both live our own lives, Galla."

"I just—I just don't want anything to happen to either of you," Galla wheezed nervously.

"Calm down! I can't feel you, but I can tell you're panicking," said Dagovaby. "Try taking deep breaths."

Galla obliged. "You're just—you're all I have," she said, appalled to find herself streaming tears.

Dagovaby said, "Then let's get this job done so we can be back with our people."

Galla grew calmer. She nodded.

"All right. Are you ready?"

"Well, not really, but we're doing this," Dagovaby said, his voice barely shaking.

They sat on the bike, Galla in front and Dagovaby behind.

"Rob," called Galla. "Open it up."

The bay opened, and Galla moved the bike over the gaping hole. Rob had lowered the ship just above the storm, and the upper-level winds buffeted the ship, rocking it.

"Now!" Galla shouted, and they dropped.

The wind instantly snatched the sky bike. Swept into the maelstrom, Galla held fast to the bike, and Dagovaby clung to her waist. She gritted her teeth against the pressure of his arms as he roared.

"Hold on!" she screamed. But she was not sure he could hear her, as even in the helmet the winds shrieked and the airborne grit blasted them. She fought the cyclone to regain control of the bike as its engine whined in protest.

"It's gonna destroy the bike!" she yelled. "I've got to let it ride out!"

Dagovaby shook behind her, convulsing, and she felt his grip loosen a bit.

"Dagovaby! Dagovaby! Hold on!" she shouted desperately. He did not respond. *I'm going to lose him! What do I do?*

Her own stone heated against her breast until she felt scorched, and she lifted her voice in agony. But she felt a moment of clarity in the searing heat. She seized Dagovaby's weakening arms and clenched them into her hips with her elbows. She squeezed her hands onto the bike's controls and turned it into the vortex.

They whipped around and around and down, the light dimming in the brown-grey-rust blur of the cyclone. At its base the storm flung them as a unit with such force, Galla had to let go of the bike and hold Dagovaby. She twisted in the air to land beneath him to soften his landing.

She hit the ground with a sickening crack. Dagovaby lay sprawled and unconscious on top of her, and she squirmed out from beneath him and gently turned him over. She brushed the dirt off his faceplate with her gloved hands.

"Dag!" she yelled. "Wake up! Please wake up!"

His eyes did not open.

"No no no *no NO!*" screamed Galla.

I've killed him.

She staggered to her feet and then doubled over in anguish. She could see nothing, her eyes pooled with tears, her hair twisted into her face. So she did not see, at first, that the storm had vanished.

She wheezed. She stumbled back to Dagovaby, knelt beside him, and brought her head to her knees. Her stone lay between the two of them.

"Ariel, I'm so sorry," she whispered.

What do I do? I can't leave him here.

Her stone burned hot between her body and his. She did not mind its pain, as her spirit hurt far more. She knew she must find the Device, and as she did on Rikiloi, she would deliver the little diamethyst in its pouch in her pocket. It also felt hot, like a little burning stab into her thigh.

And then she was flung backward. Dagovaby's arms had shot out and he lay like a starfish, convulsing.

Galla let out a small scream. She reached out to touch him.

"Dagovaby!" she cried. She seized one of his hands and his tremors shook her entire body. But she held fast. His eyes flicked open.

A choked sob left Galla's throat and she gripped his hand.

"You're alive!"

Dagovaby's jerks and twitches slowed, and finally he lay staring up at her, completely exhausted.

"Did we make it?" he croaked.

She laughed through her tears. "We did. So far."

Dagovaby let out a long, loud groan. "I feel like pulp," he muttered. "I'm sorry, I don't know what happened. The storm—the storm was full of voices. They overcame me and I—I don't remember anything after that."

"Voices?" repeated Galla, wondering. "I didn't hear any voices."

"Feelings," Dagovaby said. "But they—they were horrible. So much pain."

He gasped for several minutes. Galla held his large hand in her two small ones.

"Easy," she soothed. "You've been through a lot."

He turned his eyes up to hers again. Their gold rings looked dull through his faceplate, like tarnished brass. "How did I survive that?"

Galla felt her face burn.

"I'm—I'm not really sure. I think my stone—or something—made me stronger. And I tried to get us safely down. But we were thrown and—and I could only try to cushion you."

"You saved me!" said Dagovaby. He squeezed her hands. "Thank you." He turned his head back to look at the sky. "I know she must be worried."

He slowly pushed himself up onto his elbows.

"The storm is gone!" he exclaimed. "Good. I don't know if I could handle that again. I've never felt anything like it before. All that pain —just complete torment. What was it?"

"I don't know," admitted Galla. "But what if it comes back? I think we had better get to the Device, and I can deliver my stone."

"Where's the bike?" asked Dagovaby.

Galla looked up at the small hills and distant mesas, dull and dead. The sky had turned a salmon color in the absence of the storm.

"It was flung pretty far, I think," she muttered. "One thing at a time. We'll find it."

She helped him up.

A crackling sound made them both jump. Galla slapped her communicator.

"We're all right," she gasped. The comms link crackled again.

"Thank God," she heard Meredith say. "We'd lost . . . sign . . . you."

Rob spoke in broken bursts. "Trent . . . you to know . . . levels . . . ation . . ." And the comms link stopped.

Galla and Dagovaby looked at each other.

"Radiation," she said.

"Well, shit," said Dagovaby. "Can't do anything about that now. We'll have to clean up when we get back."

If we can get back, Galla thought. She let out a sigh of relief that he could not read her mind. But he watched her.

"Now what?" he asked.

Galla squinted. Little eddies of sand swept up into dust devils, obscuring their view of the horizon. "I think the Device is that way," she answered, pointing.

So they set off. As they did, Galla began to notice bumps on the ground, almost as high as her knees. They were arranged in long curves. Finally, after seeing five at regular intervals, she bent down and swept the dust off one of them.

"Look at this," she called. Dagovaby stepped over. He looked at the markings she had uncovered. "What do you think they are?"

"No idea," he said, and he shifted his feet around. "Galla, this place is disturbing. I keep getting ... echoes, for lack of a better word, of the things I felt in that storm."

Galla stood up and searched the man's face. His gold eye rings glowed bright.

"Something happened here," said Dagovaby. "And whatever it was, it's left some residual ... presence, I guess. Like memories of pain."

A deep rumbling met their ears. Galla and Dagovaby found themselves slipping as the ground beneath them shook. The arranged lumps on the ground looked more prominent, as if they had risen slightly. Galla scanned the horizon in all directions, but could see nothing but the wind-blown landscape. She shivered.

"Let's keep going," she said cautiously.

More tremors arose. Again, the shapes in the ground appeared to grow. They were soon as high as Galla's shoulders. And they revealed more markings, in some language neither she nor Dagovaby could discern. Their comms link still did not function reliably. Dagovaby recorded the images on some of these growing pillars. They pressed on, the wind rising again, and adjusted their helmets to combat the dust.

Finally Galla could see a dip in the near distance, and she could tell by the breadth of it that it must be the entrance to a Device. She remembered the size of the one on Rikiloi. The ground shook again. Now the pillars were taller than Dagovaby. And there was a pattern to them: they were all lined up toward the Device.

Galla glanced at Dagovaby, who had begun to shuffle his feet slightly. He placed his hands on his temples as they approached the huge hole in the ground.

"Are you all right?" she asked him. The veins in his forehead had begun to bulge.

"The pain," he gasped. "I can feel them again ... with every step it's stronger ... they are screaming!"

She held his arm, and he staggered forward.

"Stop," she told him. "This is hurting you. You can't go on. I can go by myself."

"I ... have to ..." groaned Dagovaby. "They ... want me to ..."

She said to him, "Listen. You might experience strange things in the Device, maybe even stranger than this. Visions. I don't know ... but that's what happened to me."

He nodded.

Galla watched him helplessly as he lurched step by step with her toward the edge of the hole. The wind whipped up and out of the entrance, its updraft hot on their faces and sharply metallic in scent. Galla could just make out a small platform, corroded and greatly aged.

"There," she said, and Dagovaby followed her gesture. "Let's see if it still works."

Dagovaby nodded, grunting in great discomfort. They eased onto the platform, and Galla urged him to sit. Her stone began to glow again, and she felt the one in her pocket grow warm. The platform screeched immediately, its sound flying into the howl of the wind, which had begun to spin again, less violently than before, but with something like intention. The platform lowered quickly, but not as fast as the one on Rikiloi had. They moved down into the depths of the pit, the wind whistling and crying and spinning around them.

They reached a landing, very like the one on Rikiloi, but lit only with a faint, sickly yellow light. Galla pulled Dagovaby to his feet. He was sweating.

"Can you walk?" she asked him, concerned he might collapse at any second.

He nodded. They entered a hallway that seemed to lead nowhere. Dark, vacant doorways led off in multiple directions. Galla and Dagovaby stood very still. Neither wanted to step forward. But her stone glowed again, and so she walked ahead in the dimness. They lifted their faceplates. The purple light from the stone cheered both of them, and Dagovaby was able to stand straight again.

"I feel them," he said suddenly. "They feel . . . hopeful," and he looked down at Galla. "It's you. They're hopeful because of *you*."

Galla's forehead creased together between her brows. Then it all hit her. She began to see flashes of scenes she had seen in the other Device, as well as new ones. A black hole destroying a planet, and pulling a vessel of some kind into it. A human male, sitting in a small ship, writhing and screaming, his eyes finally freezing into diamonds. A dome structure, covered in vines. And she heard that voice again, calming, reassuring: *"It doesn't matter how long. I want to do this. I'll be able to live as long as you."*

And then she saw a beautiful city, lush and green and violet with vegetation, with tall white columns leading to an ornate, fenced place, a huge gaping hole, which small creatures flew down into and rose from again. And in the sky, a dark shape covered their sun, and long tendrils spun out and down. The people who dwelled there, round and comfortable and robed and at peace, could not see what she could see approaching them. But then they all felt it, and the shrieks began.

A great fire bloomed on the horizon, and she watched in horror as it melted the landscape and its people. Those who survived crawled away from the shapes they could not see, which reached for them and lapped at their very souls. And everything blew away in a cloud of dust, left to swirl in little eddies.

"You came to help us," said a multitude of soft voices in whispered layers. *"We did not know, at first. No one has come here for many years, due to the contamination. Some tried to live here and operate in secret. But we screamed for long enough that they all left. But you did not leave."*

"What happened here?" Galla asked aloud, and her voice fell flat and without any echo despite the vast space behind her.

"The entity came here, and those who serve it brought us fire from the sky, so that we would bend and break, and the entity could feed."

"Paosh Tohon?" said Galla.

A long, high howl met their ears. Dagovaby looked wretched.

"I felt them *all*," he said to her. "The pain of those left behind, it's still echoing here. Like a ghost."

Galla shuddered.

"*Here we died. Everything that we loved, and lived, and dreamt, it all died. And yet the entity forced many to live, a continual feast. It took them somewhere. And we could not follow. We could not rescue them. But perhaps you could.*"

Galla shook her head. "I don't know how to do that. All I can do is leave part of a stone here, until we know what to do with it."

"*It will remain safe here.*"

Galla searched for her smaller stone, and after finding it, set it down upon the floor of the dim hall. There it shone, pale lavender in the darkness. Dagovaby looked relieved.

"Their pain is gone," he said, smiling.

"Then we should leave," said Galla. "We'll do what we can," she added, gesturing her arms around her. "I don't want to see this happen to anywhere else."

They walked back to the platform, and it rose to the surface. It jerked and clanked and fell still so that they could get out. To their amazement, their bike stood waiting for them at the edge of the abyss. Neither questioned how it had got there, and each shivered. Their comms popped, and then they could hear Rob's voice clearly.

"Everything all right?"

"Yes," answered Galla. "We're coming up."

42

RESPITE

Chucking her helmet off, Galla watched Dagovaby limp from a decontamination chamber out of the bay. She pushed her rebellious hair into a topknot, rubbed her aching back, and walked guiltily toward the cockpit. She spied Ariel's small form reaching up to the towering Dagovaby. Her green eyes flashed to Galla, and Galla swallowed. Trent approached Dagovaby and asked him to move his arms and legs.

"Nothing so bad," Trent announced reassuringly. "Ice the knee and you should be good to go in no time. Take this," and he gave Dagovaby a small slip of medicine. "Put it on your tongue, and you won't have any ill effects from the radiation. Still, it's a wonder you're not in worse shape."

"She broke the fall," Dagovaby said simply, turning to nod at Galla. Ariel wrapped her arm around Dagovaby's waist and beamed at Galla in gratitude.

"I wish I had gone alone," said Galla ruefully. "But with you there, we learned much more, I think."

The four of them headed to the round room and found Meredith there. Her fingers were crossed in repose on top of some embroidery work, a swirling slip of saffron fabric dotted with scarlet thread. Galla sighed in relief at the sight of her, but wondered at the look in the elderly lady's fading green eyes. She decided to sit next to Meredith.

"Are you all right?" Galla asked, her hands balled on her lap.

"Yes, dear, yes," replied Meredith. "Just a little tired is all. And I find my eyes are not as good as they used to be. I've not been sewing as much, and embroidering . . . well, it's just a little harder to focus. But enough about me! You had an adventure down there, I take it?"

Galla soaked in Meredith's warm interest. She could never tire of it, and felt again wistfulness, a tugging at her innermost thoughts, reminding her that Oni-Odi was gone and that she had no other true family. Ariel had a mother, a partner, and was growing a child. Galla had none of those things. And though she did not feel envy for Ariel, she felt an ache that the gap between her and Ariel kept widening rather than closing.

Meredith, ever observant, gently nudged Galla by leaning over and touching shoulders.

"Go on, everybody's here," she said softly. "Why don't you tell us what happened?"

So Galla and Dagovaby recounted the terrible winds, the voices, and the visions and emotions. A pall dropped over the group.

"Paosh Tohon destroyed that world and its people," said Galla solemnly. "It will keep happening. But we have to keep trying to stop it."

"So what's next, Captain Deia?" Rob asked cheerfully, his arms crossed and his feet propped on the table's edge.

Captain! she thought. *I like that.*

"Onward," Galla replied. "With Rikiloi and the storm world behind us, there are nineteen more worlds on our list. We work our way through the Horseshoe. It's going to take time, and we have to work our way from one side to the other. We started in an odd spot, with Rikiloi. But we'll have to make do. Maybe if we work our way to one end, we can jump across to the other and see what's in that space between."

"We're still not sure there's really anything there," Ariel pointed out.

"No, but I'm going to assume something is. And maybe, even if we can't find it, we'll find evidence that something is protected there. It's worth checking out." And Galla turned to Rob.

"Have you worked out junction coordinates for these worlds? I know it's not as straightforward as going star to star in our horseshoe," she added.

Rob winked at her. "You know it!" he replied. He took his feet off the table and leaned in on it with his elbows. "The next one is an oddball. It's a moon. But a large moon, relatively. Around a gas giant. It looks like it's still living. In fact the bio signatures for it are incredible! That'll be a switch."

"Good," said Galla, relieved. "I need a break from dead worlds. How soon will we be there?"

"Twelve days," he answered.

"That's the closest world?" gasped Jana.

"The closest one with a Device," Rob answered. "If we need anything, we can make a pit stop somewhere else."

Ariel smiled. "Good," she said, glancing at Dagovaby.

"Enjoy the break!" Galla cried. Then she noted out of the corner of her eyes that Meredith clasped her own hands tightly. A little creeping chill worked its way through Galla. What was happening with Meredith?

Before she could speak to Meredith again at the table, Rob motioned to her.

"Can we talk for a sec?" he asked.

Galla nodded. She rubbed her neck, which was sore from breaking Dagovaby's fall.

"Meet me in my office," he said. Then he saw Galla's quizzical look and rolled his eyes. "The *cockpit*."

Galla sighed and followed Rob, sliding her feet along the sleek corridor floors, lit by embedded silver lighting. Everything about the ship reminded her of Aeriod, except for its pilot. Rob walked along with a bounce, and an airy demeanor.

Rob knows he's alive, Galla thought suddenly. *Everything about him. He knows he's alive and he's mortal. There's no stagnation. He pulses.*

And that was the difference between him and Aeriod, she realized suddenly. Rob would never take anything for granted. The man had nothing other than his pilot seat. No grand home, nor grander illusions. He was a fiery spirit, unabashed. Galla felt suddenly intensely attracted to him, so much so that it startled her.

Rob turned to her in the cockpit and patted the copilot chair. Galla sat in it, discomfited by her awakened attraction. She fought the urge to fidget, and gave him clear-eyed attention. His strawberry-blond lashes blinked rapidly as he watched her.

"Galla," he said quietly, "I think we need to talk about some situations around here."

"Like what?" Galla asked, leaning forward.

Rob shook his head and sighed. "Like Ariel," he said. "Look, I had to come in here to get away from her. Maybe she's reading my mind right now, I don't know. But if she's looking at me, she's totally reading me. So."

"What's the problem?" Galla wanted to know.

"Come on! She's pregnant! How's this going to work? We have one person who's a nurse, Trent. That's just one problem. How's she going to help out when she's further along? Don't you think it's too big a risk?"

Galla fumed. "That's not up to you. It's up to her. I really think she can do anything she likes, and she's an incredible asset to the team. She's our only telepath! Also, her mother is with us."

Rob raised his hands in the air. "I'm not trying to be an asshole here, Galla, I swear," he said. "But like . . . what if something were to happen, something bad? And look. I've known Meredith for a little while and I—I don't know how to say this without sounding like a shithead. But, Galla, she's getting old. It's more obvious every day."

Galla felt a stab of anxiety and surprise. She had hoped she was imagining that there had been something afoot with Meredith. "Is anything wrong with her? She mentioned her vision not being as good."

Rob rubbed his hands over his face. He sighed. "I don't know if she would tell me or anyone else if there were something wrong," he admitted. "I'm just saying we need to think about contingency plans. I know this is a fancy ship, and it's got resources that can help us, but . . . just hear me out. If things get dicey, I don't want to be responsible for putting that family in harm's way."

"It's your job to keep us all out of harm's way. Mine and yours," Galla added emphatically, with color rising in her cheeks.

"I get it, I know," Rob answered her. "But *if something goes down*, I am going to make the call to put them somewhere safe."

"Where is safer than this ship? It's protected! They'd be more vulnerable away from it."

"That's your opinion," Rob argued. "I don't agree completely. I mean, just so you know, I have a course laid in for Ika Nui as a last resort. Okay? I'm sticking with that as a backup."

Galla took a deep breath and slowly exhaled. She repeated this a few times, as the Curator Loreena had taught her on Perpetua.

"I don't like any of this," she confessed.

"I know," Rob said, shaking his head. "I don't like even thinking about it. But you and I, we have to."

"Yes," agreed Galla. "I don't want to tell anyone else this, though, unless they ask. But if you know of anything wrong with Meredith, please let me know. I'll see what I can find out. And Rob?" She almost did not want to ask, but she had seen *something* in Trent's face she could not quite recognize when he examined Ariel.

"Yep?" he asked, arms behind his head.

"Is . . . is Trent all right?"

"Jesus, I hope so—he's our only medic of any kind," Rob quipped.

"That's not what I meant. He seemed . . . sad somehow."

Rob frowned. "Yes. Well. He . . . lost his wife on Ika Nui. She was the first person to die after Mandira was moved."

Galla gasped. "What happened?"

Rob lowered his head and sighed. "They were on an expedition, exploring the wildlife. Which is wall-to-wall there, by the way—I'm not a fan. But anyway. Apparently she had grabbed hold of some sort of plant or fungus or something, big, and it broke her skin. And . . . she reacted, she anaphylaxed."

"What?" asked Galla, her eyes wide and sad.

"She started choking, couldn't breathe, and then she died," Rob said firmly.

Galla made a low sound, exhaling as she did so, and sat stunned.

"He kept saying, 'She was laughing. I heard her laugh.' And stuff like that. It took him a long time to process it. I mean, it would for anyone, right? But maybe especially because he did what he could and he still lost her. It was a fucking *mess*."

"How devastating!" said Galla through tears. "And now, if Meredith is ill . . . how must he feel? Rob. I can't bear it if something happens to her!"

Rob lowered his bright blue eyes. "You love her too, don't you? She's everyone's aunt or mom or grandma."

She straightened up and lowered her eyes. "I never had any of those," she told him.

"Oh," said Rob, blinking. "Now it makes sense why you're so defensive. No family, eh?"

"No . . . not really, not anymore," said Galla.

Rob shrugged. "Look, I don't know what your past is—I mean I know about *him,* but aside from that. I just think we can make a good team here. Gotta see eye to eye."

"We won't always," cautioned Galla. "I'm still in command of this mission. I have the final say."

Rob dipped his head. "Noted. Now, how will we spend these next couple of weeks?" And he flashed an impish grin at her. Galla lifted her eyebrows high.

"Researching," she answered demurely. Rob snorted and shook his head. Galla smirked, rose, and left.

43

TEMERITY

Aeriod glowered at the Associates. They stood with their shadowy Summoners convened in an orbiter high above the ancient, rocky world of Ezeldae. He had answered their call reluctantly, and really only at the urging of Sumond did he heft himself back out of his asteroid castle. He knew what was coming.

"You, as Governor and mage, and host to refugees on various worlds in your jurisdiction, stand before us to hear judgment on your actions," the spindly being Ushalda hooted.

Aeriod resisted the human gesture of rolling his eyes, but barely. A habit he had picked up from his time on Mandira, though he would never admit to such "contamination" by the humans. Instead he interlocked his long fingers under his chin.

He said silkily, "And what actions do you judge? Did I not agree to train Galla-Deia? That I did, and then she continued her training elsewhere. Did I not agree to maintain the security of the worlds I govern? That entails having scouts working for me to secure boundaries, and intercept any transmissions. I have fulfilled my end of the bargain for you. Now we sit and bide our time, do we? For the Event? For Paosh Tohon to lie waiting for soul-carrion when systems shred apart? Leave me be. I've done my bit."

"Without Oni-Odi," Ushalda admonished, "we face these threats with no assistance from the last of the Seltra."

Aeriod sighed, bored. "Isn't it time you moved on?"

The Associates rumbled and hissed and shuffled at this.

"They were our templates!" cried Ushalda. "We are meant to continue their work, and preserve their peace!"

"Are we?" Aeriod asked, his eyes like half-lidded silver crescents. "And what peace would that be, exactly?"

He walked into the center of the room and whirled around on his heel, spinning his vast, black cape.

"When," he continued, "have any of us ever known peace for long? There have always been struggles. I would say we've grown soft. Otherwise I wouldn't have had to dash across the galaxy to snip some humans and a stalk of Paosh Tohon from a star system no one cared much about."

"You retrieved the necessary humans," Ushalda remarked.

"I did, again, fulfilling my mission," Aeriod drawled.

"What of this relationship with Galla-Deia? She is the last remaining shred of anything related to Oni-Odi, yet you dared pursue her?"

Aeriod's eyes flashed.

"My teaching had ended. What happened after that is none of your concern. We—" he started and he felt his breath catch, envisioning her warm eyes looking into his and her wild hair twisting into his own silver mane, her lips tracing a path along his chin, her fingers softly touching the points of his ears. "We entered a mutual . . . relationship. And—and anyway, that's over."

He exhaled. He was furious, and sick, and sad. He never wanted to talk about his time with Galla in front of these leering, inept beings. But he had always known it would come to this. It made nothing easier. His deep, low heartbeat thudded in his own ears, so that he did not hear the disapproving sounds of the Associates. *I imploded the one good thing I've ever had. And now I have to stand here and tell them about it.*

"I've had enough of this. I'm not saying anything more," Aeriod hissed suddenly. "You can count on me to keep up surveillance. But it is time to prepare my worlds for attacks as Paosh Tohon's strength builds. I can assure you, the attacks will grow more brazen. There seems to be a cult-like affiliation growing. Supporters of Paosh Tohon who see it as an antidote, as it were, to your sagging leadership."

"You dare defy us!" the Speaker of Bitikk's voice ricocheted in the chamber.

"Yes, I do, in fact, defy you!" Aeriod boomed. "You disgust me. The lot of you. You've allowed the galaxy to go soft, its denizens restive. Enemies crawl out from their holes, emboldened. You take innocent beings that could aid all of us, and you torture them *for decades,* just to see what they can or cannot do." His eyes blazed, daring anyone to look at him.

"At least I *love* Galla. And want her to succeed. I wonder if you do. Because she'll need all the help she can get. And I don't think any of you has the will. Not even half the will she has in one strand of her hair!"

"She rejected us, and you," Ushalda remarked.

Aeriod crossed the floor in a flash and lifted Ushalda up like a stick he might throw. "Enough!" he yelled.

The guards had surrounded him. He put Ushalda back down again quickly, breathing hard.

He nodded. "I see. I'll be leaving now. Soon you'll have enough mess to deal with. And you seem not to want our help. Because, believe it or not, we are all helping. You may not like our style. But soon you won't have a choice."

And he tossed his silver hair over his shoulders, waved away the guards, and marched to the bay where his ship waited. As he steered it away from the orbit of Ezeldae, he considered.

"She won't like it. And he won't want to. But I'm going to try again," he murmured to himself. He set his course for the long flight ahead.

44

AN ECHO FROM THE PAST

Shrieks. Galla shot up and threw back her quilt. She saw Meredith rise, wobbly, from her bed.

"It's Ariel," the elderly woman said hoarsely, hastening to dress.

Galla felt her throat tighten.

"I'll go with you—take my arm," she insisted, and Meredith obliged gratefully.

They sped down the hallway to Ariel and Dagovaby's quarters, and he met them at the door. Meredith's green eyes were huge, and she lunged forward toward the door, but Dagovaby held her back.

Galla demanded, "What is going on? Tell us!"

"Let me in!" cried Meredith.

"Hold on," said Dagovaby. "I will!" he hastily added, seeing and feeling the frantic concern of Ariel's mother rise within her. "First, you need to know something."

Galla perched one hand on her hip and the other under Meredith's arm for support. She craned to see Ariel, who wept inconsolably.

"She's terrified," murmured Dagovaby softly. "She began dreaming, and then I sensed fear building in her and tried to wake her up. She started screaming, saying something about 'Veronica,' and would not listen to anything I said. Then she started raving, saying, 'She's got him! She's got our baby!' and that's all I can get out of her."

Meredith pushed forward, shoving the much larger man aside. He stood gaping helplessly and reentered the room. A small crowd had gathered outside the door.

"Is she okay?" Jana whispered to Galla.

Galla frowned. "I don't know."

Trent arrived with the expression of someone yanked from deep sleep by an earthquake. He, too, rushed into the room and over to Ariel, whose mother knelt beside her and stroked her long hair.

"Ariel," Trent said urgently. "Your pulse is very high. I need you to try and calm yourself. Take deep breaths, like this," and he demonstrated. He checked her vitals.

Then he stared at Dagovaby, and then at Galla.

"What is it, Trent?" Galla pressed him.

"The baby," murmured Trent.

Galla went cold and clasped her hands to her chest.

"No, no," he said in a soothing voice to Ariel and Dagovaby. "It's nothing wrong. Just . . . unusual." Both stared at him with wide eyes, and their hands squeezed together.

"What do you mean?" Ariel asked, sitting up on her elbows. Her pale face, stained with splotches from crying, furrowed in tension and worry.

"The fetus should be approximately three weeks along," Trent said slowly, "if this were a full human baby. What I am reading on your scans, and by the look of your abdomen, this child is now entering into its second trimester."

Galla gasped when Ariel clasped her belly. It had grown noticeably.

"I—I've only worn loose clothing the past several days, because nothing else fit. I wasn't sure how normal it was," she added.

Meredith nodded. "I wondered why you were already loosening your tops!"

Ariel lay back on her pillow. Tears streamed from the corners of her eyes.

"Is it a boy?" she asked, staring at the ceiling.

Trent swept his scan-wand over her. He grinned at Ariel and Dagovaby in turn.

"You will have a boy," he said, smiling. Then he quickly frowned as Ariel began gasping and sobbing again. Dagovaby and Meredith knelt on either side of her, telling her in quiet voices to calm down.

"Veronica will get him. I saw it," she choked.

Galla felt an icy chill, and she stifled a shiver. The horror of what Ariel feared shook her.

She said quickly, "Nobody's getting your baby, Ariel. I will make sure of that!"

But Ariel ignored everyone and continued weeping. Jana and Rob, who had been standing outside the hall, sighed to each other and retreated.

Meredith looked up at Galla and said, "I think we should talk." She turned to her daughter and told her, "My dear, I will be right back. Dagovaby is here. Trent is here. We'll be right back."

She pulled Galla along with her out into the hall.

"Who is Veronica?" Galla asked, mystified.

Meredith, who looked as if she had aged ten more years in the past ten minutes, sighed wearily. She said, "Veronica was another telepath in a program Ariel enrolled in years ago. Both were lost . . . Hasn't Aeriod told you any of this?"

"A bit," Galla responded, "but he never mentioned anyone by the name of Veronica."

Meredith nodded. "Likely he emphasized Paosh Tohon. She became a host for that entity, and tried to overtake Mandira Station."

"I was not aware Paosh Tohon had used humans as hosts. I remembered it had attacked and killed other humans," Galla said, growing uneasy. In that moment, Galla realized just what they were up against. If Paosh Tohon could use a human in such a way rather than simply torturing to gain power, that meant anyone could fall sway.

"So," Galla said slowly, "when Ariel and Forster and Aeriod

purged that piece of Paosh Tohon from the human system, what happened to . . . Veronica?"

Meredith's face crumpled in wrinkles. "I assumed she was dead," she said in a low voice. "I hoped she was. But now I wonder."

Galla clasped Meredith's hands.

"Meredith, wait," she said, her voice clear and sure. "Dagovaby said Ariel was dreaming. And that dream showed this Veronica taking their baby away," and Galla watched as Meredith began to tremble. "It was just a dream. Nothing more. A terrible nightmare, but only that."

Meredith swallowed and nodded, and wiped the crinkled corners of her eyes.

"I hope so, dear," she said in a low voice.

"I'll go and talk to her," Galla declared.

They made their way back to Ariel's room, where Trent met Galla at the door.

"I think it was a very vivid nightmare," he told her. "This is not unusual for telepaths. But given the fact that Ariel is pregnant with a child whose development may be accelerated, anything to prevent trauma is a good idea. Is there anywhere she can go, maybe back to Mandira, for the rest of her pregnancy?"

Galla put both her hands on her hips.

"Trent," said Galla firmly, "only Ariel can make the final decision on what she wants to do. As the leader of this mission, I need everyone to cooperate. I need Ariel's skills. If she does not want to work, I will respect that. But I don't think that's going to be the case."

Trent balked. "I'm going to continue to insist that she not overwork herself. Know this."

"I understand," said Galla. "We will let you know if we need you. I suggest you return to your much-earned sleep, and thank you."

Trent grimaced and did an about-face to head back down the hall.

Galla stopped him, feeling ashamed. "Trent," she called gently. He turned to look at her, his face a storm of emotions. "Trent, I'm so sorry I snapped."

Trent sighed and nodded. "It's all right. Sometimes it's hard to step back from people we care about."

She looked at him with aching sympathy. Trent's eyes opened a bit more as he saw her dip her head. He could tell that she knew about his wife. He turned and walked away.

Galla reentered the room.

Ariel sat up again, smudged away her remaining tears, and looked defiantly at Galla. "I couldn't hear or read what you said, but I could read Trent," she announced. "I'm not going anywhere."

"I meant what I said to him," Galla told her, shoving her feisty hair back over her shoulders. "Nobody is taking your baby away. I won't let them. So even if—and it sounds like a long shot, but hey, space is weird—even if this *Veronica* is still out there? She'd have to go through me. And that's not happening."

She sat beside Ariel.

"I didn't know about her," she said quietly, clasping Ariel's hand. "I'm sorry. It sounds like there was some history."

And she watched as Ariel's face changed very subtly, as if lowering a veil. Galla crinkled her own forehead.

I know she knows I can't read her thoughts, thought Galla. And it dawned on her. Ariel was blocking Dagovaby. It must have been undetectable by him, for he continued stroking her arm and listening attentively.

Galla sighed. "I think maybe we should practice. Try to figure out a strategy for when Paosh Tohon strikes again. When we reach the next planet, I want you to come with me this time."

Sounds of protestation lifted from the throats of Dagovaby and Meredith.

"Oh shut up!" Ariel cried. "I'm going with Galla. I can't stand this. From either of you," she said viciously to Meredith and Dagovaby, and then looked as if she instantly regretted it. "I'm sorry. I just—I can't handle your treating me like glass about to shatter. I'm alive, I'm okay, the baby is okay." She heaved a large sigh. "I have to get on with my life despite the fact I'm growing another one—pretty quickly, it seems."

Ariel patted her belly, and Dagovaby brought his large hand to rest there too.

"I'm fine," said Ariel, partly to herself as well as to everyone else. "I think I'll sleep better now. Thank you," she said, earnestly locking eyes with Galla.

Galla lowered her head and nodded.

She walked back to her room with her hands in her pockets, an unpleasant sensation twisting within her. She thought about everything she had learned. She ached for Ariel, whose fear had seemed so visceral. But she also admired her friend for overcoming her fear enough to cope. Galla only wished she would not let Ariel down.

My friends may be in danger. I hope I can do enough to protect them.

45

DANCE LESSONS

The next world, a large moon, met them shortly after they left the junction. Galla squinted at the image before them. There were oceans on this world, and vast swaths of vegetation by the look of the green lands arcing up at them as they entered its orbit. She noticed several small shapes in orbit as well.

"What are those?" she murmured, tapping her chin with her finger.

Rob glanced up and said, "Satellites."

"Still in use?" Galla asked, feeling unsettled. She did not like this.

"They look defunct. Derelict," Rob answered, shrugging.

Galla shivered. *Why would they be deteriorated? Was there no one on the planet?*

She cleared her throat and said through the comms, "Jana, can you come up here? I want you to see something."

A few minutes later, Jana entered, looking slightly dazed. One of her eyelids twitched.

"I just went back through the data," she told Galla. "I still didn't see anything recent. As far as I can tell, no one has lived here for a very long time."

Galla nodded, but seeing Jana's eyes twitch, she said, "Rest for a bit if you like. But before you go, can you tell me what you think?"

And she gestured to the view screen. Jana rubbed her eyes and then her temples.

"What happened here?" Galla whispered to her. "Do you think those still function at all?"

"I don't know. It's possible," Jana replied.

"It's unsettling for some reason," Galla said, unable to shake her uneasiness. *Maybe they're all dead worlds, in different ways,* she thought. She crossed her arms to hide her slight trembling.

"Let me know if you need anything," Jana said, turning on her heel and leaving.

Galla thanked Jana, and stood behind Rob.

Rob slowly turned his head up to look at her, his eyebrows rising higher and higher. "Yeeeees?" he asked pointedly.

"Are you picking up anything unusual?" she asked, fidgeting with the back of his chair.

He swiveled around. "If I did, you'd be the first to know," he assured her. "What's up? Are you ready to scan for the Device?"

"Yes," answered Galla, staring at the image again. "And no. I don't know why, I just . . . I dread this, for some reason. After—after the storm world, after Ariel's nightmares . . . I'm a little . . . I feel like I—"

"Are you stressed out?" asked Rob, not unkindly.

Galla looked down at him and noticed for the first time the patterns in his blue eyes, little green spokes around the pupil in between the blue.

"Maybe," she finally answered. And she felt her shoulders fall in relief at the admission.

"You know," said Rob, "you don't have to run *everything*. It's okay to delegate. Not—not that you aren't good at it," he added hastily. "But it's a lot to shoulder."

She bit her lower lip.

"What if we go down there, and something worse happens? One of you gets seriously injured, or killed. It could have gone so much worse before," she muttered, creasing her brow. Rob stood and faced her.

"Galla," he said, "every one of us on this ship knows the possibilities. It's part of even being *out* here in space. We have to be responsible for ourselves, too. Let me ask you this. Do you *want* to lead? Or do you just feel like you *have* to, like it's your destiny?"

"It *is* my destiny," she replied simply. To her, that was ironclad.

Rob rolled his eyes. "Let me rephrase this. Is there something you'd rather be doing than this, right now?"

Galla widened her eyes and shook her head.

"I can't think of anything," she answered, baffled.

Rob took her hand. She blinked in surprise.

"What about dancing?" he asked, grinning.

She laughed. "Dancing? I don't have time for dancing. We're on a mission."

"That's my point!" Rob exclaimed. "You're go-go-go." He turned his head aside. *"Play some bossa nova,"* he commanded his systems. "Will you dance with me? Just for a few minutes. Then back to the mission; it's not going anywhere, after all."

Galla lowered her head as the undulating notes of music echoed through the cockpit. She raised her head again and commanded via the comms, "Crew, take a break from whatever you're doing. I'll give us one day in orbit before we head down."

Then she turned back to Rob. "Ready," she said.

"Ready for what?" Rob asked, crinkling his forehead.

"I'm ready to dance with you," answered Galla.

Rob's eyes shone. "Now it's my turn to lead," he said to her.

He took her through a number of steps until she could manage not to tread on his feet. They found a rhythm and made their way around the small floor space, laughing and dancing. Once Rob's face reached a bright red, they slowed and finally stopped.

Galla could not stop smiling.

"I loved that!" she exclaimed.

"Feel better?" asked Rob, still holding her hands.

"Much," gasped Galla, and she swept in to give him a quick side hug. "Now it's your turn to take a break."

"Oh no, not if you're going to take over; you need a break too,"

Rob objected.

"Fine. Autopilot it is. I'll see you at lunch," said Galla, feeling euphoric.

She met Ariel in the hallway outside the kitchen. Her friend held snacks in both hands and gazed at them with some contempt. Then she looked up at Galla and half-smiled. Galla noticed Ariel's abdomen.

"Did you grow since yesterday?" exclaimed Galla, staring at Ariel's bump.

Ariel, her face already abnormally flushed, went further red, but she snickered.

"I think so," she answered, staring down at her own body.

"That is so weird," Galla could not help but say.

Ariel met her gaze. "It really is."

The two burst out laughing.

"I'm feeling so strange," Ariel told her as they walked to the round room for lunch. "I know I need to eat, and there are some things I really want, but there are other things I would normally love and I can't stand the thought of right now." She shook her head, her long, straight tresses shimmering.

"Are you still really tired?" asked Galla warmly, wondering to herself if a day's break before heading to the planet would be enough for Ariel.

"Actually, I've been feeling a lot better the last couple of days," said Ariel. "I'm still tired, but I feel like I've entered another phase, maybe. If this little guy truly doesn't take nine months like a normal baby, I am totally fine with that!"

"And—and your dreams, are they—have you had any more like before?" asked Galla quietly, as she watched other crew members enter the room.

"No, thank Christ," Ariel said emphatically.

"Good," Galla said, exhaling. "Do you feel up for heading to the surface tomorrow?"

"Hell yes, I do," said Ariel. "Get me out of here, please!"

Galla snorted. "I'll lead the way."

46

INTERWOVEN

Galla and Ariel took one sky bike, and Jana and Trent took a second. Meredith, Dagovaby, and Rob remained on the ship. Rob brought the ship in close this time, since the weather cooperated and there were no deterrents. The two bikes dropped from the hovering ship into a warm, hazy, thickly forested landscape.

As they skimmed along, Galla turned her bike to an outcropping at the top of a cliff. She braked, and she and Ariel stepped onto the world's root-covered dirt. Galla checked her readings.

"Fine down here," she called to Rob, and yanked off her helmet. Her hair burst forth, frazzled in the humidity. Ariel laughed out loud, taking her helmet off and revealing her usual sleek, dark mane. Galla rolled her eyes.

"It's like your hair is angry," Ariel mused, coming closer to her friend and staring as the several colors of hair twisted in the heady breeze.

"Maybe it is," Galla answered tartly.

Jana and Trent joined them, and they turned and looked out across the valley below them.

"Lush place, lots of oxygen," Trent observed. "No sign of development from here, anyway."

"What are those strange gaps in the trees?" Galla wondered aloud, pointing. They all looked to see long rows of canopy gaps, like tunnels through the trees.

Jana crinkled her nose. "I don't like it." She squinted up at the sky. "Those derelict stations came from somewhere."

"See what you can find," advised Galla. "We'll head to the Device while you and Trent look around. Meet us back here in two hours. No more."

Trent nodded. Jana patted her holster, with her hacking tool. "On it," she answered.

They stepped through the glade and into the dense undergrowth. The air felt thick to Galla, and somehow harder for her to breathe. She could see clouds on the horizon, and she felt troubled. She tended to agree with Jana's assessment. Something did not seem quite right about this world.

Raucous animal sounds echoed through the dark, vine-twisted canopy. *Insects, maybe,* Galla thought. She and Ariel stepped through clearings and over roots and shoved away vines. The going was not so bad at first. Eventually, though, they hit a shadowy thicket of vines, a fortress of them curving high into the canopy and choking out much of the light on the forest floor. The two women donned their headlamps and looked around the near-wall of vines.

"We could cut through," suggested Ariel, raising her wristband, which held a small torch control called a fire blade. Galla smirked. Ariel grinned back. "Guess that would take more than two hours."

"I was thinking two years," said Galla, and they snickered.

"So now what?" asked Ariel. "We know it's this way, but we can't get through."

"Let's try to go around. There has to be an opening somewhere," Galla replied. So they headed right, and Galla noted how the vine wall curved. She felt a tinge of warmth from her stone, where it lay on her chest. "This is the right way," she said, trying to reassure herself.

They kept at it. Galla led and pushed through lingering vines. Ariel twitched off tiny insects and webs and spores, which assaulted them from every side. Suddenly Ariel froze. She turned and stared into the vine wall.

"Galla," she said in a low voice. Galla halted and turned.

"Something is in there," Ariel whispered.

Galla stepped quietly next to Ariel and peered in through the dark weave of plant life.

"Is it hostile?" she asked softly.

"I'm not sure," said Ariel. "Whatever it is, it's watching us. And I can't understand its thoughts." She sighed. "Dagovaby could pick up on its feelings better than I can. I think it might be frightened."

"An animal, then," said Galla, folding her arms.

"I don't think so, not exactly," replied Ariel doubtfully.

"Let's keep going," suggested Galla. "If it shows itself, we'll deal with it."

Ariel nodded, looking with dislike at the vines as she walked. She moved closer to Galla instinctively. The two kept pushing forward, both occasionally glancing at the vine wall, and eventually the canopy grew thinner.

"I think we're coming out of it," said Galla, sighing with relief.

"We're going to face whatever that is, and soon," Ariel warned.

Galla clenched her fists.

"Let's get this done. I'll deal with it."

And they nearly turned into an opening, ready to face anything, when they heard a distant yell.

"Who was that?" Galla cried. "Trent or Jana?"

"One of them." Ariel closed her eyes halfway and focused. "I'm not getting a good read on them at all. Shit!"

Galla hurried forward and faced a great circle of green, a carpet of sorts, completely woven from vines and leaves. It appeared to be natural plant growth, but what it covered certainly was not. They had found the Device. And they found something else staring at them from the edge of it.

Ariel seized Galla's hand. The two women looked at an oval-shaped *something*, a being that glistened in iridescent greens and purples. It was taller than they were, and it looked at them through bulging yellow eyes.

A crashing and cracking of branches and vines sounded off to their right, and Trent and Jana erupted from the forest and nearly skidded right onto the plants covering the Device. Galla stared at them and wondered at the passageway they had come through. It looked large and smooth and round, maybe an eighth the size of the Device opening. Nothing about the passage looked natural.

"Something's coming," Jana gasped, glancing behind her. Trent leaned over, his hands on his knees, and took deep, gasping breaths.

"Come to us!" shouted Galla, and the two stumbled around the edge of the Device to join her and Ariel.

Then they saw the creature that Ariel and Galla had found.

Jana wheezed, pointing behind her at the opening in the trees. "Huge," she gasped, and a great shape loomed through the trees and halted in front of the Device.

Galla could not quite wrap her mind around what she saw. It looked mostly like some kind of worm, but its skin seemed to twist in patterns. It had no discernible face or eyes, just a long set of toothlike knobs on its underside.

Galla stared from this worm to the being, which more than anything looked like a giant beetle, and then she looked to Ariel.

"What is happening?" she cried.

"I don't know," moaned Ariel. "I'm still trying to read this one over here, or it's trying to read me, I don't know. The words are jumbled."

"It came up from the valley, followed us on that trail," choked Jana. She and Trent still looked winded and badly frightened.

"There are more of them," said a melodious voice, and they all jumped. It was the beetle creature.

Ariel exclaimed, "Now I can read you! You're not frightened by the worm! But you're frightened of us?"

The creature stepped toward them, its appendages extended outward, exposing its abdomen.

"I think it's supplicating," Trent marveled. "Letting us know it means no harm, by exposing its vulnerable parts."

The worm sat motionless, but slightly raised as if waiting.

"I will not harm you," the giant insect said in voice interspersed with pops and clicks. "I am a guardian of the place. This ... worm, as you call it, is one of many thousands in our land, and we have lived here since the visitors abandoned it."

Galla approached this being. "What is your name?" she asked.

The being responded with chirps and pops.

"Beetle," suggested Ariel. "Let's just call you Beetle, if you don't mind," and she sent her own thoughts to the creature: *We mean no harm. We are here on a mission, and then we will leave. Can you tell the worm?*

Beetle raised two great, armored, iridescent wings, made rhythmic scratching sounds, and the worm responded by lowering and backing into the forest.

"Thank you, Beetle," Galla said to the creature.

Beetle approached her and looked at her with its immense eyes. Its puckered mouth, surrounded by small pincers, spoke again.

"You have come for the Device," it said to her.

"Yes," said Galla. She lifted her stone from her chest, and the light of the clearing bounced off of its facets in little purple starbursts. "I am the keeper of the stones that activate the Device. I am here to deliver a small one. Will you let me do this?"

Beetle lowered to the ground and lifted its wings as if in salute. It stood again and answered, "My time has ended, then. You may proceed."

Galla pinched her forehead together. "You've been waiting for this?"

"I have been guarding the Device since the last guardian, who replaced the one before, and so on. My kin live at the edge of the forests. But there was no one else, so we took on the role."

Galla considered. "Then who built the abandoned stations in orbit?"

Beetle bristled and shuddered.

"Brutal people came here, sought to build and pillage," it said. "They destroyed our homes and our trees. The worms, as you call them, banded together with us to stop them. The people were taking the soil of the worms. We sabotaged their works, and they eventually left."

"Their *soil?*" Jana muttered, furrowing her brow.

"The worms till the soil in vast fields. The people came to take the soil," said Beetle.

Trent nodded. "Probably for minerals, or some other resource in the dirt," he speculated.

"Has anyone been here since?" Galla asked.

"There have been crafts in the skies, but no one has landed recently, until now."

Slapping sounds startled Galla, and she felt enormous raindrops hit her head. All around them the huge drops pelted down. The storm had arrived. Beetle scurried toward the domelike vine structure it had emerged from.

"Come," Beetle called. "The rains will be gone before long, but they are strong."

The creature led them into a cathedral of vines, with a high ceiling of dark green, living buttresses. No rain reached the floor of this structure. Beetle had kept the floor smooth and clean as well, and in one area had fashioned ledges as large as beds to sit on from the vines themselves. Galla, Ariel, Jana, and Trent sat on ledges and rested.

Galla sniffed in the humid air, noting the acrid tang and the sheer greenness of its heady scent. She had never been to such a place, where everything around her seemed fecund and warm and twisting. The rain pounded above her head, and her companions drooped in the thick air.

"Why don't we just relax for a bit," Galla suggested. No one argued.

But she felt restless, so she stood and walked to the opening of the vine dome. The rain poured into the crevice of the Device, some of it bouncing off the network of vines covering it. Galla wondered just how deep these Device holes reached, and if in this case, its base would be completely covered with water. Beetle clicked up beside her, and she could not hold back a small shiver. And yet there was something familiar about Beetle's movements.

"You remind me of androids," she said. Beetle made a pop with its mouth.

"I do not know androids," the creature responded.

"Well, they're not organic, like you," Galla conceded, "but they have many moving parts. And the way you move yours makes me think of them."

Beetle tilted its head and gazed at her with its multifaceted yellow eyes that reflected the light outside the opening.

"You are not like the others," said Beetle.

Galla squinted at Beetle and felt a small crease grow above her nose, as she could not decide whether or not to frown.

"What do you mean?" she demanded, but she kept her voice low. "They know. But how do you know?"

"You look different," said Beetle simply.

"No I do not!" exclaimed Galla. Someone shifted behind her.

"That material on your head," Beetle remarked.

"My hair?" And Galla self-consciously tried to pull the quivering coils down to tame them.

"That material glows," Beetle continued. "It does not glow on the others' heads. You have a different color, and a different smell, and a different structure."

Galla felt more surprised than offended. "I do? Is . . . is that good or bad?"

"It simply is," said Beetle. "You are made of something different from them," and the huge insect swiveled its head just slightly to peer back into the shaded dome.

"Yes," admitted Galla.

"They accept you as one of theirs," remarked Beetle.

"Do you think so?" she asked, and an unusual pang swept through her. She squeezed her fingers together into a tight knot.

"They would smell of fear if they did not," commented Beetle. "You are their leader."

Galla exhaled slowly. "I hope you are right."

"They did fear me, at first," clicked the insect.

"Well, that was instinct," noted Galla.

"I feared them too."

"Did you fear me?" asked Galla.

"No."

"Why is that?" she wondered.

"Because I knew you were different. As I said. And I knew you must be here for the Device."

"Do you know who built it, and what it's for?" she asked Beetle eagerly.

"I do not," said Beetle. "Only that it must be guarded."

Galla furrowed her brow. "All I know is that I must place one of my stones in it. And then I must continue to all the other worlds with Devices, and do the same. And at some point, they must be activated."

"Will you do this?" asked Beetle.

"I . . . I think I have to," said Galla, and the furrow in her brow returned. "But I'm not exactly sure how. I just want to do this soon, because Paosh Tohon is growing. And if we can figure out a way to stop it before the Event, maybe the galaxy stands a chance."

"What is Paosh Tohon, and what is the Event?" asked Beetle.

"Paosh Tohon is an entity that feeds off suffering. The Event is a natural disaster predicted long ago. We're afraid Paosh Tohon will take advantage of the suffering created by the Event to grow even more, and infect the entire galaxy."

Galla watched the great creature. It twitched its iridescent wings.

"I do not understand this Paosh Tohon," it said finally. "This does not sound like a creature of nature. This sounds like one of the people who came to our world. To take and yet not give back. That is against nature.

"As for the Event, everything changes. And yet it is constant. That is just the way it is." Beetle's antennae stretched up a few inches. "The rain has stopped."

Galla sighed.

"Then I'm ready to go down into the Device," she said.

She turned away from Beetle and blinked as her eyes adjusted to the dim light inside the dome of vines. She found Ariel fast asleep, her long dark hair trailing over her ledge, her hooded eyes closed yet twitching. Her abdomen looked somehow a little larger to Galla than even the day before. Galla bit her lip. She hated to disturb this peace.

She began to back away and give them more time, but Ariel stirred from her dreams and her eyes shot open. They glowed, ethereal yellow-green in the dim light.

"What is it?" asked Ariel, yawning and shifting carefully up.

"I hate to wake you," Galla said softly. "The rain stopped, and I thought I might go down."

Ariel stood swiftly, and caught hold of her belly instinctively. "I'm still figuring out this balance thing," she admitted with a wry grin. "Let's go."

Galla nodded with her own grin, and the two walked softly to the opening while the others slept behind them. Galla assessed the crisscrossed vine cover of the Device.

"Why don't we use some of these vines to help us?" she suggested.

Ariel peered over the lip of the plant-riddled crevice. "To climb down with?"

"Yes!"

"Good idea," Ariel answered. "How far down is the platform?"

"It shouldn't be far," said Galla.

The two slipped and slid at the edge on wet vines, while Beetle watched from the dome.

"This is not ideal," Ariel said, skidding onto her bottom clumsily. But finally they made it down far enough that Galla could investigate.

Galla fought her way through a gap in the vines and cast a light into the depths. A faint shape appeared as the beam swept through the darkness. She sheathed her light and nodded.

"I see the platform. It's not too far."

So the two women made their way along the edge of the vine-webbed crevasse and stepped carefully down the vines to get below them and onto the platform. Galla huffed when she saw how tangled with plants the platform was. She reached in her belt for a knife and tried sawing through one of the vines. It was tough and woody.

"Well, shit," said Ariel glumly, after trying the same. The two tried small fire blades, which worked to cut through but only slowly. "These are really thick."

"I guess it's good they are, so they shielded this thing for so long," said Galla, "but it's not so good for us. This platform won't release with a basket of vines all around it!"

Ariel peered over the edge of the platform at the unsettling darkness below them. She instinctively edged back into the center of the platform, her green eyes bulging. "That's really deep."

"Yes," responded Galla, grimly searing through a particularly huge vine. The insides of the plant smelled syrupy. "I suppose we could ask the others for help, but I don't want to risk anyone else falling in or anything."

Ariel worked away on her vines and then sighed and wiped the sweat from her brow.

"It's like soup in here," she grunted. "Galla, we aren't making much progress. I think we *have* to ask the others."

Ariel closed her eyes for a moment. Then she looked up at the bright sky, and smiled when a great oval shape appeared above. Galla followed her gaze.

"Beetle!" she exclaimed.

"Ariel told me you need help cutting the vines," said Beetle nonchalantly.

"Yes, we do," answered Galla. She grinned at Ariel in admiration.

And she and Ariel watched in awe as Beetle crawled down and snipped and snapped its jaws through the vines as if they were blades of grass. Then Beetle flicked its wings and shot out of the dank hole. The platform activated. Galla's face burst into a huge smile and she clasped Ariel's hand.

"Great work," she told her friend.

Ariel smirked and shrugged. "At least telepathy is good for something!" she said.

"Thank you!" cried Galla to Beetle, and she and Ariel held on as the platform plummeted into the darkness.

47

MIND CAVE

With their hair flying up as the platform raced downward, the two women looked at each other in the starved light of a flashlight and purple stones, which had begun to glow. Galla's large stone peeked up from her shirt where she had tucked it, and the smaller stone she had brought along radiated purple light through the stitches of her belt. The two sat on the platform's center, their fingers gripping the holes in its metal, and the wind shrieked at them. Neither wished to look down, so they stared at each other's dimly lit eyes for several minutes in silence.

Galla could not guess what Ariel was thinking, and knew her friend could not read her own thoughts either, so she felt they were on even footing together in this dank pit. Still she grew nervous. What happened to Dagovaby before had shaken Galla. What would happen to Ariel? Was it wise to bring her down here? And yet somehow Galla knew she must.

"Is it like this in every Device?" yelled Ariel eventually.

"So far," Galla called back, for even though they sat close to each other, the noise of the platform and the wind from its speed pummeled their ears.

And quite suddenly the platform slowed. Galla swallowed, remembering her first experience on Rikiloi. The platform stopped and leveled at a walkway, and lights winked on in succession down a long hall. She glanced at her friend and saw the throbbing pulse in her neck. Ariel, in turn, blinked a few times and looked down at her wrist.

"Comms aren't working," she said in a flat voice.

"Ariel," said Galla suddenly. "I don't know if Dag told you, but you might . . . strange things might happen to you inside. You might see disturbing images." She bit her lip. "You can go back if you want. I can do this alone."

Ariel turned sharply to look behind her at the platform perched at the edge of nightmare blackness.

"I think the fuck not," she whispered.

Galla closed her eyes in relief and stepped forward, and Ariel joined her.

"There are doors—" she began to say, but a pulsing light rushed at them in great arcs from the hallway.

The flashes began: the future, the past, Galla was not sure, and she felt destabilized, stretched and burned and dropped and entombed. She heard a distant scream, and opened her mouth to scream back, but could not find her voice. She did find a hand, and grabbed it: Ariel's hand. She could not see Ariel because of the rings of light invading every sense. She could barely think through all the visions bombarding her. But Galla moved ahead, and pulled Ariel along.

For the first time, Galla felt grateful in some respect for her time on Bitikk. They had tortured her there, and she had not known why. *Maybe in some way, that helped me be ready to deal with this. Doesn't excuse their methods, though.*

Every step meant sensory agony. At one point she slipped and fell on one knee into something wet, and realized Ariel had vomited. Long wails of sobs reverberated from the young woman, and Galla held her hand tightly. *What is she seeing? It must be bad. I wish I hadn't done this to her,* she thought, miserable. They stepped ahead, the only certainty their clasped hands, and the warmth of Galla's stones against her body.

And then, calm. The flashing rings vanished. Galla and Ariel stood in a hallway of doors, dull and grey and flat, not at all reflective. At one end of the hallway the doors branched off, and at the other end the opening to the crevice menaced them like a great, dark mouth.

"Are you all right?" Galla asked urgently, noting Ariel's mixture of pallor and flushing. Her face was swollen from tears. Her other hand clutched her growing belly.

"I am now," answered Ariel. She shuddered and stood trembling for several minutes.

"What happened?" Galla wanted to know.

Ariel looked steadily at Galla's gem sticking up near her collarbone. Galla reached down and pulled the large crystal out. Ariel released a long sigh, and nodded to herself.

"I'm glad you have that," she said quietly.

"Why, what happened? Tell me!" Galla urged, now holding both of Ariel's hands in her own.

"It was like . . . like my nightmares," Ariel answered hoarsely, and tears came easily to her eyes. "It felt like I was on Mandira again, when—when Veronica tried to take hold of me and Forster. She was *there,* in those flashing lights, staring at me, telling me I could never get away from her, not really."

"But she's gone," Galla reassured her. "She's not here. The Device, it shows things to me. I don't understand it, but I know that whatever it is I see, it's not right *now* or right *here.* Some of it is from the past. I don't know about the rest." And now Galla felt uncomfortable. She had seen the vine dome in one of those prior visions. So perhaps she *had* seen what was to come.

"So you might be seeing . . . the future?" Ariel asked her, her green eyes demanding honesty.

Galla started. She knew Ariel could not read her thoughts, but again, her own face betrayed her. She could not lie to her, not ever. But it gave her no joy in telling her, "Maybe."

Ariel hung her head and closed her eyes. "I see," she said, and then she looked up again and marveled at Galla's stone.

"It's glowing more," she said.

Galla looked down and sighed in comfort to see the crystal's warm violet-magenta-lavender glimmer upon her breast. She fumbled with her belt and produced the smaller gem. "It's time we left this here," she said.

"What happens then?" Ariel asked.

"It waits for us to come back and activate it," said Galla, but with a measure of uncertainty in her voice that did not escape Ariel's keen ears.

"How will we do that?" Ariel wanted to know, and yet the moment she uttered those words, green eyes met copper ones in a flash of recognition.

"Telepaths," they said at the same time.

Galla held the small gem out to Ariel to look at. "You were able to focus before, and you moved an entire station instantaneously across space! I think you can do it again."

"I don't think I could do this alone," said Ariel. "I had help from Forster and Aeriod."

"We're going to need a telepath for every Device!" Galla exclaimed. "Do you think you can help find more?"

"I think so," said Ariel slowly, but Galla could see her eyes brighten at the idea.

Galla smiled. "We have a project, then." She set the small stone on the floor of the hallway, and while the tiny gem glowed benignly purple, the hallway lights began to dim.

"We'd better leave now," she said.

They walked back to the platform, sat, and held fast. Before it zoomed upward, Ariel said, "I'm glad we're friends. I didn't know what it was like to have friends, or a lover, not really. And now I do. I'm afraid, but not *as* afraid."

Galla felt as though dawn broke into her mind. She did not know what to say, but she reached over to squeeze Ariel's hand. The platform rose, and the dark depths receded below them, as they headed skyward toward a web of light.

But as they approached that sunlight, the comms on their wrists screamed at them. Something was wrong.

48

BEFALLEN

"Do you copy?" Rob's voice crackled on Galla's squawking comm.

"Yes!" she cried, watching the opening to the Device approach above her. "What's going on?"

"Thank God. The others weren't responding. You need to get back up here. There's another ship coming, and I don't know whose it is. We're coming down to get you."

And Rob's voiced fizzed off.

Galla looked at Ariel, whose eyes were round and haunted.

"Your stone," she hissed, and Galla took her own large crystal into her hands and marveled at its dark violet glow.

"What is it?" Galla asked, but she felt tiny spikes of anxiety travel up and down her back. She did not want to accept what was happening.

"I hope I'm wrong," said Ariel grimly, "but after everything . . . after Fael'Kar . . . I don't think I am. I think it's Paosh Tohon."

Galla scurried to her feet the second the platform stopped. She held her hand out and Ariel took it.

"You go first," Galla told her. She snatched a trailing vine and passed it to Ariel.

Ariel clambered up and over the vine net and glanced down. Galla nodded and seized the vine again for herself.

Hand over hand, Galla climbed. She soon realized this must have been brutal for Ariel's hands, as her own slipped a bit and her fingernails dug into the vine as she climbed up. She hoisted herself onto the web of vines and swung her legs out of the chasm. Ariel had already made her way back to the dome, where Beetle stood on guard.

Ariel glanced up at the sky, searching the break among the tropical clouds, and then dashed inside the dome. Galla looked around as well. She shuddered.

"Rob," she called on her comms, "we're out of the Device. Do you know if the other ship can see you?"

Rob's warped voice responded, "I don't know. The cloak is holding, but who knows what tech the other ship has, if they can see us or not. Get ready to board."

Galla stepped quickly over the vines at the Device's edge and onto the smooth ground near the entry to the dome. She faced Beetle and looked up into its faceted yellow eyes.

"Beetle, another ship is coming toward your planet," she said solemnly. "It's not one of ours; we don't know whose it is. Our ship will take us away soon. Can you stand guard over the Device?"

Beetle clicked and hummed. "We will guard, as we have always done."

Her wrist squawked again.

"Galla!" cried Rob. "Some small ships, shuttles—I don't know—left the main ship and are headed down here. Take cover just in case."

She faced her crew inside the dome.

"Rob will be here soon, but someone else is coming. Be ready for anything. For now, stay in the dome. I'll guard the front."

She and Beetle watched and waited, and after what seemed like hours, but in reality were only a few minutes, wind swirled around her and Beetle, and the air shifted. There hung their own ship, lowering near the edge of the Device. At that moment, two small crafts appeared and long blades of fire sliced into the back of the dome.

"Get in!" roared Rob. Galla seized Ariel and Jana's hands and ran with them to the ramp extending from their ship, where Dagovaby stood waiting.

"Go!" urged Galla.

"Dagovaby!" yelled Ariel, but he had run from the ship to the smoking dome to find Trent.

"Ariel, *go!*" Galla shouted. "I'll get them!"

And Jana, seeing the desperation in Galla's eyes, took Ariel with strong arms, despite her fighting, into the ship.

Galla turned and ran into the smoldering dome. Dagovaby had looped his arms under Trent, who was weakened and coughing, and they both wheezed and dragged forward. But Trent kept turning around.

"I hear her! I can't leave her!" he gasped.

"There's no one back there!" Dagovaby yelled.

But there was someone, or something, behind them, and Galla ran in between it and them. Through the blasted hole, she watched tendril shapes twist and turn. Two figures stood among the writhing shapes.

"Hand them over," said a helmeted man's voice, a human man!

He held a weapon of some kind in the crook of his arm. Galla could see a badge on his sleeve, something reddish.

"If you give them to us," he said, "we'll let them live. We'll make them better than before."

Galla held onto her stone with both hands and stared through the smoke.

"No."

Violet light flared from her stone and illuminated the flaming dome.

"If you don't give them to us now," the man said, "it's going to be so much worse for them."

A strange, chattering sort of laugh arose from the person next to him. Galla could not make this person out in the obscuring smoke.

Behind Galla, she heard Dagovaby struggle, and Trent rushed forward and crashed into her, knocking her onto her hands and knees.

"Phoebe!" he yelled. "Phoebe, I'm here, Phoebe!"

"Trent!" this other person cried in response. "Come with me, Trent!"

He stopped for one moment, and Galla rose to her feet and stared at him. The hunger in the man's eyes terrified her.

"Phoebe, how? How are you here?" Trent said, stepping slowly forward.

"Yes, please, come to me, Trent! Everything is better, I'll make everything better!" said the voice, and Galla could then make out a tall silhouette of what looked like a human woman.

Galla turned her head and yelled, "Dagovaby! Run to the ship! RUN!"

Dagovaby bolted out.

"Trent!" cried Galla. "It's not her! It's not Phoebe! *Trent!*"

Trent's starved, devastated face wanted so much to believe.

"I never thought I would see you again. I wanted to stop hearing that last sound, I—"

"This sound?" asked the woman, and the strange, chattering, wheezing, laugh-like sound rose again.

Trent covered his ears and screamed.

"Trent! Run away, go back to the ship!" cried Galla, holding her stone high and watching triangles of purple light scatter from its depths.

But Trent stepped forward, and Galla watched him embrace this not-Phoebe, and she knew then for certain who it was. But by the time she did, Trent had crumpled into a ball and shrieked so loudly that the sound of his torture reverberated through the dome and into Galla's mind.

Her horror and rage commingled. She yelled as she brandished the stone, and shards of blinding light shot from it into the dark, swirling shape before her and struck the helmeted man, who shrieked in pain. The tentacles that only Galla could see shrank back.

The man and the woman dragged Trent away from the burning hole and retreated to their ship.

Galla emerged from the hole herself, oblivious to the fire around her, and looked up to see something she did not understand. The sky had grown dark and fluttering, and a great wind and buzzing and whirring arose. Everywhere she looked, she could see giant insects: Beetle's own kind, attacking the two invading craft. Among them, Beetle flew and beat its wings on the ship with Trent inside.

A dreadful voice sounded then, as Trent's captors rose upward, a woman's velvety yet manipulative voice:

"Nice try. We don't need him anyway. There's too little of him left. But you can tell Ariel, we'll get her soon enough."

And a hole in the beleaguered craft opened, and out hurled Trent from above. Galla watched helplessly as he fell and struck the ground.

The attackers fled, beaten back by the giant insects, launching weapons and ultimately firing afterburners to escape. They shimmered high in the sky and disappeared. Galla ran to Trent's side.

She bent over his broken body and let out a long, anguished wail. All around her, insects landed and gingerly approached, Beetle among them.

"I couldn't save him," she cried, looking up at Beetle.

Beetle dipped down and perched beside her, and scraped its back legs together. An echoing trill sounded from those legs, and soon the other insects joined. Galla, in her shock and disbelief, could barely register what was happening.

They're keening, some tiny part of her realized. The rest of her mind swam in the enormity of what had happened. She felt affixed to the ground beside Trent, who at last bore a calm expression, one of surprise, but no longer of anguish.

The warmth and softness of human hands slipped under her arms to raise her from the ground. She flailed for a moment, and then turned to see Rob, haggard with grief and alarm.

"Come on, Galla," he said quietly, but with an edge in his voice.

"They could come back, and there could be more. We need to get away from here."

"We have to bring him," Galla protested, tears streaking her smoke-stained face.

The singing of the insects stopped.

"I will carry him onto your ship," said Beetle.

Two other insects approached Beetle, and they seemed to communicate.

Beetle turned to Rob.

"I will carry him and I will join you."

Rob scrunched his face up. "Wait, what? I don't think—"

"Beetle!" exclaimed Galla. "You're the guardian of the Device!"

"*We* are the guardians of the Device," Beetle announced, flicking its wings up, gesturing at the other insects around them. "We and the worms. One of us can go. I will go."

"But Beetle, *why* would you want to leave your home, and come with us, away from your kind?" Galla asked, summoning all the patience she could in her despair.

"You have lost a crew member, and you need another one," Beetle said simply. "It would be against nature if I did not go with you."

"I—I—" Galla stammered. Nothing else made sense, but somehow this did. "Very well."

Rob whispered in a low voice, *"The fuuuuck?"*

"But what can we do with Trent?" asked Galla sadly.

Rob shook off his irritation and said, his voice breaking, "He'll get a burial in space. We can do that much."

Beetle said, "I do not understand why you would bury him in space."

"Beetle," said Galla with warmth, "you all sang for him. You have done what you would do. Now, we will do what we must, to say goodbye to him."

And so Beetle lifted Trent with extraordinary gentleness on its uppermost arms and stood on its hind legs to carry Trent to the ship, which perched close by. Galla and Rob followed him. Galla entered the ship last, and looked all about her, and noticed then that a fleet of the worms had joined the array of insects on all sides of the forest.

"Thank you," she told the creatures. She glanced at the vine-throttled cover of the Device. "I know you'll keep it safe."

And she stepped onto the ship's ramp, her feet heavy, and her thoughts heavier still.

49

BEHEST

Meredith's expression pierced Galla. She could see the emotions flickering across the elderly woman's face in waves. Not for the first time, Galla was glad she had no telepathic abilities. She felt as though Meredith's thoughts might be too difficult to bear. She did not know what to do or say.

But Meredith did know. She stepped forward to embrace Galla, having already greeted her own daughter with extraordinary relief. Galla slumped in the woman's arms, her head falling onto her welcoming shoulder.

"I could have stopped them," she choked. "I know I could have. I just didn't know *how*."

Meredith let her cry. Galla rambled, and gasped through her tears, and poured out her regrets. "I'm so sorry," she kept saying, and she felt useless.

"If you hadn't been there, it would have been far worse," Meredith told her.

Galla stood and wiped her cheeks. "But that's the whole problem. I'm the reason Trent was there to begin with."

"No," said Meredith firmly, her green eyes fierce. "Stop that. Trent chose to go with you. We all knew this mission would be risky."

"But I—it—*she*—" Galla felt the boiling rage from before. "She tricked him," she hissed. "Made him think it was his wife."

"That is what she does," Meredith murmured. "It is not the first time she has done this. Or rather, Paosh Tohon. The greatest trick was that Paosh Tohon ensnared her in this very way to begin with. Now it uses her to do the same to others.

"But Galla, I want you to listen to me carefully, dear. You did save the rest of us by holding them off as long as you did. Try to remember that."

Galla nodded, but the feeling of anguish did not abate. She could not help but think again and again of Trent's desperate eyes, the chattering coughing, and watching Trent fall to his death. Jana tapped at her door just then.

"We've made it beyond the junction," she announced, her eyes red. "It's time."

They walked to the cockpit and crowded in. Galla sat down next to Rob. They all stared out at the open scene of myriad stars, so empty and yet so full.

Rob shifted in his seat, uncomfortable. Dagovaby stood behind him, holding Ariel around her waist. She leaned her head against him. Beetle stood just outside the door, watching curiously. Jana glanced at Galla, who turned in her seat to look at all of them. Meredith nodded to her.

Galla said, "Trent was a good man. Some of you knew him better than I. He was kind and helpful, and I will miss him. I'm grateful for his service to all of us." She swallowed and turned back to look at the inky vastness ahead of them. *He deserved better,* she thought sadly.

Meredith then spoke. "Trent was a friend, and he was hopeful even in the toughest times. We belonged to that same, horrible club, when you lose your partner and have to figure out how to go on. We bonded over that. And so much more."

Rob sighed long and loudly. He clasped his hands together in his lap and said in a cracking voice, "Thanks for letting me lord over you, buddy. You put up with too much of my shit."

He lowered his head and commanded, "Release bay airlock."

And they watched a small pod jettison out into the darkness.

One by one, everyone shuffled away from the cockpit, except for Rob and Galla, who sat brooding separately in their chairs. Several minutes passed, and Galla closed her eyes.

"Well, shit," Rob said finally.

Galla opened her eyes.

"What?" she asked. She was not ready to think about what they should do next, but knew she must make some decisions.

"Well, he was our only medical staff," Rob pointed out. "And in case you forgot, there's going to be a baby born, by the looks of it, pretty soon. We've got a smart ship, but I'm guessing it knows fuck-all about hybrid human childbirth. Who's gonna deliver that baby? Sure as shit won't be me."

Galla scowled at him. "That's what you're worried about right now? We'll figure that one out. We have another mother on board; surely she knows *something* about having babies. But what do we do next? Paosh Tohon has found us. At least, a part of it has. And honestly, the worst part: Veronica."

Rob cleared his throat. "Why is this Veronica so obsessed with Ariel?"

Galla at first felt certain, but then began to question herself. "They were friends, once. Veronica was warped into something else. I don't know why she wants Ariel so much, though."

"Probably because she got away," mused Rob.

"I think it's because Ariel is as powerful as Veronica was, and maybe she's more so," Galla considered. "Paosh Tohon would be even stronger with another powerful telepath to manipulate people to its will."

Rob tapped his chin with his forefinger. "This thing, Paosh Tohon," he said slowly, "has been a 'galactic problem' apparently mostly near the core. Now it's spread out. Aeriod described it as stalks, like metastasis. And we were able to get it away from the solar system."

"Ariel was," Galla interjected.

"Yep, with Aeriod and that guy Forster, who took off to some rain world forever with his girlfriend. A lotta good he did," sneered Rob.

"He did more than you can imagine," snapped Galla. "They began a settlement on Perpetua from scratch. His descendents still live there. Well, one of them: Kein."

"So why isn't that guy helping us?" Rob wanted to know. "If we had him, and Ariel, and Dagovaby—maybe, I don't know shit about this mind power stuff—maybe we could pull off another stunt like they did with Mandira."

"Kein's not joining us," Galla said glumly. "He wants to stay where he's at and live his life."

Rob made a disgusted sound. "Well, fuck him then!" he muttered.

Galla flinched, and then she blushed from temper. "You don't know him. It's his right to have his own life."

Rob wheeled around to face her, his face so red that his eyebrows seemed to glow.

"Listen, I guarantee you Paosh Tohon won't give a damn about his cushy life on Forest Planet or whatever. He can fart around in the trees, sure, but this thing is getting stronger and craftier with Veronica on board. It's gonna come after all of us."

"Try telling Kein," spat Galla.

"I know what I'd like to tell him," hissed Rob.

Galla stood in a huff.

"Look, I'm done arguing with you," she told him. "We have to decide if we're ready to go to the next Device world. We still have a long way to go on those. You're sure this ship is not traceable? Because if it *is,* we're in real trouble."

"Aeriod said it's not traceable," Rob replied shortly, "and who am I to question the wizard's judgment about his own ship? Especially since Veronica has found us."

It was obvious to Galla what Rob thought of Aeriod in general.

"We have to take him at his word, then," Galla declared. "I think Ariel was right," and she sighed deeply. "I think Veronica found Ariel, not our ship.

"We don't have much choice. If we try to get another ship, we definitely will risk getting caught. With Ariel in the ship, near my stones, she's safe. And I think the rest of us are as well. What I'm worried about is, will they figure out what we're doing? And stop us from doing it?"

"We'd better hope not," said Rob, and he groaned, leaning onto the console with his head in his hands.

Galla sighed. "I have to figure out how to fight this thing. I can't risk anyone else dying. I have so much training, much of which I don't even remember. There has to be a way to tap into that."

"You weren't trained for this, though, right? You were trained for that Event, or whatever," Rob pointed out.

"I wish I could remember anything at all," admitted Galla, "because anything would be more helpful."

"It's something you'll have to figure out while we're making our deliveries."

"Are you up to doing this?" Galla asked him.

"It's the only thing I *can* do right now," Rob retorted.

Galla stood to leave, and Rob caught her hand. He sat, and she stood, and they looked out again at the stars, and then at each other. Galla could feel the pulse in Rob's hand as he squeezed hers: warm and alive and strong. A dormant part of her stirred as she looked at him and his unflinching turquoise eyes. She glanced away and loosened her grip.

"I'm sorry about Trent, Rob," she murmured. She left him sitting there, and he leaned back with his eyes closed.

She met the others in the round room and found Jana staring at Beetle, who had lowered onto all its legs and folded its wings about itself. The wings twitched occasionally, and once in a while they could hear clicks. Ariel intercepted Galla's look and put a finger to her lips.

"Sleeping," she whispered.

Galla breathed in and exhaled slowly, fighting her frustration. She held up her hand and said in a low voice, "We're going ahead with the mission. Any objections?"

Everyone shook their heads.

"Full speed ahead, captain," Ariel said, her arm draped across her large belly.

Galla bit her lip and wondered about what Rob had said. With Trent gone, they had lost their only medic. Galla hoped against hope that the ship and its crew would be enough to meet the next challenge.

50

QUONDAM

Ezeldae shone, its seas glowing in the reflected light of its star. Aeriod lowered his ship into orbit and lingered there, awaiting clearance. He sat sheathed in his cape, brooding.

A series of notes sounded, granting him clearance, so he set his craft to descend and only half-watched the flames of entry as he dropped through the atmosphere. Lately his mind was everywhere, and in one place, all at once. Perpetua, the Task, Galla-Deia, and his other worlds to look after. He fretted over Ika Nui, feeling for the first time a measure of guilt at leaving its denizens alone. And he wallowed in restlessness, watching the vibrant fires outside his ship's window, thinking that those flames reminded him of Galla's bright hair, tumbling over him. He turned away from the window.

And soon enough the craft slowed and landed with a great *WHISSSSSH* on a platform high atop an iridescent tower. He wearily stepped out from his ship, and a gust caught his cape and sent it high behind him, along with his pale hair, as he marched past guards, both organic and bot. Coral clouds like shredded ramparts raced in the teal sky behind him. His footsteps felt leaden, and for the first time in his long life, he felt old.

Ushalda met him, and both bowed and raised their hands to each other in begrudging respect.

"The others await," said Ushalda in a reverent tone. Aeriod nodded and walked alongside Ushalda through the high-arched hallway, and a long set of musical notes reverberated in the great space.

Into the shadow of a great room, Aeriod swept forward and stood straight and tall, ready to accept whatever judgment lay ahead. The shadows moved with an assemblage of races, Associates and Representatives, and he could see the raiment of the Speaker of Bitikk glowing green among them. He would never like this creature, and he could never forgive whatever torment it had put Galla through on its world. But he knew its power and its sway, so he seethed in silence, for that moment.

"Welcome again, Governor," the Speaker's low, translated voice whirled through the room's odd acoustics.

"I await your judgment and instruction," Aeriod said, loud and clear and defiant.

An eddy of voices and hoots and clicks circuited the room.

"You have been called for data," responded the Speaker, emotionless.

Aeriod blinked, and crinkled his eyebrows.

"Data?" he asked, confused.

"You must give us all your sensory data," said the Speaker. "You have been called to do so, for security's sake."

Aeriod blinked again. He quickly recovered from his surprise, however, and responded, "Of course. As you wish." And he flicked his wrists and brought his hands together, and produced a hand-sized, flat, silver diamond-shaped piece. He stepped forward, bowed deeply with a smirk, and handed it to the Speaker. The Speaker stretched an appendage and retrieved it, and passed it along to one of its lackeys.

"Now that I've given you this, will you tell me why?" Aeriod asked. "And what your concern is, with regard to security? It must be important, to summon me here rather than rely on a remote link."

"First, we must analyze your data," Ushalda responded. "Please, wait for us in your quarters. We have much to discuss."

Aeriod sighed and followed two bots along a pale blue walkway to a domed room overlooking the city below. He disliked the tower and its trappings, its bots and its mechanisms and its sleek metal. In some ways it seemed to him a cheap mimicry of Seltrason construction. These people could never match those creations; even Demetraan outshone this entire world, but then again it was the final product of that ancient age. Whereas Ezeldae's design felt like an obscenity to him, lacking in anything original. He paced impatiently, wanting to be away from this trompe-l'oeil of a place.

At last two bots awoke by his door and ushered him back to the great hall. He could hear the sounds within rising and falling, and he wondered.

The Speaker of Bitikk, Ushalda, and a bank of other Associates turned toward him.

"Where is Galla-Deia?" the Speaker demanded. "Her records are not in this data."

Aeriod lowered his eyelids, and he grinned openly.

"I have no claim over Galla-Deia. Therefore I collect no data on her, or her whereabouts."

"You defy us! Now!" Ushalda gasped.

"I gave her free will, such as she may have, such as anyone might in this galaxy. I know you feel no attachment to such an idea," spat Aeriod. "I let her go."

"We need to know where she is!" cried Ushalda. "*We* have other sources that tell us troubling news, that she is visiting Device worlds and that she may have been attacked!"

Aeriod took a deep breath.

"I trust her, and her team," he answered with a steady voice. He would betray nothing of his innermost feelings here again. "She is accomplishing her Task and building her own alliance. If she needs help, she will ask for it." And Aeriod said that mostly to himself, trying to believe it.

"We have reports of a militant faction known as Valemog, which has allied itself with Paosh Tohon," said the Speaker of Bitikk. "This we did not anticipate. We see within your data evidence that this faction grows unheeded, and somehow Paosh Tohon is not assimilating it."

Aeriod spun his cape around.

"I warned you! And here you stand, claiming you did not anticipate this!" he roared. "You with your stilted, self-congratulatory airs, the lot of you! It formed under your very noses while you pontificated about what was *right* and *orderly* for the galaxy. That worked for a time, and now that time is ended. Paosh Tohon now seeds itself beyond the core systems, and your protections begin to fail. What will you do when it finally breaches all your defenses?"

The stillness of that room unnerved him. And yet he was glad that it did.

Just then, a piercing tone shot through the room, and Aeriod jumped. Some of the voices lifted into a howling din, while others sounded fraught and urgent. Bots scurried out of the room.

The Speaker of Bitikk turned on Aeriod, deep rumblings sounding from its faceted face.

"You did not give us all the data!" it screamed.

Aeriod's silver eyes flew wide.

"What do you mean?" he demanded. "What data?"

But he stopped himself and looked around at the wave of panic and fear. He did not need to hear the words, but the Speaker formed them anyway:

"The Event has begun!"

51

PORTENTOUS

Ariel and Galla stood side by side in the kitchen, stirring their tea. Galla looked at her friend, whose cheeks flamed crimson. Her abdomen had grown huge in the past few days. She held her back.

"Are you all right?" Galla asked. Ariel smirked at her.

"Well," said Ariel, "my back is killing me, my feet are puffy, my stomach looks like a small planet, and I have to pee every few minutes. Other than that, I'm fine. Hey, want to come to my wedding?"

Galla's mouth opened in shock. "Your wedding? Where? When?"

Ariel laughed loudly at Galla's face. "Right here, obviously. Maybe in about fifteen minutes? I guess I should look a little more polished, shouldn't I?"

Galla jumped up and down. "This is so exciting!" And she threw her arms around Ariel. Then she looked at Ariel and said, "I'll fix your hair. I'm good with a brush."

So they sat on Ariel's bed and Galla held the long, dark mane and pulled the brush gently through it until Ariel's hair shone. They smiled sheepishly at each other. Ariel reached for Galla's hand.

"I'm nervous," she admitted. "We've not known each other for long. But I've never felt so comfortable. There's so much I don't even have to say, because Dagovaby feels all of it. But I do like getting him worked up." And she smiled impishly.

And then Dagovaby tapped on her door. "I'm ready," he called, his eyes meeting Galla's. Ariel had hidden from him.

"I'm not!" Ariel replied. "Five minutes!" She pulled forth a long, simple gown, green and gauzy.

"Help me get this over my huge belly," she said.

"Where did this come from?" Galla wanted to know.

"Mama made it," Ariel said with a grin. She pulled the gown over her head, and Galla stretched it out and smoothed it. Then she looked at her friend.

Ariel's face glowed, rosy, mischievous, frightened, loving; her green eyes beamed and her dark hair rippled over the pale green dress. Galla felt pierced by Ariel's happiness, and part of her also felt sad, though she did not understand why.

They walked together to the round room. Soft harp-like music played over the speakers. Dagovaby, in his dark suit stitched specially by Meredith, sought Ariel with his black-and-gold eyes. Any nervousness Ariel had felt before vanished. Dagovaby blinked rapidly as Ariel approached him.

Jana stepped up and looked at all of them.

"I'm not much for words," she said simply. "But I'm happy to say a few and get these two married."

Everyone laughed, though their laughter was tinged in sadness as well, as they each stole glances at the empty chair where Trent usually sat. Jana lowered her head and whispered some words to herself, and then looked up with a smile.

She spoke for Ariel and Dagovaby: "We are gathered here, out in the middle of nowhere," and snickers rippled around the room, "to unite Ariel Brant and Dagovaby Ambrono in marriage."

Jana smiled at them. She said, "Do you take each other today in love and friendship, before us and the Universe?"

"We do," Ariel and Dagovaby said in unison, holding hands. Ariel's face was bright red. She and Dagovaby had tears in their eyes.

"Then I pronounce you married!" cried Jana.

And they kissed. Meredith's eyes streamed with tears. Rob pointedly looked at Galla, who in turn ignored him.

Ariel then suddenly looked pale, and Meredith moved toward her and Dagovaby. Dagovaby's face looked anxious. A loud *POP!* shot through the room. Galla looked in amazement as Ariel bent over and gasped, and then guffawed in spite of herself.

"My water just broke!" she cried, and then there was a rush of everyone moving forward, and Ariel's labor began.

Jana yelled, "Oh my God!"

Rob shouted, "I've got this!" and rushed to clear the table and make room for Ariel, until she screamed, "I'm not having my baby on a fucking *table!*" and shrieked in pain.

"It's coming soon," said Meredith, her mouth set. "This is a fast birth. Get some blankets! I'll need a knife, too."

Jana and Rob dashed to grab the blankets and placed them on the floor, for Ariel was straining.

And Dagovaby held his screaming bride's hand, his face strained from the shared excruciating pain, while Meredith told Ariel to push. Rob had receded, half out into the hallway and half in, his eyes averted.

Galla, however, had rushed to Ariel's other side, grabbed her hand, and let her friend dig her fingernails deep as she strained, focused, and shrieked, sometimes all at once. Soon after Ariel felt her friend's hand, however, she gasped, "That's better!" With her pain lessened, she relaxed just enough. And with a final push, it was over. Jana swept forward with a knife, which Meredith deftly took and used to cut the umbilical cord, and she presented her grandson to his mother.

He squalled in a tiny yet strong voice that echoed through the room. Ariel took him to her breast, tears flooding her eyes and Dagovaby's. Meredith, trembling, draped a small blanket around the two of them.

Galla watched dumbstruck, her very soul shaken. She could see some link between mother, father, and son, a mental link she assumed. And she felt deeply touched.

Yet she had never felt so alien as she did at that moment.

Jana smiled broadly, congratulating the new family and Meredith. Galla shook herself out of her state and joined in. Rob popped his head back in and said, "Congrats! Dag, the booze is on me in a bit!"

And then with a fussy series of clicks, Beetle waddled into the room and stopped.

"Where did this tiny person come from?" it asked. The room echoed with laughter.

It ended swiftly, for Rob abruptly rejoined them.

"Um. Guys," he said, wild-eyed. "Some really big shit is going down."

Galla and Jana jumped up.

Meredith looked up in concern. Galla shook her head. "You stay with them. We'll take care of this."

She and Jana scurried to the cockpit.

"All kinds of fucking readings going off," Rob told them.

"I don't understand," said Galla, "what readings?"

"Waves, electromagnetic pulses, you name it," Rob said breathlessly. "Something big happened out in space."

Galla gasped.

"Open a channel to Aeriod," she commanded.

Rob did not hesitate.

Aeriod's fierce, aquiline face met hers. Galla pushed down the shock of seeing him and all that it meant.

"Good," he said, "you know."

"No, I don't know," retorted Galla. "What is it? What's happened?"

"The Event," he said crisply. "You're going to experience at first a shockwave, and then many more strange phenomena. Expect refugees, fleeing the devastated areas. This will be just the beginning. The Event will last for a long time, unless it can be stopped somehow. I must go."

"Aeriod, wait! It's Ariel—" Galla cried quickly, but the screen had gone black.

52

PROPULSION

"Paul Brant Ambrono," Ariel sighed proudly, handing the clean baby to Galla for the first time. Galla placed her right hand behind his tiny head and cradled him in the crook of her left arm.

His wee head was covered in a small swirl of dark hair, and his skin was light brown. His eyes, however, opened just enough to stare at Galla, with the bright green of his mother and his grandmother. Baby Paul looked up at her with a quizzical little wrinkle in his brow.

Galla blinked through tears. She was overwhelmed.

"He's so tiny. So perfect," she said quietly, and the newborn stared at her.

"He's trying to read you!" Ariel cried, her face flushed. She had her hair back in a high bun, and Galla looked at her in amazement. Ariel, to her, had been transformed into something new. Seeing her friend's glowing face and her extraordinary love for this small being sent a wave of feeling through Galla.

"Can he really read minds, at this age?" Galla exclaimed.

Meredith turned around from where she sat working on a small quilt. She looked warmly up at Galla through her crinkled eyes.

"Yes indeed," Meredith replied. "That's how we knew about Ariel from the start. She seemed to know exactly what we all thought. And for the most part, that made her an easy baby! But when she got a bit older, she did like to play tricks on us."

Meredith's face radiated love, and Galla breathed in deeply and sighed. She bent her head down, and she kissed baby Paul on his forehead and passed him back to Ariel.

Dagovaby soon entered. He cast a loving glance to his wife and baby, and then his forehead creased.

He turned to Galla and said, "Jana and Rob are monitoring a shockwave, and it should be here within a half hour. Oh, I don't mean for you to go," he protested, as Galla stood to leave.

"No, I should, and the four of you can rest and relax while we handle the situation," said Galla firmly.

She looked at the family and found herself coursing with strong emotions. Something had awoken in her that she did not know existed. She wondered to herself if the Associates knew, though.

Galla left the room and ran square into Beetle, feeling its sharp, angled appendages crease into her skin. Beetle stood there, antennae swerving, and Galla stared at it, puzzled.

"Beetle, what are you doing?" she asked.

And she looked to see Beetle holding something above her head, to avoid her touching it. It was a small oval *something*, but what it was she could not guess.

"This is for the pupa," said Beetle in its musical voice, accentuated by pops.

Galla stared again.

"I'm sorry. The what?"

"The Paul larva needs a pupa to change in," Beetle declared melodiously. "It is quite clear Paul larva cannot make one himself."

Beetle lowered its raised arms and showed Galla an ovoid bundle, an exquisitely woven little pod, with an opening for Paul's head.

Jana stomped down the hall and called, "Beetle! Did you shred my blanket? I know it was you!"

Beetle lowered its head.

"I needed thread for the Paul larva's pupa." It gestured to the little pod. "I can weave some, but Paul larva might not be warm enough."

Jana and Galla met eyes. Jana covered her mouth and bent over and guffawed.

"You made that for the baby!" she shouted. "Oh my God!"

"Oh Beetle," said Galla gently, "it's wonderful. They'll love it, they will!" And awkwardly, she kissed the top of Beetle's left wing.

"Nice work, Beetle," called Jana, with a roll of her eyes, "but next time, could you *ask* before you destroy someone's priceless silk blanket from her aunt who lives on the other side of the galaxy?"

"I will ask next time," agreed Beetle, tapping an arm on the door of Ariel's room.

Jana and Galla walked together to the cockpit, with Jana shaking her head.

"I don't know what I'm going to do with this crew," she murmured. "Trent would have known, though."

Galla paused in the hallway, turned toward Jana, and said, "I'm sorry. I—I assumed that you were close."

"Oh, we weren't *close*-close," Jana corrected her swiftly, tossing her mohawk. "He was my friend. And only that, and only ever that. I'm not into guys. And anyway, we can all just be *friends* and only friends." And she raised an eyebrow as she turned her head to the cockpit.

Galla followed her gaze, and then blushed. She marched forward without a word, and ignored the wry grin at the edge of Jana's mouth.

"How long until the wave hits us?" Galla asked Rob, whose feet shot down from their position along his control panel. He straightened himself.

"Ten minutes," he replied, looking at the two women. "What?"

Jana sighed and sat next to him. She pressed her fingers onto her temples and shook her head.

Galla activated her mic and announced, "You have less than ten minutes until the shockwave hits. Brace for impact."

And they waited, with grim expressions, looking out into the void, seeing nothing. Then a blistering flurry of rocks pelted the ship, debris from the front of the wave. It rattled all over the ship. The wave struck, and the ship was thrown and tumbled over and over.

Rob at last regained control and pierced the wave with the ship, and the craft shuddered and protested. And then with a number of creaks and pops and flashing alerts, the ship stilled.

Galla ran out of the cockpit to check on the others. Beetle had braced its several legs into a supply cage, and slowly let one leg down at a time after it saw her. She hastened to Ariel's room, and found everyone disheveled but safe. Ariel held Paul in Beetle's little pod.

"This protected him," she marveled, and she pulled the newborn from the pod. She grinned. "I think it's time to change him, though, after that little scare! Do you think we'll have any more?"

"Not for now," Galla said, relaxing her shoulders. "But I'm not sure what to expect next. Aeriod told me this is just the beginning, and to be ready for many strange things. Rob says all the sensors this ship is connected to have gone haywire. So we may not be able to detect much of anything. And we aren't sure about the guidance.

"But listen. I hate to ask this of you, especially now," Galla said, clasping her hands under her chin. "With the Event starting, Paosh Tohon will take advantage of the suffering that it causes on the worlds closest to the rupture. And Paosh Tohon will grow stronger. We have to keep going with our plans, and get all the stones to the Devices."

"Then full speed ahead!" exclaimed Ariel.

Dagovaby sighed. "I would like more time," he declared, stroking little Paul's head. "But I think we don't have any. Go on, then."

Galla turned to Meredith, who looked more bent and fatigued than she had ever seen her. She remembered suddenly what Rob had said about her. Meredith smiled up at Galla.

"Lead the way, dear!" said Meredith.

Galla smiled at her, sighed, and left the room.

But she was troubled. Meredith looked weak.

She approached Jana, who was on her way to the kitchen. She followed her into the kitchen and watched Jana assemble a sandwich.

"I'm not letting a galactic cataclysm stop *my* lunch," she declared, as if daring Galla to say anything. Galla grinned.

"That's for sure," she laughed. Then she sobered again. "Jana, I know you weren't close with Trent, but did he ever teach you any medicine?"

Jana measured Galla's face with her dark eyes.

"He did a bit," she replied.

"I have to ask you something, and I want you to keep it private," said Galla. "Rob thinks something is wrong with Meredith, but he didn't elaborate."

"Why don't you ask Meredith?" retorted Jana.

"Because I want to know if we have any chance of healing her, and I need to know if you can figure that out," said Galla. "You're brilliant. Surely you can access Trent's medical records, and maybe something helpful from the Associates' data. There has to be some way we can heal Meredith."

Jana heaved a great sigh. She looked down at her sandwich. "I'll look into it. But Galla, Meredith should know about anything related to her own health. Including my research. So you ask her first, and if she agrees, I'll go for it. But not until then. Got it?"

"Got it," agreed Galla, and she threw back her head in relief. "Thank you, Jana."

She marched to the cockpit and said to Rob, "To the next world."

Winking, he swiveled around and engaged the engines.

53

FUSILLADE

The ship catapulted out of the junction into a rose and violet-hued nebula. Galla scanned the scene.

"You're sure this is it?" Galla asked Rob.

"I mean, check with Jana, but these are the coordinates."

Galla wondered. "How old are those records? This star has been dead a long time."

"There's a brown dwarf," noted Rob. "Maybe that's what's kept the place going. Not sure if the planet orbited the dead star, or this, or both at one point."

"Take us in closer to the planet," said Galla.

As they approached, Galla squinted. The dark sphere had no moon, though a hazy, small ring circuited the planet.

"A dim place," she murmured, looking at the slate-hued world.

"I don't like it," Rob remarked.

Galla shivered.

"Bring us into high orbit, for now," she said, and she walked out.

She knocked on Ariel's door.

"Come in," said Ariel.

She sat nursing Paul, with her eyes shut.

"You've come to ask about this place," Ariel declared.

"Can you read me, finally?" Galla asked with a smile.

"Never," said Ariel with a rueful sigh. "But I know why you are here. You don't need to be a telepath for that sort of thing."

Ariel considered her friend. "Why do you have that look, Galla?"

"What look?" asked Galla, startled.

"I just—I've seen it on your face now for some time. You look—sad, maybe."

Galla shook her curls. "I don't think I'm sad. Not really. I suppose I have a lot on my mind. And I still feel badly about Trent. I guess that won't go away."

"Just keep moving," said Ariel, adjusting her baby and sitting up straighter. "As for the planet? I don't know. Something doesn't sit well with me."

"I feel the same way," Galla agreed. "But you're not picking up on anything?"

"Not yet," said Ariel. "What's the plan?"

"I'm going down alone this time," Galla said, deciding it at that moment.

"Nope," snapped Ariel. "No way."

Galla stood straight and fiery. "I am. I'm not risking any of you. I'll be down and out quickly, and then we can leave."

"Galla, don't," urged Ariel. "Take Dag, take Jana, hell—take Beetle!"

"No," said Galla. "I'll see you soon."

And against Ariel's protests she turned and fled. She entered the small bay.

"Rob, I'm suiting up. Move us down," she said.

"Who else?" asked Rob over the comms.

"Nobody." And she sealed her suit and slammed her helmet over the head.

She heard the clanging of footsteps within minutes, and met the stern gazes of Dagovaby, Rob, and Jana.

"Like hell you're going alone!" cried Jana, reaching for a suit.

"Stop!" said Galla. "All of you. Back to your stations. And keep a watch out. Something isn't right. And after what happened to

Trent? No. I'm going alone this time. Rob, send us down, or I'll do it from here myself," she said, her voice hard, her hand over a wall panel.

"Goddammit, Galla!" Rob cried, stepping toward her, but she held her hands up and stared him down.

"Jana," she said, "I'm taking the bike. Keep a watch, and do what you have to do. I'll let you know when I'm ready to come back up."

No sooner had she spoken than something struck the ship and shook it.

"We've been hit!" Rob yelled, and he and Jana sprinted back to the cockpit.

"I thought we were shielded!" cried Galla. "How were we detected?"

Dagovaby said to Galla, the gold rings around his pupils flickering in the light of the bay, "There's something menacing, I can sense it now. Before it was just a feeling. Now it's throbbing. Hurry."

"I will," she answered. He backed away, and when he had left, she activated the bike.

"There's anti-aircraft," Rob announced over the mic.

"Get me where I need to be, and return fire as needed," Galla snapped.

"Ready?"

"Ready," she said, and the bay door opened. She turned on the bike and dropped.

Into the dark clouds she swept, and long lancets of fire flew past her on all sides, but she dodged them. Whatever shot at her could not match her flying skill, or so she hoped. She had to be fast. She switched her course and slalomed through the turbulent skies of this dark sphere.

One of the menacing fingers of light caught the tail of the bike and sent her veering, but she compensated by shifting her weight and struggled against the wind. She had entered rain clouds, and her helmet streaked with dirty rain as she descended.

"Am I close?" she yelled, for she could see almost nothing, the light was so faint and the clouds so foreboding.

Rob's voice cracked into her helmet. "You're a few miles off. Head east. Should be somewhere there."

She had reached a gap in the clouds and could see glints through the rain. There were lights below her, and low, round structures. Someone definitely lived here, and whoever it was did not want her there. She veered aside from the bolts of unseen weapons.

And finally she could see something: a bowl-like indentation, surrounded by a fortress, all of its firepower aimed at her. And still she dodged, and ducked, and swooped in. She reached this indentation and realized it was a cover over the Device, and so she veered off to a ledge and parked her bike under it. The firing had stopped.

"Ah!" she cried. "You don't want to fire on the Device! So I'm going to walk right on it, then."

She went into the strange bowl dipping into the Device. It was made of shiny grey, flexible material that dented as she walked. Then she watched as several small craft rose all around her and surrounded her from above.

A rippling voice penetrated her helmet: *"Surrender yourself or be destroyed!"*

"I don't think so!" she cried.

She cast about, looking for some entrance to the hole beneath her, but there was nothing to be seen, other than this strange, silvery covering. She tried walking along its outer edge and slid down toward its center, the rain giving no purchase for her feet.

She stood and stared up at all the craft. Beings or bots, she could not tell, began to drop down lines toward the cover of the Device, to come to her. She dodged energy grapples and skidded along.

"Surrender yourself!" the voices came again.

Galla stared up defiantly, reached inside her suit, and pulled out her diamethyst. She held it high and watched it shimmer, casting bright purple light all around her. And then she plunged the sharp tip of the stone straight into the silver cover, ripping a gash in it, and dropped through it into the blackness.

Her comms came alive with a shrill yell from Rob: *"Gallaaaaaa!"*

She watched, terrified, as the small sliver of dim light receded rapidly above her, and she held fast to her stone, the only other light at all, and could not see the other side. *It will be a long fall, and a hard landing,* she mused.

But then she slowed. She gasped, and tumbled in the air, but her falling had indeed slowed, and she found herself surrounded by her stone's light. And then she stopped in midair. By and by she heard the telltale sound of some mechanism, but whether it came from above or below she could not decide.

"What—what is happening?" she gasped.

Underneath her a hard surface bumped, and she sprawled out on her back. She found herself on a Device platform. And she watched, stunned, as the purple light all around her faded slightly, until her stone only gave off pink and lavender glints. The platform whirred for some time, and at last jerked to a stop at a door, and there winked a lit hallway.

She stumbled off the platform and swayed, fell on her backside, and stood again, dizzy. She put her hand on the closest wall, and pale lights activated all down the hall. And then the visions began, or were they only voices? Were they memories? Galla could not grasp any of it.

"Find the exact temperature."

"What was the impact? We need those readings."

"Why is this not working? Try it again. Increase the focus."

"Ignore the screams. She cannot truly feel this."

"Now lift up your arms! Spread them just so. Good, very good."

"Make your bubble. There you go. Now you can drift."

Galla sat again, her back against the wall, breathing hard. She fought back tears. Then she jolted herself back to reality; the voices stilled. She must hurry. Who knew what firepower the ship had been enduring all this time? She clumsily twitched her fingers through her little pouch inside her suit, found the small diamethyst, plucked it out, and dropped it onto the floor. She stared at the little stone, and the lights in the hall dimmed, and the two stones, her larger one and this smaller one, winked and flashed as if communicating in some strange language. She fought vertigo and swayed as she walked back to the platform.

It shot up so quickly that she felt a shriek escape her throat. Up toward the pale rent in the ceiling of this chasm she raced. She readied herself.

And out Galla burst, her stone held high, and she found several beings on the cover of the pit on either side of her. She noticed a familiar-looking badge on their helmets or breastplates. *That symbol...* But she did not have time to dwell on it. She pulled at the cover gash with the stone, and with a great ripping sound it fluttered open, sending many of these beings down into the depths.

She held fast to the torn material and slammed into the side of the Device wall, and crawled up it. Weapons stabbed the air, shooting at her, and she swung left and right to avoid them, but knew she would eventually be hit. So she took a chance and jumped, holding her stone: and she did not fall.

Instead she rose, all the violet light around her seeming to buoy her, and drifted toward her bike. She collapsed onto it, spent, and turned it on, and surrounded by the violet light she rose high in the sky, the shots glancing off of the light. Soon they changed direction, and aimed at the ship, which had come back to meet her, but this time Jana was ready.

She shot a volley of fire all around Galla's location, down into the depths of the world. Small ships rose out of the crowds to meet them, and Galla could see red markings on their sides. She entered her ship and ran to the cockpit. Jana turned the weapons toward the other ships and engaged them as well.

"Junction!" yelled Galla, and Rob thrust the ship forward at high speed, outpacing their followers.

The junction burst open and they entered its pulsating lights. They were free.

54

AMALGAMATE

Galla drummed her fingers on the table. She passed an image she had sketched over to Jana, who passed it to the others.

"That's what I saw on the man that attacked Trent," said Galla. "That same symbol. I didn't get a clear look at it. But I know that's what I saw on that planet. Every being attacking wore it somewhere. It was on their ships, too."

"I've never seen it before," said Rob.

Meredith shook her head in assent.

Dagovaby scowled at it.

"Even the sight of it fills me with dread," he admitted. "There's something about it. Some dark nature. Cruelty. Chaos. Malice."

Galla turned again to Jana.

"Can you look for this image? Even if it's not a perfect match?"

Jana nodded confidently. "I'll do what I can."

Galla returned her nod.

"So. We have a couple of problems now," she declared. Everyone shifted, as if they had been avoiding this conversation up to this point.

"First we're attacked on Beetle's world," Galla said slowly, cupping her chin with her left hand. "And Paosh Tohon is there, but limited. Only what we think is Veronica, and someone else."

Ariel stirred gingerly, so as not to wake Paul from his nap in her arms.

"I think I know who that was," she announced.

Meredith turned her drooped eyes to her daughter. Galla felt a stab of realization that she had not asked Meredith about her health.

Ariel went on, "Remember when Officer Derry went AWOL from Mandira? And they tried to stop him?"

"You think it's Derry?" exclaimed Rob.

"I do," said Ariel. She shoved a rogue lock of dark hair behind her ear. "I could sense something familiar about the two. And of course I'm pretty sensitive to all things Veronica."

She cleared her throat as if in disgust, and shuddered.

"But beyond her, there was . . . *something*. It had to be Derry."

Jana held up her hand.

"Wait. Derry's working for Paosh Tohon now?" she asked, dipping her head down to stare at Ariel with wide eyes.

"It makes sense, right?" Ariel said quickly. "He took off, and was out of jurisdiction of Ika Nui. And then he disappeared. What else would a human be doing out here?"

Dagovaby coughed and smirked.

"I mean besides you," Ariel snorted.

"Well, half-human anyway," said Dagovaby. "But I get what you're saying. There aren't many humans in this part of the galaxy. And if he seemed familiar to you, it had to be him."

Meredith let out a large sigh. "So Paosh Tohon knows we're out here. And Derry is as good as gone. But what about these other forces that attacked you, Galla? Why would they do that? Do they know what we're doing?"

"I hope not," Galla said. "It could all be a coincidence, but at this point I'm thinking there is a connection. And I want to know how they knew we were there, and fired at us, when we're supposed to be untraceable."

Jana said, "Hmm. Their shots were not very accurate. I think they detected something in the atmosphere, but couldn't really see our ship. It could be they're testing the waters. Maybe it's early on in whatever plan these folks have. Clearly they weren't overtaken by Paosh Tohon. But they're working for it, I think."

"Run that image, then, and let's see what we find out," suggested Galla.

She went on, "As for our own plans, we have to forge ahead. We aren't traceable in this ship, or so we hope. I think as far as that goes, Paosh Tohon got lucky finding us on Beetle's world."

"It wasn't luck," Ariel said in a glum voice. "It was me. *I* attracted Paosh Tohon. And had I not been on the ship in time, things would have gone very differently."

Galla shivered.

"Why would it come after *you* out here like this?" Rob asked her.

"Maybe she—it," Ariel corrected herself doubtfully, "found a way in and thought it could get to me. But you foiled it again," and she grinned at Galla out of one side of her mouth. "It's obvious that when I can be traced, like on the planet surfaces, she—it—can sense me."

"Then you stay in the ship," Dagovaby suggested. Ariel howled in protest.

"I'll do what I want!" she snapped.

Dagovaby sighed. "I know that. I love that you're stubborn, but in this case . . . something has to be done. You'll have to stay with Galla's stones until we figure this out."

Galla shook her bright head, sending her hair coasting in swirls.

"I think there's a better way. Do we have any wire? Or fine chain?" she asked.

Rob said, "I'm sure we can find something like that. Why?"

Galla stood quickly. "Come with me. All of you."

They followed her to her geode, which twinkled from within in magenta and violet sparkles.

"You can't very well fit everyone in this thing," Galla said, "but I can do the next best thing."

And she amazed them by plucking off robin's-egg-sized pieces of the diamethyst and handing them to each person. She offered one to

Beetle, who touched it with an antenna. Beetle took the stone delicately in a pincer.

"These are yours now," she told them. "Wear them constantly. They'll ward off Paosh Tohon's effects, to some degree. I should have done this before."

And she bowed her head, her hair lowered, and sighed, deeply sad over Trent. Blinking away her tears, she said, "I can't stand the thought of anything happening to any of you. Until we figure out some way to attack Paosh Tohon, we have to go on the defensive.

"But," she continued slowly, watching everyone admire their purple stones, roll them over in their hands, or hold them up to the light, "it's also clear that we need a lot more telepaths. And a lot more security around Devices to protect the telepaths and any of us who guard them. So how do we do that?"

Rob spoke up.

"I think we need to recruit who we can somewhere *away* from these planets. Don't draw any more attention to them until we can put everyone in place," he said.

"Good," said Galla. "But *where* do we find them?"

Jana declared, "The Associates. I'll search the data I got. There has to be something in their files about telepaths, other species, and all that."

Galla smiled. "Excellent. Please go ahead and start," she told Jana.

She turned to Ariel and Dagovaby.

"Will you try and seek out what you can with your powers? Or is that too much of a risk?" she asked them.

"I don't think we have a choice, unless Jana finds a bank of telepaths we can call," Ariel retorted. "Besides, I do have some experience sending long-distance signals with my mind," and she smirked at Meredith, who brightened.

"Rob," Ariel went on, "maybe you could find some systems with a lot of trade. There are bound to be telepaths in those kinds of areas."

She held Paul up to her shoulder and patted his back.

"And I can tell you which ones to avoid," she declared darkly.

Galla arched an eyebrow at her. *I imagine she knows quite a bit about what to avoid. I wonder what Aeriod made her do when she worked for him?* And she felt disquieted by even thinking this.

"I'll get on it," Rob affirmed. Galla nodded, and he left, holding his stone in one hand.

Beetle said, "I can sense things about other beings as well, should you need me to."

"Thank you, Beetle," said Galla. "I think we will need you for many things, before long. I don't know what all exactly, but no doubt you can help."

"I will weave silk for the stones, so you can put them around your necks," Beetle said.

Galla's eyes lit up. "Brilliant!" she said. "Thank you, Beetle!"

She knelt over sleepy Paul, now stretching his waking little body in Ariel's arms. Dagovaby offered to take him, and Ariel obliged. Paul latched his tiny mouth onto Dagovaby's knuckle while Ariel drank water and stretched as well. Galla reached a tentative hand over the baby's small head and stroked his dark hair. He stopped sucking on his father's finger long enough to stare at her with his great, green eyes. Galla smiled at him, and felt a gush of love for him, his mother and father, and Meredith.

"I'll leave you to get back to your day," Galla said quietly. "Let me know if you pick up anything."

"We will," answered Ariel, and the Brant-Ambrono family walked to their quarters.

Meredith lingered behind.

"You look as though you have something to ask me, Galla," said the elderly woman, with her piercing eyes. She smiled warmly.

Galla looked at her for a moment. *How does she know? Always?*

"I do," said Galla, swallowing in dread.

"Don't be shy about it—that's not your nature, dear," Meredith said kindly, giving her hand a squeeze.

"No, I know," agreed Galla. "It's just—it's something Rob said to me once."

"Ah," said Meredith, her eyes steady on Galla's.

"Is everything all right?" asked Galla. "Are you . . . *oakay?*"

Meredith gave a short, clipped laugh.

"Well, Galla, I'm getting on up there in years now," she responded. "Things just don't work the way they used to." She sighed and looked down. She held her hands together tightly, but still they trembled. Galla noticed.

"It's just—now we don't have a medic, and this ship has no bots—being Aeriod's after all," Galla began.

"So you're worried about my care?" asked Meredith gently.

"Yes," said Galla, unhappily.

"Well, don't be. I'm sure we can research what we need on this ship," Meredith said, with a wave of her hand.

"Can Jana at least provide some help with that? Maybe she could research some cures or something," Galla suggested eagerly.

"Oh, she can help, that's fine," Meredith smiled. "Now don't worry about me! You've got enough on your plate. And I can look after myself."

Galla felt her shoulders loosen.

"I'm glad," she told Meredith. "But please let me know if you need *anything*."

"Oh, I will, dear," said Meredith. "Now I'm off to take my nap, if you don't mind."

"Of course," said Galla.

And she found herself alone and at peace, but it soon vanished.

"Galla," Jana's voice buzzed on her comms.

Galla took a breath. "Yes?"

"We should talk. In private. I found something."

55

MACHINATIONS

She did not understand the pit of anxiety building inside her at every footfall that led her to Jana's quarters. *It can't be that bad,* she assured herself, while even those wisps of optimism felt snatched away as she rang Jana's door.

Jana opened, beckoned her to enter, and sat on the edge of her simple bed. Galla's quick glance around her room showed her interesting tidbits of Jana's life, and a fascination with antique objects and green crystals.

"Look," Jana said, unblinking. "I thought about just calling a meeting. But there's . . . sensitive information that you might want to know. And some info that pertains to others."

Galla raised her eyebrows.

"Tell me," she breathed.

Jana held up her data miner. "This thing," she said, "drew so much out of the Associates' ship. So I cannot even *imagine* what their own version of databases might have. And some of what I got is jumbled. But I caught a few things.

"First, I didn't know him very well, but there was a man named Forster—I'm sure you've heard the story, about how he and Ariel and Aeriod moved Mandira Station across the galaxy, and all that."

Galla nodded.

"Well," Jana sighed and rubbed her mohawk, "there's a very strange . . . file, for lack of a better word. It's got Forster and Ariel in it—I'll just show you."

And Jana placed her data miner into her desk screen, and a hologram formed. Two long sets of beads of light seemed to stretch from the ceiling, and out from them various tiny branches moved off, or ended. The sets never converged. But near their ends, Galla could see faces in the beads. On one end, she clearly saw Ariel's face. On the other, a man she recognized from the Curator's pictures appeared in a bead, and from him branched off various other beads, but ultimately it ended in a bead that showed a familiar face.

"Kein!" Galla exclaimed.

Jana stared. "So Kein is Forster's great—however many—grandson?"

"Yes!" said Galla, and she stared intently at Kein's kind face, feeling a knot of homesickness.

Jana blinked. "Okay. This is some crazy time dilation shit, but okay." She looked back at the image. "What do you think it means?"

Galla bit her lip. Why did this seem familiar? And then she felt it. Her nerves danced with shock. She had seen this same shape, in Aeriod's private tower. She had thought it was some sort of artwork, and had not looked closely. But she was certain it had been there.

"Your face right now," said Jana, "tells me I was right to talk to you in private."

"Yes," said Galla slowly. She felt her cheeks grow hot.

"Galla," gasped Jana, "your hair, and your stone—" and Jana backed up a bit where she sat.

Galla's hair had frizzed and bushed out all over rapidly, and her stone grew hot, and when she looked down it seemed to spark within.

"He knew," she hissed. "He knew! All along! All about them! And the Associates knew!"

Her fingers curled in to make fists.

"Okay, who is *he*?" asked Jana.

"Aeriod," said Galla through clenched teeth.

"Ohhhh shit," said Jana, and she stood. "What do you want to do?"

"We'll call a meeting," Galla managed to choke out, and she turned to leave.

"Wait," Jana said, grasping her arm gently. "I—I hate to do this right now. But I can't let you go without seeing what else I found. It's too important."

Galla wondered what could possibly be more important than what she had just learned. But the look on Jana's face, of concern, sympathy, and a whiff of fear—she could not shake that.

"Go ahead then," Galla said quietly.

Jana rubbed her temples. "Galla, there's a lot of information about *you* in this thing. I'm guessing there's a lot more somewhere. But . . . were you, like, a prisoner or something?"

Galla's hair fell instantly and her stone went ice cold.

"What did you find?"

Jana breathed deeply, taking in the sudden change in Galla. She closed her eyes for a moment. Then she opened them, and took Galla's hand in her own.

"They recorded you," she said in a very quiet voice.

Galla covered her eyes. Then she let her hands fall.

"Show me," she said, her voice flat.

And Jana let another display unfold in the small room, and Galla saw herself in flashes, much as she had in her Device visions. The recording had no sound, and flickered in many spots. But it was definitely her, and she was subjected again and again to various tests.

Jana could not watch again.

"They tortured you," she said, and Galla heard this as if from a long tunnel, echoing along the sides, as she tried to run in her mind away from what she saw. "And I think—I can't translate it all, but—I think they took notes. And they called you 'one of the Questri,' whatever that means. Something about the Seltrason era ending?"

"Why?" Galla managed to say. "I thought they were training me, and that was all it was, just subconscious training."

Jana and Galla looked at each other at the same moment.

"They were looking for your weaknesses," Jana murmured. "And we don't know what all they found."

Galla drew herself up as tall as she could. She would not let this defeat her. Somewhere, the Associates knew all they needed to about her. Or they thought they did. But she had not had her stone with her on Bitikk. So they could not know everything.

"Show the first holograms to the others immediately," said Galla firmly, her eyebrows stern. "As for mine, this is between you and me. I want you to keep this information a secret. We can talk about it more if you want—"

"I really don't want to see that again," Jana interrupted. "And we will only talk if *you* want to."

Galla lowered her head. "Thank you, Jana," she said. "Let's call the meeting."

And soon they sat and stared at each other across the round table.

"I want you to see what Jana found in the data from the Associates' ship," Galla announced.

Jana played the holograms, and sat intently working with a tablet while they unfolded before everyone else. Galla stared at Ariel's pale face and watched her skin flush and blanch over and over. Paul began fussing, and Ariel, to quiet him, began nursing. This calmed her for a moment.

"What the hell am I looking at?" she finally demanded.

"Two lineages of telepaths," Galla said. "The Associates knew about you for some time. Before you were even born. And so, Aeriod did too," and she glanced at Meredith. Meredith looked completely staggered. Galla felt her fists ball again.

"I don't know what it all means yet," Galla said quickly, "but I can assure you, Aeriod will answer to *me* about this. Right now."

And she sent a communiqué to Aeriod. Her rage overtook her, and she felt imperious and wrathful.

"Aeriod!" Galla cried. "Answer me!"

And he did. His silver hair seemed to wave above them, framing his ghostly face in the hologram, his black outfit making him seem headless to them. Rob squirmed. Dagovaby squinted at him. Jana ignored him. And Ariel and Meredith met the image with the exact same expression: furrowed brows and lips drawn to a line.

"I've not got long, Galla-Deia," Aeriod began, "there's too much—"

Galla stood straight and crossed her arms.

"I don't care. You need to answer for something," Galla thundered. She moved the hologram of the lineages into his line of sight.

Everyone could see his look of surprise.

"How did you get this?" he demanded.

"No, I ask the questions now. And then Ariel and Meredith can," said Galla with ice in her voice. "Is this what you had in your office? Over half a century ago? I thought it was art, and you waved it away from me."

Aeriod sighed and raised his hands, saying, "This doesn't concern you—"

"Stop," snapped Galla. "Answer the question."

Aeriod grimaced. "Yes, it is, now—"

"So the Associates knew, and you knew, about Ariel and Forster and Kein long before you met them, yes?" Galla demanded. "And you were just going to bide your time and leave Ariel floating out there alone. When you could have rescued her."

Aeriod closed his eyes. "I can't speak of this, Galla. For reasons of top security."

"*Bullshit!*" cried a woman's voice. It was not Jana's, and it was not Ariel's. It was her mother's.

Eyes green like a tornado sky, Meredith rose and shouted, "You knew all along! You knew she was out there! You knew she was alone. And you didn't tell me! And you, you drew Forster to the station, didn't you?"

"Meredith, I—" Aeriod began.

"How *dare you!*" Meredith wailed.

Ariel deftly handed the startled Paul to Dagovaby, and said,

"Please take him out of earshot. He'll hear enough of my thoughts as it is." Dagovaby quickly obliged and left with their son.

She turned to Aeriod.

"You *used* us!" she shouted. "You played a sick game, made us do what you wanted, and then moved us all away!"

"For your safety!" bellowed Aeriod. "It might not have worked at all, and indeed I really didn't think it would. Veronica was something none of us anticipated. But the Associates gave me this Task, and I took it. I took it so that—"

Aeriod looked longingly at Galla, who stood with her fists clenched and her eyes in fiery slits.

"—I had nothing else to keep me from worrying about Galla while she was being—trained," and he spat the word out with a scowl, "though I knew she was being harmed."

"You're garbage," Ariel said in a deadly calm voice.

Aeriod raised his hands again. "I gave you what you wanted," he pleaded, with Meredith particularly. "And Forster got what he wanted. I made sure."

Meredith and Ariel were in tears, and held onto each other. "How dare you," Meredith whispered over and over. "I missed decades of my daughter's life! I can't believe we trusted you!"

Galla opened her eyes and everyone gasped. Her stone threw off wedges of bright violet light.

"Enough, Aeriod," said Galla, her voice low in tone, but resonant. Even Beetle poked its head in tentatively in wonder to look at her.

"You've destroyed everything," Galla went on, staring at Aeriod's face, which looked permanently locked in surprise. "You've ruined people's lives. You've used us."

Aeriod then roared, "You have *my* ship! I've given you everything!"

"We will do just fine without you," Galla said ominously. "And the Associates. You can tell them that for me. It's the least you can do.

"Oh, and as for the ship," she sneered, "go ahead and try and take it from us. We can find another."

"Galla, please—"Aeriod begged, and Galla cleared her throat.

"Jana, Rob," she called in a cold voice, and they both looked up at her in awe. "Cut the communication, and make sure he can't get through again. Those are your orders."

"Galla—"

And the image blinked off.

56

CUTTING THE WAKE

Everyone had left the room except for Galla, Jana, and Rob.

"I found the image, Galla," Jana announced, staring at the tablet in her hands.

Galla felt as if it took every ounce of her strength after her confrontation with Aeriod even to hear Jana, but she nodded.

"Go ahead."

Jana showed them the entire clean image as a projection, the jagged red curves that seemed to them the symbol of everything wrong.

"It's Valemog," she declared. "If I had to guess, these are the most recent files on my data miner. There's not a lot of info. But they do seem to be some sort of cult-like faction that admires Paosh Tohon. And for whatever reason, they aren't attacked by it."

"Some sort of twisted symbiosis," Galla muttered, "if not outright parasitism. Maybe they just don't realize it, but that's what it will be eventually. They think they're benefiting now. They're rising and expanding. But it won't go so well for them in the end."

"Maybe," Rob said, "but what about *us*? There's not much out here. And what there is, it's either the Associates or Paosh Tohon or this Valemog. As if we needed anything else besides the goddamn

Event that we're still in a wake of. And all sensors are haywire out there, too."

"So what's next, boss?" Jana asked.

"Everyone," Galla called on her comms. "I want you all in here."

Ariel, Dagovaby, Paul, and Beetle shuffled back in. Meredith followed Beetle, and her eyes were bloodshot. Everyone else sat while Beetle and Galla stood. Galla took a deep breath, and looked at all of them in turn.

"We've seen a lot. We've heard too much," said Galla, her hands spread out on the table, her violet stone swaying, her hair curling all about her, gold-red-bronze-roan-burgundy, her eyes warm copper. She let the hair fall, and thought, *It really needs brushing*. And she blinked out two tears as she thought of Oni-Odi, far away, gone, who knew where. Her only family.

"Too many people seem to know too much about us," she said finally. "And now we've got enemies. But we have to move ahead, to survive. There's not much we can do about the Event. We have to find more telepaths, and try to stop a monster. I'll need every one of you to help"—but she smiled when her eyes fell on Paul's dark head, adding, "well, almost everyone. But if any of you want to go your own way, say so. I won't stop you."

Everyone stood.

"I'm staying in the pilot seat, Captain," Rob said, and he winked at her through his red-blond lashes.

"Not going anywhere," Jana said.

Ariel and Dagovaby looked at each other, and down at Paul. "We're with you, my friend," Ariel said.

Beetle clicked and said, "I will help as I can, though I hope my wings do not get in the way." Galla smirked.

Meredith came up to Galla and held out her arms. Galla stepped away from the table and sank into Meredith's hug. Meredith kissed her on the cheek, and then held Galla's face in her hands.

"We are your family now, dear," said Meredith.

Galla felt all of them surround her, though they were a blur of loving faces in her teary vision.

At that moment, an alarm sounded. Something was approaching.

Galla took a deep breath, sighed, made a wry grin, and then told them, "We are the Questri. The age of the Seltra is over, and now it's our turn. Everyone to your stations! We've got work to do."

THE END

PRONUNCIATION GUIDE

Aeriod (AIR-ee-od)
Auna (AWN-a)
Bitikk (bit-ik)
Dagovaby Ambrono (da-GOV-a-bee am-BRO-no)
Demetraan (DEM-eh-tron)
diamethyst (di-amethyst)
Dijj (dij); Dijjan (DIJ-un)
Ezeldae (ez-el-DIE)
Fael'Kar (fail car)
Galla-Deia (GAL-a DAY-a)
Ika Nui (IK-uh NOO-ee)
Indry-Kol (in-dree coal)
Kein (cane, rhymes with skein)
Klelk (clelk)
Mandira (man-DEER-a)
MindSynd (mind send)
Oni-Odi (oh-nee oh-dee)
Paosh Tohon (pay-OSH to-HON)
Pliip (plip)
Rez (rez)

Rikiloi (RIK-i-loy)
Seltra (SEL-tra)
Sumond (soo-MOND)
sylphlets (SILF-lets)
Ushalda (oo-SHAL-da)
Valemog (vale-mog)
Vedant (vee-DANT)
Veeldt-Ka (veelt-KA)

ABOUT THE AUTHOR

Dianne dreamed up other worlds and their characters as a child in the 1980s. She formed her own neighborhood astronomy club before age 10, to educate her friends about the Universe. In addition to writing stories, she drew and painted her characters, gave them outrageous space fashions, and created travel guides and glossaries for the worlds she invented. As an adult, Dianne earned a Bachelor of Science and spent several years working in research. She published *Heliopause: The Questrison Saga: Book One* in 2018. Dianne is also a science writer and watercolorist. She lives with her family in Southern California, and they make up a home of makers and nerds who enjoy Dianne's baked goods. *The Questrison Saga: Book Three* arrives in 2020.

jdiannedotson.com

facebook.com/jdiannedotsonwriter
twitter.com/jdiannedotson
instagram.com/jdiannedotson